Alexander is dead. Does it matter if I'm odd? We're going to be slaughtered in a foreign city, just like the Magi said. It's the dice. You roll enough and you lose." The wine was very, very good. It came to me that perhaps it had been meant for the King. Perhaps it was poisoned. There had been that tale about.

I looked into the dregs. Nothing to see. The flickering light made shapes on the surface, curled like an octopus in the bottom of the cup.

Glaukos touched my hand gently. "Drink up, my friend," he said.

I did. If it was poisoned, I was past caring.

I drank with him while the night came in through the windows, while the lamp sputtered and died. Silence settled over the palace. Glaukos talked on and on, making less sense. "Elephants," he whispered one last time, and lowered his head on his arms.

Poisoned, I thought. Of course.

From the far side of the room there was a rustle in the darkness. Two green eyes regarded me steadily. A great gray cat paced out of the shadows.

"Death," I whispered. I thought she spoke to me, words I didn't understand.

And night took me.

I woke to morning coming in through the window, and the loud annoying sound of Glaukos' snores. My head throbbed, and on the table were five-toed paw prints in red wine.

The King was still dead.

I was still alive.

by Jo Graham

*Black Ships*
*Hand of Isis*
*Stealing Fire*

# Praise for the Novels of Jo Graham

"Graham's spare style focuses on action, but fraught meaning and smoldering emotional resonance overlays her deceptively simple words." — *Publishers Weekly* (starred review)

"...A refreshingly different approach to a legend we only *thought* we knew." — *Locus*

"A bittersweet saga with enough action, romance, and intrigue to entertain and enthrall." — Romance Reviews Today

"A plausible premise, superb characters, a plot that originally extrapolates from classical literature, history, and mythology—all make for a first-class, very readable novel." — *Booklist* (starred review)

"Although most readers will be aware of Cleopatra's sad fate...the journey, and the vivid descriptions of life in the cosmopolitan city of Alexandria, make this book well worth reading." — *Kirkus*

"Charmian's shy hopes, failures and devotion to Cleopatra and Isis make her one of the most memorable 'witnesses to history' to emerge from fantasy in quite some time." — *Publishers Weekly*

"Drawing her inspiration from Virgil's *The Aeneid*, debut author Graham re-creates a vivid picture of the ancient world, a mysterious place in which gods and goddesses speak to their chosen." — *Library Journal* (starred review)

"Graham makes her world come truly alive, as the best writers of historical romances have always done." — scifi.com

"Graham...has packed the novel with exquisite detail, bringing to life a time long gone." — *The St. Petersburg Times*

"Inspired and relentlessly entertaining...an auspicious debut." — *Realms of Fantasy*

"*Hand of Isis* should cement Graham's place as a rising and strong voice in historical fantasy fiction." — *Sacramento Book Review*

# Stealing Fire

## JO GRAHAM

www.orbitbooks.net

Orbit
Hachette Book Group
237 Park Avenue, New York, NY 10017
www.HachetteBookGroup.com

First Edition: May 2010

Orbit is an imprint of Hachette Book Group. The Orbit name and logo
are trademarks of Little, Brown Book Group Limited.

Library of Congress Cataloging-in-Publication Data
Graham, Jo.
    Stealing fire / Jo Graham.
        p.   cm.
    ISBN 978-0-316-07639-5
    1. Egypt — History — To 332 B.C. — Fiction.   I. Title.
PS3607.R338S74   2010
813'.6 — dc22

                                        2009032391


        10   9   8   7   6   5   4   3   2   1

Printed in the United States of America

*For my daughter Beth,*
*who has taught me the meaning of courage*

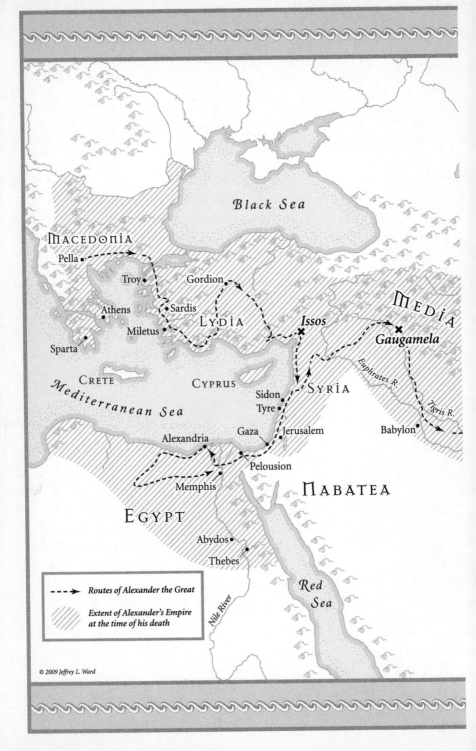

Black Sea

MACEDONIA
Pella

Troy
Gordion
Athens
Sardis
LYDIA
Miletus
MEDIA
Issos
Gaugamela

Sparta

CRETE
CYPRUS

Mediterranean Sea

SYRIA
Sidon
Tyre

Gaza
Jerusalem
Babylon

Alexandria

Pelousion

NABATEA

Memphis

EGYPT

Abydos

Thebes

Red
Sea

Euphrates R.
Tigris R.
Nile River

Routes of Alexander the Great

Extent of Alexander's Empire
at the time of his death

© 2009 Jeffrey L. Ward

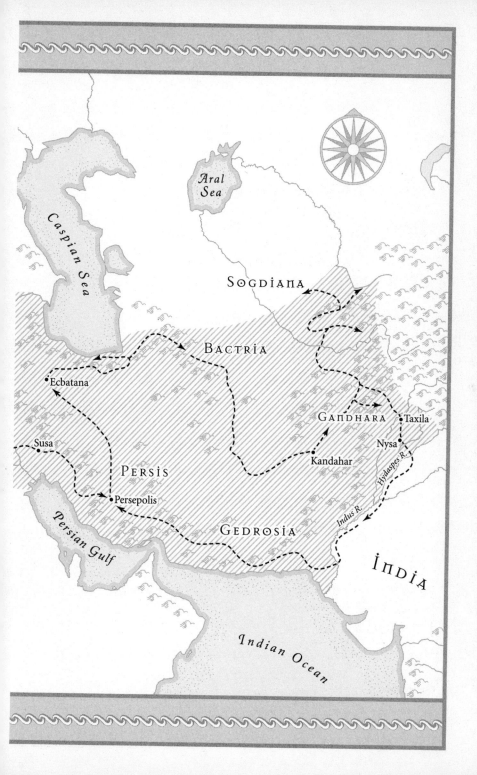

In what immortal deeps or skies
Burned the fire of thine eyes?
On what wings dare he aspire?
What the hand dare seize the fire?

— *William Blake*

# THE KING LIES
# IN BABYLON

The King was dead. Alexander lay in Babylon, in the palace
of the Persian kings, upon the bed where he had died, and
I killed a man across his body for no reason that made
any sense.

The melee had come even here, to the death chamber.

"To me! To me!" shouted Perdiccas, his head bare and his face shining with sweat. He claimed he was the heir, that Alexander had pressed
his ring into his hand.

Others said it was meant for Krateros, who was not here.

And there were other claimants, of course. His body was not cold.

I took a step back, the blood running down the channels of the
blade as I shifted into guard, rivulets of warmth across my knuckles.
The King's legs were bare below his chiton. If he had been decently covered, the cloth had slipped in the fighting. One drop fell from my blade
and glistened on a golden hair.

The young eunuch had fallen across his torso and face, shielding
him with his own dead body. At least I presumed he was dead. He was
still as death, his back bared to the swords about the bier.

"Push them back!" Perdiccas screamed. It seemed he was winning.

I stood, sword in hand. No one came near. I had no reason to attack
anyone.

A man went down, and Perdiccas and two others rushed the doorway. They pressed them out into the hall. I heard the dying man choking out his life, but I did not move. Who should I belong to? Perdiccas? He was well enough, but had never given me a word. Krateros, who had laughed at men who married foreign women and called their sons bastard?

My master was already dead.

And so I stood above the bier, listening to my breath harsh in the close air.

Outside, the sounds of the fight were becoming distant. Perhaps Perdiccas had pushed them back to the receiving hall, or toward the bathhouse.

The lamp guttered. The fragrant oil was almost gone. Soon the stench of death would fill the room.

The young eunuch moved. I saw him breathing shallowly. Having no reason to kill him, I cleaned off my sword on the fallen cloth, stepped over the dying, and left the room.

I found Glaukos in the kitchen. He had three pots of wine before him, and an onion. The knives and food lay on the table. The servants had been preparing a meal when they were frightened away.

Glaukos looked up at me, and his eyes were red. "Come to kill me, then?"

I sat down heavily on the bench. "Why should I do that, you drunkard? The world is in ruins, and you're at it again."

"You'd do best to try it," Glaukos advised. "No reason not to."

I poured a small amount into a clay cup and took a sip. It was good strong Bactrian red, dark and rich, entirely unwatered. I expect it had been intended for the King's table.

"Elephants, he said," Glaukos said. "The King wanted elephants. I said there was no way I could get elephants. You could talk to him just like that. I said no elephants, and what was he asking me about them for as I never had anything to do with elephants in my life. 'Glaukos,' he said, 'I know you can get them for me.'" He refilled his cup, tears running down his face. "So elephants it was."

"I don't want to hear about your accursed elephants," I said.

"When I showed up with those four elephants on the banks of the river…"

"Shut up about the elephants!" I said, and knocked the cup from his hand. It broke in fragments across the floor, the red wine stain spreading.

Glaukos blinked at me. "That wasn't friendly," he said mildly. He got up with the slow, purposeful movements of a man who is already drunk, went over to a shelf on the wall, and turned, holding another cup.

I stalked out of the kitchen.

The hallway was silent. If the battle had passed this way, it was gone now. Aimlessly, I wandered the corridors. In the receiving hall, the golden ornaments were stripped from the throne, a little carved table lying on its side. I went down the corridor that led to the bathhouse.

"Halt! Who's there!" I heard a shout, and the more important sound of a bow being drawn.

I stopped. The voice was familiar. "Lydias of Miletus," I said.

"Ah." He stepped into the space between the bathhouse doors. I could see four or five men beyond him, some in their harness, in reasonable order. "Take your hand from your sword hilt," he directed.

I did. "Artashir," I said.

He was a Companion though he was armed with a bow. Persians learn archery very young, and I thought it wise not to doubt he could use it, when the point was aimed at my breast.

"Are you friend or foe?" he asked.

"Of whom?" I said.

Behind him the bathing pool was blue and clear. The King had spent most of his last days here.

"Of us," Artashir said, with only a slight hesitation. He was tall and angular, younger than I, with a closely trimmed beard in the Persian fashion.

"I am no enemy of yours," I said. Truth, I hardly knew the man. We had not been in the same place until after Gedrosia, and then I had not made friends.

"We are holding the bathhouse," he said.

"For whom?"

"For the King," he answered.

I laughed, and even to myself sounded overwrought. "The King is dead. You will hold the bathhouse for all eternity."

Artashir straightened, his dark eyes suspiciously bright. "Then that is what we will do. We will wait for our orders, as Companions should."

"Wait and rot then," I said, and turned and walked away.

No arrow hit me in the back.

I could hear the battle sounds coming from the stableyard, but I had no desire to seek it out. My sword was too heavy in my hand, and the deserted palace too empty. In the anteroom to the receiving hall papers were spread, letters and dispatches, all the business of empire waiting for the King's hand. The lamps burned on in their fretted holders. In the courtyard beyond, the fountain played. I half expected it to be frozen, droplets suspended in midair. Surely the sun should not set, the droplets fall.

I wandered back to the kitchen, where Glaukos still was.

He looked up blearily from the table. "Come back, have you?"

I shrugged. "Nowhere better to go. Best to die with a friend, I suppose."

"That's the way," Glaukos said, moving over and pouring for me. Half the unwatered wine splashed out of the cup, his hands were that unsteady. "Always thought I would die with you."

I raised my cup in salute. "To death, my friend Glaukos. Death and an eternity amid the shades."

Glaukos raised his cup and looked at me over it, blinking. "You know, you've been a bit odd since Gedrosia, Lydias."

"You're calling me odd," I said. "Alexander is dead. Does it matter if I'm odd? We're going to be slaughtered in a foreign city, just like the Magi said. It's the dice. You roll enough and you lose." The wine was very, very good. It came to me that perhaps it had been meant for the King. Perhaps it was poisoned. There had been that tale about.

I looked into the dregs. Nothing to see. The flickering light made shapes on the surface, curled like an octopus in the bottom of the cup.

Glaukos touched my hand gently. "Drink up, my friend," he said.

I did. If it was poisoned, I was past caring.

I drank with him while the night came in through the windows, while the lamp sputtered and died. Silence settled over the palace. Glaukos talked on and on, making less sense. "Elephants," he whispered one last time, and lowered his head on his arms.

Poisoned, I thought. Of course.

From the far side of the room there was a rustle in the darkness. Two green eyes regarded me steadily. A great gray cat paced out of the shadows.

"Death," I whispered. I thought she spoke to me, words I didn't understand.

And night took me.

I woke to morning coming in through the window, and the loud annoying sound of Glaukos' snores. My head throbbed, and on the table were five-toed paw prints in red wine.

The King was still dead.

I was still alive.

# THE CARIAN

Once there was a boy who lived in a city by the sea which had once been Millawanda of the mighty walls, long ago in the time Homer spoke of, when Troy fell and dark raiders patrolled the seas. He was a scrawny, dark-haired boy ten years old, and his name was Jio.

Well enough, then. I cannot tell it like a poet. I am a soldier, and must speak much plainer.

Once I was a boy named Jio, and I lived in the city of Miletus. My mother was a Carian, from farther south along the coast, with flashing dark eyes and high cheekbones, honey skin, and long, tapering hands. Her long hair fell in ringlets halfway down her back, and she was voluptuous and wild, prone to fits of ecstatic weeping for Adonis, and to dancing alike. Perhaps it was because she was the concubine of a man she did not like, but who indeed chooses who they serve?

My master—my father—had a dozen sons, half of them legitimate, and grandsons nearly my age. He was a wealthy merchant of Corinthian stock whose fathers had been in Miletus four generations before I was born, but who spoke Greek in the house and considered himself a student of Attic philosophy. We spoke nothing but Greek, even in the women's quarters, because his wife would have none of it. Her children would not pick up bad habits this way. Her sons would be Greek gentlemen.

I had all of my mother's wildness and none of her beauty. I climbed the garden trees and ate the fruit, escaped over the walls and wandered the city, going to the port and watching the ships come and go, dreaming of the day that I would run away on one of them, bound for Tyre or Sidon, Pelousion or Syracuse. I stood on the walls of the breakwater in the brisk wind off the sea, my arms spread like a bird, and dreamed of flight. I dreamed at night that the wind picked me up and I soared like Icarus, over land and sea, until all the world spread beneath my wings, precious as a tapestry picked out in bright thread.

Away in Greece on the other side of the seas, Phillip, the King of Macedon, strove with Athens, and the Sacred Band fell on the field of Chaeronea to a prince of seventeen. The world did not yet know the name Alexander. I had never heard it, but already the wind was blowing, leaves flying before the storm that would come.

My father always had an eye for profit, like the canny merchant he was, and he was more than happy to trade with Macedon. Ships came and went to Amphipolis and Phillippopolis, their Macedonian captains received with wine and conversation that bordered on the treasonous. Yes, of course the Greek cities of the coast would like to be rid of Persian overlordship. My father spread his hands. But that was a futile dream, of course, unless some powerful ruler like Phillip could forge a new and stronger alliance. It might be a king like Phillip. After all, what city of Greece could accomplish that, and lift men like him up from servitude to barbarians?

Barbarians, I thought. We are all barbarians to him, with his scrolls of philosophy that he probably doesn't understand anyway. We are barbarians, his lesser children. I could not read a word. The expensive slave from Syracuse who tutored his legitimate grandsons was not wasted on me. And why should he be? My world was the world of the city, running errands and dashing about, doing as the women wished and fetching them little things from the market, eluding the old eunuch who managed the kitchen and always wanted to put me to work peeling something or washing something. There was too much in the world to waste time peeling things.

Of course sometimes when I ran off it caused consternation, and my mother and the others would go at it over my punishment. A few licks with a rod were not so very bad, and I bore them philosophically as the price of my freedom, but my mother would fall into fits and scream until the entire household was disturbed, leaping at the old eunuch and trying to claw out his eyes because he had beaten her son. I found it vaguely embarrassing.

Often it went on until my father stepped in. He hardly saw me at all, but my mother's antics left him solicitous, calling for cool water and a dark room, bathing her face and hands and whispering endearments, lifting a cup of watered wine to her lips with his own hands while his wife fumed.

Once when this happened, the old eunuch caught my eye. "Love is unfathomable," he said. "And masters all, even kings."

I took that as a lesson indeed.

My mother died when I was ten. Perhaps that should have drawn us closer in our grief, my father—my master—and I, but it did not. Instead of clinging to me, he wanted to be rid of anything that reminded him of her. And what should remind him more than their son together?

It was perhaps a week after her burial when one of the women called me in and told me to bathe right away, that the master wanted to see me. I was hurriedly scrubbed, my long dark hair combed and tied in a wet tail at my neck, and dressed in a too-short chiton of good cloth that belonged to the oldest grandson. Still pink from the bath, I was rushed into the dining room.

My father reclined on one couch, and a man I did not know reclined on another, the best one as he was an honored guest. I thought, from his beardless face, that he might be a eunuch too, but if so he was dressed like a gentleman. "This is Jio," my father said. "He was ten in the spring, at the equinox."

Actually, my birthday was two weeks later, but I was surprised he remembered my age at all.

"Come here, Jio," the man said, and I walked across the floor toward him, my hardened bare feet against the cold mosaics of the floor. "Look at me."

I did, searching his face for some clue. I did not understand. His eyes ran over my face, my overbite and sharp chin, my eyebrows growing together in one long line over my eyes, my sun-darkened skin and ordinary brown eyes.

"Turn for the man, Jio," my father said. "Lift your arms over your head."

I did, with some embarrassment, as raising my arms in the too-small chiton pulled it up so that it half exposed my buttocks as I turned.

The man's voice was amused. "What can you have been thinking? This boy belongs in the stable, not the bedroom! Graceless and completely unschooled, with a face he won't grow into until he's twenty! Yes, he has good bones, and I believe that his mother was a beauty, but I tell you quite frankly no one will take him. No, not even as a favor to you!"

"You may go, Jio," my master said coldly, and I did so gratefully, glad only that I had escaped whatever it was.

A few days later I was sold to a horse trader.


THE HORSE TRADER, whose name was Tehwaz, was not a cruel man. He was unsentimental about men or animals, but he never beat either for the pleasure in it. Man and horse should learn to obey, and that was all. He had no gentleness in him either. He bought horses and sold them at a better price. They were things for sale, and he had no affection or attachment to any of them. Of course they must be fed and taken care of, or they should lose their value.

The last boy had died of a fever, and he needed another boy to muck out stables and do the dirtiest work. Each horse must be groomed and exercised daily, and even the yearlings who were not broken must be taken out. Being confined sickens horses, he explained, and horses who are sick do not fetch a good price. Likewise, horses and men alike must be fed, and if the food was the cheapest available, at least there was enough of it.

Of course I tried to run away. Four times I tried it, and each time was caught before half a day passed, brought back to the inevitable beating. There was no anger in it, any more than there was for the colt who bit people. It was a bad habit of which boy and horse alike must be broken.

It worked. After the fourth time it came to me that there was little point in half a day's freedom, which led to four days of pain, and that I should not run unless there was some chance of actually getting away. I should have to wait and bide my time. After all, I was smarter than the colt.

And so I settled in quite satisfactorily, doing my work of mucking out, shoveling horse manure and old hay, and bringing in new hay for the feedboxes. All winter long that was what I did all day, as there were between ten and fourteen horses at any time. The muscles of my arms grew strong as I grew thinner, until it seemed to me that I was nothing but bone and muscle. I was taller, too, one of those mysterious spurts of growing coming on. By my birthday in the spring, when I was eleven, I looked like a boy no more.

My consolation and my joy were the horses. I had never had anything to do with them before, but now I spent the entirety of every day with them. Since it was I who cleaned up their mucky stalls, and I who held their halters while they were groomed, I who brought clean hay and slept in the loft at night, they were used to me very quickly. One horse, in particular, took to me, a lean Nisean mare, almost white, who was in foal to a famous racing champion.

The foal was due around my birthday, and Tehwaz had high hopes that it would be worth a lot of money. "With the dam's beautiful looks and his sire's turn of speed, he'd be a horse fit for a king!"

"Are you going to sell him?" I asked. I hoped not for a while, as I was fond of the mare.

"Not his first year at least," Tehwaz said. "And who knows? I might keep him until he's broken and I can get the best price."

"He'd sell better if he'd won a race or two so people would know what he could do," I said shrewdly, visions in my head of clinging to the back of a milk-white stallion as he charged effortlessly across the finish line, the crowd shouting my name.

"You may have something there, Jio," Tehwaz said. "We'll see."

The colt was born on the night of the equinox, and it was I who stood at his mother's head as he tumbled free. A colt, yes, but not milk white. He was almost red, with a white blaze and white feet, his mother's height, and long, spindly legs.

As he stood at her side to nurse, his legs wide-planted, Tehwaz clapped me on the shoulder. "Well done, boy. And if he's not white, he looks like his sire and that's good enough. He'll have the Nisean size! Look how tall he stands! He'll seat a man in armor when he's grown."

"He's beautiful," I said, for I had fallen in love.

From that day on any extra time I had was spent with him. Tehwaz called him Good Fortune, but I had another, better name for him. Watching him cavort in the pasture, kicking up his heels for the fun of it, charging and leaping in the spring sunshine, it looked to me as though he were dancing with an invisible twin, with the Spirit of Horse who had come to play beside him. I called him Ghost Dancer.

Late spring began to turn into summer, and we left Miletus. Now was the time to make the circuit of all the fairs along the coast, from the great horse fair at Halicarnassos to the one at Ehweh in the uplands, in the mountains where there was snow on the peaks even in the summer. Hittite lands, they said, where men had lived forever worshipping the gods of the heights. The high mountain pastures produced good horses, and we made a long passage through them, buying and selling. Ghost Dancer was not for sale, of course, but he made a good show frisking along the road beside his mother, full of high spirits. Some horses do not take to the uncertainty of each night in a different place, but he was undisturbed.

"Born for campaign," Tehwaz said with satisfaction. "Not a timid bone in him. He will fetch the best price I've ever had, mark my words!"

I did. Ghost Dancer would be sold. But not yet. Not yet. We had at least a year, he and I.

Often we would buy a horse in one place and then sell it a bit farther on, so I learned to ride many different kinds of horses, and to stay on those of uncertain temper. Often I rode Ghost Dancer's mother, with him frisking along beside, and we brought up the rear of the column keeping any new buys from straying. The skies were blue and the peaks glittered with snow. On the high currents of the air eagles patrolled, almost seeming to stand motionless at times, borne on the winds.

I might have run. But where should I go? I was city bred, and what should I do in open country alone? I did not know how to hunt or track, and I had nowhere to go in any case. And I should have to leave Ghost Dancer. Tehwaz had tethered me as surely as Ghost Dancer, who skipped along without halter or rope, following after me and his mother.

When autumn ended and winter came we returned to Miletus. I do not think my father should have recognized me if we had passed in the street. Almost two years had changed me. I was growing, and like Ghost Dancer I should be tall if the length of my legs were any indication. It seemed that everything was ungainly, and that my bones ached with the speed of their growth. There was no such thing as enough food. I ate one man's portion and was still hungry, still wanting more. We passed the winter in Miletus, and in the spring were on the road again.

Tehwaz had an offer for Ghost Dancer from one of the leading men of the city, which he laughed at. "If that is what he will pay for a year-ling that is not even broken, think what he will pay in the autumn!"

I thought, my face against Ghost Dancer's glossy hide. He was growing too. Soon we would begin breaking him, and when he had his strength I would ride him. I would be the first, I promised him. He should know no cruelty, learn no bad habits. When it came down to it, he should know nothing but love.

And he did love me. I knew that in the eagerness in his brown eyes, in the way he bugled out for me when I first came near, a small shadow of the stallion's bugle he would have soon. He would not be gelded, of course. He would be too valuable at stud. In him, every promise was to be fulfilled, strong and tall and gentle, fast and tractable and brave. Ghost Dancer would serve princes, and no less.

Besides, there was no hurry to sell him, and no stampede to buy. There had been a panic in the spring, when it was rumored that Phillip of Macedon meant to invade Asia, and that there would be a run on warhorses. It was many years since the Greek colonies of Ionia had been independent, since Persia had conquered them, but men like my father still dreamed of that time. Phillip had beaten the last of the cities in Greece who opposed his League, and had sworn a mighty vow to free the cities of Asia from Persia. He was a formidable man, and it seemed for a little while that he might actually bring an army over, but he was assassinated at a festival in his own city, and there would be no invasion. His heir was barely twenty. The satraps of the western provinces breathed a sigh of relief. It would be long years yet before Macedon was again a threat. We set off for the uplands and the circuit of the horse fairs unconcerned with any rumors of war.

I rode Ghost Dancer a week short of his second birthday, with no saddle pad or bridle, only a halter and my knees. I thought that I should make a try of it before Tehwaz did, so that I could show him that it was already done, and there should be no need for harshness. Indeed, there was not. We practiced at night, by the light of the moon, and by the time Tehwaz came round to it a month later, after my thirteenth birthday, we could put on a pretty show. We walked and trotted around the ring, Ghost Dancer with his neck arched in pride, every step perfectly responsive to my signals. Together we went through everything we knew, even stepping over bars that had been placed on the ground, the first thing before learning to jump. At last we finished right before him, Ghost Dancer's ears pricked forward and me with a grin I could not suppress.

Tehwaz nodded as he did when he had found a horse to be unexpectedly sound and worth more than he had paid for it. "You'll make a horseman yet," he said. "From now on you're exercising." He bought a new boy to muck out, and I was instead set to exercising the horses and working with them to overcome small faults, like following too closely.

Ghost Dancer, of course, was my joy, but I loved all the other horses too. I thought sometimes that the Spirit of Horse must be pleased with me.

Tehwaz began teaching Ghost Dancer the things a warhorse should know, and I learned too. My master was not as young as he used to be, and scrambling up and down banks or fording icy streams of the uplands repeatedly was not a pleasure to him. Once he had shown us both, I was set to practice with him. We charged at targets and veered off at the last second, jumped over low hurdles, rode at things that flapped or made noise, and learned to wheel at a canter about obstacles. In this way, I learned as well.

"Next year, when he is three, he will fetch enough to make me a rich man!" Tehwaz said. "And then I shall turn the fair circuit over to my nephew and spend my days at home in Miletus!"

He was triumphant, but I felt sick. Ghost Dancer should go to some other home, to a lord who might or might not cherish him, and I should be stuck with Tehwaz's nephew, endlessly pacing the fair circuit. I should be fourteen, and yet it seemed my life should be over without him.

In the spring there was no market. The lords of Miletus were called to service by the Satrap of Sardis, to join the army of the Great King that marched west from Anaya. The new King of Macedon had crossed the straits, and even now celebrated rites on the grave of Achilles at Troy. His name was Alexander, and though very young he was something to reckon with.

While the lords of Miletus marched north, we made the circuit of the early horse fairs, south to Halicarnassos. There we collected a good fee for putting Ghost Dancer to stud for the first time, which pleased Tehwaz immensely. I held out the hope that if the stud fees were high enough and regular enough he should not want to sell him.

While we were there the news came—Alexander had defeated the army of the Great King on the banks of the Granicus River, and now he marched down the coast. Cities opened their gates to him, merchants like my father professing that they had always admired Macedon and they viewed him as a liberator. The Great King's fleet intended to make a stand in the harbor of Miletus, and they had shut the city gates against him. Now Miletus stood besieged.

"Not for anything would I go into that. We'd lose our whole stock," Tehwaz said. "In fact, best to go into the uplands and let the Great King take care of this."

Of course it occurred to me to run. With Ghost Dancer I could get a long way. But he was not only very recognizable, but also very valuable, and if I were caught it would be as a thief, not a runaway. I had no desire to chance that.

We were at Emmen in the uplands when the word came that Miletus had surrendered after a brief siege, and that the gates were open and the city returning to normal. The leading citizens had made peace with Alexander, and it seemed that as long as tribute was paid to him rather than the Great King all would be well.

Tehwaz shrugged. "The lords make it go round, and it's the same to us. Still, it's best not to be in the way of an army, especially with a string of horses. We'll cut it short and go straight back to Miletus, where this king has already been."

And so we did. Tehwaz was right that it seemed little had changed. I gaped at the broken gates as we went in, at the streaks of black soot on some of the walls. The harbor was full of Greek ships instead of the Persian fleet, but the buildings of the town seemed little affected. Miletus had only held against Alexander for six days, and most of the actions had been fought at sea. I wished I had been there. War seemed very exciting to me, and I cursed Tehwaz's caution that had deprived me of the chance to taste it.

There were Macedonians and Greeks here still, though the King and the main body had moved on to Halicarnassos. The wounded were here, and the officers and men of the navy, as well as a couple of very young men who were supposed to organize supply for the army as it moved. They were not despoiling the land, but paying for supplies properly, if at about half the going rate. Still, Tehwaz said, it could have been worse. As yet I had no concept what he might mean.

Tehwaz, of course, had an eye to the main chance. The King of Macedon's army would want remounts before they started off on the long road east, following the Royal Road through the mountains toward Gordion. Remounts are expensive, and good ones hard to find. We had sold more than half of our stock at good prices before the blow fell.

The boy who mucked out came running to me while I was tending to a sore hoof. "The master wants Good Fortune turned out, looking his best, as fast as you can! There's a gentleman here and he's delaying him with wine while you do it!"

With a sinking feeling I laid aside the hoof pick and set about getting Ghost Dancer ready, pad and bridle and a quick brush to his mane. I pressed my nose against him, my arms around his neck, then led him out into the yard.

Tehwaz had just come out, several Macedonian gentlemen with him. They were all young, and all of them wore gleaming harness and swords, a fair show and not at all what I was used to. "Now, sirs," Tehwaz said, "you will not see a finer three-year-old in all the world! I swear to you he is like my own son!"

Ghost Dancer's ears pricked forward, but he did not shy at the bright light reflecting from their polished steel. He stood patient and alert, solid on all four legs.

"What do you think, Ptolemy?" one of them asked in Greek.

Ptolemy, a nondescript young man with his helmet under his arm, shrugged. "He's a big fellow. But I'm not shopping, remember? I'm just along for the company."

"Just like at the whorehouse," another of them jested. "You aren't shopping, just passing through!" The rest laughed.

One paid no attention to the joke. He was tall, with red hair, dark eyes, and a square jaw. He was looking at nothing besides Ghost Dancer. He nodded slowly, approaching where I stood with my hand lightly on his bridle. Ghost Dancer's eyes followed him, and he waited patiently while the man put his hands on him and looked at him. He took the bridle from me and lifted his head, looking at his teeth, which Ghost Dancer bore without protest. "Three years old?"

"Yes, Lord," I said.

His eyebrows twitched, surprised I spoke Greek, perhaps. "How does he go?"

"Sweetly, Lord," I said. I was half tempted to tell lies, anything that would make him not buy Ghost Dancer, but I could not. Like it or not, he would be sold, and this Macedonian lord seemed to know horses at least.

"What does he answer to?" he asked me quietly, taking the bridle off and putting it back on to see how he took the bit.

"Ghost Dancer," I said, and his brows twitched again. I had named him in Greek, not Carian.

"Well, Ghost Dancer," he said, one hand on his side, "let us see how we will get on. I am Hephaistion son of Amyntor."

I thought it was a bit strange to introduce oneself to a horse, but I stepped back and let him swing up easily. He was much heavier than I was, and wearing steel as well, but Ghost Dancer did not flinch, only waited patiently for a signal. A squeeze and they stepped out nicely, going round the yard at a walk, turning easily. They looked just alike, I thought, blood-red horse and red-haired man. I watched them walk about the yard, then trot. He put Ghost Dancer into tight circles, and I was glad that we had practiced that, and then sent him flying at a canter around the yard, his hooves drumming on the packed earth. When at last they pulled up, I saw that he was grinning.

"Tehwaz, you have not lied to me! You are a man of truthfulness! It is true that I have not seen a finer three-year-old in the world!"

The one they had called Ptolemy laughed. "You have added talents to the purchase price now! You will not have seen a more expensive three-year-old in the whole world!"

The other men laughed, and Hephaistion swung down, pausing to pet Ghost Dancer affectionately. "I know a prize when I see one, and I'm prepared to pay what he's worth."

"Then come and let us discuss it over watered wine," Tehwaz said, and I could see that he was certain of the best sale of his career. "That horse is like my own son, and he is fit indeed for Hipparch and Companion. Jio, cool him down and tend to him."

"Yes, sir," I said, and took Ghost Dancer's rein. I felt sick. I knew he would buy him, this tall young soldier. I knew it. Of course he would. Any man would. And he would not mistreat him, but I should be parted from him forever.

The other men followed them in. "Are you staying another day?" one asked the one they had called Ptolemy.

He shook his head. "No, just Nicanor is staying with Nearchus. The rest of us are back to the King tonight, only Hephaistion had to go see this peerless horse first!" He threw up his hands as though this were some joke of long standing. "So now we will be late on the road and riding through the night, like as not." They went in, and the door closed behind them.

In that moment, I knew what I would do.

It was nearly dawn before I caught up with the column. After all, they were mounted and I was not, and they had not stopped to make camp until very late, riding on into the night under the bright moon.

I had slipped out as soon as I thought the household safely abed, Tehwaz snoring softly after drinking a great deal of wine to celebrate the largest sale of his career. Ghost Dancer had brought him nearly enough to buy a galley instead of a horse, enough to retire as he had desired. I thought it more than enough to cover my price as well. If he guessed where I had gone, he would not care enough to chase after, not and risk displeasing the so generous Macedonian lord. Hephaistion son of Amyntor had spent a king's ransom on a horse.

They were not hard to follow. There were few on the Royal Road this late, and no other group of mounted men. I was grateful that they had walked the horses most of the way, but even so the stars were beginning to pale and the morning coming before I caught up with them. I did not realize I had finally come upon them, except that I heard Ghost Dancer's nicker. I was upwind from him, and my scent had come to him on the breeze. As I came over the hill I saw them, the picket lines downwind of the camp among the trees, saw his white blaze as his head went up among the drowsing other horses and he called out to me.

I forced my tired legs to run. I must reach him before he woke the whole camp. A few other heads came up as I passed.

But Ghost Dancer would not be silenced. He had not liked this at all, being away from me, and now it was remedied. He bugled out joyfully his greeting, backing up with his legs braced and tearing up the stake that he was tied to before I even reached his side.

At that they were all in arms in a flash.

One man held a knife to my throat, his arm like steel around me. I knew better than to struggle. Another was shouting, and there was a great deal of shoving back and forth.

At last a man I had seen earlier pushed through, the one they had called Ptolemy. "What's going on here?"

"We caught a horse thief in the picket lines, sir," a man replied.

"It's a funny horse thief that makes so much noise," Ptolemy observed.

Hephaistion angled his way between men, a torch in his hand, his hair still tousled from sleep. I did not struggle as the light fell on my face. "Great Lord, please hear me!" I asked in Greek.

His eyebrows rose. "Surely this is Tehwaz's stable boy," he said.

Behind me, Ghost Dancer was kicking up a fuss. I could hear a groom swearing as he tried to keep hold of him.

"I am, Great Lord," I said. "I have been with Ghost Dancer since he was foaled, and I have followed to ask you if you will take me on as your stable boy. I swear to you that I will work twice as hard for you as for Tehwaz! I will work all day and all night."

Hephaistion scratched his head, his eyes on mine. I willed him to believe me. How could I possibly have hoped to make off with Ghost Dancer? He was too valuable to lose, and anyone would recognize him on sight.

"I have helped train him, and I can do everything needful," I said. "I do not want to be parted from him. Please."

Hephaistion put his head to the side. "Are you a runaway slave?"

"I am a freeborn orphan," I lied. "I worked for Tehwaz because I had nowhere else to go when my father died. That is how I speak Greek. We always spoke it at home."

"How old are you?"

"Fifteen," I said. I could feel my heart pounding in my throat.

"What's your name?"

"Lydias, Great Lord," I said. Surely he would not ask my name if he meant to kill me for a horse thief.

"Lydias?" Ptolemy said, and I remembered he had been there when Tehwaz called me Jio. He must be a man of quick mind to remember.

"Lydias," I said decisively. "Tehwaz did not want to call me by my Greek name." In fact he had never heard it, as I had made it up.

Hephaistion gestured to the man who held me and I felt the arm around me release. "Well, Lydias of Miletus, I suppose I can afford to pay another man, since we've just sacked most of Ionia. You'll draw a groom's wages, and I expect you to care for other horses as well as Ghost Dancer. I have four others, and you will do the low work for all, until you have proven yourself."

"Yes, Great Lord," I said, and began to prostrate myself.

"None of that," he said, catching at my arm. "Yes, sir, will suffice. We don't bow and scrape in the army, even to the King."

"Yes...sir." I swallowed "Great Lord" in my throat before it came out.

He clapped me on the shoulder, exchanging an amused look with Ptolemy. "Well enough then. Welcome to the King's service, Lydias of Miletus." And so I was reborn.

# ASHES

The King lay dead in the care of the embalmers, dead three weeks, and yet I lived.

We left Babylon by night, under Ishtar's horned moon. I did not care where I went. One place was as good as another, but I had orders.

We mounted up in one of the palace courtyards. It was after midnight, but the lights from the great temples still showed. Glaukos, one of my men, sidled over as I adjusted the pad across my horse's back. "Are you sure this is right?" he asked, jerking his chin at the darkened windows of the palace.

I shrugged, tugging on my bag to make sure the strap held. "General Ptolemy's as much right to order us someplace as anybody else. He's one of the Regents, isn't he?"

Glaukos nodded, still chewing on his lip beneath his helmet. "It doesn't seem right," he said.

"Nothing does." I turned and met his eyes. "Look, man. The King is dead, and that's how it is. The fornicating Regents are all going to kill each other. Somebody's already knocked off Queen Stateira, and everybody's just waiting to see if Roxane will drop a son. If she does, well and good. The Regents will only kill each other. If it's a daughter, then it's war. And if you hadn't noticed, we're sitting on about twenty million Persians who'd like to be rid of the lot of us. This is not good!"

He opened his mouth and then shut it again.

I lowered my voice and spoke to him close. "Now, nobody's saying you have to have a head for politics. We follow orders, and Ptolemy's still giving orders that make sense. We're the fucking cavalry, Hephaistion's Ile with his name for all eternity, and we do what we're told. Ptolemy's made Satrap of Egypt, and how do you think he's to do that without a single man actually in Egypt? Our job is to seize the fortress at Pelousion and hold it for him. And if it gets us out of Babylon, well and good."

"How we going to seize a fortress with sixty men?" Glaukos wanted to know, his chin forward stubbornly.

I didn't blink. "That's for me to figure out, isn't it? Seeing as how I'm the Hipparch and you aren't."

"And better you than me," he said, but he set about making ready again.

I heard a noise and looked up at the portico, but it was only Ptolemy coming down, a couple of people with him. His head was bare, but he wore full harness. Everyone wore full harness now, even in the palace, even to sleep.

"Ready?"

I nodded, my voice low. "Ready, sir. We'll be out the gates before anyone has a chance to ask questions."

He handed me a pair of scrolls. "Good. Here's the letters for the governor at Gaza and for Artamenes at Pelousion. I don't know if he'll yield, but we got on well before. If he does, don't challenge his authority about anything civilian." Ptolemy stopped and ran a hand through his damp hair. His hairline was already receding a bit. "You must do what you think best after a point, Lydias. I don't know what the situation is. The word of the King's death can't have reached them more than a few days ago. You'll be riding on the tails of the news."

I put the scrolls in my bag. "And you'll be behind us."

His eyes met mine for a moment. "I hope so," he said.

I nodded.

"But not until Roxane is delivered at least," he said. "Three more months. And then…" Ptolemy let his voice trail off. There was no point in discussing something so far away, so shrouded in blood.

"We'll hold Pelousion for you," I said, for want of something to say.

Ptolemy looked about. "I have something for you to take with you as well," he said, and one of the cloaked figures with him stepped forward. Under the dark cloth I saw her eyes, Thais the Athenian, the hetaira who had traveled with Ptolemy for ten years now, since they had crossed into Asia.

I must have looked surprised, because she said quickly, "I can ride, Hipparch. How do you think I've kept up all these years?"

"I'm sure you can," I said.

Her cloak moved, and I saw the child standing beside her, so close that one cloak covered them both. She held a second in her arms, sleeping against her shoulder.

I opened my mouth and shut it again.

Ptolemy's voice was low. "I am entrusting Thais and our children to you, Lydias. Convey them to Pelousion."

"We have no litters or wagons," I said. "General..."

Ptolemy's eyes flickered to Thais. "Thais can ride," he said. "And if you take Chloe up before you, you will not lose speed. She won't be afraid. Thais can wear Lagos in a sling against her. That's what she's always done."

I nodded sharply.

"Thank you, Hipparch," Thais said in her rich voice. "We will not delay your business. I promise you that."

I mumbled some pleasantry or other and stowed the last of the things in my bag, conscious that behind me Ptolemy had knelt beside the child, who had thrown her arms around his neck while he spoke softly in her ear. He stood up, lifting her, a little girl seven years old or so, almost a bundle in her dark cloak.

Thais bent her head toward his, and I caught his words as he straightened. "I'll see you soon in Pelousion, dove," I heard him promise, and I heard the catch in his voice and knew he expected to die.

I ground my teeth together and swung onto my horse's back. "Ile, mount!"

There was the bustle of everyone getting up, the rattle of lances, one trooper holding the bridle while Thais mounted, surprisingly nimble.

Ptolemy handed the younger child up to her, and I caught a glimpse of his sleeping face, a boy perhaps a year and a half old, wrapped tight in a sling that would hold him against his mother's body. Then he helped the little girl up before me. "Hold on right there," he said, putting her fingers where they should be. "Just like you do for me. The Hipparch Lydias won't let you fall."

"The Hipparch Lydias hopes not," I said, wondering how in Chaos I was supposed to hold on to her if I had to use my sword. Still, it should not come to swords at the gate.

"Good fortune," Ptolemy said, and I touched my heels to my horse.

The streets of Babylon were broad and empty. We rode in loose order, Thais behind me and in the center. The baby was not visible at all beneath her cloak, bound to her in the cloth sling. She seemed at least to be able to ride at a walk. Sati had never ridden. She was afraid of horses...

I pulled myself away from that thought. "When we get to the gates, boys, I'll do the talking. But if they try to stop us, don't engage. Just push straight through. They're not mounted, and they won't catch us."

I saw the nods, Glaukos passing the word back.

Before me, the child sat very straight, her body swaying a little with the gait, relaxing into my chest. It went without saying her father was desperate. He must see nothing but death for her in Babylon.

"If we have to run, I need you to hang on tight," I said, and she nodded. I could not see her face.

"I'll hold on," she said, and there was no tremor in her voice.

The guards challenged us.

"Hephaistion's Ile of Companion Cavalry," I replied, "on the orders of the Regents."

"We've had no orders," the officer of the watch said. The gates were open, but there were ten or twelve men on duty.

"Well, I have!" I said arrogantly. "We're Companions, man. People actually tell us things."

The officer bristled, but he didn't draw as we approached. "General Perdiccas said no couriers were to leave without his permission."

"Do I look like a fornicating courier?" I sneered at him. "I don't need General Perdiccas' permission. I told you, the Regents sent us." I raised my left hand, the reins in my right about the child. "Forward!" I touched my heels to her flanks.

We surged forward through the gates, Thais and all, several of the guards dodging to get out of our way with oaths and curses.

The Royal Road was empty ahead of us at this time of night. "Forward!" I shouted. "Put some distance between us!"

Archers could fire from the gatehouse, of course, or the towers, but if we were fast we'd be out of range before they were ready. I did not hear the song of a single bow as we cantered, the wind rushing past us, falling into the familiar wedge out of habit with me at the point. The child's hood fell back and her dark hair tangled in the wind, my arm tight around her, leaving Babylon behind.

Above, the stars shone down and the Royal Road was a ribbon of light before us, leading us west. Somewhere, days and weeks ahead, was the sea, was the desert that guarded Egypt. Under Ishtar's stars we flew.

WE FOLLOWED THE Royal Road westward through plains and hills, a company moving quickly from one waystation to another. A courier could have overtaken us, changing mounts frequently, but none did. Perdiccas did not care so very much about sixty men. Either that, or he did not see the value of challenging Ptolemy openly for such a little thing.

Or perhaps, I thought on the twelfth day as we crested a rise and looked ahead at the descent, it would suit him well for Ptolemy himself to leave for Egypt. The fewer generals who remained in Babylon, the fewer there would be to challenge him.

Never before had such a great prize been so lightly held. Alexander's empire stretched across half the world, from the Adriatic Sea to the cities of India, uncounted millions of people, uncountable wealth. No one had thought the King would die. After all, he had survived battle after battle, and he was only thirty-two years old. Who would have supposed that he would die of a simple fever?

Or perhaps it was not so simple. Poison, murder…Whispers became rumors in the last days in Babylon. Too many people had too much to gain. His only child lay still in the womb, and the Regent for an unborn prince had many years ahead of wielding absolute power before the boy's majority could even be thought of.

Who could ever know, I thought. Even I, who was there, even I who fought beside his own bier as Companion turned on Companion for control of Alexander's corpse, did not really know anything beyond rumor and innuendo.

It was said that in the King's last hours he had named General Krateros his heir, but Krateros was halfway to Macedon, leading the veterans home who had been promised retirement. He had an army, and he would not yield place to Perdiccas easily. I did not dislike him, precisely, but he had had much to say in the past about the half-breed children of Macedonians and campaign wives that I did not like. It was the same as calling my son bastard, and that I would not take, even though my son was dead.

In Macedon itself, the King had left Antipatros as Regent, an old man who had faithfully served the King's father before him. I had never met him and knew little of him, other than that he was said to be a skillful and true man, though quite advanced in age. His son, Cassander, I did know and disliked heartily. He beat his horses, sometimes for no flaw at all but merely in temper. One hears things as a groom, and one sees things one's betters bother to hide from their peers. I had come up from those days, but I had not forgotten. A man who treats his horses cruelly will treat men cruelly if the opportunity comes, and will treat women and eunuchs the same as his horses without a thought. If backing Antipatros meant siding with Cassander, I should rather be elsewhere.

Perdiccas himself had much to recommend him. He had been of the party not tied to the old ways of Macedon, willing to learn as much as take from the peoples we had encountered. I could not explain precisely what there was to dislike in him. He was courteous, a reasonably good officer, and now he championed the cause of Alexander's unborn child. If he were ruthless, what is that in a soldier? And what use to say that Hephaistion would have been better? Hephaistion was dead.

Hephaistion, of course, should have put nothing before Alexander's true-born heir. He should not have sought power for himself, but rather held it in trust as a sacred duty from his king, as he had always done. And as the Chiliarch, essentially the Grand Vizier of the empire, he should have had the power to do so. But Hephaistion was dead not even a year, and in his absence who should I follow?

As well Ptolemy as anyone.


AT THE HALTS I handed the child off to her mother and the little girl thanked me prettily, her head down so that all I could see of her was the top of her head. She did not seem likely to cause any trouble. Nor did she seem frightened in the least, rather raising her eyes to all we passed and sometimes asking me about the things we saw.

The fourth night we made camp at a reasonable hour instead of pressing so hard. Men and horses were all tired.

After the watch was set I went round the camp one last time. The horses drowsed heads down in the picket line. We had no tents, and the night was clear and not so very cool. The children slept in a little bundle on the ground, curled around each other like puppies. Thais the Athenian sat beside them, her arms about her knees like a boy, looking up at the night sky. Her himation was around her shoulders, her head tilted back, her blonde hair gleaming in the moonlight. I came and sat near, but not too near as to foster misunderstanding.

She looked at me sideways and smiled as if she had guessed my thought.

"I do not intend offense," I said.

Thais nodded. "I know. Ptolemy said you are not a man to steal that which is entrusted to you."

"No," I said.

She looked up again, as though she drank in moonlight, her pale eyes filled with it.

"Still," I said, "you should be wary." She was alone in this place with me and my men, with none of her own except the children. She did not know me, nor any who served me, except that Ptolemy had trusted me. I was not sure I would have.

Thais looked amused. "I have traveled with the army for ten years now," she said. "I think I know the look of men I should trust and those I should not."

"Can it be ten years?" I blurted. "You must have been a child when you came out."

Thais laughed, a clear, crystal sound. "I was twenty," she said, "and you flatter like a gentleman."

"I do not mean to flatter," I said rather stiffly, uncertain whether she meant it or not.

"I see that you don't," she said, and her voice took on another tone entirely. "I was eighteen when Ptolemy came to Athens with Alexander, you see. He came to see me on a bet. Someone had bet him that he would not seek out an Athenian hetaira, trained to arts of love and philosophy alike, that such would shut her door in his rude Macedonian face."

"I take it you did not," I said.

Thais gave me a rather piercing look. "Ptolemy studied with Aristotle and he did not waste his time," she said. "When Alexander's father hired a tutor for his son he did bother to hire someone of some note."

"And Ptolemy was one who shared in those studies." I had known of course that the prince's friends shared his tutor, that the prince might learn disputation properly and nobles be honored by their sons' inclusion. But Ptolemy must have been too old. Nearly nine years Alexander's senior, he would have been a young man when the prince was a youth.

Of course there had always been the rumor that Ptolemy's mother had been King Phillip's lover when they were both very young, that his seed had taken in her before she was married off to Lagos, a country gentleman known for his mild temper and loyalty to the throne. But perhaps there was nothing in it. Certainly she had borne Lagos children, and there had never been a whisper of any impropriety. But this oldest son, her firstborn — why had Phillip sent him to the schoolroom when he must have been twenty-two? Was it mere courtesy to Lagos for his years of good service, or the only thing he could do for a son he could never acknowledge?

I expected that Ptolemy himself did not know. And how could one ever know the truth of what had passed forty years ago between people now dead?

"I came out to Asia with Ptolemy," Thais said, and she smiled. "My friends said I was mad to leave the beauty of Athens to take to the road with a wild Macedonian who would like as not abandon me in some strange city."

"He is not that sort of man," I said, thinking of the way he had bent over the child in Babylon, her arms around his neck in farewell.

"He is not," she said. "I knew that then, and I know it now. If he has entrusted us to you, then he is certain what you are made of."

"Then he knows more than me," I said, "for I do not know what I am made of."

"Do you not?" Thais looked at me curiously. "Do you have a family of your own?"

I swallowed, but my voice was still rough. "My wife and son died in Gedrosia. He was just learning to pull himself up. He had not yet taken his first steps when…" I stopped, swallowing again.

Thais' face was white in the moonlight. "I am so sorry," she said. "I did not mean to remind you."

"I do not want to forget," I said, looking up at the dark sky. "His name was Sikander. He had black hair that curled over his brow, and the most beautiful laugh, just like his mother's. I do not want to ever forget."

"I am so sorry," she said.

I closed my eyes. "My wife, Sati, believed that we are all reborn somewhere in the world, in circumstances that reflect the life we have lived and the good we have earned. If that is so, then I may know that they are somewhere in peace and plenty, and it is only my selfishness that I mourn them. Instead I should celebrate that they are escaped from suffering and live instead in some quiet land that has never known war."

"I am not sure there is any place like that," Thais said gently.

"I know," I said.

Thais shifted, and I thought for a moment she meant to touch me, but of course she could not do that.

I swallowed again, my face stretched toward the stars. "But I cannot help but wonder when I look into the face of every young child I see, if it is Sati or Sikander. If they are here, still standing in the dust of armies."

"I understand," she said quietly.

I opened my eyes. "I will see you safe to Pelousion. I have given Ptolemy my word."

Thais nodded gravely. "And what will you do then?" she asked.

"Hold the fortress for Ptolemy until he comes," I said. If he comes, I thought. If he is not murdered in Babylon as he expects to be. But he will face that more bravely knowing he has got his woman and children clear.

"We will wait in Pelousion for Ptolemy," Thais said. Her eyes met mine, and there were no tears there. "He's harder to kill than you might think."


We crossed into Egypt by night. No one bothered us, but then even in the wadis and dangerous places where bandits were known to lurk, none would attack so large a group of armed men. At that time there were no markers at the border, but I knew where it was nevertheless. We rode between cliffs that did not quite overshadow the road. It was rock, not sand here, red, not golden in the sun. It would be easy to lose one's way. One rock looked like another.

And yet I knew when we crossed into Egypt. The fine hairs on the back of my neck stood up as though we were being watched. Our horses grew more restive.

At last, I saw something gleaming pale as bone in the moonlight, a sphinx the size of a small horse half buried in dirt, strange words and symbols graven upon it. It stood beside the road, a broken plinth on the other side showing where its mate had been.

"Halt," I called.

I dismounted and walked forward. Its empty carven eyes regarded me. Perhaps in an ancient day it had marked the triumph of some pharaoh, or had stood guard over this stretch of road, a silent sentinel at the edge of Khemet.

I took out a skin of good wine and poured a generous libation into the dust before its feet. "Guardian of Egypt," I prayed aloud so that my men might hear, "we cross into your lands not as enemies, but in the service of the Divine Alexander, whom you welcomed at Siwah as the son of Amon. Let us pass, we pray, and guide our steps true to Pelousion."

I inclined my head. The night wind brushed past me like a great cat, stirring my cloak against my legs. I almost thought I heard it whisper, *Pass, Lydias, and know you shall be changed.*

Well, I thought, that is not such great peril.

I lifted my head. "We ride," I said, and mounted up again.

# KHEMET

The first time I came to Egypt it was as a stable boy. A little more than a year had passed since I had run away from Miletus and joined Ghost Dancer in the service of Hephaistion son of Amyntor, but it seemed a much longer time. It was the time in which I turned from boy to man. To be sure, I was still not quite seventeen, but a year and more with the army had changed me though I had not yet seen battle. The boy Jio was long gone.

I had crossed mountains and plains, trundling along in the baggage train with the spare horses and tents, and seen the dreadful wounded of the Battle of Issos. I had sat months before Tyre as we besieged it and watched the slaughter after, the apportioning of captives. There had been no cities sacked before in this campaign, only the genteel occupation such as there had been in Miletus, but Tyre had resisted for many months. And so for the first time I heard the shrieking of the women, saw the frightened children hurried into lines for the slave markets of Damascus and Apamea. I understood, then, why Tehwaz had said it could be worse.

I learned other things as well. I tried my hand with a bow and found it more difficult than it looked to shoot a waterbird on the wing for our dinner. I learned to use a sword. I was terrible, no doubt, but when the day was done, particularly during the long months we sat outside Tyre, some of the grooms and servants got up games, wrestling or pretend bouts with a sword, aping the recreations of our betters. I did not have my full height yet, but I was tall enough and lethal quick. A sword weighed less than the shovels and rakes I had been handling, and was better balanced too.

Thus when I came to Egypt, I was like a colt on the edge of adulthood, broken already to ride, but not yet steady, not yet at his full weight.

In Egypt, there was no slaughter. The Egyptians hated the Persians, who had conquered them again after a brief period of independence only eleven years earlier, and rather than resist they greeted us with celebration. Even for us in the baggage train, there was something rather spectacular about entering Memphis in procession, riding Ghost Dancer at the end of the line, while people threw flowers down upon us and girls blew us kisses. Ghost Dancer pranced, his head held high.

I might have preened a little myself. When a girl broke from the lines along the street and ran out to give me a flower, her face upturned like a rose in the sun, her dark eyes lively with laughter, I could not understand a word she said, but I saw the movement of her breasts beneath her white shift and felt myself in that moment a man indeed. Egyptian women do not go veiled like the women of Miletus, and they may talk to anyone they choose. I found it disconcerting—so much beauty so close at hand. I did not know what to say. The world of the stable is a male world, and I had not so much as spoken to Tehwaz's daughters. To do so would have been to deserve a beating.

As for Memphis, what can I say? It was grander than Tyre and older still, the great pyramids standing guard in the desert nearby, already incalculably old. Her temples, her streets, the great walls along the river that stood seven times the height of a man wrought of golden sandstone that glowed in the sunset—what may I say of Memphis that has not been said a thousand times by every traveler who has passed through her gates? I thought her the most beautiful city in the world, and to enter thus, with song and trumpet, even the servants' brows bound with victory wreaths, was a wonder unimaginable. I came to Memphis like a child coming home.

Now I came to Pelousion not as a child or as a servant, but as a soldier.

Artamenes, the governor, was a Persian gentleman in middle age who had been confirmed in his post by Alexander, who had heard nothing ill of him. He heard me out with some trepidation.

"Now see," he said, "how am I to know that these orders are legitimate?"

"Ptolemy has been confirmed as Satrap of Egypt by the Regents, and he is one of their number. He will be here himself soon, after the Lady Roxane is delivered of her child."

Artamenes stroked the end of his beard. "And if the child is a girl?"

I spread my hands. "That is in the hands of the gods," I said piously. "If they meant for Alexander to have a son, it will be."

"And if not?" he asked.

"Then no doubt the King's brother Arrhidaeus will be crowned, since he should be the next heir." I hoped he had not heard that Arrhidaeus was feebleminded. I certainly had no doubt that if it came down to Arrhidaeus on the throne of Great King in the absence of any other heir, Persia would revolt.

"I see," Artamenes said, and I struggled to keep my face bland. Just a common soldier, who had no idea about politics.

"That's as it may be," I said, "but all I know is that Ptolemy is the new satrap, and he's given me orders to join you here at Pelousion and to cooperate with you in all ways. I hope that my troops may be of some assistance in whatever challenges you face." As though, I thought, they answered to anyone but me.

Artamenes nodded. "There is the issue of Cleomenes in Memphis. You probably do not know that I had written to the King several times about him. He lives like a king himself on the taxes of Egypt, and does not do what is needful. He does not repair the roads and makes excuses when grain is sent for."

"I had not heard," I said. "Is he also Persian?"

"Greek." Artamenes frowned. "I suppose he was some friend of someone's to be appointed to this position, but I tell you he fleeces the Great King in a way that is unseemly."

I looked grave. "I shall be certain to tell the new satrap, General Ptolemy, all that you say."

Artamenes raised his chin speculatively. "Are you close in his confidence, then?"

"Should he have entrusted his harem to me otherwise? His chief concubine and his children?" That was not the way it had happened in Babylon, of course. And Thais would no doubt be incensed to be described as a chief concubine, rather than a free hetaira, but I had been raised in the Satrapy of Sardis, not in Greece.

"That is true," Artamenes said contemplatively. "One might only trust one's brother with such, or a bosom friend whose loyalty is beyond reproach." I saw his estimate of me going up. "We shall make you welcome in Pelousion, then, that the new satrap may know that whatever Cleomenes' doings we are loyal here. The women's quarters will be made ready for the Satrap's harem, and there will be rooms for you and your men in the fortress proper, that you may convey to General Ptolemy that all has been done in accordance with his wishes."

I inclined my head courteously, the little half bow of one nobleman to another, not to a superior. After all, we were brothers in Ptolemy's service, and knew what was due one another. "I am grateful for your courtesy. And if it is not too much of an imposition on your time as a busy man, I should appreciate being shown the administrativa of Pelousion—where you draw your taxes from, the roads and navigational hazards and the disposition of the port—those things that a conscientious servant should make it his business to learn."

"It would be my pleasure to show you those things, Hipparch," he said, and so we came into Pelousion.


My quarters were far and away the grandest I had ever had, with fretted screens of carved wood letting in light and air from an inner courtyard made up as a bower. A fountain played. There were no statues, just clean beautiful lines, and fig trees shaded a little garden of flowers. My room had a gigantic heavy bed, two chests of fine cedar wood, and a desk and chairs in the Persian style. If I had not known I was in Egypt, I should have thought myself in Persia.

I did not rest easily. Perhaps it was being in a strange place, or perhaps that the bed smelled vaguely musty, but I tossed and turned for a good while before at last sleep took me.

I dreamed, and in my dream I stood on a plain of sand under the full moon, dunes retreating from me, ridge after ridge of them marking the trackless desert. In the distance glimmered the walls of a city, cold as death in the moonlight, and I thought that it reminded me of some city I had known, rendered still and nacreous as a city of the dead.

The night wind whirled around me, kicking up dust devils, speaking to me with haunted voices. Bone and night, old spirits haunted the darkness before there was fire, whispering creatures made out of wind. They toyed with me, lifting my hair and tugging at my clothes, speaking of despair and silence, of lying down on the cool sand to die beneath the moon. There was somewhere I needed to go. There was something I needed to do, only I could not remember what.

With a rush like a breath of wind they slid away like shadows at the sound of her coming, and I looked up to see the Sphinx. She was no longer stone, but tawny-furred like a lion, padding toward me on great paws, her human face strangely beautiful.

"You have returned to Egypt, Lydias of Miletus," she said, and her voice recalled not that of a woman, but the pure tones of a eunuch. "Beware, for it is a perilous time to be abroad, either in the Two Lands or their analogies in dreams."

"Why?" I asked, shivering. "I did not feel anything bad here before, and I have done no wrong in Egypt."

"They are loosened," she said, her voice sounding like bronze. "All the spirits of the Red Land that should be bound. Pharaoh's death has unbound them, and more besides. Here and elsewhere they are abroad, and death walks the night."

"Why?" I asked again. "Where did they come from?"

"They were made by people," she said. "All the dark spirits and Furies, all the hags and spiteful cursed things. You made them. You imagined them, and thus brought them into being. You gave your fears flesh of a kind and set them free in the world."

"We made them?"

"Yes." She nodded. "People made them. It is easy for people to imagine monsters, to give them power. It is easy to imagine guilt and fear and pain in tangible form. And when you do, you make them real. In Egypt they were long ago bound to the Red Land by Pharaoh's power. Alexander could hold them, as pharaohs have for a thousand years, but he is dead and they are freed. His heir must take on the responsibility and bind them."

I lifted my eyes to hers under the stars of this heaven, where even their patterns were strange. "There may be an heir. But if so, his heir is a baby. We don't even know if Roxane carries a boy or girl."

"Alexander's son will never rule the Black Land," she said, and her eyes were blue, blue as faience. "Egypt must have a pharaoh, not a disinterested overlord who will not see to what is needful. With Pharaoh's death, all is released and they roam through the world. Do you not see that all will be taken by the Furies? Do you not see that all the creatures of your mind will feed on blood and grow strong unless they are called to order and returned to the bindings that should hold them?"

"What must happen?" I asked, though I felt that somehow I already knew.

"Horus must bury Osiris in all honor and come forth by day as Egypt's champion," she said.

"Lady, those are riddles," I said. "Cannot you tell me plainly what you want me to do?"

"Bring the King to Memphis," she said. A cloud passed over the moon, veiling her, and as it passed I woke.

I sat upright in the big Persian bed. It seemed stifling hot and close in the room after the cool desert I had dreamed. I got up and went to the window, looked out over the garden. The moonlight limned every leaf, every bud.

"Egypt," I whispered. "Khemet." I did not quite know what she wanted of me.

It was only a few days before we had a strange visitor. Artamenes and I were sitting in his study while he showed me the maps of the roadways that led through the Delta, to Tanis and Pi-Ramesses and other places where it was not possible to go directly by river without going far south out of one's way, when a messenger entered.

"Lord Artamenes," he said, "there is a priest here come downriver from Memphis who says he has come to speak with the Companion Lydias."

I straightened. "I do not know a priest," I said.

Artamenes' eyebrows rose. The Persians and the priesthood of Egypt had not been on good terms. Some matter of killing sacred animals, I thought. But as far as I knew, we had not offended the priesthood in any way.

"He says his name is Manetho and he is a priest of Thoth," the messenger said. "Lord, will you see this man?"

I thought that Artamenes would refuse, but I got to my feet first. "I will come," I said. "Perhaps he has some news of Cleomenes it would be useful to receive."

Artamenes nodded. "Perhaps that is politic, then."

I nodded pleasantly and went down.

The man standing in the courtyard of the fortress looked as though he had just stepped off the wall of a temple or a tomb. His head was shaven, and he wore an elaborately pleated linen skirt. His brown shaven chest was crossed by a cheetah skin, which he wore over one shoulder. He did not bow at all.

"I am the Hipparch Lydias," I said, and came out to him. "You wanted to see me?"

"I did," he said. "I am Manetho, and I have come from Memphis to speak with you. Is there some private place where we may walk?"

"There is," I said, and led him toward the inner garden. The fountain should make us difficult to overhear, and I did not really fear that he would try to knife me. I could take my chances with that. "But you must have left Memphis more than a week ago. How could you know I would be here?"

He turned and regarded me solemnly. "We had word that Alexander the Son of Amon was dead, of course. It is reasonable that a man would come to Pelousion soon, and of course I asked the gate guards your name. Did you expect some other answer?"

"Of course not," I said.

We went into the garden. I saw him look about, his face studiously neutral. It was a very, very Persian garden.

"Do you come from the Great King of Persia?" Manetho asked.

"I come from General Ptolemy, the Satrap of Egypt," I said carefully.

"And who does he serve?" he asked.

"The Council of Regents," I said. "Who hold the empire in trust for Alexander's child."

"Or his brother," Manetho said.

I nodded. "If necessary."

Manetho sat down on the bench beneath the fig tree, and it came to me that he was quite young, at least five years my junior. "Egypt will not serve a Persian king," he said.

"Are you here to warn me of an uprising? Or to threaten one?"

"Not at this time," Manetho said tranquilly. "We have no prince who shall serve. Nectanebo is dead, he who was our last Pharaoh before the Persians returned and crushed us. His line is gone." Manetho spread his hands. "There are many noble leaders in Egypt, some from Upper Egypt and some from Lower Egypt, but none who can do the thing that needs to be done."

"Which is?"

"Keep us free," he said, and his brown eyes met mine. "Is freedom so little to strive for?"

I nodded slowly. "And what you want is the Satrap Ptolemy to guarantee Egypt the freedoms that Alexander restored, which you did not have under the Persians? Such as the free practice of your own religions and the worship of your gods?"

Manetho nodded. "No doubt you have heard how the Great King of Persia slew the Apis bull and laughed when we wept. But you may not know how it has galled beneath their yoke, following their laws and their ways. We do not lock up our women or let men have ten wives. We do not hold man and wife yoked together when they have decided to part or make eunuchs of young boys. They have taken Egyptian women as concubines and said they may not depart if they wish, and have castrated our sons." He shifted on the bench, and his mild face was at odds with his words. "And then Alexander the Son of Amon came and restored to us what was ours. It is said that throughout his lands he let every people live according to their customs."

"That is true," I said.

"We will not live under Persia again," Manetho said. "I tell you that as a fact, so that you may tell General Ptolemy."

"General Ptolemy has no wish to interfere in Egyptian custom or law," I said carefully, "save in those towns or places founded primarily by Greeks. You know that this new city Alexander founded, the one which is to bear his name, was intended to attract merchants from many lands who may be expected to bring their own customs with them, and to operate under a code of law that was laid down — civic law, one law for all, so that there are not discrepancies in the punishment of crimes between people just because their native language is different or their heritage. I do not think Ptolemy will be willing to abandon that."

Manetho searched my face, and there was something in him suddenly that reminded me of the King. "I see that," he said. "Are you then a man of government?"

"I am a plain soldier," I said. "Not a priest or a philosopher."

His eyebrows rose. "And yet you know something of governing."

"I have traveled in many lands," I said, "and in each I have seen something to like. I do not say this gives me wisdom or has taught me how to govern. I only seek to represent my master."

"And yet it is said that one can tell a great deal about a master by the conduct of his servants," Manetho observed.

"That is also true," I said. "In which case you should perhaps consider General Hephaistion, as until his death I served him for many years."

Manetho tilted his head back, looking up at the fig tree above. "I understand Alexander ordered a temple built for him in Alexandria. I do not believe the work has begun."

"I am sure Ptolemy will follow the King's wishes," I said rather shortly.

Manetho nodded politely. "As one should. Have you been there yet?"

"To Alexandria? I was there when it was laid out, but have not been back."

I had stood holding Ghost Dancer's rein when Hephaistion came out to see why the King must do the work of a digger and had found him, hat off and sunburned, laughing and talking with the men who were setting out the lines of the streets with stakes and string, the surveyor with his angles and tripod. I stood holding the horse, letting the sea wind lift my damp hair from my neck, watching the wild seabirds wheeling in the air. Ptolemy was anxious to be off, fidgeting, while Alexander would not be satisfied until he had done all himself. I watched, looking out over the cerulean depths of the Middle Sea, watching the black-winged gulls calling on the wind over the vast natural bowl of the harbor. It seemed for a moment that the world tilted beneath me. Perhaps it was only that beauty moved me.

"Perhaps you will go," Manetho said.

"If General Ptolemy sends me," I said.

"Just so," Manetho said, and took his leave.

After he was gone I walked in the garden a while longer. It was true that if I had not known I was in Egypt I should have thought I was in Persia from the garden. They had erased anything not their own.

And yet it was still fair.

The curves of the fountain were not Egyptian. The fretted screens with their elaborate carving were straight from Susa or Persepolis, that palace that Alexander had burned long ago, Thais throwing the first torch. The flowers that grew—I did not know their names—were things I had seen in Babylon.

And still it was beautiful.

Must beauty only have one form? I wondered. That is like saying that all women must be pale, or all boys doe-eyed. Is there only, as the Persians believe, one right way to live and that is the Truth, all else being Lies? And if many things can be true, how can a man know which way to live?

I wondered, beneath the fig tree, but my heart answered already. By following your heart, I thought. By giving heed always to love and honor. Really, that was all the answer I needed.

I had spoken truly when I told Manetho that if a man's worthiness can be determined from the actions of his servants, that he should consider Hephaistion rather than Ptolemy. After all, I had only served Ptolemy a few short months. If I had a model for how a Companion should behave it was Hephaistion, and if I had learned anything of governing it had been from him.

I had been sixteen and a horseboy still at the Battle of Issos, and had taken no part in the fighting. Afterward, Alexander had ridden down the coast with all haste, making for Egypt, accepting surrenders of the cities along the way as he went. In Sidon the Persian satrap ran at the rumor of our approach and the gates of the city stood open to us. Alexander stayed only a single night before he went on southward, leaving Hephaistion to order things in his wake.

Among the things that needed to be done was an arrangement made for the governing of the city. It was Alexander's custom to only appoint a Macedonian or Greek governor if the task was exceptionally challenging, a city that had resisted with great force. In other cases he returned the governance to some local person of worth who would rule according to their own customs, and thus avoid leaving a trail of anger and resentment behind us, simmering always in our rear.

So it was in Sidon that Hephaistion held a dinner for gentlemen of the important families, seeking to know which might be worthy of being made Sidon's king. Although many men pressed their claims, two young men told him that it was long custom that the king must be of a certain lineage and royal line, as that line was blessed by Ashteret of the Sea, who we call Aphrodite Cythera, and only one of that line might fruitfully rule the city. Hephaistion inquired about and found that a man of that line remained who was well spoken of, though he had fallen on hard times lately and was employed as a gardener.

He sent for this man, named Abdalonymus, but he refused, sending word that he was in the midst of pruning and could not take the time.

At this many men would have been angry, but Hephaistion laughed and called for me to bring out Ghost Dancer, as he would go to Abdalonymus if he would not come to him.

We rode to the outskirts of the city on a beautiful morning. These were not great houses here, but modest dwellings of a room or two, though sturdily built. As I followed Hephaistion along the street I wondered at one we saw first from a distance. Its roof was overgrown with climbing roses, trained in a riot of red and pink, and every bit of the yard was planted tightly, fig trees and almond trees and weeping peach trees bending their heavy branches. Cucumbers and melons and all good things grew tied carefully to trellises, and the bees were in the lavender. It was the most beautiful tiny house I had ever seen, each plant perfect and perfectly cared for.

I went to hold the general's rein and he dismounted. I saw that he was as awestruck by the beauty of the place as I was. There are gardens, and then there are paradises.

A middle-aged man on a ladder was up in the peach tree. Hephaistion came up below. "Are you Abdalonymus?" he called up.

"Yes," the man said without looking around.

"Will you come down and talk with me?" Hephaistion asked, his hand on his hip.

"Nope. I'm busy." He didn't even glance down, just kept on doing what he was doing. "What do you want?"

"To make you King of Sidon," Hephaistion said, and there was a note of amusement in his voice.

At that he did look around, a pair of shears in his hands, keen bright eyes in a stubbled face. "Why?"

"Because if this is how you care for what is yours, you are the man to rule the city," Hephaistion said. "Will you come down and talk with me? I am Hephaistion son of Amyntor, and the King of Macedon has charged me with finding a good shepherd for this people."

At that he came down. "What if I don't want to be King of Sidon?" he said.

Hephaistion rubbed his nose ruefully. "Well, I can't make you be King of Sidon, can I? But someone's got to be. Better for all if it's a man who builds and brings fruit rather than a man who despoils, don't you think? If you don't, whenever something goes wrong you'll wonder if you might have mended it."

"Hephaistion son of Amyntor?"

"Yes."

"Come inside, Hephaistion son of Amyntor. Have some wine and fill me in a bit about this king job," he said, and they went into the house, Hephaistion hanging behind as a young man should to let his elder precede him.

I stood in the street under the peach tree, holding Ghost Dancer's rein.

# DREAMS AND NIGHTMARES

Roxane was delivered of a son, a healthy enough child they said, who was promptly proclaimed Alexander IV. This averted civil war for the moment, which surely would have erupted if the baby had been a girl. The Regents settled in for the long term — it would be sixteen years before the boy could wield real power, almost an eternity. Rather than remain in Babylon, Ptolemy arrived in Pelousion ten weeks later with nearly a thousand men.

His baggage train was larger still. Most of the men had brought all their goods and their families as well. I watched them file into the walls of Pelousion, the women with their wary eyes, veterans of too many camps and too many years on the road, their children running around them like puppies, taking in the sights. The oldest were nearly youths and maidens, ten or eleven years old, fair-skinned and light-haired, children of Greeks and Ionians. Then there were the dark-haired children of Carians and Persians, and the green-eyed children of the Medes from the middle of the campaign. One or two honey-skinned women fell to their knees in thanksgiving, women of Egypt who had at last come home.

Next there were the Bactrians and Sogdians, small-boned and quick like their ancestors on the plains near the Caspian Sea, and the sons and daughters of the Indians with their dark eyes, still carried or riding in carts as they were too small to walk all the way. Last were the

Babylonians, worn in slings on their mothers' hips, or swelling the bellies of the women in the carts.

Sikander would have been three and a half, I thought. He should have been riding in a cart beside his mother, waving and pointing at the high gates painted with blue and gold. My heart ached in my chest.

Alexander had dreamed of establishing an Ile to be called the Successors, made up of the sons of his soldiers, boys from many lands who should all learn together and all fight together as brothers, as though humanity itself were nothing but a tribe. It had not happened. And yet here, watching the children of Ptolemy's men enter into Pelousion, I knew I saw a new thing. They did not see Greeks and Persians, Egyptians, Medes, Bactrians, Indians. They only saw each other, the playmates of the journey, gabbling together in a bastard Greek liberally spiced with words from their mothers' tongues. They did not see Humans and Barbarians.

Standing there upon the wall, waiting for Ptolemy, I saw it in a flash, all that could be, all that Alexander had intended. His sacred fire was gone, broken into a thousand sparks, and I saw them all in the tired faces of women of a dozen nations eager to find the best quarters, in the faces of their children.

"A new thing," I whispered, and felt it prick through me like pain.

"Yes," Ptolemy said. I had not heard him join me on the wall, Thais beside him with her arm about his waist beneath his traveling cloak. The sun had burned his forehead where his hair was receding.

"General," I said and turned, pulling myself together.

Thais' blue eyes were compassionate, and I thought that she guessed what I felt, that my wife and son were not among them. "The Hipparch Lydias was the most gracious companion possible," she said. "I am grateful for his escort."

"Thank you," I said.

Ptolemy looked out at the rapidly filling courtyard. "I don't know what we're going to do with them all tonight, but I suppose we'll work it out."

"They've worked it out before a thousand times on campaign," Thais said practically. "Let me go down and tell the leaders among the women where the water supply and the privies are, and that they can cook in the courtyard but not in the stableyard." She gave him another quick squeeze and started along the wall to the stair, pulling her himation up to cover the back of her hair.

Ptolemy sighed. I thought he looked tired and strung out.

"How many are there?"

"Hundreds. I suspect that some of them aren't with men in my Ile or phalanx. But if they've lost their men or been abandoned by men who went with Krateros, they've got to go somewhere or beg in Babylon. They've no place there, and I suppose they think their chances are better here. Alexander intended a school for the campaign orphans, but..."

"It will never happen now," I said. I had been a child sold as a slave. And now I knew what good fortune it had been to be bought by Tehwaz.

"Death can come for us at any time. I'd like to think someone would take care of Thais and the children."

"I imagine Thais does a fair job of taking care of herself," I said.

He smiled at that. "She does. But Chloe and her brother, Lagos..." He took a deep breath. "It's not good in Babylon, Lydias. Krateros and the Macedonian party want to put everything back the way it was, just go home to Pella and forget that any of this ever happened, except for being richer men."

I nodded. There had always been that faction, Macedonians who had followed their king to make war on the Persian barbarians, and who could not understand why, having won, there was anything to think of besides the money and going home. They had been the ones who had the least patience for ruling, and who had grumbled that the King adopted too much Persian dress, ate too much Persian food, and had too many Persians about him.

Ptolemy continued. "Perdiccas wants to be Great King of Persia, and he's got a bunch of Persian nobles backing him. He has a Persian wife from one of the greatest families, and he's making a play for Alexander's sister Cleopatra at the same time. Add to that a bunch of half-baked contenders who want the entire pudding, and you have a disaster. Everyone wants to be Alexander."

"No one is," I said.

Ptolemy looked at me sideways. "That was a happy conjunction of circumstance and talent that will not happen again."

"The gods willed it," I said.

"Yes, that too. But in any event, the effects of the experiment are unreproduceable."

"And Roxane's son?" I asked.

Ptolemy looked out over the courtyard, where Thais and his daughter had joined the others below. Thais was gesturing and talking with three women, one a dark-haired Indian in a threadbare printed sari. "Do you really think he will be allowed to grow up? Is it in anyone's interests for him to live more than a few years?"

"It's in Roxane's interests," I said, and felt my stomach clench.

"Roxane, yes," he said. "She's a tiger. Just exactly like Alexander's mother, Olympias. She murdered anyone who got in her way. If you wanted to live, you gave her no reason to fear you." Below, Thais seemed to have made clear where the privies were, involving elaborate hand gestures for women who it seemed spoke little Greek. "Roxane had Queen Stateira killed. Which is the reason Oxathres won't support Perdiccas. Stateira was his niece, and he is not about to be of any party that countenanced her murder." Ptolemy shook his head. "Which means if it comes to war the Persian nobility will split along blood and clan lines. That's why Artashir came with me. He will not support anyone who is with Roxane. Not only have we split along the lines one would expect, the old-style Macedonians against the new men, but now this as well. Artashir and Perdiccas should be of the same party — Perdiccas was always one of the new men, always one who got on well with Persians. But if he's with Roxane, then he's lost Stateira's kin."

"That's not good," I said. I had expected that it would fall out with the old Macedonians, the men who had served Alexander's father like Antipatros and Krateros, against the younger Companions lately raised to prominence by the King. But if both those sides were split as well, then who knew how it might end?

Ptolemy went on. "And meanwhile Athens and several other cities in Greece are on the verge of revolt against Antipatros."

I let out a long breath. "Civil war in Persia and Greece both. What does that leave us?"

"Egypt," Ptolemy said.

"And when Perdiccas and Antipatros both call for troops?"

Ptolemy ran his hand through his hair. "We'll face that when we come to it. In the meantime, we must do our best to put Egypt in order. Now what is this problem I hear about Cleomenes? He's a friend of Perdiccas, so I must walk softly there."

"There is more," I said. "A priest named Manetho has come from Memphis, and I think you should talk with him." And so I told him all I knew.

WE LEFT FOR Alexandria by sea a month later, leaving a garrison at Pelousion. Ptolemy had more men coming, another phalanx and their baggage train that had started later, some thousand men. They would reinforce Pelousion when they arrived.

In the meantime, we and the men and their dependents who had first come to Pelousion would go on to Alexandria. As it was a new city, Ptolemy was offering each man land as part of his pay, a bonus for signing on with him. Each man should get a house lot of a size commensurate with his rank, thus settling the city. Alexander had done this, giving land in new cities to veterans who were retiring. Ptolemy gave it to men who were serving as well.

"They will serve all the better," he said to me, "when it is their own homes they are defending."

"And the women will bless your name through all eternity," I said.

When I had seen Alexandria last it had been nothing but string and stakes. Now I could begin to see the shape of the city to come. Broad streets crossed at sharp right angles, some already clad in white sandstone pavers. The city curved around the natural harbor, the first quay already built, while another was under construction, heavy concrete piers sunk in the mud of the harbor but not yet topped. Out on the barrier island there was a watchtower, but the city walls were not yet built. I could see where they would go, pierced by great gates.

The neighborhoods were odd—each street laid out, treeless, with perhaps one house in ten rising from the dirt, bare walls freshly painted or plastered, with occasionally a struggling vine staked up. The other houses were no more than bare dirt with a stake in it painted with a number.

I saw the women walking in groups through the streets, their children puttering along, trying to find the right number, then stopping and pointing when they did, imagining the houses that would go there, counting the distance to the houses of friends. "Here will be your house and there will be mine."

Sati would have liked it, I thought. She would have wanted a fountain and a peach tree. I had brought her peaches, once, and she had laughed and kissed me, the taste of peaches on her mouth.

One of the public markets had been built, and the stalls were crowded with traders up from Canopus and other towns, bringing vegetables and fish at exorbitant prices. Something would have to be done about that, I thought. Although there was something to be said for making yourself welcome with your spending money.

The temples were no more than roped-off cordons. Quays were more important just now than temples.

Of course much of the construction was not evident. The huge cisterns that should store fresh water and the sewers that underlay everything were not visible. The vast mountains created by dredging in the harbor were beneath the surface. All of those things could not be seen, yet when it was finished Alexander's city would be the most beautiful in the world.

The original plan had included a palace, and orders were left to build it, but very little had actually been done. The building was long and low, looking more like a stoa or a marketplace than a palace. I supposed another story could be put on eventually. Situated as it was at the base of the Lochias Peninsula, the far right end of the crescent of the harbor, the site could not have been more lovely. It caught the sea breezes, and from the portico looking left the entire city spread before one.

Ptolemy had an office in what looked like it should have been a market stall, three walls and a side open to the portico, and I wondered again what designer of marketplaces had been given the palace to build. But then there had not been architects of note here, after Dinocrates left with the King.

He looked up from his work when I came in, a litter of scrolls before him and a wax tablet, the stylus in his hand. "Settled in, Lydias?"

"I suppose," I said. I had nothing to settle but a tent. I had not looked at the plan to see if there was a number with my name beside it. I supposed there was. The Hipparch of an Ile should have a substantial lot, but I didn't see any reason to look at it. There was no one who would care if anything were ever built there.

"Good, because three days from now you and I are leaving for Memphis."

I must have looked startled. Ptolemy stretched his legs out under the writing table. "I need to see Cleomenes and work this out in person. He's a friend of Perdiccas, which makes it politically difficult, as he seems to have problems with Persians and Egyptians alike. Not to mention that the taxes he's supposed to have been spending on construction in Alexandria for the last three years haven't been spent here. The city walls haven't even been begun, not so much as a foundation laid. You're coming with me as my aide because I need a man who can handle the politics."

"Sir, I am no politician," I began.

Ptolemy frowned. "You handled Artamenes in Pelousion ideally. The only other who can do as well is Artashir, but I can't bring him to Memphis. Bringing a Persian will give insult to the clergy in Memphis, and I need their support. Artashir is staying here to handle the fortification issues and you're coming with me." He raised a hand before I could say anything. "Yes, I know Artashir is a mounted archer, not a siege engineer. But we must all turn our hand to new things as our duty requires." He looked at me and his eyes twinkled. "Besides, is politics so different than dealing with horses?"

I laughed. "I suppose not," I said. "Only we cannot geld for bad temper!"

"I'm considering it," Ptolemy said.

WE SAILED UP the Nile on a fast galley, one of the narrow-draft lateen-sailed ships the Egyptians build for river traffic, and so I returned to Memphis for the second time in my life. Arriving from the Saite branch of the river, the city seemed even more imposing than I remembered. The walls were massive, with enormous square gate towers, and below them the levees that held back the river in the flood season were three times the height of a man.

As we passed the city, ready to come about to the docks below, Ptolemy gestured to a massive iron grate set in the levees. "I wonder what that's for?" he asked.

It looked like it was designed to be lifted, and I said so.

Manetho, who had accompanied us from Alexandria, had come up to us, and he smiled. "That's where the Temple of Sobek is. He's the avenger of wrongs, and takes the form of a crocodile. The grate goes into the pools where the sacred crocodiles live. The small ones can come and go through the grate, but the large ones stay in the temple pool."

"How big are the large ones?" I asked, as the holes in the grate would have been big enough for a boy to swim through.

Manetho shrugged. "Three times the length of a man, the biggest of them. The oldest are more than a hundred years old. We protected them from the Persians when they were here."

"I see," Ptolemy said, and looked impressed.

I didn't particularly think a crocodile a hundred years old and three times the length of a man needed much protecting.

CLEOMENES WAS ABOUT Ptolemy's age, which is to say around forty, clean-shaven in the Greek fashion, fit and obviously vain of his appearance. He really had no need to flex his arms so much in his short-sleeved chiton except to show off how much time he spent in the gymnasium, and how he had certainly not run to fat like many men in sedentary jobs.

Ptolemy, who had not made time for the wrestling matches and weight lifting of the gymnasium in years, was irritated, though he hid it well. I had certainly never trained in the gymnasium as a boy, nor been welcome until lately, so I had even less patience for it. I thought that a man who had so much time to spend on the perfection of his muscles must not do a lot of work.

He was very accommodating, helpful and eager to go over the tax rolls with Ptolemy, delighted for us to be his guest at any number of entertainments. There were banquets and symposia, concerts and dancers. Of course Manetho and the other Egyptians were not invited. Cleomenes had kept the Persian custom of not including the natives. I thought that perhaps that was not wise, but Ptolemy kept his own counsel and attended each entertainment, though his good humor seemed to be wearing a little thin. He should rather spend time with the tax rolls and the other work of the governor. I suspected he was being diverted.

The eighth day in Memphis, Cleomenes arranged a hunt in the desert. We left very early. The sun had not yet risen above the wadis of the eastern side of the river and the sky had only begun to pale. The men stood about in little groups, laughing and sharing a jest and bread. I dismounted and left my horse with a groom.

Ptolemy looked up and offered me a flask. "Sport of the pharaohs, eh?" He was dressed in chiton and leather, not full harness. Who could walk about the desert during the day wearing steel?

I took it and drank sparingly. Strong unwatered wine for breakfast made my head spin. I shrugged. "Hunting is hunting, my Lord. And it is best to be seen to do as the pharaohs, of course." It had occurred to me that at least Ptolemy could appear a proper overlord.

"It will be good hunting, I hope," Ptolemy said. "But it's the cats I'm not used to." A short distance away, three cheetahs paced on light leads of scarlet leather, their handlers beside them.

I raised an eyebrow. Their thin leather cords wouldn't stop the chee-tahs for an instant if they wanted to go. It was their training that kept them within the bounds of the leads. "I've never hunted with them before," I said, my eyes following their pacing, lean muscles moving beneath perfect, mottled hides.

"You can see them in the paintings on temple walls, back a thou-sand years," Ptolemy said. "But they don't capture the beauty of the animals."

"Not hardly," I said, admiring the way one sleek female turned, her graceful tail carried high like a pleased housecat. She looked at me then, and I did not look away. Green eyes met mine, as though it were she who assessed me. I tilted my chin, but did not break the stare.

She moved toward me then, her handler following, telling her to stop. Ptolemy reached for the knife at his belt reflexively.

I looked into her eyes. I thought that she might be the mother of cats herself, so steady and intelligent was her gaze.

"My Lord, don't move," the handler said as the cheetah reared up on her hind legs, resting her forepaws on my shoulders. Her claws pricked through the linen of my chiton, just barely testing the skin, her green eyes raised to mine, her massive jaws almost at my throat.

I was not afraid, and I did not need the handler to tell me that. She looked at me keenly, measuringly, her hot breath against my face. And yet I felt no menace in her, only curiosity.

"No, my Lord," the handler said again, as I heard the scrape of Ptolemy drawing. "Wait."

She bent her head, butting at my chin with the soft fur of the top of her head, nudging at me like a cat. I leaned forward, butting back with my chin at the top of her head, my cheek rubbing against her. For a moment we stood thus, like lovers locked in an embrace.

Then she disengaged, her paws leaving my shoulders as she dropped down and ambled a few steps away, where she sat down unconcernedly to wash.

Ptolemy let out a breath, his sword in hand. "That was... interesting."

The handler was looking at me closely. "She wanted to see you, my Lord. And you must never run from a cat."

"I know," I said, my eyes still following her with admiration. "She's gorgeous."

The handler said something under his breath, and went to collect his charge.

"What was that?" I asked. I had not quite gotten what he said.

Ptolemy looked amused, and something more. "He says you are favored of Bastet, my friend."

"Oh," I said.

We rode into the desert before the sun was high. By noon I had decided this was a rather hopeless endeavor. How any game should be found with twenty men in the party, and a dozen horses, I could not guess. No doubt we looked grand, but in hours we had not seen anything besides a hawk on the wing, far above hovering on the hot air that rose from the desert. Perhaps we weren't supposed to really catch anything. Perhaps it was all to look good.

Cleomenes seemed unperterbed. At midday we halted in the shadow of an overhanging cliff and ate and drank from a fairly sumptuous hunter's spread. Then we rested a while replete in the shade.

Ptolemy was being gracious to Cleomenes, but I thought he was getting annoyed. An entire day lost riding around the desert at a snail's pace doing nothing! Even the cheetahs looked bored and drowsed, washing their paws in a desultory fashion.

Afternoon came on with long shadows. I was fascinatedly watching the trainers with their animals, and only half heard Ptolemy talking to Cleomenes, saying that perhaps we should be getting back.

"But you have not caught anything!" Cleomenes said. "And I have heard that there are lions near here. Men have seen them! I would consider myself disgraced if you returned without bagging anything!"

"You must be easier on yourself," Ptolemy said dryly. "And anyway, how could we possibly get a lion with all this parade? In Macedon we hunted lions on foot, with five or six men."

Cleomenes laughed heartily. "You must think us very soft here! I can't bear that! Let us send away the parade, as you call it, and hunt lions as a king should, just us with our spears!"

And dogs, I thought. In most places they used dogs, but we had none with us, as the cheetahs would not abide them. The hairs on the back of my neck rose.

"It's gotten so late," Ptolemy began.

"It's early yet," Cleomenes said, and began giving orders to send the cheetahs and their handlers back, as well as the men and horses who had brought our lunches out.

I was not pleased to see the cheetahs go. The beautiful female turned as she was led away and looked at me with a steady gaze, as though in warning. I loosened my sword in the scabbard. It did not escape me that if he wanted to kill Ptolemy, the fewer witnesses the better. I was one he should have to kill, at least.

I was watching Cleomenes and that was my mistake. I hardly noticed as the shadows got deeper. I certainly did not watch carefully where we went.

At last one of the trackers found some dung that he said was that of a lion. It was at the edge of a wadi, a steep ravine of reddish rock with a dry stream bed at the bottom. Perhaps that was why I found it hard to breathe. Perhaps that was why I was not attentive when Ptolemy said that we would go down. I was trying to think of a reason not to.

*A dry stream bed, a shaded ravine to camp in during the heat of the day…*

My blood ran cold and my breath came in starts. My chest ached with stabbing pains, and my vision swam. I wondered if I were dying just there, and what Ptolemy would say if I did. I would stay on my feet as long as I could, act as though all were normal. And so we were at the bottom of the cliff before I was aware of more than my feet on the path.

"I think we should go around to the left," Ptolemy said.

This is not the same place, I told myself. This is not that place in Gedrosia. This is not that place. This is another place in another country. It only looks superficially the same. I would be the master of my own heart. I would not let this choking panic make a frightened animal of me, make me prey.

I followed him.

We went up the dry stream bed. The sun had entirely disappeared behind the walls of the wadi. Dusk was upon us and night was falling.

"I don't see any spoor," Ptolemy said. He stopped, one foot up on a boulder, and scratched at where one of the high straps on his boots had rubbed his leg. His face was hot with sunburn and exertion. "Chaos take this!" he exclaimed. "I've had about enough of this wandering around. We're going back to Memphis."

I must have said something appropriate. He had not noticed. Breathe, I told myself. Deep breaths. This is not that place. See how it is evening, not morning?

Night. Night was coming up. I could see the first faint star.

"Cleomenes?" Ptolemy called out. "Tell the trackers we're going back."

There was no answer. I sat down on a rock. I hoped I only looked tired. There was an excuse for that.

Ptolemy called, and called again.

There was no answer.

He climbed up a little ways that we had come and shouted again. Then he looked down at me, and I saw his face tighten from annoyance into something different. "They've gone," he said.

I looked up.

Ptolemy came back down, careful on the loose rocks. "They've left us."

Everything dawned on me. "With no horses and not knowing the way back."

"And no water," Ptolemy said.

"Where any accident might happen," I said. "Snakes, a fall of rocks…"

"A misstep that breaks a bone," Ptolemy said. "A tragic accident. It could happen to any man lost in the desert."

I looked at him and he at me.

Somewhere above, echoing off the walls of the wadi, we heard the answering roar of a lion.

# UNDER THE MOON

**W**e should follow the dry stream bed," Ptolemy said.

I nodded. A dry stream bed would eventually lead to a larger channel, and a larger channel would lead to the Nile. Once we had found the river, it would be easy to find our way back to Memphis.

We began to walk. The ground was pitted and uneven, littered with fallen stones from above, and the going was difficult, made more so by darkness. We stopped after a little distance when Ptolemy twisted his foot, and I stood by while he cursed and rubbed it.

"We can't wait until sunrise," he said.

"I know," I agreed. We did not know how far the stream bed might twist around in the wadis. While as the bird flew we could not be more than half a day's ride from the Nile, it might be much farther as we had to walk following the track. If we climbed up the walls of the wadi and attempted to go over the top, not only would we have a dangerous climb, but we would not then know where we were, except for general direction. And when the sun rose and the heat of the day began we would feel the lack of water. Going on in the cool of the night was the best decision.

I had not heard the lion again. I hoped that meant it was far away and uninterested in us. Unfortunately, I knew perfectly well that the lion you hear is no threat. It's the lion you don't hear that is silently stalking you.

I do not know how long we walked. The moon rose high above the cliffs, a faint crescent in the dark sky, tilted like a reaper's sickle. We came to a place where the stream bed descended steeply, and I thought I heard the faint trickle of water. We climbed down, half sliding on the crumbling red stones. There, at the bottom where another dusty channel joined it, was a thin thread of water. We cupped it in our hands and lapped at it like dogs. I wished that lunch had not been quite so salty, though it was now many hours past.

From somewhere quite nearby a howl went up. Jackals.

"Shit," Ptolemy said.

Jackals do not normally bother men, but we were two alone and had probably come into their territory.

I could see them slinking along the rocks, not moving at the quick trot they usually do, dark in color. In Egypt, jackals are the color of sand and stone. These were black and they moved like shadows. In the darkness their eyes glowed with an eerie light.

"What are they?" I said. They seemed to gather out of the stones themselves.

"I don't know," Ptolemy said grimly, and then he shouted, "Back to back!" The first of the jackals leapt.

We stood shoulder to shoulder. I was a little taller than he, but he was more solidly built. If we had been a chariot team we should have been decently matched, I thought irrelevantly. And then the jackal leaped for my throat.

I caught his teeth on my left forearm, feeling the sharp edges score just above the leather wristband I wore, though he could not bite down. The sword in my right hand came up and I struck at him, a blow that should have opened his belly, only he was not there.

Another jackal dodged snarling at my other side, and I hit her backhanded across the face with the hilt of my sword. Behind me, Ptolemy staggered back against me a step as one landed with its full weight against his shoulder. He threw it off with a heave, and it hit the ground with a crunch that should have broken its back.

Only it wasn't there.

I did not lose it in the movement of the battle. I saw it falling, and then I saw bare ground.

"They're not real!" I shouted, stepping around in guard.

"They really bite," Ptolemy replied, though I heard the incredulity in his voice.

They did bite. The cuts on my left arm were bleeding, not badly but enough to notice.

For a moment they backed off, circling. We stood together, our shoulders almost touching.

"There are too many of them," Ptolemy said. His breath was coming in quick gasps. Jackals hunted in small packs, but I had never seen more than six or eight together, including pups. There were at least twice that number now, lean black jackals with eyes that reflected the nacreous sheen of the moon.

"They're not real," I said. There was something in this that reminded me of my dream in Pelousion, of the Sphinx. I felt something click into place like a sword sliding home in its scabbard. "They're creatures of the mind, come to feed on our blood and fear, monsters we imagined."

"And how do you suggest we get rid of them?" Ptolemy said, turning to keep his blade on one lean dark form that ventured close.

"Stop fearing," I said.

Ptolemy laughed grimly. "You first."

I took a deep breath and straightened out of guard. Somewhere, sometime I had known something like this, had been someone who could have dismissed them out of hand.

Once, I had been someone who did not fear the dark places. Sati had told me that—that all I had ever been lived still in me, like a bird's memory of the egg, or a butterfly's memory of the caterpillar it had once been.

Somewhere within me was everything I needed.

My heart beat in my throat. I looked into the eyes of the nearest one, dropping the tip of my blade. "You have no right to touch us," I said. "We are Companions of Alexander the Son of Amon, he whose word bound you. We do not fear death."

The creature snarled, stalking to my left.

I followed him around. "Go back whence you came. You cannot harm us."

Beside me Ptolemy straightened. There was a bleeding scrape down the side of his face, but it didn't seem serious. "You cannot touch us," he said. "Go back to the deep desert and do not trouble us!"

The creature laughed, hyena rather than jackal, and it seemed to me that it spoke. "You are not Pharaoh, Ptolemy son of Lagos. Alexander lies unburied in Babylon, and we are free!"

"They're not attacking," I whispered.

He nodded. "Keep them at bay," he said out of the corner of his mouth. "Try to work downhill. I'll keep talking."

"You have it," I assented grimly.

"You were bound by Alexander," Ptolemy ventured. "So you must obey his men. I am one of the Regents for his son."

It snarled. "Son there may be, but Alexander is not Osiris descended. He lies still in Babylon, and there is no kinsman to escort his soul to Amenti or to open his stoppered mouth. Until that happens, only he can bind us, and we are loosed upon the world."

I inched downhill, Ptolemy retreating with me. Ahead, beyond the edge of the wadi wall, I saw something I could have sworn was not there before. A house stood in the shelter of the cliff, a plain mud-brick dwelling such as the peasants build, but it had a low wall with a gate about it, and from the high narrow window I could see the glow of firelight.

The jackal laughed again. "It will be many years before we are bound, son of Lagos! That child in Babylon may never set foot in Egypt, or if he does it will be twenty years before he can wield the power of Pharaoh, before we have Horus and his bright eyes to fear!"

There was something queer in Ptolemy's voice. "But only his heir may bind you? Surely more than once in the past there has been a pharaoh who was a child."

Closer. I could see the house more clearly now. I could smell the scent of the smoke. The house had a stout door, and the windows were all small and high. I wondered whether if we ran the pack would be on us before we gained the gate.

"In the past when the King was a child, a kinsman walked the paths of Amenti in his stead and helped Osiris descend. But there is no one who can thus speak for Alexander. We are free, and none can bind us!"

"The house," I said low. "We must run."

I saw him nod, and then as one we turned and ran.

A howl went up from the pack, but we did not heed it, only pounded for the house as quickly as we could with them in full pursuit. I could almost feel their breath on my heels. I ran over the uneven ground, sure that if I fell they would be upon me, hearing Ptolemy behind me.

I reached the gate first and flung it open, Ptolemy passing me and pounding on the door. "Let us in! Let us in!"

I threw the gate shut, catching the pack leader in the chest as I did.

The door to the house swung open under Ptolemy's hands, and I plunged after him, almost colliding with him as he spun about to shut the door and drop a bar into place. I leaned against it, listening to the thud of a heavy body against it, the throbbing of the blood in my temples.

They howled, but the door did not give. It was good, solid wood, and the bar was strong.

"I do beg your pardon," Ptolemy said, and I turned to see who he was talking to.

Beside the hearth was the house's only inhabitant, a young woman in the late stages of pregnancy, wearing a printed linen shift. She looked up serenely from the chair beside the fire.

"We mean you no harm," Ptolemy said, sheathing his sword. "We would not have broken into your house like that except that we were in peril of our lives."

I sagged against the door. Surely she should be terrified, screaming? A woman alone in such a vulnerable state, with two bloody armed men bursting in suddenly, the hounds of Chaos after them? And yet her beautiful face was untroubled, the firelight playing across her honey skin.

"Come and sit by the fire," she said. "You must be tired. There is water."

She lifted a painted pitcher and poured some out into a clay cup that she held, offering it to Ptolemy and me.

He took it, a curious expression on his face. Ptolemy's eyes met hers over the rim of the cup. "What is in it?"

"Only water," she said. Her hair was done in dozens of tight braids, and the beads on the ends of them rang as she moved her head.

He drank and handed the cup to me, though his eyes never left her.

I looked down at it and then up at her. "From what river?" I asked her.

She smiled then, a delighted smile like a young girl given a present, or a mother when her child has done something especially clever. "From the Nile," she said. "Would you remember all, Lydias?" Her eyes were like a thousand stars, and I knew Her.

"Gracious Queen," I said, and sank to my knees.

Ptolemy wavered beside me. "Who are you?"

Her eyes flickered over his face. "Lydias can name me, can't you, Lydias?"

"You are Isis," I said, and my throat was dry. "You are the Lady of the Living and the Dead, the Mother of the World."

"Mother of the World," She said, "and of worlds unborn, desirer of all the things that may yet be." She looked up at Ptolemy, who still stood beside me. "Come and sit by me, Ptolemy of Egypt. The gods of the Black Land have a proposition for you."

He put his head to the side, considering. "I will hear your proposal, Lady. But first I want to know if you are real."

Isis laughed. "You may touch me, and I will seem real to you. And tomorrow I will seem like a dream. What is real, Ptolemy of Egypt?"

"Are you really here, or are you in my mind?"

She laughed again, and Her voice was pure delight, like water over stones in the desert. "You are very stubborn. I am real, and I am in your mind. Cannot both be true at once?"

"I don't know," he said.

Her beautiful face was serious. "Should I tell you that you created the gods from your thoughts and gave us life? That we are the mirrors of your souls?"

"I should ask you then what a soul is," Ptolemy said.

Isis' eyes sparkled. "Aristotle has taught you well in disputation. And so I will answer you as best I can, knowing that one day you will understand the answer. A soul is a unique quantum pattern, both energy and matter, formed and deformed by physical energy."

"Like the creatures outside," I said. "They exist because people dreamed them and gave form to their night fears." I did not understand her words, but I thought I understood her meaning.

Ptolemy looked at me sharply.

She laughed, and Her eyes fell on me. "This is one who sees in metaphors and does not doubt his own senses. Welcome, Lydias, you who have been priest and priestess in years past. The Black Land has need of you, and you of her."

I dropped my gaze. Hers was too bright.

I heard Ptolemy sit down on the rude bench beside the hearth. His voice was steady, serious and unafraid. "What is your proposition, Lady? I will consider it with good will, provided it does not conflict with other oaths or duties."

"Very well," She said, and it seemed Her words hung in the air as She said them. "Here is what we offer. The gods of Egypt will give you the power to subdue the creatures unbound by Alexander's death, and to hold Egypt against all contenders now and throughout your lifetime. We will make you Pharaoh, Lord of the Two Lands, and establish the children of your body as the legitimate royal house of Egypt. In exchange, we require that you be Pharaoh in truth, that you seek no sovereignty outside the ancient borders of Khemet, and that you keep faith with the people of Egypt as a shepherd should, ruling the land for the benefit of My children."

Ptolemy took a ragged breath and I raised my head.

His eyes were on Her. "All my life," he said, "I have not coveted a throne. I have seen the misery it brings, and how grappling after the wheel of fire brings men and women to ruin."

"It did not bring Alexander to ruin," She said.

"That was Alexander." Ptolemy smiled thinly. "I have known from the day of his birth what he was."

Isis looked interested. "You would remember that, I suppose."

"I was eight years old, Lady," he said. "It was the day my mother told me that Queen Olympias wanted to kill me." He cupped his hands around the water and lifted it to his mouth again. "There were rumors. My mother assured me they were not true, but there were rumors all the same that she had lain with the King, that I was his son, not the son of Lagos. I must never excel, my mother said, or Queen Olympias would kill me, seeing me as rival to Alexander. I must always blend into the background, fade into the crowd. I must never do anything that might draw her attention. And so that is what I did." He drank deeply from the cup.

"Surely Alexander must have heard the rumors too," She said.

"Of course he did. Olympias told him as soon as he could walk that he must stay away from me because I would try to kill him. He did not run from me the day I met him because he had too much pride to back down from a death fight." Ptolemy put the cup aside and smiled. "He was six and I fourteen. Of course I did not try to kill him, and of course he did not run. We agreed that our mothers were stupid, and that we should not let any silly rumor rest between us. That was not, Alexander said, the way a king should behave."

"And so neither of you should behave thus." Isis looked pleased. She put Her feet up on the edge of the hearth, easing Her pregnant belly.

"I will not usurp his son's throne," Ptolemy said. "I may not be able to preserve the empire, or even his son's life, but I will not be the man to begin it. I will not take what belonged to Alexander." His eyes were bright. "I will keep faith with him."

"Egypt needs a pharaoh," She said. "We need you, Ptolemy of Egypt. You are a man who has the strength and the wisdom to rule, and somewhat more. You have the self-restraint. You can keep Egypt free from foreign overlords who will bleed her dry and crush all that she is."

"Am I not a foreign overlord?" Ptolemy raised an eyebrow. "I am Macedonian, not Egyptian, Lady."

"You will become Egyptian," She said tranquilly.

"Alexander did not."

"That was Alexander." Isis smiled. "He is a wind through the world, and no land can contain him. But we will not see his like again soon." She put Her feet down and leaned forward, Her face growing serious. "But Alexander still lies unburied in Babylon. He is not free to descend to Amenti, to rule in the West as Osiris, or to return to these lands if he wills. He must be released, Ptolemy. You cannot keep him with you by refusing him a funeral."

"I know." Ptolemy glanced sideways at me. "But the Council of Regents cannot agree. Roxane wants him buried in Babylon, in a great tomb that will be the foundation stone of a new dynasty begun by her son, and Perdiccas backs her. Queen Olympias and Antipatros, the Regent in Macedon, want him returned to Aigai to lie in the royal tombs beside his father. There's a story going around that he asked to be buried at the Temple of Amon at Siwah, though I have no idea how that could possibly be accomplished. Alexander cannot be buried. At least not now."

Her eyebrows rose. "He has been dead eight months. Is it then the custom of the Greeks to leave dead bodies embalmed and lying about, denied proper burial and decent mourning, because the heirs must quarrel over the property left behind?"

"I did not say it was seemly, Lady. Just that it is."

"Bring the King to Memphis," I said, and then started. I was hardly aware I had spoken until the words poured forth and they were both staring at me. It was what the Sphinx had said in my dream.

Ptolemy laughed, though I thought there was a nervous sound in it. "And how would I do that? And why?"

Isis nodded. "Memphis is the center of the Black Land. If Alexander lay in Memphis in the tomb of a hero, it would be a powerful talisman for Khemet. And you, his heir, would reign in peace."

"I am not his heir," Ptolemy said, and his eyes met Hers unflinching.

"Are you not?" She asked.

"No. I will not usurp his son's throne." He had a stubborn set to his jaw for such a mild tone.

It was the goddess who looked away first. "And if the child dies?"

Ptolemy glanced down at his hands. "If the child dies through no fault of mine, then I will consider what you say. Arrhidaeus cannot rule, and he will be only a front for powerful men behind him."

"Cannot you at least act as a Regent and a kinsman should?" She asked. "Cannot you at least claim the power to bind all his death has unleashed in Khemet? Can you not bring him to Memphis and give him proper burial? Do you not at least owe his soul its freedom?"

Ptolemy closed his eyes. "You are saying the soul of Alexander itself is bound?"

"He was crowned as Pharaoh, and as Great King besides, a living god. He cannot put that aside without proper rites. Otherwise, yes, Alexander remains bound to the body that once he inhabited." Isis tilted Her head back and the beads in Her hair rang again. "That is what the rites are for, Ptolemy of Egypt! That is what they do! Horus departs from the dead pharaoh so that he may pass into the West."

"And if I bring him to Memphis?" Ptolemy opened his eyes and looked at Her. "Can he then be released?"

"If you do what is needful, yes."

"Can I do that without usurping the throne?"

I remembered what the creatures outside had said. "Surely there is a way, when the heir is a minor. Surely Ptolemy could stand as proxy for the boy." I looked at him. "Would that be suitable?"

Ptolemy nodded slowly. "I would be willing to stand as proxy." His eyes met Isis' again. "As long as it is understood that I am not seizing the throne."

"That is understood," She said gravely.

"Then I will consider all we have said, Lady," he said. "How shall I tell you what my answer is?"

Isis smiled, and there was no anger in Her. "I am very easy to find. Rest here, and in the morning find your way home."

It seemed to me that the fire grew dim, and that I curled somewhere safe and warm. With some still waking part of my mind, I wondered why that was, but then I slept.


I WOKE LYING beside Ptolemy on the floor of a peasant's hut of mud brick. I sat up slowly and heard him stir. The sun was not yet over the walls of the wadi, but above the sky was a clear and flawless blue. I felt rested, as though I had passed the night dreamlessly on the most comfortable mattress.

And yet.

I looked about. I could see the sky through the roof where it had fallen in, a tangle of broken birds' nests in a corner. The hearth was empty except for long cold embers. No one had lit a fire here in years. This house must have been deserted for decades.

Ptolemy sat up, and I saw him thinking the same things.

I spread my hands. There was a long gash down my left arm, the mirror of the one on his face. They looked as though perhaps we had slipped on rocks in the night or cut ourselves on some sharp edge. Such things could happen easily enough, climbing about by fading moonlight.

Ptolemy blinked. For a moment I thought he would ask me something, but then he did not. He got up and brushed off his clothes, looking out the broken door of the house, down the ravine. I could not see his face.

"Look," he said.

I came and stood where he was.

Below, the ravine opened out, and I could see green, the edge of the cultivated fields that lined the Nile. We could not be more than a mile from the river.

"So close," I said. Of course we had not seen it in the night.

"Come on, Lydias," Ptolemy said, clapping me on the shoulder. "Let's get back to Memphis. Bath, breakfast, and dealing with Cleomenes."

"I shouldn't think he'd be glad to see us," I said.


He wasn't. Ptolemy sent for him before noon, freshly bathed and shaven. Cleomenes came in with many exclamations of relief.

Ptolemy cut him off. "I do not need to hear all this. Your plan has failed, and now you will bear the consequences." He looked over at Glaukos, who stood with his hand on his sword by the door, senior soldier of the bodyguard.

"Execute him."

# COMPANION

The full extent of Cleomenes' crimes did not become evident until later. Examination of his papers and dealings exposed them. Not only had he appropriated the taxes intended to pay for the fortifications at Alexandria, but he had skimmed off a tenth of the soldiers' pay, and taken bribes up and down the Black Land from anyone who wanted their cases heard in court.

Ptolemy was more than annoyed. "How are we to convince people that we are just, when we have such as him for an example? What can Alexander have been thinking?"

I did not answer that, of course, knowing a rhetorical question when I heard one. But Cleomenes had been appointed in the last months of the King's life, upon the recommendation of Perdiccas, after the death of Hephaistion. He had been so consumed with his grief that no doubt he had agreed to whatever Perdiccas recommended. It did not matter to him.

Kings, I thought, cannot be men. Men are subject to grief and sadness and neglect their duties when life holds no luster for them. If I should die, or if I should simply lie down and not get up to attend my work, what should happen? I should inconvenience those who must take up my job, but I should do no real harm to the realm. Kings cannot be men. They must be gods.

And I, I was nothing but a soldier.

Y<small>OU MAY WONDER</small> how it was that I became a soldier when I had
been nothing but a stable boy, how I came to stand so close to one who
might be Pharaoh. It was, like most things in the world, something that
happened a little at a time.

I have told you how I became groom to General Hephaistion, and
yet I have said so far little of the man. I hardly know what to say. If
I say he was the boldest and the best of Alexander's Companions, I
illustrate nothing except my own devotion. Let me begin then with
this—when I entered his service after years of harsh servitude to
Tehwaz I worshipped him as a boy will a hero who has suddenly taken
an interest in him. I was used to work, but I was not used to thanks,
and his occasional words of praise for a job well done threw me into
confusions of happiness. I had mucked out well! I had Ghost Dancer
groomed for parade in a way that was pleasing!

I suppose I writhed under praise like a colt who wants to obey and
be made much of but has never known anything besides harshness.
I took common kindness for a gift from the heavens. I should have
walked through fire for him if he had asked me.

Instead, what he asked of me was far more reasonable—to keep his
horses well, even on the march, and to attend to them as I would my
own children. When, a year later, he made me chief groom, I was filled
with pride and threw myself into improving yet again, talking to the
King's Master of Horse whenever I got the chance and absorbing any
bit of horse lore I might learn.

I also learned to use a sword. Once, some other boys and I were
practicing, whacking at each other with blunted old wrecks and
laughing, when Hephaistion came along. Perhaps it was something in
my stance, or just that I had always done a good job, but he stopped me
very seriously.

"Lydias, come here," he said, "and learn how to guard properly."

I stood beside him and he corrected my grip on the hilt in my
hand.

"Like that," he said. "Lightly. The first thing a man does from nerves is clutch at the hilt as though he were going to cut grain. Lightly. Let the sword rest in your hand, an extension of your arm. The blade should be almost in line with your forearm, not off to the side like that."

I tried to hold it as he said, and it seemed that the sword weighed less when I did.

"Don't squat." He walked around me, looking at my stance. "Stand naturally with your knees bent, athletically." Hephaistion put his hand on my back. "Straighten your back." I felt his touch through my chiton and suddenly found it intensely distracting, though it meant nothing.

"Better," he said. He came around my right side, frowning. "Like this." He moved my elbow back closer to my body. His passing touch raised goosebumps all over me. "Don't wave your elbow around either. How does that feel?"

"Good," I said. The stance was better, but I hardly knew how to name the blush that rose in my face.

Hephaistion nodded. "Looks better, too. Keep practicing! You've talent enough." He smiled and sauntered off.

I hardly knew whether to flush with pride, or with something else entirely.

Of course I knew he was the King's lover. Everyone knew that. They'd been together since they were boys, sacrificed together at the tombs of Achilles and Patroclos at Troy when they'd crossed into Asia. It was not that I thought something might happen. How should it? When he had Alexander, why would he even look twice at a groom? My unease had nothing to do with that.

Truth to tell, when it came to love I was behindhand. When I had belonged to Tehwaz there was no one I could have wanted I could possibly have looked to. Now, with the army, there were chances aplenty, both with the other boys and with the camp followers and prostitutes that shadowed us, part of the living, vibrant thing that was the baggage train.

And yet I held back. I was shy, and to boldly hand over my pay and get it done behind a wagon seemed less than I wanted. I was shy, and the other boys my age seemed low creatures compared to the beauty of the Companions. I wanted beauty and love both.

It came to me, watching Hephaistion walk away down the picket line, stopping to have a word with this man and that, that to have beauty and love both I must be worthy. No man I could desire should want an untidy sloven of a groom, and an untidy sloven of a groom should not aspire to a good wife.

A wife. I did not want a dull-eyed woman tumbled by half the army behind a wagon, but a wife. In my mind's eye she was beautiful, her face clean and bright with delight to see me. I should feel her trembling hands in mine as she pledged herself to me, meet lovely eyes glowing with anticipation.

That night, as we camped beneath the stars on the long march into Persia, I looked up at the moon glowing serenely above the hills. I took the wine from my ration and walked out into the hills, away from the camp, away from the others, and poured it out in libation.

"I do not know what words to say," I whispered. "I do not know even which name to call you by. Lady of Stars, make me worthy of love!"

The night wind brushed the hair back from my forehead like a gentle hand, like a mother's hand remembered from earliest childhood. *Sweet boy,* She whispered, *all you need is a chance.*

I bent my head and prayed for a chance, for the opportunity to make myself all I could be.

I HAD MY chance, though not in the way I had imagined. It came in blood, not love.

We marched northward, into the heart of Persia. Somewhere soon the King would force a battle with Darius, the Great King. Sometime soon we would meet him.

When it came, it was not in a place of our choosing. The plain of Gaugamela was wide and flat, covered only with a little grass and scrub, without rivers or significant hills, perfect for the Great King's chariots. And he outnumbered us significantly. Talk in the camp made it five to one, which I mentally revised to two or three to one, long odds but not impossible. And yet there was no talk of defeat. We had defeated him before, at Issos, and watched Darius run away, leaving his family behind him, even his old mother. Two or three to one? What is that, when we have Alexander and they Darius?

Hephaistion did not ride Ghost Dancer in the morning. Ghost Dancer was the youngest of his warhorses, the one still being trained up. For a battle such as this, he wanted Zephyr, the most experienced horse that he had brought from Greece. I made Zephyr ready, checking his tack three times to make sure everything was sound. Then I cleaned his hooves again while we waited for Hephaistion. A stone in his foot today could be deadly.

It was just after dawn. The day would be scorchingly hot, but now there was a breeze and the sky was pale blue, streaked with high thin clouds, all the world gold and blue in the sunrise. Surely in some language there were hymns for this, for gold and blue, a battle day. But I did not know them.

The generals had gone to watch the omens read before the army. I stood with Zephyr in the picket lines. Ghost Dancer stomped restlessly. He did not like it that some other would seize the glory. I petted him and he tossed his head, looking at me as if to say, you and I, Lydias, we could be about this business too.

"We could not," I whispered, holding his head against my chest. "It's not our time yet."

He stamped as if to disagree. I was eighteen and he four. Four is too young for the best warhorses, but in a pinch he could have done.

Hephaistion was coming from the sacrifice, his red hair shining in the sun. He was grave, not cocky. "All right, Lydias?"

"Yes, sir," I said. "Zephyr is as sound as any horse ever was."

"Good lad." He clapped me on the shoulder and swung up easily, gathering the rein in his left hand. He looked down at me. "Take good care of the others."

"I will, sir," I said. Just because it was a battle day did not mean the other horses wouldn't need to be groomed and exercised as always.

An hour after sunrise they were all gone, and a strange hush fell over the camp. Just us servants remained. The cooks were busy, for men coming from battle would be hungry. Somewhere a dog barked, sounding loud in the empty camp.

I groomed Ghost Dancer head to toe.

Out there on the plain the battle would be beginning. We could see nothing, except the birds gathering on the high currents of the air, circling the place where the slaughter had begun. My palms sweated. Ghost Dancer tossed his head.

I led him out for some exercise. Perhaps walking him a little would calm him.

We walked through the camp, stopping here and there to talk with someone, with a woman baking bread in the ashes of the fire, her children playing around her. Beside the hospital tents some men were digging pits to put the arms and legs in. Farther along, toward the King's tent, were the tents of some of the officers.

The bright sunlight glittered off the hair of a woman who stood before one tent, her hand shading her eyes as she looked off where they had gone, her blue veil around her shoulders, lifting on the breeze. Her face was as serene as a goddess carved in stone, but her eyes were sharp. Not entirely Aphrodite, I thought. Athena has touched her too. A general's woman, I thought. I did not know her name yet.

Her head lifted suddenly, and I looked where she did.

A long cloud of dust was rolling toward us. Yellow and roiling, it took me a moment to realize what it must be.

The Persian cavalry had broken through our left wing, between the squares of infantry where General Parmenio held desperately.

And now they thundered down on the camp.

Someone screamed. Not her. She had already vanished inside the tent.

I saw them coming out of the roiling yellow clouds of dust, lean Persian riders on fast horses, swords flashing with blood. They had already been through the infantry lines.

Ghost Dancer let out a loud call, a challenge, and his eyes were wide.

I swung up without a thought. Had not Hephaistion charged me to take care of all that was his?

Behind me, I heard the baking woman scream her child's name, sweeping him up. The doctor looked out of the hospital tent, a long knife in his hand. Everything seemed to happen incredibly slowly.

The forms in the dust resolved. A young man with a black beard, a tan horse rendered golden by the dust, riding straight for me, his sword pointing at my heart.

"Here!" There was a shriek beside me, and I looked down to see her, the woman in blue, holding out a sword to me. I wrapped my fingers around the hilt and ripped it from the scabbard, a dressy thing with an inlaid pommel, doubtless left by its owner in favor of a more serviceable blade.

And yet it was light in my hand, light as fire.

I did not thank her. I touched my heels to Ghost Dancer instead and at last let him go.

A goose fled from our hooves as we flew like an arrow from the bow. My man had marked me, and I had marked him.

We came together in a clean pass, right side to right side, my sword blocking his, the weight of the impact shuddering all along my arm. Ghost Dancer's shoulder was against his horse's shoulder, and he shoved. The Persian horse lost his footing, stumbling.

And with the stumble I disengaged. In the second he answered his horse I thrust my sword into his neck.

I wrenched the blade free, his blood fountaining over me. Another Persian was coming up, and I spun Ghost Dancer around. He met the Persian with raised hooves, half in the middle of the turn, just as Xenophon says a horse should do, his weight on his muscled haunches. With the strength of the horse behind me, I severed the Persian's sword arm.

Ghost Dancer leapt again, and for a moment I thought I would fall. He had gotten me out of the way of two riders who converged. One should have been on each side of me, but now one of them was between his fellow and me, rendering the far one useless.

I don't think he realized what had happened before I cut him down.

Behind, at the door of the hospital tent, the doctor was fighting off a horseman. He should have been slain in a moment, had not the horse become entangled in the ropes tying the tent to the stakes.

I turned Ghost Dancer around and we came up behind him like thunder. Ghost Dancer slammed into the entangled horse, who fell thrashing, pinning his rider beneath him. The doctor scrambled after with his knife.

I looked back. There were more coming. Many, many more. Fifty, a hundred...

I realized that Ghost Dancer's back was soaked with my urine, but it hardly mattered. There were no other horsemen in the street. I hoped the baker and her children had run, that the general's woman had run. Surely this had bought a little time.

I saw them looming out of the dust. Many, many more.

"Come on, boy," I said, stroking his mane.

And then I touched my heels to his side.

We plowed into the first man, block, block, guard and thrust. Again and again. Blood ran down the fancy sword, overflowing the channels and sticking my hand to the pommel. Thrust and guard. Endless and slow, a forever.

Ghost Dancer was heavier than many of their horses, and his weight gave my hand strength. Cut and batter.

And then above it all I heard something different, the high clear note of horns. The dust swirled. More. There must be more.

Out of the dust plunged the horsemen, sun glittering on steel. It was not more Persians. It was our own Companion Cavalry, Alexander on his black horse, his high white plume shaking.

I saw it for a moment, and then something struck me on the shoulder, hard enough to grind my teeth together and fling me from Ghost Dancer's back. I lay in the dirt dazed, not even rolling to the side to avoid hooves. My shoulder was an explosion of fire.

Hooves circled around me, and in a moment I thought I knew those feet. I had cleaned them enough. It was Zephyr. Hephaistion stood over me, trading blows with a Persian. Their horses danced.

I watched him cut him down, Hephaistion's face serene and intent, as though the beauty of the swordplay were all, not a man's life.

He leaned sideways out of the saddle then, looking at me. "All right, boy?"

"Yes," I said, struggling to my feet. I still had the fancy sword.

He nodded sharply, and I thought he would have said something.

Behind him, I saw the lancer charge.

Most of the Persians had been armed with short sword. This was one of the lancers, and his light little horse almost floated over the ground. I did not have time to think. I did not have time to call out. Perhaps I was still befuddled, or perhaps it really was that fast.

The lancer hit Hephaistion square on, the point going deep into his right shoulder just below the edge of the harness.

Zephyr went up, hooves flailing, trying to prevent the Persian from closing.

Hephaistion fell, the muscles in his arm no longer working, blood blossoming everywhere.

I staggered out, the sword still in my hand, trusting that Zephyr knew me, that he would not turn on me the tactics that Xenophon says a warhorse is supposed to display with his rider down.

Thrust and block, thrust and block again, on foot against a lancer on horseback, the whole business partly fouled by Zephyr's antics.

Thrust and block, my head spinning, my feet slipping in the dust.

Zephyr screaming as the lancer slammed him full in the face with his shield.

Something hit me and I fell, only half aware that the body next to mine was Hephaistion, struggling to get up.

And then there was a bugle challenging all the world. I looked up. All I could see was Ghost Dancer's belly as he stood in front of us both, teeth bared.

I passed out, and saw no more.

I WOKE TO screaming.

I lay in the hospital tent, and the doctor was taking off a man's arm. I lay staring at the tent above and did not even try to rise. We must have won, I thought, if I am here and not given field mercy. I must have a chance, if I have not been given field mercy.

And with that I slept.

WHEN I AWOKE again it was night. A boy held cool water to my lips.

"Careful," the doctor said. "You must be very careful giving water to men with head injuries. They may not be able to swallow and may breathe it instead. Just wet his lips."

I made a croaking sound, and opened eyelids that must have been made of stone. The entire world tilted around me, refusing to come into focus.

"Ah," the doctor said, and I realized it was the same man I had seen earlier, during the battle. "Do you know who you are?"

"Lydias," I whispered. The water was so good. "What happened?"

"That is the best thing you can hope for," the doctor said, instructing the boy. "He knows his name, and he seems oriented."

"I can't see," I said, and there was a note of panic in my voice.

"Can't see light or can't focus?" He sounded concerned, and gestured for the boy to bring a lamp. I could see its bright flame, and something of his face beyond, though everything wavered as though underwater.

"Can't focus," I said.

He held the lamp up, moving it back and forth several times.

"See?" he asked the boy. "The pupil in his right eye is dilated and doesn't respond when I move the flame closer and farther. That's common with head injuries."

"Am I blind?" I felt panic seize me in its claws.

"No," the doctor said. "If you're coherent, there's not much bleeding in the brain. And the eye will usually heal in time. Give it a few weeks. In addition to that, you've got stitches in your scalp, and your left shoulder is bound. You took a blow on your back that's broken your left clavicle. But you'll see well enough in time, I expect." He laid the lamp aside.

"Drink some water, and lie down and try to sleep." His voice was wry. "You're one of the lucky ones, son."


I WAS. MY sight was blurry, but I could tell it was improving. My head hurt and the stitches itched, but the worst was my taped arm with which I could do nothing. The doctor told me the next day that I should not lift my arm for at least a month and a half.

"I've set it," he said, "but it's not like a leg or something. It's your shoulder in the back. The pieces will shift out of place if you move it around. That's why you're strapped." Long pieces of linen went round it, tying it tightly.

I fretted until he said, "Leave it alone if you ever want to use that arm again."

At that I stopped, for what use is a one-armed groom?

I fretted over the horses too, until the third day.

I woke when someone sat down on my pallet, opened my eyes, and saw General Hephaistion.

He looked worn and ill too. His right arm was in a sling, a pad of bandages against his shoulder.

"Sir," I said, and tried to get up.

"Be still, Lydias," he said. "You've earned lying down. They've just let me up myself."

"The horses?"

He laughed, putting his head back, and the long tan line of his throat exposed. "Trust you to worry about what's important first! Ghost Dancer is entirely well, having stood over us until the King came. Zephyr's got broken teeth, and he's lost the sight in one eye. I'm afraid his days of war are ended. It's his time to go out to stud."

"I'm so sorry, sir," I said, knowing he had put his horses in my care. I knew the blow that had hurt Zephyr. It had been taking that shield in the face. "It is my fault."

"Your fault that you helped save the camp, and that you may have saved my life as well?" Hephaistion looked amused. "I gave Ptolemy his sword back, by the way. He thanks you for defending Thais."

I gulped. I suppose I had kind of stolen a general's sword.

Hephaistion shifted. "The King would have words for you, but I told him I'd rather have them myself."

"Please," I began, ready to offer some sort of excuse, I knew not what.

His brown eyes were grave. "Lydias, you are unsuited to be a groom in my service. I know that you have done your best, but it cannot continue. From now on you are a soldier, not a servant. I raise you to the ranks of Companion Cavalry, to fight in my Ile beside the best men I know."

My blurry eyes filled with tears and I could not speak.

"We will have to find a horse of your own for you when you can ride, Lydias of Miletus. And a sword. We are going after Darius, who once again fled the field, leaving his wounded behind, and I will need you at my back." He clasped my hand wrist to wrist, one man to another. "Welcome to a valiant company, and know you have earned your place."

I should have raised his hand to my lips and kissed it in thanksgiving, only that was the sort of thing a servant did. I was a soldier now. "I shall never disappoint you, sir," I said instead.

"I know," he said, as though he were certain of it.

# THE HEART OF THE
# BLACK LAND

There was a great deal of work to do in Memphis in the wake of Cleomenes' execution. The finances of Egypt were chaos, and it was anyone's guess what had been paid and what hadn't. It made matters worse that there had been two sets of records of everything—Cleomenes' own records, and the official ones, which the Egyptians kept in their own tongue, written in Demotic, which Ptolemy did not read.

It was a month and a half later or so that Ptolemy sent me to Upper Egypt. He wanted opinions, he said. Documents he had, hundreds of petitions for the satrap about this and that, tax rolls and lawsuits, facts and facts and facts. What he didn't have was any real sense of the place or the temper of the people. None of us had gone farther up the Nile than Memphis when we were here with Alexander, and now it was too dangerous for Ptolemy to go so far from the coast, when there was such uncertainty with Perdiccas and the political situation.

Instead, he sent me to be his eyes and ears.

"Lydias," he said, "you do not give offense, you keep your own counsel, and you're cleverer than anyone expects a plain soldier to be. I need opinions as well as facts. Go and form some."

And so in the dry season before the Inundation I sailed south, up the Nile and into the past.

For me, in memory, thinking of those days is like remembering falling in love. I rose at dawn and watched the sun rise over where life and death met, the stark line where the fields of Egypt ended and desert began. In the clear morning air the scent of bread baking came over the water, smoke rising from village ovens. In the fields the gleaners were taking up the last of the harvest.

The first day up from Memphis I watched a little boy six or seven years old, a gaggle of geese around him, his stick in his hand. When he saw our brightly painted ship he waved, a brown-and-white hound jumping up and down beside him. I lifted my hand to him in return, and as he waved again, following us a little way along the shore with his unruly dog, I felt something loosen in my chest.

The second morning we saw the hippopotamuses. We slowed and went through them carefully, a great herd of twenty or thirty beasts with absolutely no fear of us, swimming as though it were nothing. I could not stop grinning. I had thought surely there were not such strange beasts so close to the homes of men, but there were villages all about, and the hippopotamuses seemed undisturbed. They were not as large as the elephants I had seen in India, but they reminded me of them somewhat. I could not stop grinning, even as we left them behind us and went on to Herakleopolis.

I stopped there, and then at Oxyrhynchos, and again at Hermopolis, talking to nobles and priests, talking to those Persian officials that the King or Cleomenes had confirmed in their posts. Hermopolis was the last place going south that there were Persian officials, and they talked of Upper Egypt as though it were a distant and barbarian land. "Be sure," they told me, "to always have sufficient bodyguards. Especially in Thebes. One of the Great King's men was killed in broad daylight in the markets of Thebes, and no one would say anything, even when witnesses were put to torture."

I thanked him kindly for his advice, and resolved to have no bodyguards at all in Upper Egypt. I was the first thing they should see of Ptolemy, the first opinion they should form. I would not go with Persian hauteur, but try to conduct myself as they might expect a servant of Pharaoh to do. To that end I put off helmet and harness in favor of a beautifully worked white chiton over which I wore my sword belt, and had my arms and legs shaved by the servants in Hermopolis. It was truly not so odd, as I shaved my face every day, and to the Egyptians shaving the rest of one's body was considered no more than a matter of good hygiene. In Greece, of course, only fancy boys shaved entirely to look younger than they were, though shaving one's chest or back was something of a fashion, to look smooth and clean on the floor of the gymnasium. The Macedonians would have considered it effete, which is not to say that some of them wouldn't have done it! To the Egyptians, however, I simply would look well groomed.

It was the day after that, the morning we left Hermopolis for Abydos, that the strangest thing of the journey happened.

I stood on deck enjoying the breeze of our passage in the warmth of the day. It seemed to me that the landscape was subtly changing as we moved south. The ribbon of green along the river was narrower, and beyond on the western side it seemed rockier, more wadis and cliffs than sandy desert. I was wondering how far it was to Abydos, and wondering if I should try to ask the ship's captain. His Greek was very limited, and my Egyptian more limited still.

Ahead, around a curve in the river, I saw a city emerging. As we drew closer I saw it was larger and more magnificent than any we had come to since Memphis, with a huge carved pylon gate ornamented with paintings and a wide avenue cutting through the city toward a palace nestled like a jewel among gardens and pools.

Surely, I thought, this must be Abydos, though it seemed both larger and more antique than I had anticipated. Was it possible that we had passed Abydos entirely and now approached Thebes? The magnificent temples of Thebes had been much talked of.

Yet as we drew closer I doubted it. The docks along the river were empty of barges and ships, and I saw no people walking along the shore. The vast avenues seemed deserted.

A chill ran down my back. As we passed the beginning of the gardens even the trees were silent of birds. The fountains did not play. The droplets of water hung in the air, glittering like drops of glass.

I walked astern quickly to the captain. "What is that city?" I asked him in my halting Egyptian.

He looked away, at the tiller in his worn hands, and said something I did not understand.

"I didn't get that," I said.

The captain met my eyes. "Cursed," he said in Greek. "Cursed. Do not look, understand? Leave the Dead City alone." He spat over the side.

I turned back to look again.

The city I had seen was gone. Instead, a broken pylon emerged from the sand, a few stubs of broken columns near the riverside marking where perhaps the entrance to gardens had once been. Wind whipped golden sand over brown dunes, mounded in ways that did not seem entirely natural. The city was gone, gone a thousand years ago. Above, a hawk turned on the wind. Below, the river flowed past a few pitiful ruins.

I stared. Where were the gardens? Where were the palaces and streets I had seen? Gone, all gone beneath the sands, beneath the Red Land reclaiming this place.

"The Dead City?" I asked the captain.

He did not so much as glance toward it. "Leave it be," he said. "Evil lives there. Long ago, the gods were angered by one who was their enemy, and the Black Land nearly destroyed. Leave it be, I tell you. It is a cursed place."

I nodded.

The ruins were slipping away behind us. Soon they would be lost to sight again.

"Babylon," I whispered. That was what it reminded me of. Had those palaces echoed, the king dead and evil unleashed on the land? Did they echo still? Would Babylon echo thus, a thousand years hence?

THAT NIGHT WE slept on the river, rocking on the currents of the Nile, and I dreamed.

I dreamed I rode a chestnut horse in a vast baggage train, following carts full of supplies, full of wounded men. It was late summer, and about us the fields were green in the sun. I rode a chestnut horse named Lady, and I wore a curved sword at my side. It did not seem strange to me, not even the woman's body I had in that place, athletic and older than I was now.

We crested a rise, and I drew rein to look.

Across the plain a city waited in the sun, gleaming walls and the high glittering domes of temples, shaped like onions and painted scarlet and gold. The city waited like doom in the sun, beneath the blue sky. I stopped, and I saw. In the shape of the walls I saw the shadow of Babylon, the shadow of the City of the Dead. Ahead, the column and the baggage train curled like a dark serpent.

It was not Babylon, of course, but some other city still unbuilt. I dreamed, and I knew I dreamed the future.

"What is this place?" I whispered. The plain, the city, the marching column wavered, as though a mist stood between me and them.

I stood on the rise above the column, looking down at them.

"That which may be," She said, and I turned to see Isis standing beside me, Her dark hair plaited in many braids and covered with a veil of silver, like the moon in mourning. "Lydias," She said.

"Gracious Queen," I said, and dropped to my knees.

She raised me up with Her hand beneath my elbow—my own body, once again myself.

I glanced over the rise and saw her from the outside, the woman on the brown horse, her hair the color of sunlight cut close as any Greek boy, her sunburned nose and sharp blue eyes, a body that moved like a boy or a eunuch, though she must be close to forty. "Is that me?" I asked.

"It may be," Isis said. "The future has many paths, and the gods cannot see which will come to pass. For that we must rely on oracles, who see straight the choices of men."

"You don't know what will happen?" I asked curiously.

She shook Her head ruefully. "No. We may know what is likely, or know reasons that you do not yet understand, but we cannot see what the choices of men will be. This future is far from now, and many choices lie between now and then. I could not see this, if you did not open the way." She lifted Her chin, gesturing toward the woman on the horse. "From you to you. From you to a woman who was once Lydias and is struck by something that reminds her of you."

"This is very deep water for me," I said. "How can it be that I will be a woman?"

Isis smiled. "Do you think the soul has gender? Or are men and women not both human?"

"Some philosophers say not," I said. "But I am not an educated man, and I do not know such things. I can only tell what I see. Men and women are human alike and suffer the same pains." I remembered something then, something She had said when I dreamed in the desert with Ptolemy. "Gracious Queen, You hailed me as priest and priestess both. Is that what You mean?"

Her smile grew broader. "The gods see the past clearly, as it is only a matter of remembering. Yes, you have been priest and priestess both to the Black Land in the past, wife of Amon and priest of Thoth, and more besides. You are not a stranger to us, Lydias, though you come with a foreign name and face. We know you, as your King did."

"Alexander," I said. "Is it true that he is bound?"

She nodded. "Yes. Is it not the belief of many peoples that the soul remains until the funeral is accomplished? How may he pass on when he is unburied? And while he is unburied, the spirits Pharaoh hold in check run rampant through the world."

"Is that why I saw the Dead City?" I asked.

For a moment I thought She looked startled. "It may be. Chaos walks the land, and death and disease will follow. Ptolemy could bind it, if he wished."

"If he were Pharaoh," I said flatly. "I cannot push him to that, and I will not. No man should be king who does not want to take up the burden."

Her eyes flashed. "And does that not happen always? What prince chooses that his father shall rule? A prince must take up the duty he is born to, just as every man must. When you are assigned to a duty, do you whine and say that it is too hard?"

"No," I said, "but I chose to give my oath as Companion, and I will keep it while my breath lasts. Ptolemy will not usurp a throne to which he has no right. He is not a man who will say, I want it and so it is just."

"Which is why he should be Pharaoh," She said. "Do you think I should seek a despot for Egypt's throne? This land has known suffering enough."

She paced away from me, and beyond Her I could still see the column of horses and carts, the long line of the future baggage train winding its way down the hill toward the city, dark blue coats and strange short staves held to the shoulders of each soldier. The woman on the horse watched, her eyes as blue as the skies of the Black Land.

Her back to me still, Isis spoke, and Her voice was low. "I wonder. Will you forget me, Lydias, when two thousand years have gone?"

I looked back to the woman again, her seat on the strange leather pad on her horse's back, the way she held the reins easily in her left hand, as though she had done this two thousand years, for more campaigns than I could imagine. "I don't think so," I said. "I don't think I'm good at forgetting."

I woke to the sound of the boatmen's calls as we came into Abydos, their voices echoing over the water as we came alongside the dock.

The sense of strangeness stayed with me all the way up the Nile, to Thebes and back.

They had not loved Alexander in Upper Egypt. They had not known him. To them, he was just a name. A good name to be sure, as they had not liked the Persians, but the hand of the Persian Great King had rested lightly on Upper Egypt, and Persian law had never really been enforced. In Memphis and the Delta they hated the Persians, and welcomed Alexander with open arms. In Upper Egypt, they were cautious.

I was well received, to be sure. Everyone was quite polite, though I felt that I often missed half of what was said, and resolved to learn Egyptian as fast as I might. Yes, of course everyone was glad to hear that the infant son of Alexander lived and was well. Yes, of course everyone was loyal to his satrap, Ptolemy. It was good to hear that Egypt should be governed by Egyptian law.

And yet beneath it all was a current I did not like. Something was wrong.

I did not get an idea until my fifth day in Thebes, when I woke before dawn to the sounds of servants outside in the courtyard, and the weeping of women. Peering from the window, it seemed that they were clustered around a body that had been brought in by two men carrying a sling, family and friends running to rend their clothes and lament over it.

Later in the day I asked my host about it.

The priest of Amon looked troubled, and he did not meet my eyes. "A peasant," he said in Greek. "Nothing to be concerned about. Killed in a fall in the desert."

"Ah," I said. It was certainly true that one might be. The wadis on the western side of the river had steep cliffs. A man might fall to his death easily enough. But why the secrecy, the fear I saw in his face?

It was evening, and the lamps were lit when I retired to my chamber. One of the young servant women was standing on a stool hanging the freshly washed curtains at the window, though she begged my pardon when I came in.

"I did not mean to be still at my work," she said, clambering down. "Please excuse, Gracious Lord." I thought her Greek was rather better than her master's, and her eyes were red from weeping.

She stood about, as if waiting for direction. I wondered if she had been instructed to remain at my disposal, and if she found the thought of pleasing me so displeasing.

"Why do you weep?" I asked carefully. "Is it that the man who died last night was kin to you?"

Her dark eyes filled with tears. "My uncle," she said. "Please, Gracious Lord, your pardon. I am unseemly."

"No, not in the least," I said, taking care not to come too close to her so that she might mistake me. "We may be foreigners, but we hardly consider it unseemly to mourn your uncle's death. Surely that is understandable. How did he die?"

"A lion," she said, and dropped her face into her hands. "They say it was a lion."

"A lion?" That a peasant man of no doubt some years should be out in the desert with a lion in the night seemed unusual.

"A lion," she said, her voice choked. "We saw the claw marks where its talons had torn him."

"Ah," I said.

She looked up, and her young face was fierce and her voice low. "It wasn't a lion, Gracious Lord. It was the Night Spirits. They are back and they grow stronger! No one will go outside the walls at night now, unless they must. They come from the West, out of the Red Land, and they hate men! Already they haunt the other bank of the Nile. Take this as a warning, and do not go out at night or you will be like my poor uncle!" Sobbing, she ran from the room.

I RETURNED TO Alexandria with the flood, the Nile rising as we journeyed down her broad breast. We left the river before we reached Alexandria, for it was not being built on the river but rather on Lake Mareotis, where there was a better harbor than in the shallows of the river mouths. I was shocked by the change in seven short months since Ptolemy and I had left for Memphis.

When I had left, most of the streets were nothing but muddy tracks, stakes and rope marking out where houses and shops should go. Now it was a city.

To be sure there were still streets unpaved, still lots with nothing on them but a stake and a number, but from the dirt rose houses of mud brick, some painted and decorated a bit, or walls half finished with tents pitched in the middle of them to make a roof. The streets rang with the sounds of carpenters' hammers, with the shouts of children running and playing, with the sounds of barter in a dozen languages in the makeshift markets. It was as though the baggage train were given permanence, the volatile movement of the camp rendered in brick instead of canvas. The scents of cooking rose on the night air. I could have sworn I smelled curried lamb.

I made my way to what was supposed to be the palace to report to Ptolemy, past awnings pitched on new paved courtyards, taverns serving wine to soldiers and townsmen alike. I even thought I saw a couple of Jews and wondered where they had come from. A vast building site stood empty, a sign on it proclaiming in Greek that it would soon be a gymnasium by subscription for the sons of the city, with tutors and coaches to be hired as soon as money permitted, please apply to Phaidon of Achillas' Ile for prices and information, discounts to be given to fathers who enrolled more than one son at a time, and half price for the third.

For the sons of the city, I thought. Not for young Greek gentlemen. And how should it be? There were hardly any Greek women here. Most of the sons would have mothers of other nations, Persian or Median, Egyptian or Indian. Unexpectedly, I felt my throat close.

Here I should be nothing unusual, half Greek and half Carian. Here I would not have been a by-blow to sell off as a slave, but a son of the city. These boys would not be sold away as I had been, but go to school. They would read and write and see no difference between the son of a Carian and the son of an Indian. In course of time, they should marry one another's sisters, and we should be a new people altogether. Alexandrian.

If we had time. That was the question. Would this fragile thing prevail, or be burned to ashes in the first war?

Standing there in the night, beside a muddy lot that would one day be a gymnasium, I closed my eyes.

Oh my city, I prayed, oh spirit of the city, Spirit of Alexandria, I do pledge myself to this, that I shall do as best I can to preserve you for all the sons of our sons. I will do my best.

I felt the night wind curl around me, heavy with smells of raw wood and fresh fish, of cooking and horses and people. The city embraced me.

*Home*, it whispered. *Lydias, you are home.*

Home, I thought. I have a home, and it is here.

And then I opened my eyes and went to report to Ptolemy.

I DID NOT expect him to be still in his office and still about his work. He looked up when I came in. "Oh, good, Lydias. You're back in good time."

"I am?" I feared I had a mixed bag of news to tell him from Upper Egypt, and some of it could hardly be welcome.

Ptolemy put down the paper he was holding and gestured to the stool on the other side of the table from him. "Have some wine," he said. "I need to talk to you. I've just had a letter from the embalmers."

I poured some out from an amphora that stood near and added the water from the pitcher. "Embalmers?" I asked blankly. I could not think what embalmers he meant.

"When Hephaistion died, Alexander sent for the finest embalmers to preserve his corpse until the funeral. Those of course came from Egypt, from the priests of Anubis who are entrusted with such things. Since the King died a few short months after Hephaistion, the embalmers were still in Babylon. That's who was sent to preserve his body."

"Oh," I said. I had not given much thought to that, in the chaos of the palace in Babylon.

"They're still there with it now, and Manetho is in contact with them, as I am in contact with others highly placed in the King's entourage." Ptolemy put his painted cup down on the edge of the table. "And so I've learned something unwelcome. Olympias has made common cause with Perdiccas."

"Shit," I said. "I thought they were deadly enemies, with Olympias wanting Alexander's body in Macedon and Perdiccas wanting it in Babylon."

"Olympias hates Antipatros, the Regent in Macedon, more than she does Perdiccas. And Perdiccas has Roxane, and the only thing that Olympias cares about: that her grandson gain the throne of Macedon over any other contender and rule as king in Pella. To that end, she's made Perdiccas an offer he'll take." Ptolemy paused, meeting my eyes. "Perdiccas will send Alexander's body to Macedon, and Olympias will send Perdiccas the only thing more important — Cleopatra, Alexander's only full sister, as his bride."

I blew out a breath and took a sip of wine before I spoke. "We're screwed. What's the next move?"

Ptolemy nodded. "I've opened correspondence with Antipatros. He liked me as a boy, and he's agreed to send me his daughter Eurydice as my wife."

"That helps some," I said. Cassander's sister, I thought. I had never liked him at all, but perhaps his sister was not the same. Perhaps she wasn't a bloody-minded bully. She might be entirely different. There was no point in asking what Thais might think of this. It was a marriage of state, and had nothing to do with her. "Is that enough?"

"No," Ptolemy said, putting his elbows on the table. "And here's where we come to your job."

"I'm not much of an envoy for arranging marriages," I said.

"Not that," Ptolemy said. "You're going to steal Alexander's body."

# A CLEVER PLAN

I'm going to what?" I asked dumbfoundedly. It does not do to ask your commanding officer if he has lost his mind.

"Steal Alexander's body," Ptolemy repeated.

"How am I going to do that?" The picture it presented was simply grotesque. "Just pick it up and walk off with it? Surely there are guards, and it's not as though no one would notice him missing…" I could hardly imagine it. Alexander lay in Babylon, in the palace of the Great Kings, the greatest hero of the age. There must be attendants, servants, guards…

Ptolemy poured more wine into my cup, making it stronger. He looked at me sideways with dark humor. "No, not just pick him up and walk off with him. A mummy is a heavy thing, anyhow. I don't know if you've ever picked one up."

"I can't say I have," I said, wondering if he'd been lifting mummies for practice, or if it were merely his usual thoroughness.

For good measure he added more of the wine to his own cup, sipped from it, and set it down. "Perdiccas agreed to send the King's body home, to Olympias in Macedon. To that end, he's had a huge hearse constructed. It's enormous, with gilded everything and a gold sarcophagus weighing about the same as an ox. It takes forty horses to pull it, or some absurd number like that. It's guarded by a good eight hundred men."

"That makes it so much easier!" I said, lifting my hands to my head. "Thank you so very much! Now it all seems clearer!"

Ptolemy laughed and touched his cup to mine. "Lydias, I swear to you I am not mad! Listen to what I have in mind, and then tell me if you think it's impossible. We will take it apart together."

"I'm listening," I said, spreading my hands. "I've never known you to be mad before."

Ptolemy grinned and took a sip. "The plan is this: the hearse cannot travel quickly. It's too large and too heavy and can only go by Royal Roads. And it cannot travel the mountains in poor weather. It must cross Asia in summer, because even a little ice or mud will make the mountains impassable. It's too late in the year to leave Babylon and make the journey now."

"True," I said, thinking of the mountains near Miletus and the uplands along the Royal Road to Gordion. We did not even travel the horse fair circuit except in spring and summer, and that was without heavy wagons. Summer was already ending in the uplands, and in a few weeks rains would come. It was not too long before they would wake to ice in the mornings in the high mountains. Here in Egypt it was easy to forget that winter was coming.

"It will have to leave Babylon in the spring next year, so that the passes are clear. How would you go?"

I closed my eyes a moment, seeing the maps in my mind. "From Babylon I'd take the Royal Road to the coast and then turn north onto the Royal Road to Gordion, the way the dispatch riders go. It's the smoothest road with the gentlest grades, which would matter dragging a huge hearse. Then from Gordion I'd turn north toward the Hellespont, instead of taking the route through the cities of Ionia. That would minimize my time within striking distance of the sea."

"And the closest point to us?"

"Not very close," I said. "There's no reason to go as far south as Tyre, or even Damascus. I suppose the closest would be near Issos, where the road comes down out of the mountains and turns north." I could see that pass in memory, the road cutting cleanly between steep cliffs, then broadening as it breached the last rampart and descended to the plain. It was there that Darius had chosen to face Alexander all those years ago. It was a very good place for an ambush.

"You're going to hijack the hearse," Ptolemy said.

I opened my eyes and nodded slowly. "Where the road comes out of the hills and comes down toward the sea." I picked up my cup again and took a drink. "A few problems. That's not Egyptian territory, or anywhere close. If we seize any controlling position or garrison anything nearby, Perdiccas will know exactly what we're doing, and either won't send the hearse at all or will send it with an enormous escort."

Ptolemy shook his head. "We can't garrison. It's got to be fast. I'm going to send you with an all-cavalry force. Enough to overwhelm the escort, but not enough to take and hold towns. You've got to do it quickly."

"And turn south for Egypt," I said. The road turned north, but it also ran south, to Tyre and the cities of the coast, to Ashkelon and Gaza and finally Pelousion. That was the way I had come when I had left Babylon with Thais. I knew that road.

"For Egypt," Ptolemy said.

"It won't be fast," I said. "Not after I have the hearse. Then I'll be stuck moving at a slow walk. It's a long way. And as soon as Perdiccas hears he'll pursue."

Ptolemy nodded seriously. "And there is no knowing exactly where he'll be when he hears, or how fast he'll come. He could be in Susa or Babylon, or he could be much closer. If I were Perdiccas..."

"You'd come after us with only cavalry, hell for leather," I said. "Figuring that we'd be all cavalry too, because we couldn't have gotten any heavy infantry there in time." I took another deep drink, my brow furrowed. "It's too far. He'll catch us before we make Egypt. If we get a good lead, we may make Ashkelon or Gaza, but Gaza's fortifications don't amount to shit since we knocked holes in the walls ten years ago. There's a gap in the curtain wall you could drive a herd of cattle through. I can't hold Gaza with cavalry."

"I know," Ptolemy said. "If you make Pelousion it's different."

I shrugged. "Oh, Perdiccas could try to take Pelousion with cavalry until the moon turns green! The problem is that I can't make Pelousion. It's too far. Once I'm stuck with the speed of the hearse, it will take me weeks down the coast instead of days. He'll catch us well short of Pelousion." I looked at him. "How many men were you planning to give me?"

"How many do you need?" he asked. "You'll have to hold him off."

"Depends on the size of the initial escort too," I said. I thought about the cavalry that had stayed with Perdiccas in Babylon, the men who had once fought beside me. "I shouldn't think he'd have more than fifteen hundred or two thousand to send, not right away. He'd have to pull some in from Susa and points east to find more than that, all cavalry. And he won't want to do that. Speed is more important."

"We have nine hundred and fifty-six," Ptolemy said. "Counting every man. The survivors of Hephaistion's Ile and my own. Krateros' Ile stayed with him. That total includes some Persian horse archers who came over for dynastic reasons, and a few men out of this unit or that who didn't like Perdiccas. I could give you something like eight hundred, one full-strength Ile."

"And Perdiccas can't do better than twice that," I said thoughtfully. "Not if he wants to move immediately. And it's realistically more like a thousand he'll actually send, or twelve hundred."

"I can't tell you how to do this, Lydias," Ptolemy said, pouring more wine. "I can't tell you where you'll meet him, or how many men he'll have. You're going to have to work it out as you go." His eyes met mine firmly. "That's why this needs to be you."

I took a deep breath.

"You can work independently. You can think for yourself. And you'll have to. There are too many ways this could go."

I steepled my hands before my face, rested my chin on my fingers. "To get the most time it will have to be a complete surprise. If they send a messenger to Perdiccas before we actually have the hearse, it will cut days off his response. It has to be completely clean. Just how good are these embalmers of yours?" I frowned. "And are they likely to know the schedule and the guard strength? Anything about the camp or the marching order?"

Ptolemy shook his head. "They won't even be with the procession. They asked permission to return home to Egypt, and Perdiccas gave them leave to go. They have to go now, and they'll be back before the hearse leaves Babylon. He's not stupid. He knows they're Egyptian, and that having them accompany the body is asking for trouble."

I shook my head.

"Fortunately, they're not my only contact," Ptolemy said. "There is someone more highly placed who will be accompanying the body. He'll know the details of the march. If you can reach him it will simplify matters a great deal."

"Who's that?" I asked, knowing I asked Ptolemy to give me the man's life. Perdiccas would not hesitate to execute a traitor immediately.

He did not hesitate, only dropped his voice a tone involuntarily. "Bagoas the eunuch, who was Alexander's."

Of course I knew who Bagoas was, though I had never actually talked to him. He had been Alexander's favorite, and as such had possessed considerable influence at court. He had come to Alexander with the rest of Darius' trappings when we had conquered Persia, and though he had been a favorite of the Great King, that was before, he had lost nothing by it. He was beautiful, of course, but more than that he was discreet and calm, able to smooth over small troubles and set the touchy Persian nobility at ease with just the right level of deference and respect, just the right gestures from the King. Like a Greek hetaira, he could be counted upon to make certain that all the proper things were done.

Alexander had used him well. The Persian nobility had expected to find Alexander a boorish conqueror eager to sate himself on luxury, ruining half of what he touched like a pig in the house. Instead, they were greeted by Bagoas with precisely the shade of formality their status required, ushered into the presence of Alexander, the new Great King, who took their prostrations as his due and behaved in all ways as one would expect the King to. And instead of going home to foment armed rebellions over insults paid, they were pleasantly surprised. Much of this was due to Bagoas, who had the King's ear.

Of course this was the very reason why others hated him. A beautiful Persian gelding at the King's side? What could be more indicative of the depths Alexander had sunk to? First he wore trousers sometimes, and then he held audience for Persians in the Persian style. But having a eunuch about, like some sort of Eastern king, was really too much.

Myself, I saw little harm in it. It was, like the palaces and the food, something that came with Persia. And like the palaces and the food, Bagoas was certainly nice to look at. I could admire beauty, even if I had not been of a rank to be running to royal audiences.

Now I raised an eyebrow to Ptolemy. "You trust him? What does he have to gain with you that he doesn't gain from Perdiccas? After all, Perdiccas is from the pro-Persian party too."

"It's not just Perdiccas' side. It's Roxane's," Ptolemy said. "She tried to kill him more than once when the King was alive." He shrugged. "Jealousy."

"You know this?" I asked. We were taking a huge risk on the word of someone I did not know.

Ptolemy's eyes were grave. "I know this. I was there when it happened, once, and when the King found out. She hated him because Alexander trusted him more."

If Hephaistion had been jealous of Bagoas, I had not seen it. But then no one was trusted more than Hephaistion.

"If you're sure he can be relied upon," I said.

Ptolemy nodded. "Bagoas needs to get out of Babylon and away from Roxane. Like Olympias, she has a long memory and she's proven that she's capable of poison. His days are numbered if he stays near her, and he'd be a fool to actually accompany the hearse to Macedon, where he would spend his days as a figure of fun or as a toy for Cassander. He's better off here by a long shot."

"What did you promise him?" I asked.

"That he would be a funerary priest of Alexander, and that he

would have a pension here in Egypt, to stay by the King and tend him."
Ptolemy shrugged. "Little enough. But it was what he asked for."

"Then I suppose we're settled," I said.


And so it was that I passed the winter in Alexandria, watching the city grow around me and drilling relentlessly the men who would ride with me.

The embalmers arrived at midwinter, with further details about the hearse if not about the escort. It was the size of a small ship, with the same breadth, made in the form of an Ionic temple. The entrance was at the rear, so the draft animals would not foul the stoop, between two golden lions. Inside, the roof was barrel-vaulted like a tomb rather than flat like a wagon, and the sides were painted in magnificent jewel colors, one side showing Alexander on his horse leading the Companions, another a fleet of galleys under sail. A third showed war elephants preparing to charge, and another showed Alexander in the guise of Great King, in his magnificent chariot. Lord of Greece, lord of Persia, lord of India, and lord of the Middle Sea—all that he had been. Except Pharaoh of Egypt. That was not lost on me. Perdiccas might extol glories which he intended to claim, but he did not hold Egypt and did not think he would.

Politics, I thought. All is politics. And what am I becoming that I see politics in the funeral murals? More than a simple soldier, for all that's what I thought I was. Now I must become a general. Upon this raid on the funeral procession the fate of the kingdom might rest.

While the fields of Egypt greened before the harvest, we drilled and practiced, making one Ile of the men of different units who must come together. We may face some rebel claimant, I said. No man there knew what we planned. Perdiccas must not hear the faintest whisper in advance.

Not even Artashir, whom I trusted, was told. He had manifested an unexpected talent for overseeing the building of the city, for getting cargoes of stone to the places where they belonged, and for making certain that the city walls and the breakwaters rose according to the drawings. He read three languages, and had studied mathematics. The angles of walls and weights of fortifications were no more than columns of numbers to me, but each day he had his head stuck between those of builders and carpenters and masons, consulting over whether this load of stone would be better there or there.

Born and bred in the uplands of Media, Artashir had been a gentleman long before Alexander came to Persia, the second son of a minor nobleman with mountain estates. He had been one of the Thousand, and stood against us at Gaugamela in command of horse archers, those lethally quick soldiers who wore silk instead of steel and could deliver a blistering barrage of arrows from a distance, then gallop away before the infantry could close.

But after Gaugamela things had changed. When Bessos had over-thrown Darius as Great King and usurped his throne, the kin of Darius had made peace with Alexander to punish his murderer. Artashir had come over then, with Oxathres and others who had ties of blood to Darius. He'd become a Companion sometime in India, though I wasn't certain when as I had been with Hephaistion's corps, not with the King. As to why he'd come with Ptolemy, I suspected it was over Roxane. She'd had Queen Stateira murdered in Babylon, right after Alexander's death. If Artashir was kin in some way to Darius, he was certainly kin to his daughter Stateira too, making her murder a matter of family honor. He could not serve her murderer, once Perdiccas and Roxane had made common cause.

Thus he had come with Ptolemy, bringing all his household with him. It was, I thought, rather extensive.

Not long after I returned to Alexandria, Artashir invited me to dinner at his house. I was expecting something rude and in keeping with the life of the camp. After all, the city was new and still more than half unbuilt.

To my surprise, his house was more than a tent pitched on a lot with half-finished walls. A streetside gate opened into a courtyard where a fountain played. Around it some short bushes were arranged in imitation of the grand gardens I had seen in Persia. Inside, his dining room was cool and comfortable, walls whitewashed but with decoration begun only on one side near the ceiling, three couches arranged in Greek fashion with little tables. Two lamps burning fragrant oil hung from the ceiling.

His wives would not eat with us, a custom shared by the Greeks and Persians alike. Only hetairae eat with men, except in the privacy of the home, though that custom had gone somewhat by the wayside in camp. The Egyptians, like the Indians, consider such restrictions foolish, which unfortunately had led to many respectable women being taken for prostitutes.

Instead, well-watered wine was served by Artashir's oldest son, Mardonias, a dark-haired boy of nine or so who looked scrubbed within an inch of his life and poured carefully, a grave and serious expression on his face.

"Well done," his father said quietly when he was done, and he gave Artashir a quicksilver grin before he tripped back off to the kitchen.

I leaned back on my couch and took a sip. It was very well watered indeed, but it is not really a Persian custom to bring the wine in before the meal at all. The wine, like the couches, was a compromise.

"He's a well-grown boy," I said. "Mardonias? Is that a family name?"

Artashir nodded, stretching his legs out on the couch. He wore linen trousers and tunic rather than a chiton, which I could see the point of on horseback, though I could never get used to not having my legs free. "It is. Mardunaya, actually. Though it's Mardonias in Greek. We are descended from that Mardunaya who was a general of Xerxes, and who married the Great King's sister. Hence we descend from Darius the Great."

"Yes," I said, "we know the name in Miletus." And we did, of course. Miletus had been part of the Persian Empire when Mardonias had staged his fleet there for the invasion of Greece. "How many children have you now? I'm sorry. I think I've lost count."

"Three sons and two daughters," he said. "He's the oldest. I was married to Amina before the war, and then I married Rania in India."

"I can't imagine having more than one wife," I said. "It seems like it would get very complicated."

Artashir shrugged, looselimbed. "It's not as complicated as one might think. Amina picked Rania out, actually. They're as affectionate as sisters and even share a bed." He grinned. "Sometimes I don't think they need me at all, devoted to each other as they are."

"Oh," I said. There was a word for that in Greek, but I couldn't imagine how one could say Sapphic in Persian.

"We all get along," Artashir said. "Though it will be good to get Mardonias in school. He's the only one old enough, and it's more than time he learned how to get along."

"A Greek school?"

Artashir shrugged and took a very small sip. "It's the school of the city. The men he will command or be commanded by his whole life will be boys there. He must learn his place." Artashir sat up, his handsome face animated. "We knew what we did when we came here, Amina and Rania and I. We knew we would never return to Persia. But hopefully we have brought the best of Persia with us." He looked up at the hanging lanterns where they cast shadows on the wall in the evening air. "Some men try to stop change. It's like stopping a wave, keeping the sea from the shore or the snows from the mountain. Better to recognize what must happen, and choose what you would keep with Mitra's blessing."

I had taken breath to reply when suddenly there was a huge crash from the kitchen, followed by the shouting of women and the screams of children.

Artashir and I both leapt up, and I followed him into the kitchen, where a scene of chaos reigned.

A black-winged seagull, flapping madly, careened around the kitchen with a fish in its talons. Two dark-haired women screamed after it, one trying to swat the gull and the other to grab it, while a small girl about six years old struggled to close the heavy windows. Underfoot, a little boy about two screamed at the top of his voice, "Bad bird! Bad bird! Bad bird!" Mardonias grabbed a heavy pot and swung it about, looking as though he was going to more likely hammer his sister than the bird.

Artashir grabbed the pot. "Don't do that," he said.

The darker of the two women pulled the other window closed with a bang while the littlest boy set up a wail.

Hissing and spitting, an enormous black cat made a leap for the bird. He missed, but he did succeed in snagging the fish. The bird let go and dived out the still open window, narrowly missing the little girl's hair. She shrieked.

In the middle of the table full of half-chopped vegetables, the black cat took a delicate sniff of the fish and then licked it deliberately.

Artashir and the two women exchanged comments in voluble Persian, Artashir still clutching the pot.

I reached down and picked up the crying child, who was now screaming and holding on to my leg. "There now," I said, remembering the Indian words I had learned. "Don't cry, small boy. It's all done now." He was heavier than Sikander had been, nearly a year older.

At my voice saying familiar words, he stopped crying and looked at me gravely, huge round brown eyes in a plump little face. It made my heart ache.

"I think that about covers dinner," Artashir said, shaking his head with a smile on his face. He gestured toward the middle of the table. "Alexander triumphs."

Sitting on the vegetables, the big black cat looked up from the fish scored by the gull's claws and took a bite, his green eyes on us.

"Pardon?"

"The cat is Alexander," one of the women said, her brown hair escaping from its pins. Her Greek was accented but perfectly fluent. I thought she must be Amina, the senior of the wives. "Mardunaya named him. He showed up right after we moved in, and we suppose he lives here now."

"Here and ten other houses," Artashir said. "The Egyptians revere cats and they're used to coming and going in people's houses as they like."

"He fought the bird really bravely," the little girl said.

"He did," Artashir agreed. "And Alexander gets the spoils. I don't suppose any of us want to eat that fish now?"

We all looked at it. Alexander looked back.

"It does seem a little the worse for wear," I said. I handed the little boy back to his mother, the younger wife Rania.

"I'm afraid we do not have dinner suitable for guests," she said, blushing furiously at the humiliating breach of hospitality.

"We could go for a walk," I said to Artashir. "We could go walk around for a while and come back later. After all, it's rather early for dinner."

Artashir's eyes went from one woman to another. "That sounds like an excellent plan. We'll go for a long walk."

And so we did. Once we were out of earshot of the house I couldn't help laughing. After a moment, Artashir started laughing too. He laughed until he was nearly crying. "The bird, the fish…"

"The cat," I said. "And the children."

"It's chaos, Lydias," he said. "But good chaos."

"I know," I said, sobering.

He did too, brushing his long hair back from his eyes. "You still mourn?"

I shrugged.

He drew me into an embrace, hands on my back like a kinsman. "I cannot tell you to ever forget, for I never would forget if I lost Rania or Amina, or any of the children. But one can love more than once. Loving a second child does not reduce your love for the first. I do not love Mardonias the less because Cyaxara is his little sister."

"I do not even know how to begin," I said. "You make the complicated seem simple."

He released me and we strolled in silence down to the harbor, where the breakwater was under construction. It was growing dark as we walked along it, the waves piling against the mole a man's height beneath our feet. The wind off the Middle Sea lifted my hair and plucked at my chiton as if to give me wings.

"It's dark out to sea," I said.

"Lift your eyes to the heavens," he said.

I tilted my head back and watched the stars appear bright against the indigo sky, the Hunter with his belt of fire rising clear of the sea.

"Do you ever wonder," Artashir asked quietly, "what the first men who came this way thought? When they came down the Nile in little reed boats and walked along the shore looking up at the sky and out at the sea?"

I looked at him sideways, his eyes on the stars, keen and alight, and for a moment it seemed to me I had stood like this with him before, in some distant dream. "I expect they wondered if the sky was just another ocean," I said.

"I expect they did," Artashir said, his hands clasped behind his back, looking up at the heavens.

"Maybe it is," I said, and as I said it I knew it was true. "We will build a boat of steel and silver to navigate the high oceans of night, and you will pilot it, and we will go there someday."

"I expect we will," Artashir said, "if Alexander wills it." He clasped my hand wrist to wrist. "It is good to have such a friend as you, Lydias."

"It is," I said. "My friend always."

Artashir looked at me sideways. "Always is a very long time."

"I know," I said.

# WİNGS OF FİRE

Summer had at last come to the uplands, and even the highest passes ahead were clear of snow. Here, however, in the lowlands by the sea not so far from the field of Issos, it was burning hot in the daytime. At night, it was bearable.

I waited in the shadow of a stone, a darker shape indistinguishable in the dark. The night was moonless, but the stars were very bright. Sothis had risen behind the peaks and was ascending the heavens as I waited, my cloak drawn tight about me to prevent any glint of steel. It would not surprise me if I waited the night through, as I had waited the past two nights. We were not certain how close the funeral cortege was. Which of course was the entire point of my being there. I could have sent any other man instead, but if this went as we had anticipated, it could hardly be entrusted to a trooper.

It might be tonight. Four days ago we had met a merchant who said that he had passed the hearse on the road west, a splendid procession, the oxen drawing the heavy hearse moving at a slow walk. His wagons had passed it easily and left it behind. It might be tonight.

To my surprise, I had little time to wait. The Dogs had hardly lifted clear of the peaks when I saw a movement below. Someone was coming along quietly, barefooted and cloaked.

I waited. It might be some local shepherd bound on a nocturnal errand or up to no good. It might be one of Perdiccas' scouts. In which case, I had the drop on him, and my knife in my hand, while presumably he did not yet know precisely where I was, only that if Ptolemy intended to do anything he must also have scouts out.

It wasn't a shepherd. As he ascended the path his hood fell back, and the starlight caught his face, the clean lovely lines of it unmistakable. That kind of relentless beauty didn't just wander in.

I made a small sound and stood.

He tensed, and for a moment I thought he would flee.

I pushed my cloak back, hoping he might remember my face, though it seemed unlikely. The gesture itself was what counted.

From his posture, I saw him relax, and he took the last steps up quickly and lightly.

"Bagoas," I said, and offered him my hand as though he were a man.

He hesitated, then took it. His grip was not mean for all the lightness of his bones. "I do not remember your name," he said.

"Lydias of Miletus," I said. "You would not. I was not often with the King after you joined us. I was in General Hephaistion's command."

His dark eyes lingered on my face. "I think that I met you in Persepolis, after we came back from the desert."

"You did," I said, and once again it tasted like ashes in my mouth. "I lost my wife and my child in Gedrosia, and do not like to think on it."

"Your pardon," he said, and came and sat in the shadow of the rock. "I did not know, or if I had, I had forgotten."

I took a breath. "Where is the cortege?"

"Less than half a day's pace on the road," he said. "Half a day for the wagons, that is. I walked it in a little less than two hours of the night, I think. You could do it with horses in an hour, and come down on us after the road descends to the plain. The escort is a thousand foot soldiers, but lightly armed, and they do not march in harness in the heat of the day."

I raised an eyebrow and sat down beside him. "And how should General Ptolemy know that you do not plan a trap?" It was really a rhetorical question. We were in too deep to hold back now. A thousand men was more or less what we had expected, all infantry. If they were not in harness and could not efficiently form defensive squares we could go through that, especially with surprise on our side.

Bagoas sounded weary. "And if I planned a trap, why should I put myself in the midst of it?"

I shrugged, and offered him my water skin. He drank, and we sat together under the stars. It was not really a question, after all. Ptolemy was already committed to this scheme, and so was I.

In a little while he spoke. "What has Perdiccas done for me?" he asked. "What, that I should betray my lord's wish that he should lie in Egypt? Perdiccas seeks an excuse to move his army over the Dardanelles and challenge Antipatros, or to claim the hand of Alexander's sister. That is not my lord's business or mine."

He did not speak of Roxane, nor did I expect him to. "It must be nice for it to be so simple," I said, and was surprised by the wistful sound in my voice. "Your lord's wish. Instead of the snarling of dogs."

"Do you not serve Ptolemy?"

I nodded, and took a drink from it myself. "I do. He's a good general and a good ruler. But he is not my lord. Not in the sense you mean."

"I should hardly think so," he said, and there was amusement in his tone. "After all, you are a man and a Greek, not a barbarian slave."

I let the "Greek" pass. Perhaps I was, though no one born in the pure free air of Attica would consider me such, half Carian and half Ionian. I shrugged. "He is the best that remains. And I must place my service somewhere. Perhaps in time Egypt will come to feel like home. Indeed, I do not think I would have chosen as I did, were it not for Egypt."

"Perhaps it's a place, not a person," he said quietly. "There are men who love their home above all else, even their gods. But Alexander is my god, and I shall see his wishes followed, whether I deal with Ptolemy or not."

"Ptolemy will take him to Egypt," I said. "He will be interred in Alexandria, in the city of his founding, in a tomb where men will worship until the end of time. This is Ptolemy's intent. I swear it."

"If that is his intent, I am well content," Bagoas said. "And if he will allow me to serve there all my days."

"If that is your desire," I said, "he has no reason to gainsay it."

I passed him the water skin back, and he drank again. He seemed in no hurry to leave, and I said so.

Bagoas shrugged. "I will not go back into the camp until dawn. Getting out was easy — no one seeks to prevent people from leaving — but returning at night would be difficult. I will walk straight back in at dawn, when the watch changes and camp is breaking, as though I had walked out a few minutes before looking for a moment's privacy. I might as well wait here as closer the camp, where I am more likely to be discovered."

I nodded. Truly, he was a pretty thing, but not empty-headed in the least. I could see why the King had wanted him.

"I shall be with the assault," I said. "It will be all cavalry to spring the trap before the sun even stands high. Keep down and don't get in the way of our business. I would not see you hurt."

Bagoas nodded gravely. "I know how to do that," he said. "I will stay with the coffin."

"It will be a hot fight," I said. "Do that. I will tell my men to leave you."

"You are a troop leader?"

"I was," I said. "When the King was alive. Now I lead Ptolemy's cavalry," I said. Lately they had begun to call it Lydias' Ile, which always disconcerted me a little. I was not used to being Hipparch, and wondered if I ever would be.

Just on the edge of the horizon I could see the faint dark shade of the sea. The stars would not pale for hours yet. When they did, it would be on a blood day. Another one.

Bagoas leaned back against the stone, his fine features limned by starlight. "Why do you do this?" he said curiously. "If not for Ptolemy? Is it for the King that you risk your life for his cold body?"

Perhaps it was the quiet that caused me to answer truthfully. "Because General Hephaistion would have wished it."

"Ah," he said, and in that word was a wealth of understanding that I did not want to hear.

"If I have worshipped at a lesser shrine, what is it to you?" I said.

"Nothing," he said. He was quiet a long moment. "I remember now where I saw you. Not Susa, but Babylon."

"Yes," I said. I did not think of that, either, the funeral pyre and the coins on his closed eyes, his long red hair spread upon his shoulders.

Bagoas was quiet a long time, and only the flicker of his lashes in the darkness told me he was still awake. At last he said, contemplatively, as though he discussed something long ago and far away, "We did not hate each other, I think. He and I."

"No," I said. "I don't think so. And if you did, it's nothing now. When the world is a ruin, it hardly matters who hated who once."

Bagoas nodded.

"And he did not love me," I said. I did not know, of course, if Alexander had loved Bagoas, but there were other things I was more certain of.

"Does that matter?" he asked.

"No." I looked at him sideways. "Of course not." I got to my feet and extended a hand to Bagoas so that he might rise. "Come, then. We must be gone to keep the faith with the dead. I will see you before noon, where the road comes down to the plains. Keep your head down and stay with your lord. I will be there."

"I know," he said, and gripped my hand in farewell.

WAITING WAS THE hardest part. At midmorning we were ready, an Ile eight hundred strong, divided into two parts. Half our force waited drawn up on the south side of the road under cover of cedar trees, at the bottom of the long incline where the road came down out of the mountains. The other half waited on the north side of the road drawn up close against the mountains in a tight gully. My scouts, dismounted, had climbed the slope above. Two of them waited there, able to see the top of the last rise. They would provide the signal.

I held my hand to my forehead, looking at them. They both waited as well, their eyes trained on the road.

Waiting. The sun climbed up the sky. My horse drowsed. I would have liked to have ridden round a bit, working off the tension, but if I did then everyone would start moving. Better to be still and present an air of cool confidence. We had to wait for them to reach exactly the right place.

The sun had just slipped west of the zenith by a hair when one of the scouts came down the hill a few paces, the mountainside blocking his body from the road. He lifted both his arms and waved to me.

I waved back.

They were coming.

The scouts slid down the hill, all but tumbling in their haste to get back to their horses.

They were coming. And we must wait. We must not spring the trap too fast and give their infantry the gates of the pass to defend.

Two years, I thought. He has been dead nearly two years. Surely the world cannot have been without Alexander that long, but it was so. It had been two years since I stood beside his bier in Babylon.

Waiting. The men about me were restive.

"Patience," I said quietly, and I thought I saw admiration in the eyes of one young man. Cool. Collected. Confident. Though my heart pounded in my chest. I was not young anymore, a green boy spoiling for battle. We could wait.

The first ranks came out of the pass. Bagoas had not lied. The infantry marched without their armor in the heat of the day. They had their sarissas, but no steel hats or breastplates.

"Let them pass," I said to Glaukos almost in a whisper. "Wait."

They started down the hill, heads rising at the cool breeze from the sea that at last reached them. We were not so far now.

There was the hearse. An enormous team of oxen pulled it, glittering winged Victory on each corner, holding forth golden olive wreaths, the outside of the hearse painted scarlet and gold. Drivers walked beside the beasts, steadying them on the incline. They trotted a bit faster, urged by the weight of the hearse behind them. It was a magnificent sight.

The first ranks were reaching the bottom. Now I must be careful. They were not a half mile from the men waiting beneath the cedar trees. Waiting too long...

The soldiers following the hearse appeared, marching in good order. Twenty. Forty. A hundred. The baggage wagons and provisions would still be in the pass, but that would not matter.

My mare's ears pricked forward as though she knew an instant before I did.

"Forward!" I raised my sword hand and shouted as loud as I could, my voice cutting through the stillness. "Alexander!"

Like a wave we broke from cover, sweeping downhill like a torrent on the rear of the ranks.

"Alexander and Ptolemy!"

The wedge resolved itself, each man falling into his proper position, a flying wedge with me at the point, four hundred horses in wild career. The beating of their hooves was like a heartbeat, like the blood singing in my veins, like drums leading the dance.

Fire kindled off my sword point, held like a beacon. Behind me the wind tore away their answering shouts. "Alexander and Ptolemy!"

If I had lifted into the air I should not have been surprised.

The ranks before us turned about seeking their places. They were veterans too, and not easily spooked, but they were not in steel and they were in column. I didn't think they'd manage to form up before we were upon them, and I was right.

Only a few sarissas were leveled before we reached them. I swung between two of them. The ranks were too far apart for them to be an effective barrier. Once we were inside the long reach of the sarissas, they were essentially defenseless. The sarissas were too long to fight hand to hand.

My mare went up with a squeeze, the first man borne down beneath her hooves while I took the second with my sword, straight into his unarmored chest.

And then the wave broke.

Far ahead, on the other side of the hearse, the first ranks turned back to face us just as the other half of our men burst from cover of the trees, bearing down on the flank of the column in the front.

I was wind, I was flame, I was fire on the mountain. A fighting rush lifted me and held me, guard and thrust, guard and thrust and thrust again.

Someone grabbed at my left leg, but my mare went up again, tossing him off as the thresher tosses barley.

Ahead of me, the golden hearse shimmered like a mirage, Victory leaning down with her golden wreath.

"To the King! To Alexander!" I yelled, the old rallying cry of the Companions, heard on many a field from one end of the world to the other. This was the last time. Never again would he be in the midst of the battle. Never again.

We swept toward the hearse. Now the resistance was light. My mare stepped nimbly over fallen sarissas. The veterans, wise in the ways of this, had dropped them as useless. Those who resisted had drawn sword instead.

"To the King!" I turned about when I gained it, my back to the golden lions that guarded Alexander's body, sword raised high. "To the King!" Once again I stood before his body, as I had on his deathbed. I wondered where Bagoas was. I hoped he'd kept clear.

"Throw down your weapons and we'll give quarter!" I yelled. "Throw them down!" A cluster of cavalry was around me, fifteen or twenty who had charged straight through. We had the hearse.

In ones and twos, and then in larger groups, they began to surrender.

An infantryman with a bloody nose and beard whom I vaguely recognized elbowed his way to me. I thought he was probably the officer in charge. "What are the terms? And who do you serve?"

"We serve Ptolemy of Egypt," I said. "And the terms are this. Lay down your weapons and you are free to go with your baggage and your provisions. We keep the King."

He shook his head, sweat running down his face, and looked back toward the head of the pass where the baggage train had stopped just short of the slope. I could see the lead wagons, the white flash of a woman's veil. They were returning to Macedon. Of course they had brought their families with them.

I dropped my voice. "Come on, man," I said. "Be reasonable. You keep your women and your earnings, your wagons and your food for the road. All we want is the hearse. Which you can't stop us from taking." I saw him hesitate. "Is it worth dying for at the end like this?"

He looked back at me again, and his eyes were very blue. "For the King."

"The King will lie in honor in Alexandria, the city of his founding," I said. "I give you my word on that. You know General Ptolemy. You know he's a man of honor and means no desecration."

"And your name, Companion?" he asked. "Are you a man of honor?"

"I am," I said. "I am Lydias of Miletus, Hipparch of Ptolemy's Ile, and you may count my deeds to my name."

He looked at the glittering hearse again, as though to fix it in his memory, and sighed. "I accept your terms."

After that it was simple. We had lost only three men, so thoroughly had the rush succeeded, and forty-five wounded. Most of the wounds were slight, and I thought that only six of them were truly serious, enough to lay a man up for weeks at a time. Their losses were heavier, and they camped to make a pyre for the dead near the field of Issos where so many had been slain before.

The sun was falling into the sea as we saw the last of them, kindling flame while the women and the servants put up camp, the bright fires licking at the cedar gathered from the wood.

We did not stop. We turned south, the hearse rolling along in the midst of our column. We would not stop, now. It was a long, long way to Egypt.

Victory glittered gold in the last rays of the sun.

Issos, I thought. My King, here is your great field. And here we are on the march again, as you would not have minded. What tomb could ever hold you, who spread your wings above all the world?

I HAD STILL been General Hephaistion's horseboy when the Battle of Issos was fought, and I had no part in it. Better men than I have told that story, including Ptolemy, who served upon the field. For my part, there was little to the battle itself except the long, tedious wait, and then the mad rush at the end when the wounded started coming in, after the Persian lines had collapsed.

Issos was the first time that Alexander faced Darius, the first time that Darius fled. He left behind his entire camp and all of his treasury that he had brought with him, talents and talents of coin and all the goods the Great King travels with. But far more importantly, in his fear at our victory he left behind his wife, his old mother, his two young daughters, and his son, a baby not yet walking. It may scarcely be credited that he did so, though it is true as I was there, that he was so poor a king and a man, as their fates were plainly written. His son should die on our swords, and his mother and wife should be playthings for our men. The fates of the two princesses, then aged ten and twelve, did not even bear contemplating. That any man should flee and leave his family thus, king or not, seemed incredible to me at the time.

When the word went round the baggage train that we had captured the camp of Darius and all his family, I could hardly believe it. And like any boy of sixteen I hurried to see.

We traveled light, and while the King had a tent and things of his own, it was nothing like the tent of Darius. The tent of Darius could have been a palace itself, with eight rooms hung with silks and floored with gorgeous patterned rugs that each must take two years on the loom. There was a bathing room with an enormous bronze bathtub chased with silver and tens of little glass bottles full of oils, hanging lamps with colored glass panes burning sweet-scented oil, and a massive bedchamber with furniture of ivory, including an ingenious folding toilet chair. I had never seen the like, and the other boys and I examined it with many crude jokes until the Royal Pages threw us out.

"Look here," they said. "This all belongs to the King now, and he won't want your grubby hands all over it! This isn't an exhibit at the fair for a bunch of stable boys! This isn't Darius' anymore. It's Alexander's."

At that we all shuffled our way to the entrance, into the falling night outside. It was the prize of our betters, but we had at least gotten a good look at it.

"What do you suppose it's like," one of the other boys asked, "to take a crap in an ivory pot?"

"About the same as anywhere else," I said. I was distracted by the tent next door, almost as big and sumptuous, but heavily guarded. There were Silver Shields infantry cordoned around it, and the officer in charge was General Perdiccas. "What do you suppose..." I began.

From within rose the sounds of women's voices raised in lamentation, and I knew what it must be. Here was the family of Darius, a prize reserved for the King to dispose of, along with his scented oil and his toilet chair.

Several horsemen were approaching, and I immediately recognized Hephaistion's warhorse Zephyr, as I spent a great deal of time with him. I hurried forward to hold the reins as he dismounted. One of the Royal Pages took the King's reins.

Alexander got down awkwardly. While he had obviously washed since the battle, he was limping from a wound to the right leg. It had been stitched and bandaged neatly, but he stumbled when he tried to put all his weight on it.

"You need to go lie down," Hephaistion said, catching his arm. "You've lost enough blood, and if you tear the stitches open you'll have to go back to the doctor again."

"I'm fine," the King said testily, shaking his hair back out of his face. It was damp and clung to his brow. "Don't hover."

Hephaistion took a step back, though he seemed unbothered by the rebuke. "If you think it will look better for the King to fall over in front of Darius' tent."

Alexander raised his head, like a dog pricking its ears. "What is all that wailing?"

Perdiccas stepped forward from where he stood in front of the tent belonging to the royal ladies. "Darius' women, Alexander. They're mourning him. They think he must be dead to have left them."

Hephaistion snorted. "Darius is alive and well and riding for Babylon on the fastest horse he can find." What he thought of that kind of cowardice was plain to see.

"Darius' women?" the King asked. "Who, besides his wife?"

"His two daughters," Perdiccas said. "Stateira, age twelve, and Drypetis, age ten. And his elderly mother, Sisygambis. They say his wife's a beauty. The most beautiful woman in Asia. I haven't seen her myself yet, so I don't know. Their eunuchs are around them and say that we'll have to kill them to get them to step aside, so we're guarding the outside of the tent and they're guarding the inside. I thought we'd wait until you came to clear out the eunuchs."

And to give the royal ladies time for suicide, I thought. A ripple of approval ran through me for Perdiccas. That was well done, to give them time to die without rape. Though it would take a strong woman to kill her own daughters and infant son.

The same thought obviously occurred to Alexander, and he traded glances with Hephaistion. "I should tell them they have nothing to fear," he said.

Hephaistion made a gesture of assent. "The sooner the better. And then you can go lie down."

"I've been telling people she's yours," Perdiccas said cheerfully. "It's a fine thing, isn't it? The Great King's wife for your concubine? And the daughters too of course. Only Alexander could do that!"

"Could he?" he said dryly.

"She'd probably come around to it if she's a sensible woman," Perdiccas said. "In exchange for her daughters' lives. Persia at your feet, the Great King's wife on her knees, begging for mercy! Your father would be proud of you."

Alexander put his head to the side, and I thought there was a current there that Perdiccas was missing. "He would be, wouldn't he?" he said, and went to the entrance of the tent.

Hephaistion brushed in front of him. "Let me," he said. "Those guards are sure to be nervous, and the last thing we need is you stabbed by a eunuch." He swept aside the tent door, followed by the King, Perdiccas, three guards, and me. Why not follow? No one had specifically told me not to, and I wanted to know what would happen.

"King Alexander is here to see the royal ladies," Perdiccas announced loudly.

The tent was much the same as Darius', with silk hangings and thick carpets. Four eunuchs armed with knives stood just inside, the older man nearest the door with his mouth set in firm determination. A cluster of women stood at the opposite end, the royal ladies and their attendants presumably, their faces decently veiled.

Only one was not. She must have been sixty-five, with keen sharp features unblurred by time, her dark blue gown embroidered with silver thread in endless stars and whorls. She stood between Alexander and the rest.

The eunuchs looked to her, and at her nod stepped back from the door, their knives at their side.

The queen mother, I thought. There was something in her face that reminded me of some other, or perhaps it was simply that she was impressive in her grief and pride.

Hephaistion looked at the eunuchs. "Do any of you speak Greek?"

"I do," the older one said. "It is my privilege to translate for my queen."

Her chin rose and she took four steps. The Great King's mother sank to her knees in front of Hephaistion, her hands upraised in pleading like a carving on a temple wall, the translator's words an echo behind her. "Hear, Alexander of Macedon, the pleas of an old woman! Hear the words of one who is lost!"

Hephaistion looked confused. "What? I'm not…"

The eunuch blanched, and spoke to the woman in swift Persian.

Her shoulders tightened, and her eyes flared, and she turned on her knees to begin again.

Alexander stepped forward and took her upraised hand. "Never mind, mother," he said. "He is Alexander too." He raised her to her feet, smiling. "I came to tell you that you and the other women are under the guard of my Silver Shields, and it is death for any man who molests you. You have nothing to fear. I will not even see the queen until Darius presents himself to me and I may return his family to him. Then I will receive him as a subject, and you will be united unharmed with him."

Her eyes roved over his face, and she asked one word in Persian. The translator rendered it as, "Why?"

"Because I'm Alexander," he said, and turned to leave.

We all scrambled out before him, me fastest of all, so that I would not look like a gawker who had not been about his work. I wasn't fast enough. His eye fell on me. "You, boy," he said. "Lydias, is it?"

"Yes, sir," I said, gulping.

"Do you know why?"

I pulled myself up, conscious of Hephaistion's curious expression. If I were going to make a fool of myself to the King, I should not do it by half. "Yes," I said. "Anyone can kill."

He smiled, a quicksilver expression that laid me open to the bone, and clapped me on the shoulder. "Good lad," he said, and, leaning a little on Hephaistion's arm, went into the tent of the Great King.


Now he lay in a golden hearse, a prize himself for which men died.

A thought struck me and I rode alongside the hearse, slipping my leg over my mare and transferring to the back stoop without a stride lost. No one had yet been inside.

A net of gold screened the door, and I lifted it with a hand still stained with blood from the fight.

A gilded lantern hung from the ceiling, throwing patterns of light and shadow over the walls. The paintings seemed to move in the dim light, galleys sailing on an endless sea, pennants bravely waving.

"Bagoas?" I said.

He rose up in one smooth motion from where he had been sitting on the floor at the sarcophagus' head. "Here," he said.

"I see that you are well," I said. The lantern light made planes of his face, casting a shadow like a flower on his cheek.

"I kept down, as you said," he replied. "It was neatly done."

"Thank you," I said. I looked down at the golden lid of the sarcophagus. "I must look," I said quietly. "To be sure."

After a moment he nodded. "I will help you," Bagoas said. "It's heavy."

Together we moved the lid back. It slid on invisible tracks, not nearly as difficult as it seemed it would be.

In the dim light Alexander looked as though he were sleeping. The embalmers had not wrapped him in linen as they do in Egypt. Instead, he looked entirely lifelike, his pale hair on his shoulders and his eyes closed, his golden breastplate over a bordered chiton of Tyrian purple. I would not have thought him dead. I would have thought he might wake at any moment, might suddenly speak.

"They did their finest work," Bagoas said, looking down expressionlessly, and I thought he must have looked many times. Perhaps he had pressed his lips to those cold ones, hoping for a breath of life.

I nodded. I could not speak. I did not know what I should say to him. Should I ask his pardon or his blessing? Instead I just inclined my head, as though waiting for orders.

After a moment, when of course they did not come, I looked up and gestured to Bagoas. We slid the lid back into position.

I said nothing. What can one say? I had never known what to say to family at a funeral. All words are hollow.

Bagoas had spent nearly two years tending the dead. He did not need my words. Instead he led me to the back stoop. "We go to Egypt?"

"We do," I said. "We will stop in Damascus and leave our wounded there, the men who are in no shape to ride. And then we will stop for nothing until we reach Pelousion."

His eyebrows rose over those startling green Median eyes. "We will make Pelousion?"

"Not without a fight," I said with a tight smile. "But we will reach it. I will give you my oath on that."

He nodded, a courtly gesture that reminded me of Artashir. "I believe we will, Lydias of Miletus."

I swung back on my horse and headed back to the front of the column. Dusk was falling. Behind me, Victory was plunged into night.

# LADY OF THE DESERT

They caught us just beyond Gaza. It was not a surprise, of course. I had scouts out from the time we left Tyre. Each morning when we started on the march at sunrise, I sent scouts riding back from our position with orders to go half a day's ride to the rear. At noon they would turn and catch up with us. We would have moved, of course, but their pace was so much faster that they would arrive a few hours after we made camp. It was a long day for them, and I used fresh riders each day, rotating through the duty roster, but it was not dangerously taxing, even in the heat of the summer. Every other day we would leave a pair of riders where we were, with orders to wait either six days or until they saw Perdiccas' troops and then return to us. Thus we had constant intelligence to our rear.

We were nearly at Gaza when the first of those brought us word. They had left Ashdod just as the first of Perdiccas' men straggled in, exhausted and seeking supply. They had an Ile and a half of men, about twelve hundred all counted, commanded by two Companions I knew, Attalos and Polemon. They had arrived almost without halt from Babylon, and their horses were exhausted. Attalos had ordered that they rest one day in Ashdod to resupply and attempt to find remounts to replace the horses that had gone off.

I nodded, thanked the scouts, and sent them off to rest. Then I walked out to the perimeter of our nightly camp, away from the fires and the gilded hearse.

Bagoas found me there. He came and stood a short distance away and did not speak.

I looked up at the stars, moving too slowly to see, but nonetheless wheeling through the night. A trooper I could have ignored, but it would be rude to ignore Bagoas. Of course he wanted to know what would happen.

"Three days, maybe four," I said.

"Do we stay in Gaza?" he asked.

That was the heart of the matter. We would be in Gaza in one more day. I could try to hold the town, send a rider to Pelousion for infantry reinforcements. Two days down to Pelousion, with no remount but riding as hard as the horse would stand. Four or five days back for the infantry. I should have to hold Gaza for three or four days. With damaged fortifications and cavalry only. Still, Attalos and Polemon would have only cavalry too, and would certainly not have any siege equipment.

Maybe. Maybe it could be done. Or maybe not. Common sense said it might be the safest course.

And yet. *Egypt*, the night wind whispered to me. *Egypt. Gaza is beyond the bounds of the Black Land. You must bring the King to Egypt.*

And yet. Perhaps it was just a cavalryman's hatred of walls. I did not want to be besieged in Gaza. Farther along, on the road, there might be opportunities. At least it would keep it open, keep it moving. Even if they did succeed in taking back the hearse from us, the closer we were to Egypt the farther they should have to take it back. And then they would be hampered by the speed of the hearse. Then they would have to worry about a sortie from Ptolemy at their rear. As far as they now had to go, even Ptolemy's infantry would catch them still south of Ashdod.

"We go on," I said.

---

Two DAYS AND a half later the sun stood high in the sky. The road had turned away from the sea. It ran now between steep cliffs, red and ochre, where stunted bushes clung to ledges and grew in the shelter of overhangs. I saw it, and I knew where we were.

The stone sphinx watched from the left hand side of the road, the shattered pedestal on the other side showing where its mate had been.

*Egypt,* something whispered.

As I walked between them I felt it as though I had broken an invisible thread, dashing past the judges to win the race. The boundaries of Egypt. Here some pharaoh of long ago had set up the sphinxes as a border guard. Last time I had passed this way I had known that, but this time I felt it like a vibration beneath the ground, the ancient magic of the Black Land roused and waiting.

I stopped the column and we poured out a libation of the best wine and I offered prayers. Then I stood back respectfully beside the sphinx while the column began moving again. If I had had my eyes closed I would still have known the moment the hearse passed the border.

It was like distant thunder, like rain in far-off mountains, like the sounding of the sea. The gods welcomed Alexander to Egypt.

My palms prickled with the power and I shook them out. If I were a priest, I thought, I should know what to do with this. I should know how to control this power, to raise the very land itself against pursuit. But I was a soldier, and I did not know.

Instead, I mounted up and we moved on again, taking my place at the head of the column.

We HAD ONLY gone on a little ways when I heard a lion roar. My horse's head went up, her ears swiveling toward the sound. I looked around.

On a ledge halfway up the cliff a tawny lioness was reclining, her golden head raised. As I looked up, her green eyes met mine. She did not leap up or appear startled by the appearance of the long column of armed men, nor did she challenge us. She simply looked.

I reined in, pulling to the side of the column. Her eyes did not leave me.

I did not look away. "Lady of the Desert," I said. "Please pardon our trespass on your place. We are only passing through and will soon be gone."

She blinked lazily, her eyes bright, her front paws before her in exactly the same posture as the sphinx.

As the sphinx.

Bagoas had come up beside me on foot. "Is it an omen?" he asked.

"Or a goddess incarnate," I said. She was truly a magnificent animal, the largest lioness I had ever seen, well fed and sleek, her hide almost glowing with good health.

Bagoas glanced about. "How did she get up there?" The walls of the wadi were very steep, and did not give footholds even for a lion.

"She must have come from another side," I said. I looked around, pushing myself up on my horse's back to look.

Her eyes never leaving me, the lioness got up, stretching purposefully. Slowly she ambled a few paces, then stopped and looked at me. Deliberately, she walked up a gentle incline behind her, and then walked along a track I could not see, passing behind fallen boulders. After a moment I saw her again. She halted, looking down at me from the track.

"There's a way up there," I said. "A way along the side of the cliff. I wonder where it comes out."

I followed the lioness back along the road, passing the hearse and the men who rode behind. Now and again she paused. The track she followed was almost invisible, dipping now and again behind outcroppings. For a while I thought I had lost it and her entirely. Half a mile or more I did not see her. The path she followed had gone behind rocks.

I came around a turn in the road, and there she was, sitting in the middle of the road behind where our procession had passed. Beside her a gentle slope led up and then curved around a red boulder.

The lioness blinked and lay down, her paws before her.

And suddenly I saw all I needed to.

"Thank you, Lady of the Desert," I said. "Thank you."

The lioness got up, and with a swift leap dashed away among the rocks on the opposite side.

I dismounted. Bagoas had followed me on foot, saying nothing, and now he watched the lioness leave without flinching. Lions will not generally attack an armed man on horseback, but an unarmed man on foot is another thing. My estimation of his courage went up, though I should have expected it. Alexander would not suffer cowards.

My horse sweated and rolled her eyes nervously at the scent of lions, but she obeyed. "Come on, Bagoas," I said, and led my horse toward the gentle slope that led to the track.

"What are you doing?" he asked.

"Seeing where it comes out and if you can lead a horse along it." I led my mare uphill and around the boulder.

It was possible. I should not want to try it in darkness, or at anything other than a careful walk, but it was certainly possible to lead a horse along it. We passed the spot where I had first seen her, then passed the hearse itself.

Glaukos called up to me. The track was more exposed at that end. At the northern end you could not see it from the road.

"I'm trying something," I called back. "Go on. I'll catch up."

Around the next bend the track descended to the road again, coming out just ahead of the cortege.

Perhaps in some earlier day this had been the original path, before the broad road was built by a long-dead pharaoh so that merchants and soldiers could travel more easily. It was disused, but still passable.

I waited while the column came up. Glaukos approached me. "What's that about?"

"We're going to ambush them," I said. "Send twenty men and the hearse on ahead. Tell them to ride through the night and put as much distance between them and us as possible. Everyone else stays here."

"Ambush? With horses? In this?" Glaukos gestured up at the steep sides of the wadi.

Bagoas smiled, and I thought he understood.

"There's a track that goes back that way," I said. "About three miles. That end of it can't be seen from the road. You're going to take two hundred men that way, in single file, leading their horses. You'll see where it descends again. Don't go quite that far. Keep them up the trail, where it's out of sight. Keep them quiet. When Perdiccas' men come through here they'll be going fast. They'll be able to tell from the freshness of the dung that they're nearly on us. They won't be stopping to scout. They'll go hell for leather trying to catch us by surprise. As soon as they go past you, come down and form up on the road."

Glaukos grinned. "Then come down on them from the rear like a wolf on the fold. Where will you be?"

"We're going to hold here," I said. "The wadi is narrow enough, and it looks like there are some thorn bushes we could cut and make a barricade with to break the charge."

"A barricade of thorn bushes isn't going to slow them down much," Glaukos said.

"It will if they're on fire," I said. "All this brush is dry. It will burn."

"And then they'll be caught between you and our charge," he said.

I nodded. "That's the shape of it. Now get to it! They're not more than half a day behind us!"


THEY CAME DOWN upon us an hour short of nightfall. We were ready.

Our first warning was the sudden starting of birds, a hawk spiraling suddenly into the air crying indignantly. And then there was the thunder of hooves and they came round the bend.

"Now!" I shouted, flinging my torch into the brush, ten other men following suit. The dry tinder caught with a roar.

Before their cavalry's headlong dash a wall of fire sprang up, flames licking up blown by the hot wind that rose at exactly the right moment, sending flames flying like banners toward them.

I stepped my horse back. Even she shied at the flames.

It broke the charge utterly. No horse will run straight into fire. The front riders pulled up, fouling those behind them, men swearing and shouting. One horse, less nimble than the others, ran straight up on another and they both fell, thrashing about with loud, frightened cries, their riders pinned beneath them.

The second cohort ran almost on top of them. They pulled up, horses rearing and pitching. It was sheer chaos.

Meanwhile, on the other side of the barrier our men waited in good order. Our horses did not like the fire either, but they were not being asked to do anything about it, and had seen it kindled as they had seen our campfires lit each night. We waited. I wished I had Artashir and a troop of Persian archers. They would be perfect targets.

Their officers were shouting, trying to get them untangled. The last cohorts had stopped short and now milled about, attempting to stay out of the way in the narrow wadi. They were not in good order either, and with their attention on the struggle in front of them they were not watching behind. They would not hear Glaukos over the shouting until he was practically on top of them.

Already the flames were dying back, the tinder-dry brush consumed quickly. In a few minutes there would not be enough left to hinder them. It would not be long before someone tried it.

I marked Polemon, whom I knew, astride a black horse, surveying the flames and measuring the dying fires, his horse lifting his head so that the bells on his bridle shook. A big horse, I thought. A black Nisean, with strong legs and a stout heart. He could make the jump now, but they would not all follow. It would not be long.

"Form up!" I heard Polemon yell. "Form up!"

"Wait," I said to the senior cavalryman beside me. "Wait. Let them come for us."

How long would it take for them to form up? It seemed moments, and an eternity at the same time. But surely it hadn't been long since we lit the brush. The flames had not died entirely.

"Form up! Are you Companions or what?" I heard Polemon shouting, trying to get people back into line. One of the fallen horses seemed to have broken a leg and was thrashing about right in the middle of where they would need to be. It would divide their charge in half, splitting to go around him. "Form up!"

"Sir," the trooper beside me began.

"Wait," I said, raising a hand. "Wait for my signal."

And then I heard the sound of hooves, and a great shout as Glaukos and his men thundered down the wadi behind them, swords drawn and in full charge.

They broke into the back of Polemon's men like boulders falling down a mountain, the screams of injured horses competing with the cries of men.

Orders or not, every man looked around.

"Forward!" I shouted, and touched my heels to her sides as we started forward across the smoldering ashes.

After that it was hard to tell what was happening more than a length from my own horse, cut and thrust and guard, the nimble mare dancing over the fallen. Blood was in my eyes, in my hair, and I could see nothing except the plunging horses around me, a trooper of my own to my right on a big bay horse.

"Forward!" It was hard to tell who was whom. We all wore the same armor, friends and foes alike, all had familiar faces. We had been friends, not two years ago. We had all fought for Alexander.

Polemon appeared out of the chaos, his helmet askew on his head. I saw him mark me and was not surprised.

He came straight for me, but at the last moment the movement of the battle shifted, so that we should pass wrong-sided, left to left rather than right to right. I tried to switch over, but his horse was bigger than mine, and in a moment our horses were shoulder to shoulder. He lifted his sword, but it was an awkward thrust, fully across his body.

I could not parry all the way across in time. I saw it rise, and the seconds elongated.

It was nothing but animal reaction to throw my left arm up to guard my head. So close were we, and so awkward the thrust, that I caught the guard just above his hand, the full weight of the descent with the horse's weight behind it caught on my left hand, the wrist bent entirely back. I heard the bones break, snapping like dry twigs.

And then we were past him, the pass incomplete, my horse taking her head from the suddenly slack reins.

"Retreat! Retreat!" Someone was shouting. "Retreat and form up!" I thought it was Polemon. All about us in the wadi men were down. Perhaps he thought more of them were his.

My arm was on fire, my hand completely useless. I gathered the reins in my sword hand, holding both together.

"Don't pursue!" I shouted. "Men of Ptolemy's Ile, do not pursue!"

"Form up!"

Everyone was shouting to form up.

I wheeled the horse about one-handed. We needed to back off, give it some room and see what we had compared to them. There was no dishonor in yielding the field. One bit of this wadi was like another.

"Ptolemy's Ile, back up!" I shouted. I guided my mare back over the embers with my legs, my left hand entirely unresponsive. I could not move my thumb at all.

"Back up, you fornicating slobs!" That was Glaukos, shouting at the first ranks, getting them back.

"Pick up the wounded," I directed. "Anyone you can carry."

"Form up!"

We backed down the wadi slowly, our eyes on them. They were also backing off a little.

I could not tell who precisely we had lost, but it looked as though many more of them were on the ground than of us.

They did not pursue. I did not think they would, not with night falling, a bitter mauling, and no idea what further backup we might have. They would not pursue until morning.

I looked about for Glaukos. "Put an hour's ride between us. We need some breathing room."

He glanced down at the reins in my sword hand, and a furrow came between his eyes. "You hurt?"

"I broke my fucking wrist," I said. "But I can ride." Truly, it did not feel so bad at the moment, merely useless. But battle makes it so. I have seen men continue on mortally wounded, seeming not to feel the wounds that have already killed them.

Night was coming swiftly down as we stopped at last, an hour along the track. I sent scouts back immediately, but there was no pursuit.

"Numbers," I said. "I want numbers from every column leader. What have we got?" By now it was starting to throb, and when I glanced at my wrist it looked misshapen, bones in entirely the wrong places beneath the skin. I could only move the last two fingers at all. The thumb and the first two did not respond.

Troop by troop we formed up. The numbers were not as bad as they might have been. Sixty-seven wounded, including myself, forty-one of whom needed camp and medical attention immediately. Twenty-six men missing, presumably dead on the field. Polemon and Attalos would burn them honorably with their own dead, I thought. We were not so far gone from the time we had been brothers.

Glaukos frowned. "Roughly one man in eight wounded or killed," he said.

I tilted my head to the side. "Tolerable for facing fifty percent above our own numbers."

"We can try to hold on here," he said.

I shook my head. "We don't need to hold ground. We need to keep them away from the hearse. It's all about delay, my friend. The hearse needs to get to Pelousion." I looked up at the stars coming out brightly. It seemed years since last night. "Three more days down to Pelousion, at the hearse's pace. But they're not supposed to stop tonight. They're supposed to drive the oxen on with only a short rest." I looked about. "Get me the two gamest men you've got. They need to go ahead at their best pace, catch up to the hearse and pass it, and go on to Pelousion. They'll carry orders for the infantry phalanx there to march this way to meet the hearse. That should get the hearse coverage in…" I closed my eyes for a moment, calculating. A full day and a bit more for the riders to reach Pelousion, their horses tired as they were. Given that the phalanx marched in a few hours, they should meet the hearse in two days, a critical day before the hearse could reach Pelousion. So we needed a day's delay.

Had we already bought it? It might be. It looked as though Perdiccas' forces had made camp for the night. We needed to ride on and get a night's march on them. We would have to leave the wounded who could not travel behind with an escort. I thought it would be safer for them than dragging on through the night. Polemon would behave with that much honor, and besides they knew nothing he did not, save that Ptolemy had an infantry phalanx at Pelousion, which he should have guessed.

No, I thought. The question Polemon will be asking is where is the phalanx? He does not have the men to take it on, not all cavalry on a solid phalanx, not in this terrain. Of course, twelve miles from Pelousion the road comes out of the wadis and into the river delta, with plowed fields watered by canals and drainage ditches. It is that last twelve miles that will be the hardest.

"We push on," I said. "The badly wounded will stay behind, and the fourth cohort will stay with them to tend them. Otherwise we ride through the night."

WE CAME UP to the hearse at dawn. By then my arm hurt, stabbing pains running all the way up and into my shoulder and chest, hurting with every breath, with every step of my horse. They had stopped for three hours, letting the oxen breathe a little.

"Make camp," I said to Glaukos through gritted teeth. "Walk the horses down and put out scouts. We rest till noon."

Glaukos looked at me, and I wondered if I looked as tired as he. "Are you all right?"

"No," I said, low. "But I have to be. Just let me rest a couple of hours. I'll be ready to go again."

I WOKE BEFORE noon, conscious that someone was sitting beside me. My arm was on fire, and I shivered, though it was bright sun.

"Water?" Bagoas said, and handed me a cup.

I drank it down with my right hand. "Thanks."

He nodded. "There is bread too."

"Later," I said, feeling that I could hardly stomach anything just now.

"You will be lightheaded," he observed.

I opened my mouth to insist I wouldn't be, but thought better of it. I probably would be. Instead I took it.

He nodded and got to his feet with one graceful motion. Glaukos was coming over. Behind him I saw the stir of breaking camp, the mounting up beginning.

"Ready, sir?"

"Ready," I said. I looked about for Bagoas to thank him for the bread, but he was already swinging up on the stoop of the hearse, nimble as a gymnast.

Glaukos had to help me mount, and I ate the bread as we rode. We stuck close to the hearse, urging the oxen to a better pace, our eyes on the road behind.

An hour short of nightfall our scouts to the rear came up, reporting that they had seen Polemon and Attalos' scouts, two men following us who had wheeled about and cantered back the way they came when they rode after them.

I blew out a breath. Less than a day behind, perhaps only half a day. Perhaps only a few hours.

"We ride through the night," I said. "Anyone who can't keep up, fall out and come along as you may."

By midnight, when the stars were high, I wondered if it would be me. I rode in a waking dream, the pain in my arm throbbing like distant drums. But my horse followed after the others, and as long as I could stay on her I should ride. She, at least, was sound.

Spirits came beside us. I saw a lean black dog loping along beside the hearse like a shadow, its golden eyes bright as stars. Above, against the distant stars a white ibis flew by night, its wings ghostly under the moon. A lioness paced us, her padded feet silent on the stones, ever watchful, looking behind.

I saw them by moonlight, and the lioness nodded to me gravely, Her green eyes bright as Bagoas'.

The gilded hearse glittered palely under the Huntsman rising, Sothis lifting clear of the hills in the sky before dawn. On the roof of the hearse was a hawk, its wings folded and head down, Horus bound to Alexander's body as the gods of Egypt escorted him home.

"Ride," I whispered. "Help me ride, Lady of the Desert."

The lioness paced beside my horse, Her head at my knee. "I will help you, Son of Egypt. I will walk with you. I will be there when you kindle fire."

"Fire," I whispered. I was made of fire, and the night was made of whispers.

"The powers of the Black Land rest in your hands," She said. "Powers of earth and air, powers of water and fire. You guard Horus Undescended, and yours is the strength to wield it."

"I do not know how," I said.

The lioness looked at me, and I wondered if a cat could smile. "You do," She said. "You will remember when you need it."

THE SKY PALED. Morning was coming. From the high cliffs a hawk lifted calling, spreading his wings in the clear bright air.

"They are behind us," I said. I could feel them, as though the ground beneath their hooves was my own body. "They will be here soon."

I pulled myself up on my horse. "Glaukos! Send the hearse ahead at all possible speed. We will go to that incline and wait. Get in line to receive cavalry!"

Glaukos looked startled, as we had not had scouts come in.

"Hurry!" I shouted.

Now I saw the incline better. The wadis opened out. Beyond, there was a smooth descent and the green of plowed fields not far away, the lazy line of the Damietta branch of the Nile meandering through. The road turned north again to meet it, toward the pale half-shell line of the sea in the growing dawn. Where road and river and sea met was a dark lowering shape — the walls of Pelousion, now less than twenty miles distant.

I heard the drivers pushing the exhausted oxen, exhorting them with whips. We formed up. Glaukos took the commander's position, and I stood behind. I could not fight with my useless hand at all. My fingers would not even close about the reins. We stood, and behind us the hearse rattled downhill.

And then I saw them, halfway across the plain, a dark streak on the road, like a snake against the green land, Ptolemy's phalanx in column, marching toward us at double time. But they were still five miles distant at least.

The blood thundered in my ears. I stood above all on the breast of the wind, soaring like the hawk over the land. I could see them coming down the wadi at a quick trot, Perdiccas' cavalry still some eight hundred strong.

"Stand to receive!" I shouted, feeling myself jolt back into my damaged body.

Glaukos looked back at me worriedly, as we had so far seen nothing to receive.

I looked straight back at him. I could feel them riding down the wadi, preparing to go into the wedge the moment they were clear of the confining walls.

"Stand to receive!" Every man did so, six hundred or a bit more.

The game was up, I thought. Even if they overwhelmed us, the infantry would catch them in a day once they were burdened with the hearse, and they'd never stand against a thousand heavy infantry.

Whether I lived or died, I had already won.

"Ready to charge!" I shouted. We would not receive. We'd charge them in column before they were clear.

Horses stomped, each man falling into position, Glaukos on the point.

The sun rose from behind the wadis before us, glittering on my sword point and on the distant sea.

Fire, and the memory of fire.

It seemed I could shape it, craft it like a lance. The first rays of the sun blazed off the Victory that adorned the hearse, rattling down the hill behind us.

"For Ptolemy and Egypt!" I shouted.

At that moment the first cavalry came clear of the wadi and checked. They had expected to come down on our rear as we hurried away, not to meet a charge.

We stood like an arrow to the bow. The air trembled around me, waiting for the word forward.

I raised my sword and fire ran down the blade. To kindle fire, She said. To throw it like fear, like a lance into their hearts. The power of Egypt ran through me, blue and gold, licking along the edges of the blade, as though I were nothing but a channel for the mighty flood.

My horse stamped. If I swept the sword forward, I would loose the arrow. The wave would break. We would charge as one man.

The fire ran through me, light and clear and painless as water. *Ptolemy and Egypt.*

And they checked. They stopped at the mouth of the wadi.

Before them we waited on the road, six hundred strong, ready to charge on their first cohorts. Beyond, the hearse labored. And beyond that, coming closer every minute, the infantry at their best pace, sun glancing off the bright points of their sarissas.

I saw Polemon. And I saw what he saw. He had already lost.

His eyes met mine, and he nodded gravely, one Companion to another. And then he wheeled his horse around and kicked it, cantering back into the wadi. His men followed.

"Stand to receive!" I heard Glaukos shout, changing our formation in case they changed their mind.

It was the last thing I heard before I slipped from my horse insensible.

# HOT EMBERS

I woke inside the walls of Pelousion, in the great Persian bedchamber I had occupied before. I felt strangely disoriented, as though I could not quite order my thoughts, and my mouth was dry. I tried to speak.

"Here," a voice said, and a pair of hands lifted cool water to my lips, supported my head so I could drink. "Just take a little. You are still feeling the opium, I expect."

The water splashed on my lips, and I got some in my mouth. I swallowed. "Opium?"

"For the pain so that the doctor could set your hand." The voice belonged to Bagoas, who bent over me, his chiton clean and his hands washed, not dusty from the road. We must have been in Pelousion for some time. "He said there were ten bones broken in your hand and wrist and left unset for days so that the swelling made it hard to attend to. He gave you opium to ease the pain while he worked."

"Ten bones," I whispered. Ten little tiny bones that all must work together.

"He's bound it tightly and will check in a few hours to make sure none of the bindings have shifted. You must keep it still for a long time."

I looked down at my arm where it lay against the covers, the wrappings making it twice its normal size. A stick ran from the back of my hand up my arm nearly to the elbow, making sure I could not bend my wrist, while other wrappings bound my thumb and first two fingers to smaller sticks, only the ends of the last two emerging.

I could not feel any pain. But then I could not really feel my feet either, and there was nothing wrong with them.

"The opium probably makes you sleepy," Bagoas said. "You can sleep. Ptolemy is here and the hearse is within the walls of Pelousion. You have fulfilled your duty. You do not need to worry anymore."

"Ptolemy is here?"

"Yes," he said, and laid a damp cloth to my brow, easing me back on the pillow. "Ptolemy has already been to see you, but you were still resting. He will be back in the morning, I expect."

"Night?"

Bagoas nodded, his long dark hair swaying where it was held back by a clasp. "It's late the same night we came out of the desert. It is all one day. Ptolemy and his men came up after you fell, and we brought the hearse into the fortress. The doctor set your hand, and you have been sleeping since nightfall."

"So tired…" I whispered. All those sleepless days on the road, night blurring into day in a blaze of fire.

"Rest then," he said. "I will stay with you."

"Why?"

Bagoas settled down on the side of the bed, his back against the carved headboard, sitting beside me. "I owe you a good turn, don't I?"

"I suppose," I said, and closed my eyes to the waiting dark.

Well, I thought as sleep claimed me, that is another thing that was Alexander's that I have had. I have slept beside the eunuch Bagoas.

WEDDINGS ALWAYS BRING out the worst in people, and of all weddings that was most true of Alexander's wedding to Roxane. If he had married a princess, it would not have been the same. Indeed, when later he married Stateira the daughter of Darius who had been Great King of Persia, only the most diehard traditionalists scoffed, but Roxane was not a princess. She was the daughter of a hill chief in

Sogdiana, a beauty sixteen years old who any other warlord would simply have taken as a prize and who might have held his favor for a few years if she were lucky.

But Alexander could never do anything in the normal way. He saw her, he wanted her, and by all the gods of Olympus, he meant to marry her. He was the King, and no one could stop him no matter how unseemly or inappropriate she might be.

Of course she was beautiful. That went without saying. She had long, curling dark hair, black as a raven's wing, as dark as he was fair, and pale skin like milk with a touch of honey. Her eyes were hazel shading to green. She was tiny and fine-boned, a head shorter than Alexander, who was not tall. Perhaps he was moved by her beauty. He would not be the first man to lose himself thus.

And so they were married in a feast fit for a bandit chief, on the cliffs of Sogdiana in a mountain stronghold lately taken, with slaughtered cattle for the wedding feast roasted plain over the fire.

For my part, it was a feast like any other, except that the wine was rawer and more potent. If there were no sweets for the feast, at least there was plenty of wine. There were bridal torches and braziers of incense to give scent and light to the feast, the sweet smell of the meat mingling with myrrh of Nabatea carried at vast expense to give honor to the gods. Inside the hall, the air was thick before the proceedings were half ended, before the procession sang the King to bed with bawdy dances and shouts in Macedonian of what he should do when he finally got her dress off her, stiff with embroidery and covering her from fingertips to ankles.

Roxane did not blush. I suspect it was because she didn't understand a word of it. Her head was high and proud, her cheeks clear as alabaster. It was Alexander who blushed and called back, trying to answer jest for jest.

I admit that I was already a little drunk.

Four years had passed since Gaugamela, when I became a soldier and a man. In those four years we had conquered Persia. From the mountains of Macedon to the cataracts of the Nile to the steppes that bordered the Caspian Sea all that had ever been claimed by the Great Kings was ours, the largest empire the world had ever known.

I was twenty-two, and the boy Jio had long since been left behind. Lydias of Miletus was born a cavalryman, a Companion of Hephaistion's Ile, veteran of ten fields. I served at the command of a man I respected above all, Hephaistion son of Amyntor, the boldest and most loyal of all Alexander's men.

Which is not to say that he was all bluster. I watched, and saw how he brought the Persian lords who had not supported Bessos over to us, how careful of their honor and pride he was. I watched while he chose a just man to rule over Sidon at Alexander's order, picking a man only distantly related to their past kings but who had the reputation of being a laborer both honest and clever. If I knew anything of governing, it was learned from Hephaistion. There was greater gain in not setting a conquered people on edge when it was not needful, in not driving men to the verge of rebellion in our rear. There was greater wisdom in adopting the customs of those governed to some extent, for useful things may be discovered by all peoples.

Of course most people did not agree, not even most of the Companions. Krateros and Parmenio and many others kept to the old Macedonian ways, and thought it shameful to wear trousers like a Persian, or eat duck roasted in pomegranate sauce rather than plain over the fire as their mothers had made. They did not mind the spoils of Persia, women and treasure and good things, but that was all it was—treasure to bring home that would make them men of consequence in Macedon.

Half Carian and half Greek as I was, raised in Miletus under Persian rule, I had been given always to understand that Greek was best, and that the rest of the world but a pale and imperfect imitation of the way things were done in Attica. I myself, half Greek, should never be as good as if I were whole, myself a pale copy of the man I might have been if I had not been so flawed.

Now, I wondered. Carian was not such a terrible thing to be. There had been cities in Caria for a thousand years, and Miletus was older than Athens. Millawanda it had been, a Hittite city with massive walls, before Athens was founded. And Egypt was older still, ancient as the dawn of time, and Babylon with her mighty walls was only the latest of the citadels of the peoples who had ruled that land. It was a fine thing to be Greek, but as I saw more of the world I thought that it was not the only fine thing to be. Truly the world had many marvels in it, and Persia had its share.

Besides, if Hephaistion son of Amyntor thought it no disgrace to dress like a Persian noble, how should I? If he clasped Oxathres to him in friendship, what dishonor did I court by acknowledging that my mother was Carian? If I, nothing but a half-breed castoff, sold as a slave without a backward glance, could be given a man's place and a man's honor as Companion, then why should not any man aspire to such? Indeed, my heart whispered in the night, what heights might I myself aspire to?

All this was because of General Hephaistion, lover of the King.

In my worship of my hero I thought him very old, but at that time he was only twenty-nine, if past the full beauty of his youth. He had recently let his red hair grow in the manner of the Persian nobles rather than the Greeks, and he was clean-shaven, with frank brown eyes and a rather high forehead. In his boyhood he might have been classically pretty, but even without the fresh young looks the Greeks prefer he was a handsome man. It seemed that the King thought so too, for he never had another lover.

Of course there was the eunuch Bagoas who was a royal favorite, but that was not the same thing at all. First of all, a slave is not a lover, and secondly a eunuch can hardly be reckoned a man. The Greeks do not understand this at all, but raised in Miletus as I was, I did. Eunuchs are a third sex, neither man nor woman, but more like to women than men in that they do not bear arms and concern themselves primarily with domestic labor. For Alexander to have a favorite from the harem that had belonged to Darius was nothing to Hephaistion, and not even to be mentioned in the same breath with him, a lover who commanded armies, a companion who stood forever at Alexander's right hand, Patroclos to his Achilles.

However, royal favorites had attained power before, counselors and governors for kings who spent more time in hunting and feasting than in the less amusing aspects of being king. Bagoas was not to be entirely discounted.

I was surprised, then, to see him at the wedding feast. I remember that I wondered at the time if Alexander had honored him to soften the blow of the wedding, and thought it odd that Alexander should have him at the tables like a man and a Companion. Perhaps I would have spoken to him, but by the time the crowd had begun to sing and dance outside the bedroom doors I had lost sight of him and did not see him again.

Indeed by that part of the evening most of the guests were as drunk as I. Only Ptolemy seemed marginally sober among the men of rank, and he was flushed and loud. My head spinning from the wine and the incense, I pushed my way outside away from the music and the shouted songs. The cool air would clear my head.

Outside, the night was welcoming. A cold moon was rising away over the mountain peaks, and Orion the Hunter struggled up the sky with his belt of stars. Below, the valley fell away in crags and defiles to the thin band of the river reflecting the skies like a fillet of silver. I walked some way, away from the shouts and torches. My head was pounding, and I vaguely hoped I wouldn't be sick. Perhaps if I sat down somewhere quiet...

Hephaistion was sitting on a stone that jutted out from the parapet wall, a cup in his hand while the light glittered off his white chiton, his feet dangling over a drop of a hundred feet. The slow, careful way he lifted the wine to his mouth told me he was very drunk indeed.

Maybe, I thought, it was a bad idea to drink on the edge of a hundred-foot drop.

Carefully, I climbed out to where he was. Hephaistion looked at me unsurprised, as though we met thus every day. "Oh, hello, Lydias."

I sat down beside him, not looking over the edge. I certainly didn't want to fall over. "This isn't a very good place for a drink," I said.

"It's a fine place for a drink," Hephaistion said, and lifted the cup again. "Quiet." He waved a hand about loosely. "Not all that singing. Do you sing, Lydias?"

"Not very well," I said truthfully.

"That's a shame," Hephaistion said. His hair had escaped from the clasp that held it, and fell across his shoulders glittering like old copper in the moonlight. "Singing is a good thing."

He was very, very drunk. "Don't you think it might be a good idea to come back on the parapet?" I asked.

"Why?"

I toyed with saying, because you might fall, but thought that might be taken as a challenge. "Because that's where there's more to drink," I said.

Hephaistion threw his arm over my shoulder. "That's an excellent idea," he said. "You're always on top of supply, Lydias."

"Thank you," I said, trying not to get pushed over. "Come on then. Let's crawl back."

We crawled along the stone until we reached the parapet, then climbed over. I lay on the ground against the wall, staring up at the stars. I don't particularly like heights, and it came to me abruptly that climbing out there had been spectacularly insane.

Hephaistion sat on the wall. "Where's the drink?" he asked.

"Around here somewhere," I lied. I hadn't actually brought any out with me.

He hunted around for a bit, then sat down next to me with his back to the wall. "Can't find it," he said.

"Oh."

"Must be drunk."

"We're all drunk," I said. "I've never seen you drunk before, but then I suppose you've never seen me drunk either."

He considered, his head to the side. "Don't suppose I have. I don't drink that much, usually." I waited and he looked up, his face to the stars. "Fifteen years, Lydias. Since we were fourteen years old. Never once have I been untrue."

I opened my mouth and shut it again, not knowing what to say.

"I've always known he'd marry. He's the King. He has to. It's a king's duty. And the gods bear me witness that I have never wanted his duties to be any heavier than they had to be! But…" He did not take his eyes from the skies, the moonlight illuminating his features like marble.

I did not know what to say, so I said nothing.

He shoved his hair back out of his face. "You ever been in love, Lydias?"

I swallowed. "Yes."

"Did it hurt?"

"Yes," I said. I looked at him, the unforgiving moonlight showing every line on his face, the stubble on his jaw, the creases in his forehead that no doubt in time would be wrinkles. "But there is no point in being jealous of things we were not meant to have. Better to behave with honor and be worthy of the trust we are given."

Hephaistion looked at me then. "You're a good man, Lydias."

"I try to be," I said honestly.

"Most don't," he said, his eyes on my face still as though he sought to read something there despite our wandering wits. "Most men just do as they please and don't worry about being worthy of a hero."

"Most men are less certain that they stand among gods," I said.

Hephaistion frowned, as though he had suddenly seen something in my face he had not expected, heard some echo that puzzled him. "Alexander?"

"Is not the only one worthy of worship," I said. I did not know if I would dare, but I was rather suspecting that I would. Fortune favors the bold.

"Who, then?" he asked, a genuine look of confusion on his face.

"Cannot you guess?" I asked, and kissed him.

For a moment he stiffened, confused, and then melted into my arms.

This was not the fumbling of uncertain boys who do not know how to get what they want. He knew what he wanted and exactly how to get it.

I was flying, I was drowning, and when he took me with my hands before me, bent over the parapet, staring down into the moonlit drop, it hurt like a hundred victories.

His hands were around my waist beneath my chiton, working on me, and I could have screamed out his name in my release before his. And yet it was a tenth, a hundredth, of all I could have wanted. I could have wanted this a thousand times.

Instead, shaking, I unbent from the wall and slid down it to sit beside him. He was shaking too, and it took me a moment to realize that he was crying.

I put my hand on his arm, and he took my hand, squeezing it until the bones ground. "Do not be sad," I whispered. "Please don't be sad!"

Hephaistion closed his eyes then, putting his head against my shoulder though I still rang like a bell from his slightest touch. "I'm sorry," he said. "I should not have done that, still less to one I would call a friend. Did I hurt you?"

"Not very much," I said.

He shook his head and sat up, his shoulder against mine. "I am sorry," he said. "Lydias, I ask your pardon. I am very drunk, and I…"

I looked away from him, my hair falling over my face so that he would not see the tears in my eyes. It was not that I regretted it, not in the least. "We were both very drunk," I said.

He took a breath, and I leaned back against his arm, feeling his heart racing still. Above, the moon leaned down, cool and implacable.

"Your hair smells like incense," he said quietly, and laid his cheek against my hair.

"I expect it does," I said. "From the feast."

"Yes." For a long moment there was quiet. I did not want it to end, but simply to rest on him this way, leaning together. I did not want it to ever end.

He took another breath. "I have behaved badly," Hephaistion said. "It's just that you are beautiful, and I thought that you were offering…"

"I was," I said, "and you must think nothing of it. What is a moment of release between friends? These things happen."

So I spoke lightly, not saying what was in my heart, not begging that he should love me, not saying that I had loved him since the day I first saw him, not begging that he should say that I was the one he had waited for all his life. Of course I was not. I had known that always, and I did have my pride.

And yet he said that I was beautiful. Perhaps he believed it.

"So they do," he said, straightening up, his arm dropping from my shoulders. "Only they do not usually happen to me. Alexander..."

I did not know how he would finish the thought. His lover would be jealous? His king would be angry?

"It is nothing," I assured him. "We will not speak of it again."

Hephaistion took a deep breath and pushed the hair back from his face. "Truly?"

"Truly," I said. "It was only the wine."

"Of course," he said, and gave me half a smile. "You are a good friend, Lydias."

"There is nothing to regret," I said and met his eyes. "Think of it no more. We will not mention it again."

And we did not, not once from then until the day he died.

Sometimes, once in a while in the years that followed, I would turn and catch his eyes on me or see an expression cross his face that should not have been there. But we never spoke of it. He was Alexander's.

Still I did not regret it. I never have.

# SACRED FIRE

Ptolemy came to see me in the morning. I was sitting up, thanks to Bagoas' help, eating barley gruel with honey. The opium had worn off somewhat, and my left arm and hand hurt a lot, but my head was clearer and I was hungry.

Ptolemy sat down on the side of the bed. "Don't try to get up," he said, waving away my attempt to rise. "No need. I'm glad to see you looking better."

"The hearse?" I asked.

"Is safe," he said. "I've heard from Glaukos and Bagoas here how you brought it in. I don't have words to commend you highly enough. That was masterful."

I opened my mouth and shut it again. He did not avoid my eyes and was entirely sincere. "Thank you, sir," I gulped. "What about my wounded men?"

"They arrived last night," Ptolemy said. "I sent the infantry to go get them with carts, and they met them halfway. Five men have died from their wounds, and will be burned tonight in all honor. I expect you will want to be there."

"Of course," I said.

"But it does not look like we are going to lose you, which is something," Ptolemy said, scratching his head. "Though the doctor tells me you will not be fighting for half a year."

I took a breath. "So long?"

"That long to heal entirely. He said the splints should stay on two months, and then you will have to regain the use of it. You won't be able to fight until you can manage a horse left-handed again."

I blew the breath out. I knew that, of course. With one good hand I could either ride or use a sword, but not both.

"So it is as well," Ptolemy said, "that Perdiccas cannot come tomorrow. He will require months to assemble an overwhelming army." He nodded as I looked up. "Perdiccas cannot afford to lose the King's body, not if he intends to lay claim to all of the Persian Empire. He will come in person, in force, with all the might of Asia at his disposal."

I opened my mouth and then shut it again, putting the bowl of gruel down among the bedclothes. "You knew this would happen if I were successful."

"That it would be a challenge to him? Yes." Ptolemy's brown eyes were grave. "How not? But what other decision is there? If it is between Perdiccas and Antipatros, the Regent in Macedon, I have no choice. Perdiccas is allied with Olympias."

"Because of that old rumor that you might be Phillip's son? Olympias would still put stock in that?" I could scarcely believe that would be true, but it might be that Olympias truly believed that Ptolemy was Alexander's half brother who sought to claim his empire.

Ptolemy looked for an instant as though he intended to say something, and I felt Bagoas stiffen at my back. Then he spread his hands. "Who knows what Olympias thinks? But I have known Antipatros from boyhood on, and an alliance with him is much more palatable than anything else. He has agreed to send me his daughter, Eurydice, as my wife. And thanks to you we have Alexander. If we can defeat Perdiccas in the field, I think he will come to terms rather than press it."

"And those terms would be?"

"That Persia stays out of Egypt."

I wondered if he remembered what Isis had offered him, or if that had really happened. Perhaps I would have asked him if we had seen the same things, if those things were real, had Bagoas not been in the room. Perhaps he would have done the same.

A glance passed between us. I thought he did remember.

"And leaves you as satrap," I said.

"Until Alexander's son comes of age," Ptolemy said.

"If he does," I said.

Ptolemy nodded. Whether or not he had shared that vision in the desert, the essentials were the same. He would not usurp what was Alexander's son's, but he would guard Egypt as the gods of Egypt themselves wanted. And would he free the King, who even now was still bound to his body by the sacred rites of Egyptian kingship? "And what of the King?"

Ptolemy stretched. "There's a barge being built here. When it's completed we'll take the hearse aboard and take him south to Memphis by river. That will be much easier than overland."

"Safer too," I said with a sigh of relief. I knew nothing of boats. The barge would not be my problem, and I had had quite enough of dragging the hearse.

"Indeed. You've seen the state of the fortifications in Alexandria. If we took him there it would be an easy matter for warships to enter the harbor and take him back by sea." Ptolemy shook his head. "The King cannot come to Alexandria until the city walls are complete and we have some kind of fortification on the breakwater."

Bagoas stirred, and Ptolemy looked at him. "I am assuming you will want to escort the King to Memphis and stay with him until his place in Alexandria is ready."

"Yes," Bagoas said gravely.

"And you will come to Memphis as well," Ptolemy said to me. "By the time the barge is ready you'll be able to travel."

"Of course," I said.

I might as well go to Memphis. I would not be able to command my Ile in Pelousion for months yet, and it would be better to have something to occupy my mind rather than standing about the fortress watching other men do what I could not.

———

Thus I came to Memphis once again, this time on a regal barge painted in gold and scarlet. The hearse sat amidships, its gilded Victories shining in the sun, while the massive barge was rowed upriver.

We did not go fast, hardly even at a walking pace, and people from every city and town came out to watch it pass, waving palm fronds and singing. I did not know, yet, that it was how they used to salute their own dead pharaohs before the Persians came, that it was how they saluted Osiris himself at his own festival.

At Memphis the hearse disembarked, and there was a delay of a day as it was determined that the hearse was wider than the city gates. With the gates themselves taken off their hinges it could just squeeze through the opening. I helped with that, familiar as I was with the way the hearse moved, standing beside it and shouting to the drivers as it passed through, less than a hand's width on each side, trying not to scrape it on the stones. Very, very slowly we got it in. At last the stoop slid through, and the men who were detailed to return the massive bronze-clad gates to their hinges ran out, ready with pulleys to lift them back into place.

Slowly, down the widest avenue in the city where we had paraded as liberators all those years ago, the hearse made its way to the Temple of the Apis bull, which was both holy and had wide doors and a fairly open sanctuary within, without too many intermediate columns. If, like most Greek temples, the façade had been supported by columns, we should never be able to get the sarcophagus between them without bringing the roof down. Instead, it was more open and the columns more widely spaced, a grander scale in keeping with the god it is holy to.

The story of the Apis bull has been told by many travelers, but it is unique to Egypt, and therefore worth repeating. In Egypt it is believed that the gods often take some mortal form to walk the earth and to participate in the pleasures and pains of their creation. Sometimes those forms may be human forms, and they may join their mortal avatars as they will, but sometimes they are not human. And why should they be? Are animals less worthy of the gods' attention than the rest of their creation?

Thus the gods may sometimes take animal form, according to their nature. Ptah, who we thought was perhaps like Hermes, often takes the form of an ibis or some other bird, so that he can fly over great distances on his mighty wings and know all there is in the world. Bastet takes the form of one of her own sacred cats, because cats can go anywhere and may go into any house, hearing all that people say and comforting those in need, especially children and women in childbirth.

Osiris, the Lord of the Underworld, chooses the form of a black bull. Now and again there is a bull calf born somewhere in the Black Land who, by his sacred markings, is known to be the current avatar, Apis. When he is found there is great rejoicing, and he and the cow his mother are taken with all ceremony to Memphis, to the temple where he shall live out his life in ease and gladness, with all of every good thing there is on this earth. After all, when the people of the Black Land are visited by a god, should they not show him every honor and welcome him with the best things they have? He has fresh grass and grain, a choice pasture under the blue of heaven, and the best cows in all the Black Land to keep him company and eventually bear his calves. The calves of the Serapeum are the best of their breed, strong and fair and gentle, and much improvement has been made in the stock of the Black Land this way. His mother is with him, and they dwell in comfort all their lives.

When the Apis bull dies, he is mourned seventy days, just like the king, and his mummified body is laid to rest in the communal tomb beneath the Serapeum, accompanied by the wailing of flutes and the lamentations of women. After he has lain there seventy days, a hunt goes out from Memphis, seeking a perfect bull calf, black and sturdy, with the same white markings on his nose. Somewhere among his people Apis has been reborn.

When the Persians conquered Egypt they killed the Apis bull as a symbol of their overlordship. This was one of the things that earned them the hatred of the people.

Of course it was not the only temple in Memphis, nor even the greatest. Memphis was an ancient city, already two thousand years old, and there were temples upon temples twined together, with houses and buildings clinging to their outer walls where they might have stood for five hundred years. Some of the temples themselves were so old that one entered them by going down short flights of stairs because the street level was much higher than it had been when they were first built.

Ptolemy did not stay in Memphis but a few days after the ceremony. He went back to Pelousion, the better to be in contact by land and sea with all that happened. Perdiccas would respond, and the sooner we knew what he was doing the better.

Which left me at loose ends. Never, not since my boyhood before my mother died, had I been without duties. Now I had none, other than the general order from Ptolemy to "rest and get better." How did one do that? I wondered.

I had no duties and nothing to worry about. I had a room provided in the palace Cleomenes had used, and my meals together with the small garrison or with the governor's staff. I had my pay, and nothing I particularly needed to spend it on. There was nothing to concern myself with, other than fretting over my wrist and hand and wondering how they were healing beneath the bandages and splints.

It was an odd feeling, having nothing to do and no time by which it must be done. The first few days I woke at first light in a panic, certain that I had missed grooming the horses or leading one out when it was needed, or that I had missed assembly and my Ile must be standing waiting for me.

But of course they weren't. The day stretched before me entirely empty.

I took to wandering the city, buying breakfast for a copper coin in the marketplace, and eating it walking along the walls and seeing the view. I walked all around the city this way in a few days, making a circuit of the walls and looking at the river.

After that I hired a man to take me down the river a little way to the great pyramids, for they are rightly called one of the wonders of the world. Tall as mountains, they looked as though they were capped with electrum, but my guide assured me that it was only polished stone. He told me some story about how they had been built long ago by the god Horus to commemorate his victory over a giant scorpion, or perhaps it was a scorpion man who was king, or a king named Scorpion, but I did not think the story was worth very much. There would be better stories from better sources than men paid to make them up for credulous travelers.

I went then to the temples, or at least to such parts of them as the curious might penetrate, the outer courtyards and galleries, rather than the sanctuaries of the gods. Some of them were almost like small towns, with refectories and dormitories for the priests, gardens and bathing pools and everything they might require. For a small donation one could walk in the gardens, which I found peaceful.

The twentieth day after I came to Memphis I found myself in one of the courtyards of the Temple of Thoth. It was one of the smaller ones, with worn carvings on the walls that surrounded it, their colors faded and in need of repainting. How long did it take to fade like that in the stark sun of the Black Land? A hundred years? Two hundred? And surely the carvings were older still. A rectangular pool stood in the middle of the courtyard, surrounded by tall date palms and other things, while a weeping peach tree dipped its leaves almost in the water. There was a bench under it in the shade, and I sat there and closed my eyes.

I listened to the buzzing of the bees and wasps drawn to the almost ripe peaches, to the very faint lapping of the water against the sides of the pool. The sounds of the city seemed far away. I could hear the pulsing of my heart, smell the peaches and the water, feel the cool stone against my legs. This is what eternity feels like, I thought. For a moment the world stood still.

Beneath the beat of my heart, I could hear it, could feel it — the pulse of the Black Land, the ancient tide of energy and strength in this place, like the tugging of a current far out to sea.

This was what I had touched in those moments when I stood before the hearse on the road, when the power seemed to fill me and flow through me like a mighty river. Then, it had poured into me, dashing me in its path like a leaf in the stream. Now it seemed instead that I floated on the breast of it, safe as a child in the embrace of the sea.

How had I drawn on it, I wondered. I was no priest who had learned how, no prince with the blood right. How had I done it?

Tentatively, like a man floating on a pool may lazily move one hand to propel himself in the water, I reached out. It was not difficult. This was not command or mastery. It was simply moving in a familiar element, gentle as floating on a stream. I did not need to control the current, only follow it. The answers were so close, so easy.

"Lydias of Miletus?"

I opened my eyes.

Bagoas stood in the shade on the other side of the pool, the shadows of their leaves making dappled patterns of light across his hair.

"Hello, Bagoas," I said. It did not seem odd for him to be here, almost as though we had promised to meet.

"Why are you here?" he asked, his head to the side like a young hunting bird, his green eyes curious.

"I am on leave until my hand is well," I said, lifting my bandaged arm. "And I like these gardens. I came here to remember."

Bagoas smiled, and he came and sat in the shade by me, the width of two men between us, wary as the hunting bird I had named him. I did not move, only waited while the reflection of light from the surface of the pool played across his face. "I remember too," he said. "I will not forget my Lord while any breath of mine endures."

"That too," I said. And how could one not think of Alexander, when the world still echoed with his footsteps, like a ruin scoured by the wind?

Bagoas crossed his legs, and though the movement was swift it was not as limber as a boy. It came to me then that he was not nearly as young as he looked. He must be my age, or nearly so. He had been a handsome youth when he entered the King's service, but that was ten years ago. He glanced at me, and his voice was low. "What is it you remember?"

The light flickered on the surface of the pool, flashes of fire from water, the memory of fire. I could see the shapes stirring just beneath the surface, as easy to reach as opening a door to the distant past.

"I remember a boy who played the harp," I said, and could see him in my mind's eye, a pretty boy of fifteen or so with curling dark hair and eyes to drown in. "A boy who played the harp before the king, while the prince stood by, watching as if he had seen the other half of his soul. The gods meant him to be king, and so he was, even if it were over the bodies of his kindred, of his wife's father, of his beloved." I saw the hall around them, the courtiers in their old-fashioned robes struck silent by the beauty of the music, the tall prince and his sister watching with the same expressions on their faces while I stood, a leashed cheetah at my side, her soft fur against my leg.

The ripples on the surface of the water shifted, reflecting the sky of the Black Land, walls trim and neat with new paint and sharp carvings, a pair of benches beneath four trees. Here, in this place, only removed in time, only trembling just below the surface. So very close.

"And I remember this place, and a prince I loved and served when Troy was no more, when across the wide seas we sought a new home. I wanted to return here, to the Black Land, and I have." Like leaves falling silently on the wind, a piece fell into place. "I knew, when Hephaistion came to Miletus, that I must go. My prince had need of me again. It was Hephaistion I followed then, you see, though he wore a different face and a different name."

"Kalanos..." Bagoas began, and I started. I had almost forgotten he was there.

I tore my eyes from the water with difficulty. "Yes, Kalanos," I said. "The Indian sage who came back with us from the lands of Raja Puru. He said things like this. My wife said things like this. Perhaps I listened too closely. Or perhaps I lost my mind in Gedrosia."

Bagoas was silent, but I saw the thought on his face. Many men had. Many men had lost their minds for far less reason than I had. And my mind was not so valuable after all. Who did it harm, if I were god-touched?

I had not spoken of it before, and now it seemed I could not stop. "Do you know what I dreamed in Gedrosia, Bagoas? After Sati and Sikander were dead, when all we could do was stagger onward in the heat while the wind tore the flesh from our bones?"

Bagoas shook his head, his face drawn.

I could see the reflections of light in his eyes, just as in the water. "I dreamed of snow," I said softly. "I dreamed of snow in my veins, snow crusting my eyelashes and the mane of the horse beneath me. I followed my king through endless plains of snow, a curved sword of steel and ice at my side, the horse picking his way around the dead, through whispering powdered winds until my woman's body seemed to fray into nothing but wind, into silence and cold. An endless retreat into nothing, into the heart of winter, a procession of shadows under a black sky. As though I stood on that plain of ice and reached back for me, drawing heat from Gedrosia." I looked away and shook my head, knowing how I must sound. "Men think strange things when they've been out in the sun too long."

"They do," he said, and his breath caught. "Perhaps you should have been a priest instead of a soldier."

"If my wife, Sati, was right, and we are born many times, should we not all play all parts?" I asked. "I should play priest and soldier both, eunuch and prince, wife and camp follower and servant of the gods."

"To what end?" he said, and his face was shadowed. "And have it be more than ceaseless suffering."

I thought for a moment, but I was raised in Persian lands, and perhaps I understood a little. "You abhor the Lie and revere Truth," I said. "Does not that sacred fire demand service, no matter what its form, should it be garbed as an Apis bull, or as the sole god of Judah or as Magi's flame? Are we not servants of the light together, working toward the good?"

Bagoas' mouth quirked. "I am my Lord's servant. Nothing more."

I lifted my eyes, seeing in the wind stirring the tree branches above the crux of the matter, the question that I had never dared to think. Here, surrounded by the stillness of the ancient Black Land, it was possible to put into words. "And who does Alexander serve?"

Bagoas shook his head. "You are above yourself to ask such questions."

"I am above myself," I said. "I have been above myself since I left Miletus. And so there is nothing to stop me from daring all."

"You do not wish to live?" Bagoas smiled grimly, though his eyes did not leave my face. "That is what stops most men from reaching above themselves."

"Not particularly," I said, and in that moment I realized it was true. I had given myself up for dead in the sands of Gedrosia, with my family. The man who had walked the earth since then was a revenant, an unburied corpse who awaited only the fatal thrust. With nothing to lose, why should I fear anything? Why should I stint at any throw?

I thought it was pity I saw in his face. "Then you will die, or you will return to life."

"You know this?" I said.

"Oh, yes." Bagoas spoke lightly, but the tension in his slender shoulders said otherwise, and in that moment I saw him as if for the first time as someone like me, not a beautiful and impenetrable riddle.

"You were very kind to me in Pelousion, and I had hoped," I said, and I stumbled over the words, "that we might be friends."

His eyebrows rose, and he seemed to recede without actually moving. "Friends?"

"You misunderstand me," I said quickly. "Friends. Nothing more."

"Oh," he said, and I thought that he colored. "It is only…"

I shrugged. "It is only that you are beautiful and everyone wants to see what you are made of. But it was only friendship I offered, not patronage. I should think I would know better than that."

His mouth twisted. "But you are a man," Bagoas said. "Men do not call themselves friends to Persian catamites."

"Thais the Athenian is a woman, which is worse," I said. "And I do not disdain her friendship. Nor does Ptolemy begrudge it, knowing I am no rival."

"You would be a fool indeed to be your own general's rival," he said, but I thought I saw his shoulders relax.

"I would be," I said, stretching out my legs before me. "And while I was not bred to courts or kings, I think I have that much sense." I looked at him. "I am sorry. I did not mean to offend you."

"You didn't," he said, and for a moment I thought Bagoas looked awkward, his usual grace deserting him. "Nor did I mean to insult your friendship. I would be pleased if you would dine with me tomorrow night."

"I would be glad of the company," I said, and was surprised to find that I meant it.

# HETAİROS

Bagoas had a room in the Temple of Apis, in the quarters along the back courtyard that were reserved for priests who served full-time, as though he were a votive priest of the god Alexander. Which I supposed was what the Egyptians had made of his status. After all, dead pharaohs usually had votive priests, whose job was to manage their funerary chapel and conduct the rites for them. Doubtless they could not figure out what else to call Bagoas. He was not a royal widow or former concubine. No doubt in Persia they had a word for the eunuch favorite of the former king, but they did not in Egypt.

In Egypt priests outrank soldiers by quite a lot. His room was much nicer than mine, with two or three little carved tables, a beautiful wooden screen in the Persian style with flowers and birds, four or five hanging lanterns with panes of colored glass, and a large dining couch with embroidered pillows that must also serve as his bed.

I had hardly walked in the door before he was serving out cool watered wine as a host should, apologizing for the humbleness of the meal to follow.

"I have been eating in the barracks," I said, "so no doubt I will think it wonderful, no matter what has happened to it."

Bagoas blinked as though he had not expected me to take his protests seriously. Perhaps they were meant for form, not an actual warning that something was wrong with the dinner.

"The last time I dined with Artashir," I said, "a seagull stole our dinner. And then the cat got it back and…"

Bagoas blinked again.

"It's not very important," I ended awkwardly.

"Come and sit," he said, and showed me to the best place.

I do not like to think that I said anything else absurd. I should like to think that I was witty and knowledgeable, the perfect combination of diplomat and soldier. In truth, I do not know. The wine was stronger and better than I expected, and the beautiful dishes of perfect almonds closed together again around bits of lemon and goat cheese, the trimmed lamb with coriander, and all the rest had precious little oil and bread to them, the things that keep the wine from going to one's head. It's an old trick, to eat oil and bread before drinking if one wants to stay sober.

But everything was good, and the tastes but whetted the appetite for the wine. By the time the honey cakes came out, and the sweet dark wine from Chios unwatered and unspoiled, I doubt I could have safely crossed the room. It did, however, have its advantages.

"My arm is not hurting for the first time in months," I said to Bagoas. It was wrapped and splinted still, but for the first time in a long time I was not aware of it throbbing and aching. "It actually doesn't hurt."

Bagoas smiled. "Perhaps it does you good to relax." His face was flushed, though his speech was perfectly clear.

I leaned back on the cushions. It was so very nice not to hurt.

"What usually hurts?" he asked.

"My arm," I said. "My hand. And my shoulder. And my back. And I suppose my legs and my neck usually do too."

"It sounds as though you could use some rest," he said, and I thought he seemed amused.

"I'm not sure how to do that," I said. The room seemed to be spinning just a little, so I lay down on the couch, my back to Bagoas, my arm propped on one of the big pillows. "I've tried to sleep late but the sun wakes me up."

"Maybe you need thicker curtains," Bagoas said.

"I don't have any curtains," I said. The stamped linen of the pillows was washed soft, and it begged me to close my eyes.

"Why not?"

"They didn't come with the room," I said.

"Don't you have a servant to buy some for you?" he asked. His hand brushed against the sleeve of my good arm and rested on my back.

"I have two grooms," I said. Of course I could not take care of my own horses with my arm like this, nor exercise them properly.

"And who takes care of you?" His hand moved in kneading motions on my shoulder, warming muscles that normally ached.

I shrugged, as that was really an unanswerable question.

"Surely the Hipparch of Ptolemy's Ile could afford a bodyservant."

"I suppose," I said doubtfully. "I've never considered it."

"Someone to wash your clothes and hang your curtains."

I wondered if he thought my chiton was dirty. I'd washed it myself the day before. It was simply hard to think, what with the wine and the way he was methodically loosening each muscle in my right shoulder. "I don't know," I said, half asleep. "I was never allowed in the house, so I've no idea what should be done about curtains and things like that. Those are for house slaves."

His hands paused only half a second. "You are not a slave now," Bagoas said.

Having said it, I might as well stand on it, I thought. "No, not now. But I haven't any idea how those things are supposed to be done. How should I? I was sold for a horseboy when I was ten because I wasn't pretty enough for the bedroom."

This time his hands did not stop in their smooth sweep. "I might have liked to have been a horseboy."

"You could have been me," I said, "and I you. It is only our fates that separate us, and the choices of others when we were boys."

"That sent me to be gelded and you to shovel manure," he said. His voice was calm, though his strong fingers dug into my back.

"But then you should not have had the King, nor known all that you have," I said. "Would you rather it were that way?"

"Would you rather be me?" Bagoas asked.

"I don't know," I said carefully. "Maybe." To have stood at Alexander's side was no mean thing.

Bagoas' hands swept over my spine, changing to the left shoulder. "You're stubborn. You might have survived."

I smiled and bowed my neck to his hands. "That is what I would say as well. A cavalry trooper doesn't have a safe life either."

"I see that," he said, his fingers hesitating on the knots below my left shoulder blade. "What have you done to yourself here?"

"Gaugamela," I said. "I broke my shoulder. It works well enough, but it hurts a lot in damp weather."

"Little enough of that in Egypt," Bagoas observed.

"Another good reason to stay here for the rest of my life," I said.

"Do you like it so much, then?" Under his hands I felt myself relaxing, almost drowsing.

"Oh yes," I said. How should I explain how I was coming to love it, this place that was not my home and yet filled my dreams?

"Except for the sun," he said, and I could hear the smile in his voice. "You might like it better with curtains."

"Mmmm," I said.

"I could go with you to buy some."

"That would be very nice," I said, and slept.

Despite my acute embarrassment in the morning at having fallen asleep on Bagoas' couch, he seemed not to be angry. Indeed, he dragged me out to the markets early, claiming that he must make good on his promise to help me buy curtains.

I stood bemusedly in the marketplace. "I had no idea there were so many kinds of curtains," I said. "Dozens of fabrics, different kinds of clips…"

"Choose some cloth you like," Bagoas said, "and we will get them made up for you. And you may as well order some pillows at the same time."

"Should I? I like pillows." I did like pillows, and I had none. But I had never given any previous thought as to where they came from.

"Pillows," Bagoas said with a smile. "And perhaps a carpet too."

"Carpets are nice," I said. I had never thought of myself as the kind of man who owned carpets, but admittedly they were nice to walk on.

Bagoas stopped between market stalls and shook his head, his long dark hair caught at the back of his neck in a clasp. "You are a senior officer now, not a plain trooper. You need to give some thought to appearances, for Ptolemy's sake if not for your own. People will take the measure of you, and that will reflect on him."

"That is true," I said. I had thought about that very clearly when I represented him in Upper Egypt, but I had not considered it here.

"You would not want the Egyptians to think him a parsimonious master who does not pay his men enough to live on," Bagoas said. "I am not saying that you must keep great state, but a decent house and a few servants is not excessive. He pays you, doesn't he?"

"Well, yes," I said. "I suppose he pays me well. But I don't usually draw my full pay. I just leave it in the treasury and draw enough for whatever I think I'll need."

"And so Ptolemy gets the loan of your pay at no interest." Bagoas smiled again. "You will never be a wealthy man."

"I have no desire to be," I said, shrugging. "There's not much I want that money can buy. Can money bring the dead to life again?"

"No," Bagoas said, and his eyes were grave. "But is there nothing worth living for?" He gestured around the busy marketplace, the walls of Memphis golden in the sun, the river winding north toward Alexandria and the sea. "Nothing?"

"No," I said. "There are things. Keeping faith. That is one thing. And…"

And how could one wish to die when one stood in Memphis on a blue morning, with a freshening breeze pulling at us and Bagoas watching me with his green eyes? If Death came for me, I should greet her with equanimity, but I did not wish to die. Which rather surprised me. It was not as simple as it had been before I came to Egypt.

I looked down from the walls and met Bagoas' eyes. His handsome face was still. I wondered when he had wished to die, and why he had not, but that is not the kind of thing one can ask in a public market-place. Perhaps it is not the kind of thing one is ever meant to know, but I was certain he had gazed over that brink.

And in that moment I saw him entirely anew. Alexander's lover, a Persian, a peerless courtier—all those things I had seen, but now instead I saw a man my age at loose ends with nothing before him except the endless service of a dead king, a lifetime of attending to a body in a golden coffin, the walls of a foreign temple closing around him. There should be no more travel, no more mornings in the high mountains when the air paled to silver, no more precious rooms redolent with incense where decisions were made that affected thousands. I might come and go, a trusted officer and sometime diplomat, and while I lived I should not want for things to do or promises to keep. But Bagoas' story was ended. He had belonged to Darius and then Alexander. And now he was nothing.

"You have been so kind to me," I said, as he stood there in the street holding the cloth for the curtains. "I cannot thank you enough for it."

He had seen the change in my face, but did not guess the reason. "You are very welcome, Lydias," he said. "You need someone to look after you."

"Maybe I do," I said.


İT WAS ALMOST evening when the messenger found me bearing words from Ptolemy. I told Bagoas I should have to leave in the morning for Alexandria, as it was too late in the day.

"Well," he said, "putting your room to rights will have to wait. You will have dinner with me again?"

"I would like that," I said. He had carefully not asked what Ptolemy wanted, but I told him over dinner.

"He wants me in Alexandria immediately," I said. "To help him greet his bride."

Bagoas choked on his wine. "Bride?"

"Bride," I said. "Antipatros' daughter, Eurydice. She's eighteen years old, sent out from Macedon as a token of alliance. He's forty-three, and he's been with Thais for sixteen years." I helped myself to more duck. It was very, very tasty.

Bagoas spread his fingers. "That has nothing to do with it, does it? Surely he won't treat her badly after so long together."

"No, of course not," I said, thinking of the way Ptolemy had bent over the children when he sent them from Babylon, the way he and Thais exchanged glances as though pages of text were written in a look. "He loves her truly, and they have a daughter and two sons, with the new baby. But surely she must feel it, when he puts a bride in her place. And if the point is to get an heir…"

"He will have to put a good face on it," Bagoas said, and did not look up from his meat. "Kings must."

Belatedly, I realized what point I had run onto and changed course frantically. "What I can't understand is why he wants me there. I don't know anything about welcoming highborn brides!"

"Perhaps he wants you there to stand beside him," he said. "A friend with no other interests in the matter. Is this girl supposed to actually take over the running of the Household?"

I put my cup down. "I'm not sure there is a Household, not in the sense we had with the King. The last time I was there no one had really gotten around to building a palace yet. More of a stoa. I hope that's changed, as I expect the bride will want four walls."

Bagoas put his hand to his forehead. "Rooms? Furniture? Linens? Servants? She can be expected to bring her own clothes and some other things with her, but surely Ptolemy doesn't want her to walk into bare rooms. It looks…"

"Cheap," I said.

"You should see to that before she gets there."

"I have no idea what should be done!" I said. "Bagoas, you can tell me but…"

"Is there no one you could ask to help you?" He raised the pitcher and poured out more wine for me.

I thought for a moment. "I suppose Artashir's senior wife, Amina. She was raised as a Persian gentlewoman. She might not know how things should be done for a Macedonian, but she ought to be able to fit out a Persian bride and know what to get." In the old days I could not have spoken to her, a respectable woman and wife of a nobleman, but things had changed in the baggage train and in this new city. I didn't think Artashir would mind if I spoke to his wife and asked her advice.

"That would work," Bagoas said, and changed the subject.

It was not until I was halfway to Alexandria that I wondered if he had wanted me to ask him to come instead.


Eurydice was pretty enough, I thought. She looked a good deal like her older brother, Cassander, who I did not like, but that was nothing to hold against her. Her hair was light, like his, and she had a long, straight nose and flat cheekbones, Illyrian or Epirote in features. You could see the fierce blood that had come off the steppes, the same way you could see it in Alexander. But then, his mother was Epirote too. They had married into the noble houses of Macedon quite a lot.

In manner Eurydice could not have been more unlike Cassander. Where he was pushy, always the first horse at the trough, so to speak, Eurydice seemed shy. She was hesitant to speak, more even than I thought natural for a young girl so far from home. But perhaps I had gotten used to the campaign brides, who if they had not been something out of the ordinary wouldn't have been there in the first place.

I was sent with an honor guard to meet her ship and escort her to the palace, and I presented myself in my best chiton and shined breastplate, scrubbed and pretty as possible. When she replied to my offer to place myself at her service, I could barely hear her.

"We are most complimented by your service," her attendant said, standing behind her. "Very proper." Her frank brown eyes met mine. "I am Eurydice's aunt, her mother's sister. My name is Berenice, and I have come with my niece to help her in her duties."

"The Hipparch Lydias," I said, bowing again. The aunt was thirty or so, plump and dark-haired, with a direct look about her and color in her face from the sea wind. "There are rooms prepared for you ladies, if you would accompany me?"

"Antigone! Magas!" She turned and called, and two children came running from where they had been standing at the ship's rail, watching the sailors make fast, a little girl about eight and a boy perhaps two years younger. "It's time to go ashore! Eurydice, let me fix your himation."

The children skidded to a halt, poking and giggling, their eyes round at my gleaming steel harness.

Berenice looked around from where she was repinning Eurydice's veil. "My children from my first marriage."

"What has brought you here?" I asked. Surely a woman with young children would not want to cross the seas.

"Enough of being a poor relation on my former brother-in-law," she said, but her eyes were laughing. "And I've all but brought Eurydice up. So I thought we'd try something new."

The girl smiled, and her face was transformed, more like a bride and less like a sacrifice. It came to me that she must be terrified.

I made myself as agreeable as possible. "It is a great honor to welcome you to Alexandria on behalf of Ptolemy. I know that he has been eagerly awaiting you, Lady. I hope that you will find our city and your quarters to your liking. There are no official functions planned tonight, as it was thought that you might like an evening to rest and get your shore legs back before the wedding tomorrow." I glanced up at the aunt. "I'm afraid we are still under construction, as it were. I have arranged for a noble lady, Amina the wife of General Artashir, to show you your rooms and to help with anything you may require."

"That is very nice," Berenice said.

Eurydice looked up at me. "This Amina...is she..."

"Persian," I said firmly. Her brother, Cassander, had been of the party that objected the most when Alexander took up Persian ways and allowed Persians to serve beside Greeks. I did not know whether these were merely Cassander's opinions, or reflections of his father's.

If it were the latter, and Eurydice now came up against all she had been taught, I must be definite that her husband's opinions on the matter were quite different. Ptolemy could not afford a bride who would make trouble with any of his subjects. "We are a city of many peoples, Lady, as Great Alexander's court was. But I assure you that Amina's Greek is quite good, and she will be able to help you communicate with the Egyptian servants, and with the Persian and Bactrian ones."

"Why not all Greek slaves?" the girl asked.

I spread my hands. "Very few of our servants are slaves, Lady. They're simply too expensive to import, and few Egyptians are slaves and they do not speak Greek in any event. Most of the palace servants that Amina and I have hired are luckless women from the baggage train, the wives of men who have died or who are too crippled to work. They are cooks and laundresses, maids and seamstresses and the like. They work for a wage and bread and board for their children. If they have boys old enough, some of them are working in the stables or doing other work of the house. It is much cheaper than importing slaves from Greece, Lady. And I am sure they do better work too."

"Very sensible," Berenice said with a nod. "It's a different world, Eurydice, and we shall have a lot to learn."

"If you will come this way, ladies?" I suggested.

THE NEXT DAY I stood beside Ptolemy, one of four Companions who stood as kinsmen while he married Eurydice. I thought the wedding went off well enough. The food and the dancing had a very Persian flair, thanks to the management of the redoubtable Amina, who I thought could probably provision an army on the march without breaking a sweat. The bride was all Greek, her pale blue chiton and himation with worked borders looking like a statue of Artemis. Or perhaps Iphigenia.

I poured a quick libation in the corner where nobody would notice, to ward off that thought.

Ptolemy looked grave rather than exuberant as a bridegroom should be, but then he was forty-three, and not prone to display at any time. He sat beside her at the wedding feast, turning to her to talk in low tones.

Of course Thais was not there. He had spared her that.

I was both surprised and flattered to find myself in the position of kin. But I suppose Ptolemy had no real kindred there, and there was value in having myself, Manetho, and Artashir all in prominent positions.

When we had sung the bride and groom to bed, it was our job to make it clear that Ptolemy did not want a crowd outside the door all night, listening and being rowdy, so we cleared them out and sent them back down to the hall for a last round of drinking, and then out into the night.

Amina came up while I stood with Artashir, making sure no one crept back in.

"We survived it," Amina said.

"We did." Artashir ducked his head against her shoulder, his forehead against her as she smiled down fondly at him. "Lydias and I should probably stay here the rest of the night, but you could go home."

"I don't mind staying alone," I said, and was surprised to find a strange jealousy uncurling in my midst. "You can go on. I'll stay here with the guardsmen until at least the turning of the watch."

"You don't mind?"

"Not at all," I said, and watched them leave, two tall, well-matched figures, his arm around her waist.

Would there ever again be someone waiting for me?

# ROSES

I went to see Thais the next day, early in the morning.

They say transplanted roses never bloom, but they did in the garden of Thais the Athenian. She had made a bower on new soil, enclosed by fine stone walls, fig trees, and exotic apricots shading a bench. Or at least they would shade the bench when they were taller. Now they cast fleeting shadows across the sandstone. Roses were trained in the shadow of the wall, rising from a bed that smelled strongly of horse manure.

It made me smile. Without it, I should never know this paradise was earthly.

Thais came forward to greet me, her veil about her shoulders, neither as modest as a Greek woman or as brazen as an Egyptian. She was thirty-five, but the beauty that had captivated everyone lingered still, the firebrand who had burned Persepolis.

"My dear lady," I said, and inclined my head in greeting.

No doubt she wondered why I had come, and she was not one to play around it. "Lydias," she said, and her eyes were a little sharp. "Have you come to show me that I am not entirely forgotten?"

"I am here only for myself, not Ptolemy," I said. "I have no idea where it stands between you, but I am steadfast in my friendships."

At that she looked surprised. "Come and sit down, then," she said, and led me to the bench, she sitting at one end and I at the other. There was no one there but us, and a young maidservant digging in a rose bed at the end of the garden. "You are wondering where it is with us."

"It is not my business," I said awkwardly. "But I have always liked you very much."

"And you thought if there were bad feelings you might mend them." Thais smiled at me and shook her head. "It is a kind thought, if it were needful. But this is not the first time, you know. Ptolemy married Artacama, the daughter of Artabazos, in Persia when Alexander commanded it."

"Yes, but that was by the King's command," I said. "This was not."

"It was needful," Thais said, "if he is to be Pharaoh of Egypt." I startled, and she raised an eyebrow. "Do you think he has not told me what the gods of Egypt offered him? But I am not a concubine to a pharaoh. I am a free hetaira, as I have been since he came to my door in Athens. I will not live in his palace with his wife, arranging her banquets and taking care of her clothes. I will live in my own house, with my children, and if he wishes to see me he can come here."

I looked at her in amazement and admiration.

Thais played with a fold of her himation. "Like Aspasia before me, I have my dignity. And if I surrendered that I should not have his love."

"I believe he loves you deeply," I said. Certainly there was nothing in the wedding the day before that suggested he had gone to Eurydice with even lust.

"And I him," she said. "Though it is not true that I have wandered the world for him. Rather that he gave me a way to do what a woman can otherwise not. He gave me my freedom." Thais put her head back, as if to drink in the blue sky of the Black Land above.

"Freedom is the greatest good," I said.

She nodded. "And now we will see what comes of it. In time my daughter should have been a hetaira after me, and our sons acknowledged and made soldiers or set up in business. But the only children of Pharaoh are a different matter than the illegitimate children of a general."

"Yes," I said, "and perhaps one day there will be some other heir, but for now…" I spread my hands. "I did not know he had agreed to the gods' bargain."

"He will agree," Thais said serenely. "Ptolemy will have no other choice."

The child I had taken for a maidservant got up, dusting off her hands on the front of her chiton, as if wondering whether to come over or not. "Mother?" she called, and I realized that it was Chloe.

I should hardly have known her otherwise. More than two years had passed since our wild journey from Babylon, an eternity in a girl her age. She was tall like her mother, with Ptolemy's nondescript brown hair. And then she looked at me.

I do not think I had ever seen her full in the face, in daylight. Her eyes were storm gray, irises rimmed in black, wide and colored like tempered steel, like winter skies, eyes Praxiteles had sculpted, eyes no one had ever captured in paint. She had Alexander's eyes exactly.

There had always been the rumors, of course, that Ptolemy was Alexander's brother, that his mother had been Phillip's before Phillip was King. I did not know if they were true or not, and I had doubted all these years that Ptolemy knew. Now I knew that he had. The truth was in his daughter's eyes.

"You see?" Thais said softly. "He is the nearest kin after Alexander's son, brother of the King that was."

"Alexander must have known," I said, realizing. "And Bagoas." And now she trusted me to know this.

Thais nodded. "And Hephaistion. Chloe was an infant when Ptolemy took the road to India. I stayed in Susa. It was supposed to be a short campaign, and I could not take the road east with a baby three weeks old. It was almost five years before he returned." Thais spread her himation on the bench, and Chloe came and sat beside her with her arm about her waist. She had heard this story before. "I waited almost five years for him in Susa, hoping that he would live and love me still."

"And he did," I said, my voice choking. Ptolemy had come out of the desert of Gedrosia to find Thais and Chloe waiting for him.

"Of course when he saw Chloe he knew. She had been a newborn when he left. She looked like any other baby. But when he saw her, he knew. And Alexander knew."

"That was a very dangerous thing to leave in his hands," I said. To put in the hands of a childless king a brother with an army at his back and an heir…

"He was Alexander. He said they had promised long ago to behave as brothers should, and there was nothing to change that. When our son was born a year later, we called him Lagos after Ptolemy's stepfather, something that ought to quell rumors."

"Bunny doesn't look like me," Chloe said. "His eyes are brown."

"Yes, darling," Thais said, pulling an errant leaf from Chloe's hair. "Both her brothers have brown eyes. But that would not stop them from being pawns in the succession."

I shivered. It all fell into place. Ptolemy had been desperate to get the children out of Babylon before someone noticed. Before Roxane noticed, and thought Chloe was Alexander's. Before Perdiccas noticed and weighed her worth. Before any one of a hundred other men jumped at an opportunity dropped in their lap. He had been desperate enough to entrust them to a plain soldier and a wild ride to Pelousion.

And Bagoas. He knew. I had seen it in his hesitation at Pelousion, when I had scoffed at the rumors. Either the King had told him, or he had seen for himself. Hephaistion would have been told.

I looked at Chloe, and she looked back with those amazing eyes. "She cannot be a hetaira," I said.

"Twice royal, twice on the wrong side of the blanket, she is too great a prize," Thais said. "And Perdiccas…"

"Father has to win. For me," Chloe said, and her face was solemn.

She was a child of the baggage train, not a highborn girl sheltered from every storm. She knew, though she was still a child, not a maiden. She knew what her fate might be.

"Well then," I said with a smile for her, "we will have to win. For you."

In a year or two she would be a woman. Already I could see it in the bones of her face, losing the roundness of childhood for her mother's beautiful cheekbones, in her slender hands that were already taking a woman's shape. No doubt beneath her loose chiton her body was changing in other ways as well. She was not so much younger than Eurydice, her father's bride.

"We will win for you, Chloe," I said.

SATI HAD BEEN seventeen when I had come to Nysa. She was a young widow, and she was begging in the street. Her husband had died of a sickness in the spring, and her husband's family wanted no more of her when it was clear she was not with child, one more mouth to feed in a time of uncertainty and war. Her own parents were dead, and so she had no place to go.

I was twenty-two. Not even a year had passed since Alexander married Roxane, and in that time we had crossed into India and fought a great battle. One of the princes of India, a king named Raja Ambhi, had sent emissaries to Alexander offering to do homage if the King would help him against his neighbor and ancient enemy, Raja Puru. Thus it was that Hephaistion and Perdiccas were sent ahead with their troops to arrange bridging of the mighty Indus River so that the main army might come up. I was in Hephaistion's Ile, and while cavalry had little to do in the business of building a bridge, we were necessary to maintain a screen lest the enemy come upon us unaware. And so I was sent to Nysa.

We had good billets in the small fortress belonging to a kinsman of Ambhi, and our pay was up to date. We arrived just at the onset of the monsoons, and while the engineers swore and bickered and sweated trying to bridge the swollen river, the cavalry had an easy time of it.

The first time I saw Sati she was begging by the gate, the water running in long rivulets down her face, her saffron scarf plastered to her hair. She sat among the old and the covered in scabs, and I could not help but look at her twice. How should someone so young be reduced to so little? I knew well enough, I supposed. There are always winners and losers. But I thought from the proud tilt of her head that she was not quite defeated.

A few days later someone hired some prostitutes to come in after dinner, to dance and to sit on our couches the way hetairae would grace our betters. The girl who played had hard eyes, and the dancers had their professional smiles. Except Sati. Every movement spoke instead of acute embarrassment. I watched her, her great dark eyes the twin of mine, her hair like black silk down her back exactly like my mother's. We could have been brother and sister, so alike were we.

I remembered how she had hated him, my father and my master, how she had come from his bed with marks in her lower lip where she had bitten down, how she had flinched when I put my little arms around her.

When the girls stopped dancing and went to the couches I watched how Sati perched on the end of Glaukos' couch, hesitantly, as though she were staying as far away as possible.

Laughing, he took her by the arm and tried to draw her in for a kiss, and I saw the fear in her eyes before she yielded.

I hardly knew what I did when I got to my feet and crossed between the couches, giving Glaukos a gentle shove. "This one's mine, my friend."

"Yours?" Glaukos looked up at me, a few drops of wine clinging to his beard. "You never want one."

"I want this one," I said, and took her by the arm. I could feel her pulse hammering in her thin wrist.

"Maybe you don't get her," he said.

"Maybe I do."

I was much soberer than he. Perhaps he considered that, or perhaps there was something in my eyes he didn't like. Glaukos sprawled back on the cushions. "Fine then. She's too skinny to be much good anyhow."

I hauled her out of the hall to the hoots of several of my men, into the little room upstairs that I rated as an officer. She said something half a dozen times, but I did not understand a word. I shut the door behind me, bending because of the low ceiling.

A little light came in blue from behind the shutters closed against the rain. The room was barely the length of a man, taken up almost entirely with my tack and bed. She stood with the back of her knees against the bed, and I saw her swallow.

"You will pay?" Sati said in halting Greek.

"Yes," I said, and opened my belt pouch, spilling a bunch of coins into her hand, much more than she was worth.

She looked at them and swallowed, her chin lifting. She took off her veil and let it drop to the floor.

"No," I said, and my voice was rough. "No."

She knew enough Greek to understand that, and she frowned.

"An old war wound," I said. "It's left me impotent. I don't want my friends to know, so I pretend to go with women. Just pretend we did it and all will be well."

Her eyes flicked down my body and up again, and I saw she didn't believe it for a minute. "You are very strange," she said.

"So are you," I said. "Why are you here with these women?"

Sati shrugged. "What else is there? I can beg and die, or I can go with soldiers." Her Greek was better than I had thought. She must have already picked up a lot in the time we had been here.

"Can't you..." I cast about. "Cook and clean or something?"

"Show me the man who wants me for cooking and cleaning," she said, her eyes sharp. She held out her arms, and I could see the way her clothes draped over her slender body, a bit of pale skin showing at her waist between the drapes. "Show me one who wants only that."

"I could," I said and swallowed. Perhaps I would want more, but I was not a beast even if every movement she made caused my blood to sing.

"You could?" She did not believe me, but there was the ghost of a smile on her face. "Because of your old war wound?" She looked pointedly at the front of my chiton.

"Yes," I said. I took a step back, but my back was against the door. "Why are you doing this?"

"When my husband died I had a choice. To die or not. I choose not." Her eyes were steady. I had thought she was like my mother, but I was wrong. She was far stronger.

"Can't you remarry?"

She put her head to the side, smiling, her dusky lips curved like a bow. "You do not know India. Who would marry me, a bad-luck bride who brought death to a strong young man two months from her wedding day? My husband was handsome and had never been ill, but he died before the moon was full twice."

"I would marry you," I said. "I mean as a matter of rhetoric."

She didn't know the last word, but her smile grew a little, though her voice was brittle. "And you would die young, soldier. Your next battle would take you, and She would carry you down among the armless ones to wait in the shadows. I am poison."

"You are not," I said, though a chill ran down my spine. "I do not fear your Lady of Shadows, though I give Her libation in blood often enough. She will have me when She wants me, and not a moment before."

I saw her eyes flicker, and I knew in that moment what she loved most in any human being. Courage. She would never want a man who was less than she, no more than I would.

"Most men fear Her."

"I am not most men," I said.

"Perhaps you have been Her beloved in ages past," Sati said contemplatively. "To have no fear of Death."

I came around and sat down on the end of the bed. "I do not fear Death's Queen, though I revere Her. Do you know the story?"

"I know one story," she said, "for I am named for her, Sati who was first wife to Lord Shiva. But I do not know if your story is the same."

"Once there was a maiden," I said, "and her name was Kore. She was the daughter of earth and sky, and there was no more beautiful woman in the world."

And I told her the story, while the monsoon beat down against the windows, how the Lord of the Underworld in his pride and loneliness had seen her walking in the fields and had seized her in his black chariot, taking her underground to be his queen. Sati drew near and sat down too, her feet crossed beneath her knees, while I told her of Death's kingdom and the land of the shades, and of how her mother had sought her in vain while all the earth died.

"She found her then, in the endless caverns beneath the earth, where starlight shines on fields of grain that neither grow nor wither, for there is no time there. And there, her mother made a bargain with Death. Half the year Kore would live beneath the earth as Death's Queen, and the other half of the year she would dwell above and walk under the sun, maiden once more. And that is how it came to pass."

There were no more sounds of revelry from the room below. It was late.

"Now I will tell you," Sati said, and her eyes sparkled. "I will tell you my story, how the Princess Parvati was born and how she sought and won Lord Shiva through many penances and through many travails on this earth, for she had been his bride before, and love is the thing that is without end. I will tell you my story, if you wish to know."

"I do," I said. "I want to hear all the stories."

She told me stories while night turned toward morning, and I told her stories too. There were gods who took the shape of monkeys, and I told her of the Titans, and Prometheus who stole fire and gave it to men. She told me of Prince Rama and how he rescued his kidnapped wife though a hundred kings stood against him, and how she came with him in his exile to live with him in hardship in the wilderness. We fell asleep just before dawn on the faded cotton bedcover, her head against my shoulder and my hair across her face.

We woke to morning and rain, and the sounds of the Ile about their business, the day's scouts turning out for their patrol below. I watched her wake and stiffen suddenly as she remembered where she was, saw the fear fade from her eyes when she saw me.

"I was thinking," I said as I sat up. My little room smelled like damp leather from the tack, and there was no breakfast.

"Thinking what?" she asked, and a shadow crossed her eyes. In the night it had seemed simple to tell each other stories in the dark, her soft voice counterpoint to the rain.

I opened my mouth and then closed it again. Fortune favors the bold. "I was thinking that today is a good day for a wedding."

Sati blinked. "Whose wedding?"

"Ours," I said. "Will you marry me this morning?"

# BAGOAS

I returned with Ptolemy to Memphis barely a month after his marriage to Eurydice. During my month in Alexandria I finally had the splints and bandages off my arm, and I was not pleased with what I found.

My left hand was withered and shrunken, bulges of bone standing out at odd angles in my wrist, my first two fingers skeletal. I could move it, some. My wrist moved down a tiny bit, flexing forward a few degrees. I could close my fingers slightly. I could hold a piece of fruit cupped between fingers and thumb, but when I turned my hand over it dropped to the ground. My fingers didn't have the strength to even hold a lemon.

I felt a rush of rage at the doctor, who was beaming. "There! See how nicely that's coming along?"

"I can't use it," I said, and my voice sounded strangled.

"Not yet, of course," he said. He took my hand in his and worked it gently, frowning only when he tried to rotate my wrist back and it would not move at all. "You've got to exercise it and let the muscles heal."

"How long?" I asked, staring at the twisted thing. "How much?"

"Another half a year, if you take care of it and work at it. How much?" He stretched my last two fingers out where they had crabbed over. "I don't know yet. You'll have some use of it, certainly."

"Enough to ride? I have to be able to ride with this hand." The reins had to lie across my palm, and I needed the full strength of fingers and wrist to manage a horse in battle. "I have to be able to use it. Will I?"

He shook his head, though his eyes were direct. "I don't know," he said.

I closed my eyes. Which meant not. I knew that. With one good hand I could either use a sword or ride. Not both. What use is a cavalryman who cannot ride and fight at the same time?

"We will have to see how it heals," the doctor said. "A few more months of light duty while you exercise it and get the muscles back. We'll have to see."

AND SO I returned to Memphis with Ptolemy by barge in the growing season, when the Black Land was greening with the gifts of the river. My room was waiting for me, though when I first entered for a moment I thought I was in the wrong place. Green curtains stamped with leaf patterns in white hung at the windows, and the bed was piled high with green and white pillows. A pair of hanging lamps swung from a stand, and there was a thick carpet underfoot. It took a moment to remember that these were the things I had ordered to have made up just before I left. During the month I had been in Alexandria they must have been finished and delivered. It looked much, much more comfortable.

I looked about with satisfaction and spread out my papers on the table. Reading was still laborious for me, though I was learning. I was told by all that it was much easier to master if it were begun in childhood, but while Ptolemy and Artashir had been at their respective lessons, I had served Tehwaz and learned other things.

There was a quiet knock on the open door, and I turned around.

Bagoas stood in the doorway, his dark hair in a long braid down his back, wearing a new tunic of white Egyptian linen over his Persian trousers, a compromise of dress, but one that suited him. Persians do not wear white often, except for religious services. I did not think it was forbidden, just not done. "I heard you were back."

"Hello, Bagoas," I said, straightening up and smiling. "I just arrived. How have you been?"

"Well," he said, and smiled back. Perhaps it was the white tunic giving a glow to his face, but he did look well. "I wondered if you'd join me for dinner. I heard that Ptolemy is dining privately tonight and there is no banquet."

"Yes, no banquet until tomorrow," I said. "Ptolemy and I arrived too late in the day to invite all the local notables. So I am free tonight. I can come with you."

"Good," he said, carefully not glancing at the scroll unrolled on the table.

"It's not secret," I said. "You can see if you like. Ptolemy wanted me to look at some of the draft language for the process of electing magistrates for the city of Alexandria."

"Electing magistrates?"

I nodded. "As I'm sure you know, when Alexander founded cities he left them with constitutions for their governance. Alexandria's wasn't finished when he took the road east, and he never got back to it. So we are working on it now, filling in the holes and making it work now that we have a better idea of what the city will be."

Bagoas looked bemused. "Doesn't Ptolemy intend to rule his own city himself?"

"Well, yes," I said, "but under the constitution. How can we have a city with men from a dozen lands living there and not have a constitution that lays out one law for everyone? If we didn't, and let each group do things according to their own laws, we should have a situation where the same crime was treated entirely differently depending on who did it! That wouldn't make sense, and it would breed unrest and resentment between peoples."

"But surely Ptolemy can appoint the magistrates, as Alexander always did. He would appoint just men, I think."

I shrugged. "Yes, he would. But will his grandson?"

Bagoas spread his hands. "How can anyone know that?"

"No one can," I said. "That's the point." I opened the scroll and laid it out. "We are building something here that must be stronger than any one man. We are building something that will endure for hundreds of years withstanding good kings and bad. It's always the same problem, isn't it? A good king comes to the throne and for a lifetime his kingdom prospers. But inevitably the crown passes to someone who isn't a good ruler, who is drunk and spoiled or simply not up to the job. And then the kingdom and all its people suffer. We are trying to build something that works regardless of who is king. If Ptolemy's grandson were an idiot, still the magistrates of Alexandria would fairly prosecute crime." I pointed out the map I had spread beside the scroll. "See how the city is divided into twelve districts? Each district elects a magistrate, and the magistrates hear the prosecution of crimes in rotation, with three courts in session at once, one for civil matters like wills or property disputes, one for petty crimes, and one for grand crimes. When you come before a magistrate, it may be the magistrate from your district, or from any of the others, but each district is equally represented in the rotation of cases."

Bagoas' brows knit together. "And any man could be a magistrate?"

"Any free man resident in the city, yes," I said. "He must run in the district in which he lives."

"Artashir could be a magistrate?"

I shrugged. "He could be. I can't imagine why Artashir would want to run for magistrate, but if he did there wouldn't be any reason he couldn't be."

"He's Persian."

"Yes." I met his eyes. "The law of the city is for everyone."

"What if a Jew ran from the Jewish district?"

I blinked. I had not truthfully thought that far. "I don't see why he couldn't be," I said slowly. "There would be nothing in the law to prevent it if he were duly elected."

"And then he would enforce Jewish law?"

I shook my head. "He would enforce the laws of the city. Jews may certainly keep to Jewish law above and beyond the laws of the city, but the laws of the city do not recognize Jewish law. For example, we have it in the laws of the city that if a butcher uses false weights to defraud customers, it is a crime. If he willfully disguises one kind of meat for another more expensive to defraud customers, it is a crime. But the laws of the city do not say that cattle must be butchered in accordance to Jewish law. Should a Jewish butcher wish to work in accordance with Jewish law and to advertise that, he may as long as he also observes the laws of the city in respect to weights and measures. The magistrates will not enforce that his meat must be butchered in accordance to Jewish law, but will consider use of false weights a petty crime for which he would pay a fine and return to the customers their money."

Bagoas met my eyes. "And you truly think men will accept this?"

"I hope so," I said simply. "I do not see how else we can proceed. And it has worked before in the cities of Greece. It is not as though we have invented democracy."

"Democracy hasn't worked," Bagoas said. "In Athens it turned into Demosthenes' demagoguery, and elsewhere it has failed, wrecked on the rocks of wealth or its inability to defend itself against stronger nations with kings. Persia burned Athens, if you remember, and that was Xerxes, not a great king."

"Which is why we will have both," I said. "A pharaoh to rule as Lord of the Two Lands, to wield the army and deal with other nations, and a constitution for the city that does not depend on Pharaoh. Add to that a third leg, the ancient bureaucracy of Egypt that has existed for a thousand years through its temples and priests, and there is a three-legged stool that will stand. It will endure even if there is a bad king for a few years. It would take twenty-five years of bad rule to set it adrift, we hope. And bad kings rarely reign so long."

"I had not thought you a dreamer, Lydias," Bagoas said, but there was something in his eyes that wanted to believe.

"Come to Alexandria," I said, "and you will see the dream made real. Alexander dreamed the Successors, an army of the sons of every nation. That will never now be real. But come to Alexandria and you will see his dreams enfleshed. You will see it in the sons of the city and in her stones, in this thing we are building. There is nothing like it in the world, and men will gape at it as they did at the first man who kindled fire and brought it into his cave. A dangerous thing, a strange thing."

Bagoas' mouth twisted, and I could not tell if he meant it for mockery, or if he remembered some other conversation with someone else, not without pain. "The face of things to come."

"Yes," I said.

WE ATE IN his room, sitting together on the large couch. It was piled up with pillows and a magnificent leopard skin, which I did not think he had gotten in Egypt. In fact, much of this must have come from Persia, and I said so.

Bagoas' eyes smiled over the rim of his wine cup. "As heavy as the hearse already was, I didn't think it would be much heavier with a few things of mine."

"You are the only man in the world who would be kidnapped with your luggage," I said, shaking my head.

"There were things I did not like to lose," he said, stroking the leopard skin. "This was a gift from Alexander, and I will not see its like again." He spread his hands. "Besides, what should I do, arriving in Egypt with nothing?"

"I'm not complaining," I said. I looked down at the sweet cakes still remaining on my plate and said what I had known I must. "I'm sorry I didn't ask you to come to Alexandria with me. I should have. I didn't think of it until I was halfway there. We could certainly have used you."

Bagoas shrugged. "It wasn't your place to. If Ptolemy wants me he can send for me."

I put my cup down. "He would not want you to take it as that sort of sending for. Ptolemy is a little strange, you know. He has no interest in boys at all, and for that matter I have never seen him with any woman besides Thais. And besides, I don't think Ptolemy thinks you're his to send for."

"If not his, then whose?" His smile was pretty, but it did not touch his eyes.

"I don't think you're anyone's," I said carefully. "You were the King's, but I cannot imagine who could say you are theirs now. You are a free man."

"I am not a man at all," Bagoas said gently. "There is no such thing as a eunuch who does not belong to someone, any more than there is such a thing as a woman who belongs to no one. If I do not belong to Ptolemy, who then do I belong to?"

"I don't know," I said. "But you could come to Alexandria if you wanted."

Bagoas leaned back on the cushions, one tapered foot on the edge of the couch. "We are all bound by our duty, Lydias. You act as though one can just choose who one will be."

"We can choose our duties," I said. "When I was married, I had a duty to my wife. But it was a duty I had chosen when I married her. I have a duty now to Ptolemy, but it is a duty I chose when I swore myself to his service. I will uphold my duty to the best of my abilities," I said, lifting my crippled hand into the light, "but it is not unwelcome. I decided to follow Ptolemy because I thought he was the best Companion remaining."

"That is the privilege of a man," he said, and his eyes were shadowed. "Women and eunuchs do not choose, but belong to those who own them. Do you think if I were Artashir I would not choose the same? But I am not Artashir."

"You know full well there are more ways to serve a king than in arms," I said, and an inspiration struck me. "You see how we are struggling to get a government working, much less a court! You are what we need in Alexandria. You know how courts work, how to plan things and get things done, and how to do all without offending people. Ptolemy has never had a chief of staff except in a military sense, and I am as ill suited to the job as anyone else, having never even lived in a great household, much less run one! We are about to face diplomats from all the kingdoms of the world, and I do not know what needs to be done! Nor does that young bride, eighteen years old and not speaking a word of anything besides Greek. If you were in Alexandria, Bagoas, you could take charge of Ptolemy's Household. I assume you could work with Amina in the women's quarters without offense?"

Bagoas opened his mouth and then shut it again. "Yes," he said quietly. "I could. In Persia and in most of the kingdoms of the East that is a eunuch's job. If one is lucky, when one's looks have faded and one is no longer a royal favorite, one learns how to run the Household. Amina is a Persian lady of noble rank. If she is the principal lady in waiting to Eurydice, she would expect to work with the eunuch who runs the Household."

"There is also Eurydice's aunt, Berenice," I said. "She seemed very sensible to me, though she only speaks Greek too. But I think she will be useful in time." My left arm was cramping where I leaned on it, the muscles in the lower arm beginning to ache again, and I shifted, lying more on my side and shoulder, though it turned my head away from Bagoas. "Come to Alexandria. I will speak to Ptolemy about it. Will you come if he asks you?"

His voice was low. "I will come if he asks me," Bagoas said. "But I am not asking you to do me favors or intercede with me at court."

I stretched my arm where it was cramping. "I am not doing you favors," I said. "I have a job I do not know how to do, and you are the one who does. Consider rather that I am recruiting someone who will make my work easier. If you take the problems of the palace and Eurydice off my hands it is I who will owe you a debt of gratitude." Raised in Miletus as I was, I understood the obligation of favors. I did not want Bagoas to owe me, especially when the coin he had to pay was not something I should like to claim. At least not as obligation. I ducked my face against the couch pillows under the cover of stretching my sore shoulder.

And should I want it if it were offered freely, not in repayment of favors?

I should be mad not to, I thought. Where in the world was there another so beautiful, whose company I enjoyed more? Would not any man be mad to refuse those green eyes and that whiplash-fine body, honed by years of dancing and acrobatics? I had seen him dance once, in the games after Gedrosia, and though my heart had not been in it, I could hardly have missed how beautiful he was, each long, slow walkover demonstrating perfect control.

We had both aged since then. I thought with a shock that it had been nearly five years. It didn't seem so long. But Alexander had been dead two and a half years, and Sati almost five. In two months I should be twenty-nine. Surely Bagoas was not much younger.

Of course I would want him. But I knew enough to say nothing. It is that way, in friendships with women or eunuchs. If one truly wishes for friendship, one must never admit the possibility of anything else.

"You would like Alexandria," I said, my face still turned from him, stretching casually against the couch pillows.

"And what is it that I would like?" he asked. He sounded relieved that we ventured back onto safer ground.

"It's beautiful," I said. "The harbor is a perfect crescent, white sand and blue water. And along the main streets the city is growing, with fine houses and markets and everything else. When it's done it will be the most beautiful city in the world. And Alexander will have the most magnificent tomb ever built, better even than the Mausoleum at Halicarnassos. Believe me when I say the Egyptians know how to build tombs!"

At this he laughed as I hoped he would. "I have been to see the pyramids," he said. "And the ones at Saqqara near where the tombs of the Apis bulls are. Is it true that Ptolemy means for Alexander to lie there?"

"Only for a little while, perhaps," I said. "Until his tomb is ready in Alexandria. But for now he must remain within the city walls of Memphis."

"Perdiccas."

"Perdiccas," I agreed. "He will come in a few months, as soon as he has had time to assemble his army. And I am useless." I stretched out my hand on the cushion. It would go flat only with effort.

"Surely not useless," Bagoas said, and I felt him shift behind me. "There is more to you than your hand. Must you be in the front of the charge? Cannot you command from the rear?"

"I suppose," I said doubtfully, trying to straighten my forefinger entirely. "It's not done."

"In Macedon," said Bagoas, taking my hand in his and straightening it gently, his fingers digging into my palm where it was sore. "But why would Ptolemy want to be rid of the man who stole the hearse and brought it to Pelousion? Even if you can't fight on horseback there is nothing wrong with your mind." He flexed my fingers again, working the muscle below my thumb. "Does that hurt?"

"Only in a good way," I admitted. "Mostly it hurts all the time, my hand and my wrist and my arm." It was good to be appreciated, I thought. It was a nice piece of work stealing the hearse, and I did not at all mind being told so.

"Let me see what I can do," Bagoas said, shifting about again so that he sat beside me, one hand on my arm above the elbow.

"I am sorry I fell asleep on you when you worked on my shoulder before," I said. "It was the wine, and it was very late."

"Well, you are supposed to relax," he said, and I heard the smile in his voice. He plucked at the back of my chiton. "Take this off and let me get at it properly."

"If you don't mind too much," I said. I had never known the removal of clothing to be the duty of the conscientious host, but I thought that while fortune favored the bold generally, it would not in this case. Better to let him set the pace, and to be certain what he wanted. I twisted about trying to pull my chiton over my head with my one good hand.

"Let me help." He untwisted my sleeve where I had gotten tangled up and took it gracefully.

I had never adopted the Persian fashion of trousers, except occasionally to ride, so this left me in nothing but my skin, stretched out on my stomach on the couch. Not that I felt I had much to hide. After all, you're always nude in the gymnasium, and ten years on horseback does develop your posterior.

"Here." He pulled the leopard skin from the end of the couch and tucked it over me from the waist down. "You wouldn't want to take cold."

"No, of course not," I said. I was beginning to see where this was going as he began to knead my sore shoulder with scented oil. Not many people keep a bottle of scented oil within hand's reach during dinner! Even I am not quite that dim.

I found it difficult not to drift into a stupor under his expert attention. "It smells wonderful," I said. "What is it?"

"Lemon," Bagoas said, "and some other things. Nabatean myrrh oil, which warms the skin, rose and star of the sea."

"You're so much better than the boy at the gymnasium," I mumbled.

"I should think so," Bagoas said, and there was a smile in his voice. "In Persia we do think one should be properly trained before one is sent to the Great King." I had never heard him speak of his life before Alexander, and I wondered at it. I did not suppose that it could have been very pleasant, serving Darius. He was perhaps not a cruel man, but a vain man and a coward does not make much of a master. I had been a slave myself, and there were certainly many men I would not have cared to serve in the bedroom.

"Did you have lessons?" I asked, wanting to know more of him without putting in at any bad bit he should not like to remember.

"I did indeed," he replied. "It is a great deal of work. There's a good bit more to it than being pretty. There are pretty boys in every marketplace."

"Yes, I see," I said. Thais had said much the same once. There are pretty slave girls everywhere, but an Athenian hetaira is something else entirely.

"I had lessons in this, how to serve at the bath and at the table, and in all of the ceremonial of court, and of course in dance and music, though I fear I am not much of a musician." His hands were both gentle and thorough. "Some eunuchs keep a sweet voice all their lives, but I had not much of a voice to begin with. Something of a disappointment," he said, and I heard the edge in his voice again.

Yes, I thought. A disappointment like a colt one has bought because its sire was fleet as the wind, only to find out the colt takes after its dam. We are no more than that, when we are slaves. We are no more than the colt.

"I think a beautiful voice is overrated," I said.

"Do you?" he said, and I heard him smile.

"I can't sing either," I said.

"No one expects a cavalry general to sing."

"Well, is there much call for the Master of the Household to sing either?" I asked.

"I am not yet Ptolemy's Master of Household," Bagoas said, but there was no heat in it. I had steered away from that edge.

Then he began to work on the backs of my thighs, and I found it difficult to keep a thought in my head.

"Turn over," he said at last.

I took a deep breath. "That will be rather...um..." I said, trying to turn over while keeping the leopard skin strategically draped. "I can't help it that..."

I looked up to see him smiling down at me, his long black hair nearly sweeping across my chest. "I can be more discouraging," Bagoas said, and leaned down and kissed me.

At which point there was really no more need for words.

# THE GATHERING STORM

I dreamed, and in my dream I stood in the desert. Above us, the dawn sky stretched pale blue, the last stars disappeared. We had marched all night. It was easier thus, with so little water.

Now we camped in a steep wadi whose sheltering walls would give us some respite from the sun. I took my helmet off and scrubbed my whole left hand across my sweat-damp hair. Sati had already pitched our tent and was putting a handful of lentils to soak in a scant handful of water. Sikander was playing in the dust beside her, one little hand clasped around a pretty stone. The horses drowsed heads down in the picket line. We would have some rest before the next night's grueling march.

I turned because Ghost Dancer had suddenly gone up on his hind legs, fighting Hephaistion's groom. I started toward him, wondering what was wrong as he jerked the bridle from the boy's hand and took off at a full gallop, his long, lean legs covering ground.

Behind him, I saw it, a sudden puff of vapor in the air up the wadi and behind it a rolling sound like thunder. Somewhere, perhaps hundreds of miles away, a violent rainstorm had broken, and now all that water came roaring down the narrow channel of the wadi straight toward the camp.

The boy groom shouted, and I saw one of the King's squires turn around.

Slowly, so slowly as though we all moved underwater, I saw Sati lift her head, saw her brows knit together.

I ran. I always ran. In this dream as in life I ran so slowly, so end-lessly slowly.

She dropped the pot, the precious lentils spilling on the ground. I saw her scoop Sikander onto her hip, saw his mouth open in a startled wail.

I ran. I ran toward them, straight toward the wave high as temples that crashed down, tossing horses in the picket lines like straws, tents and men and all. I ran straight toward the wave and Sati ran toward me, Sikander on her hip.

My arm closed around her and the baby, and the wave broke, her mouth open in a soundless scream.

The water tore me loose and threw me hard against something, the weight of my steel breastplate holding me down. Holding me under-water. Holding me underwater.


I woke gasping for breath stretched beside Bagoas and struggled up from covers and pillows.

I sat on the side of the bed and buried my face in my hands.

Bagoas said nothing, just put his arm around my back, and when I said nothing began to stroke the back of my neck. I wondered how often he had done this before, and for whom.

"I can never get there any faster," I whispered. "No matter how many times I do it, I never get there any faster."

"You never will," he said.

"I know," I said. Even in my dreams I would know that was not true. "They were burned on a pyre with the other dead, their ashes scattered to the desert winds." I bent my head. "I should have died. I should have died too."

"You were simply lucky," Bagoas said. "As was I." He had been there too. But he was not a child and he could swim.

"I am not sure that I am lucky," I said. "I am not sure I would have wanted to live."

"If you had not, who would remember them?" Bagoas asked.

Tears fell from my eyes. "No one," I said. Who in all the world would mourn the passing of a bad-luck bride, of a baby who lived ten months under the sun, who was nothing to anyone except me, because he was my son? Who would ever remember them?

"Their memory would blow like their ashes except for you," Bagoas said. "So you must live and remember, and perhaps one day tell another son of his brother that was, that he may pour a libation too."

"I will never have another son," I choked. "I will never marry again."

"You should," Bagoas said, his hands working gently on the back of my neck. "You need someone to take care of you."

"I do not," I said.

Bagoas chuckled. "Yes, you do. You should find a good woman to take care of you. You are meant for a family."

"And you?"

Bagoas shrugged. "What has that to do with us?"

"I know it's usual, but it seems so very complicated." I lay back down at his urging, and he leaned across my back, his long hair brushing my shoulders. Most men had a wife and a lover both, but I had no idea how I would find the energy. It seemed hard to manage both at once without bad feeling and neglecting one or the other. It was on the tip of my tongue to mention Alexander and Roxane, but I thought better of it.

"I am not looking for a patron," Bagoas said, stretching. "I don't want that."

"I know," I said. Like Thais, he had his pride, and would come and go as he pleased. Like Ptolemy, I respected that.

I did not suppose he had ever had the choosing of it before, to say yes or no as he wished. I could not imagine that the King had been unkind, but he was the King, and one does not say no.

"Perhaps Ptolemy can find someone for you," he said. "I imagine he would if you asked him."

"I'm not about to ask Ptolemy for a bride," I said, but I wondered. Who but me should remember, and should I be the last? Did I have any love left to offer a young woman, a new baby? I would not want to marry and give her nothing except memories and bitterness.

"Maybe something will come up," Bagoas said. He pressed his lips to my shoulder.

"Maybe it will," I said. It seemed less wrong to put those things on Bagoas, who understood sorrow, and who was anything except young and innocent. If he could bear my scars, I would bear his.

In truth, we did not fit badly. If he found me mild and yielding, he did not complain of it. Rather he seemed to enjoy leading instead of following, playing the lover rather than the beloved. It has always been my nature to yield rather than conquer, much to the amusement and pleasure of Sati, who was at first amazed that I was not done in ten minutes, but barely begun. Bagoas, slower to pleasure by virtue of his situation, did not seem to find it amiss either.

"Don't worry so much," he said, and ruffled my hair. "You have plenty of time for all of that."

"I suppose so," I said, and wondered if I did. I had grown used to never counting the days ahead. What would happen if I did count them again, if I did say to myself, I shall do such and such in the spring? If I began to imagine a future in which the seasons turned and I were still living? Months, even years, might pass and I might live.

I laid my head down against the pillow. I did not know if I could begin that.

"Perdiccas will not come for many months," Bagoas said. "Did you not say that yourself?"

"I did," I said.

"Well, then." He lay beside me, his arm about my shoulders. "Then you have so long and you know it. Nothing will happen until then."

"That is true," I said. A few months. I could decide to live until Perdiccas came. I turned, and took him in my arms.

It was ten days later, on a day when Ptolemy had no need of me, that I found my way to the temples of Memphis again. This time I did not go the Temple of Thoth, but along the walls of the city where they rose forty feet from the surface of the river. To the west I could see the temples at Saqqara, on the edge of the desert above broad cultivated lands, lush and green with date palms. There was a lake there as well, fed by irrigation canals, where the white birds sacred to Ptah lived. A little ferry boat was at midstream, running back and forth as it always did across the expanse of the Nile. The river was deep and swift opposite the city, though upstream there was an island where the waterbirds nested.

The walls of Memphis were high at this point, and gave a good view. Just a little farther along was the Temple of Sobek, where they kept the sacred crocodiles.

There was a broad rail high as a man's chest carved with warning signs, but I could lean on it and look over at the monstrous animals in the temple pool below that gave through a grate on the Nile. Beneath the green water, scales and snouts broke the surface. One monster drew himself up on land to bask in the sun on the sandy bank provided for them. He was at least three times a man's height in length, but not slow for all that.

"They are the avengers," a voice said behind me, and I turned.

Manetho had come up, and he stood looking over the rail beside me. He looked very young for his pleated white linen, his serious expression.

"The avengers?"

"Sobek is the god of justice," Manetho said. "They are dangerous, of course. Justice is dangerous. It is a sword with two blades, and may cut the man who wields it as well."

I nodded gravely.

"You go here," Manetho said, "not the brothels or taverns? Instead you come to temples?"

I shrugged. "Why should I spend my time in brothels or taverns?"

"For the same reasons most men do." Manetho's face was mild.

"Everyone seems so concerned with finding me a woman," I said.

Manetho laughed. "What is it that you want, then?"

"Nothing you can give me," I said.

He nodded slowly. His eyes were a priest's eyes, calm and impenetrable. "Perhaps the Black Land can give you something, Lydias of Miletus. Perhaps it is Isis whose gifts you need, the Lady of Amenti with Her mercy."

"I don't know," I said, and looked down into the pool of crocodiles. I wondered if he could tell me what it meant that I had wielded the powers of Egypt on the road, that I had seen the Dead City. But I did not know if I could trust him yet.

Manetho pushed back from the rail. "Tell Ptolemy that the gods will not wait forever. He must decide." And with that he strode away, his shaven head gleaming in the sun.

WE DID NOT have much time at all. It was only a few days later that a messenger came to Memphis with all haste. He had slipped out of the port of Tyre at night on a fishing boat belonging to his brother, hoping for vast rewards. He got them, as Ptolemy needed his news badly.

Perdiccas was in Tyre with his army.

Ptolemy rubbed his brow and laid it out, while I and Artashir and Nicanor and several others tried to read the dispatch upside down. "Ten thousand infantry. Two thousand cavalry. Forty elephants. A thousand horse archers."

I caught Artashir's eye and saw him grimace. He commanded fifty, all that we still had. With the losses I had taken stealing the hearse, even with our wounded who were recovering, I didn't think we could field more than seven hundred cavalry, and perhaps not quite that. Our infantry phalanxes were in better condition. We had eight thousand. And no elephants.

"We're going to have to wear him down a little bit at a time," Ptolemy said. "Use our natural defenses."

"The river," I said.

Ptolemy nodded. "He'll have to come by road to Pelousion if he wants to cross the first branch of the Nile. And the fortress at Pelousion guards the crossing and the river mouth."

"If he has to besiege Pelousion he has a problem," Artashir said. "It doesn't matter how much he outnumbers us in elephants or cavalry or horse archers. They're not going to be any use to him."

"The defenses of Pelousion are good," I said.

Ptolemy nodded again. "And that's where we're going to meet him. Artashir will go to Camel's Fort, halfway up the Nile from Pelousion to Memphis, as our rearguard. The rest of us will go on to Pelousion. Lydias, you have the cavalry."

I opened my mouth and shut it again, my maimed hand plain on the table.

"It doesn't matter," Ptolemy said, and his brown eyes were calm. "Put Glaukos in the front of the charge if you must. But you have the cavalry."

"Yes, sir," I said, and blinked lest I tear up.

Though what cavalry should do behind the walls of Pelousion I didn't know. Scouting, I presumed. We would be the eyes and ears of the army.

I REJOINED MY command at Pelousion at the beginning of the summer, when the crops were in and the Inundation still weeks away. The Delta steamed under the midday sun, the river running slow and sluggish, shrunken by the season. When Sothis rose again in the dawn sky, so the river would rise.

Glaukos took one look at my hand, still withered and twisted-looking. "Well, you fucked that up pretty good!"

"I did," I said and came and pounded him on the back. "How've you been? Up to a tangle with Perdiccas?"

"Is it true we're outnumbered three to one?"

I shook my head. "No, you know how rumor is. Not even two to one, though he's got elephants."

Glaukos cursed long and fluently. "I hate elephants. Did I tell you about the time that Alexander sent me to get some?"

"Yes," I said quickly. "You did. So how are we looking?"

"Six hundred and ninety-six men mounted and well. Ninety-seven, counting you." He looked at my hand again dubiously.

"You're taking the point," I said. "I can't ride and use a sword at the same time yet. But Perdiccas isn't going to wait for me!"

At that he laughed as I'd meant him to. "Well, I suppose we can manage. All the real work for me, of course."

"But with my brains and your brawn…" I grinned.

"We'll get by," Glaukos said. "Of course we're probably going to all get trampled by elephants. You know that, right? When Perdiccas was in Babylon he couldn't get a bunch of the old Macedonians to go along with his plans, so he had three hundred of them rounded up and trampled to death by elephants. Put the rest of the army on notice, it did."

I'd missed that story, being in Memphis on leave and with Ptolemy rather than in the hotbed of army gossip. "That helped morale a lot, I expect."

Glaukos laughed. "It shut them up, anyway! He's a hard man to serve under. Always was."

"That's not how you bind men to you," I said. "Alexander never did it."

"Oh, Alexander," Glaukos said. "Alexander never had to."

Three years, I thought. It had been three years since Glaukos and I had ridden from Babylon, from Alexander's bier. Had we changed so much in so short a time? Now we faced one another, Companion against Companion.


A GREAT ARMY cannot conceal its passing, and Perdiccas did not try to. From the time they passed Gaza we knew exactly where they were, and how many miles they were making with each day's march. We could guess to a day when they would appear at the opening out of the wadis, looking across the great floodplain of the river delta to Pelousion.

"They'd have more trouble if the river were up," Glaukos said gloomily.

"The river won't rise for a couple of weeks," I said. We waited while they came ever closer, but I knew that road all too well. They would come to us long before the Nile could swell. "Besides, they still can't ford it here." The Nile might be broken into several main branches in the Delta, but the great eastward branch that flowed into the sea at Pelousion was never shallower than a man's height, even at the peak of the dry season. It could not be forded except at Pelousion, where the pharaohs of old had built causeways and bridges. And the fortress guarded those passes.

In that day the walls of Pelousion were thirty feet high, and though they were built in an antique style they were stout. They were not quite vertical, but had a slight beetling, each course of stone set slightly out from the one beneath it, so that if a man attempted to scale it he would be overtopped by the wall above. It also made things much trickier for scaling ladders, as the bases must then be set some distance out from the walls and would have no stability at the bottom, as they would only touch the wall at the top. These were by no means inconsequential obstacles.

The weak point was the gates, which were exceptionally wide and held with bronze doors bound with iron. But there was only one set of them. There were no inner courtyards or series of walls and gates — just the main gate that gave into Pelousion. It was there that we must concentrate our men defending it, just as that must be the point where Perdiccas would seek an advantage.

Fortunately, there were strong flanking towers, and we had some Egyptian bowmen who, while not the speedy Persian horse archers Perdiccas had, were very competent soldiers though they could not possibly withstand a charge or a marching phalanx, clad as they were in linen and armed only with bows. From the walls of a fortress they could still do considerable damage. It was for that reason that Ptolemy had sent some of them south with Artashir to the fort at Camel's Fort, as that was the next fordable place along the river. We had to guard our backs as well.

We waited and we waited. Each day my scouts reported in. Perdiccas was closer. I knew it in my bones the day he passed the boundary stones, the day he entered Egypt. I thought, from the edgy way he seemed at dinner, that Ptolemy knew too. The gods had offered him a bargain. Was it now too late? Had he decided to reject it?

I thought not. I thought that Ptolemy was cautious, and he would try this first by his own strength of arms, resorting to any other power only if that failed him.

Some of our scouts, the cleverest men, were given special instructions to slip into Perdiccas' camp at night and pass among the fires listening to rumors and spreading some of their own. It was true, they said, that Ptolemy had offered a bonus to any of Alexander's men who would leave Perdiccas and come to him—a year's pay and a house of their own in Alexandria, the same terms his men had been offered. No hard feelings. If they came to Ptolemy they would be welcomed as brothers with no questions asked.

One of our scouts mistakenly tried this among the Silver Shields, Alexander's oldest veterans, and was killed for his pains, but another came back with twenty men.

They had a great deal of news. I sat at Ptolemy's council when they told it out. Perdiccas had brought Roxane and the child with him.

"He is afraid to leave them in Babylon," the man said. "They are the focus of so many plots and upheavals. He didn't dare to leave them while he marched on Egypt, so he has brought them with him, the King's mother and the baby king."

Ptolemy nodded gravely, but I saw his jaw clench. He must be two and a half now, this baby boy Alexander had never seen, Ptolemy's nephew, cousin to Chloe and Lagos and Leontiscus. The most valuable blood prize in the world.

And his mother, who had murdered Queen Stateira before Alexander's body was cold.

"No one is to touch them," Ptolemy said. "Is that clear?"

I nodded. "Surely Perdiccas will keep them well back from the fighting. They are too important to him."

"If we had the boy and his mother..." one of the men began.

"Then we would have what?" I asked. "A deadly woman we must keep prisoner while she plots?"

"Why keep her?" Glaukos asked, scratching his chin. "It's the boy that matters."

"And would we win the loyalty of a child by killing his mother or keeping her from him? Would that not result in raising a sovereign who would hate us, and who eventually would wield power in his own right against his jailers?" I snapped back.

Ptolemy held up a hand. "Peace," he said. "Gentlemen, this debate is fruitless. Perdiccas is the Regent, not I. And Roxane is his ally, not his prisoner. There is no point in beating this about." Yet I saw he was troubled.

As we left the meeting Glaukos walked next to me. "If we win he's got to kill the boy," Glaukos whispered. "Anything else is too dangerous."

"Ptolemy will not do that," I said. I was certain of that, but of little else.

A FEW MORE deserters trickled in. We knew where they were. And by now they knew where we were. The fortress at Pelousion must weigh heavily on Perdiccas. Ptolemy issued warnings for all the farmers of the plain nearby to evacuate or come into the fortress, and to bring their seed grain with them. If they left it, it would be food for Perdiccas' elephants, and they would have nothing to plant with when the flood receded.

We watched and drilled and waited.

My hand improved some little measure. I could hold something in it if it were still and not heavy. But I knew I could not control a horse in battle. Not yet. Perhaps never.

And then they were there.

We watched from the walls of Pelousion as they came down out of the wadis, spreading across the plain in a great crowd, Companion Cavalry at a bright trot ahead, a full Ile scouting before the main body. I thought I knew Polemon, mounted on the same black horse.

The numbers we had received were right. Two thousand cavalry, a thousand horse archers. Ten thousand infantry. In the center, like mighty islands topped with platforms manned by archers, were forty proud elephants come with their handlers from Raja Puru in the plain of the Indus as allies of the Great King.

"I hate elephants," Glaukos said.

"I know," I said. "You think I enjoyed the Battle of the Hydaspes any more than you did?" I was not looking forward to cavalry on elephants ever again.

That night they camped before the walls of Pelousion. In evening Perdiccas himself was seen riding around, trying to get a look at the defenses. Our archers shot at him when he got too close, and he withdrew to his camp.

In the morning they started digging. It took us several days to see what they were doing, as they were too far from our walls to have any chance of sapping them. Instead they were trying to reopen an old canal from the Nile, hoping to divert part of the river and hence drop the water level in the main channel to a fordable level. If they could ford the Nile without passing under the walls of Pelousion, there would be no need to take the fortress at all.

"Cavalry," Ptolemy said.

Of course it would have to be. A night sortie of three hundred men could fall upon their scaffolding and burn their supports and sluice gates, break through their embankments and destroy their work. They might even get back to the fortress before they were surrounded, if they were lucky.

I nodded. "I'll lead it myself."

"You won't," Ptolemy said. He saw my stubborn look and went on in a low voice, looking out over the camp where it lay. "Lydias, you know it will be hot work and every man must fight. You can't. You'll slow your men down, and if you are killed or wounded again you will deprive me of a man I need."

"I cannot be such a coward as to stay here on the walls while my men fight!" I said.

"You are a general, and you may not do just as you like," Ptolemy said, and I saw the white lines around his mouth. "You must do your duty instead." He put his hand on my arm. "You will have your time, Lydias, before this is done. Do not waste yourself on the first engagement."

"Yes, sir," I said.

I watched from the walls while half of my men, under Glaukos, made the sortie. We opened the gates of Pelousion in the hour before dawn, and the men rushed upon the siege works with torches streaming. It was impossible to tell what was happening, and I paced back and forth along the wall, knocking my hand against the stones.

"Now you know what I was when you were stealing the hearse," Ptolemy said. He sounded amused.

"You were worried?"

"Of course I was. With the fate of everything resting on you, far away with no idea what you were doing or whether or not you would succeed? Of course I was nervous. Do you think I wouldn't rather have gone myself?"

"Why didn't you?"

Ptolemy shook his head, looking out into the darkness where the bright flare of torches marked our men. "Because I had to govern Egypt. I couldn't afford to spend months riding up and down the coast with the hearse, with no other plans if that failed, out of communication from Alexandria and Memphis both. There was far too much to do."

I nodded. I could understand that, I supposed. Alexander had governed from the field, but who else was Alexander? And perhaps, I thought, he would have governed better if he hadn't, and we would not now face a disintegrating empire.

"Look there!" Ptolemy said, pointing. "I think they are coming back."

It did look as though some of the shadows moving against the fires were larger, though no flames were closer. Of course not. They would have thrown down their torches when they turned for home, the better to minimize the targets in the dark. Glaukos was no green boy either.

I ran down to the courtyard to watch them come in on blown horses, a few clinging to the backs of their mounts despite arrow wounds. One lovely Nisean chestnut came in with his rider, all game and heart, a huge arrow lodged in the shoulder of his right foreleg. I didn't know how he could run, but he had. His rider was dismounted and beside him in a moment, his body pressed to the horse's side, shouting for the grooms and the horse doctor.

Glaukos pulled up next to me, blowing hard. "We got it, I think. Hard to tell in the dark, but we burned all the wooden pilings and I don't know where they'll get more in this country. Wrecked their diggings as much as we could. I had to get out of there fast, though. Before the infantry could get between us and Pelousion." He slid down from his horse.

"You did right," I said, clapping him on the shoulder. "Your job was to wreck the works, not engage the infantry."

Ptolemy had come up beside me. "Any idea what your losses were?"

"Not yet," Glaukos said. "I couldn't see a fucking thing."

"Let's form up and get a count," I said.

In the end I was pleasantly surprised. We'd only lost three men outright, though we had twenty who wouldn't be fit for a fight anytime soon, and thirty-six horses lamed or injured.

When the sun rose we got a look at the results. The fire had spread from the works to the stored timber, and as Glaukos had said, I didn't see how they would replace it in Egypt. Large trees do not really grow here, and they had brought their bridging timbers from Lebanon.

From the walls Ptolemy and I saw Perdiccas inspecting the damage as well, his gilded breastplate unmistakable even from a distance. We watched from above, untouchable on the walls of Pelousion.

"That's bought us some time," I said with satisfaction.

Ptolemy nodded, but his eyes did not leave Perdiccas. "Yes. But it hasn't bought us victory. We have to defeat him, not just hold even. And I don't see how to do that yet."

"Neither do I," I said.

# ALEXANDER'S LEGACY

The next morning I was awakened abruptly before dawn by a boy I didn't recognize, but I gathered by his manner that he was one of the new squires. "Sir? Hipparch Lydias? General Ptolemy wants you immediately."

I sat up, shaking the sleep from my head. A glance at the window showed me that the sky had just begun to lighten. "Where's Ptolemy? Has he called to arms?" If he had I had not heard it, nor any of the bustle that should accompany the whole garrison turning out.

"On the walls, sir. And he's not called to arms, just sent me to get you."

That was better, I thought, throwing my chiton over my head but not stopping for harness and helmet.

The last stars were still showing as I mounted the stairs to the wall, but the east showed flushes of pink. Ptolemy was standing at a parapet, looking toward Perdiccas' camp. He said nothing, just waited for me to see.

They were gone. The last of their campfires were dying to ashes, while around them the camp stood empty except for the inevitable rubbish and garbage left behind by an army.

"Gone," I said.

Ptolemy shook his head, a gesture both respectful and annoyed. "Perdiccas is good, Lydias. I'd forgotten how good. If he couldn't crack Pelousion he has better sense than to sit here."

"Up the Nile," I said.

Ptolemy took a breath. "Up the Nile, looking for the next fordable place. And the river is still low."

"Camel's Fort," I said, thinking quickly. "Just above Phakussa. As he well knows. He and some of his men were here with Alexander too."

"He's held back to his infantry's pace, and the elephants won't be fast." Ptolemy turned, running his hand through the thinning hair on his forehead. "They'll be traveling up the eastern bank. I want you out of here by midmorning with all the cavalry. Go straight up the western bank to Camel's Fort and reinforce Artashir. I'll be right behind you with the infantry. You'll get there ahead of him, and the gods willing so will we. You know where he's going, don't you?"

"Memphis," I said, and I knew it in my bones. He had to recover the King's body, and Memphis was the key to Egypt. Perdiccas would not waste time taking border towns when the real prize lay before him. He had learned from Alexander too.

"Memphis," Ptolemy said. "So get going, Lydias. Leave your wounded and dismounted men in Pelousion. They'll be fine here. I'll see you at Camel's Fort tomorrow."

I ran for steel and harness, calling for someone to fetch me Glaukos. Tomorrow. Only if Ptolemy attached wings to the infantry, I thought. It was a day's ride or more down to Camel's Fort and the town of Phakussa, and the road was not the best, which was why everyone went by boat if they could. There was a good road immediately south of Pelousion, but halfway along it turned west to Tanis and Bubastis, on the next easternmost branch of the Nile. Those were much larger cities than Phakussa, which largely served as a shipping center for river traffic from Pelousion to Memphis, and as a market for local farmers.

I could beat Perdiccas to Phakussa. I was sure of that. An all-cavalry force could move, even on bad roads. Artashir had archers there. What we would lack was the heavy infantry, the very thing you need to defend a fort.

And Camel's Fort was not Pelousion.

The old pharaohs had built mighty walls at Avaris and Tanis, and even Bubastis had some serious defenses. Those had been the bulwarks of the Black Land. Camel's Fort had been built by Nectanebo II when he resisted the Persians, and was little more than a guardpost on the western bank of the river just above the country town of Phakussa. The outer wall was nothing but a palisade of wood with sharp ends stuck out of the ground surrounding a small fort of mud brick on stone foundations. It was not a place one would pick for a battle.

WE RODE. AT noon we passed through the town of Sile, at the base of the lake the easternmost branch of the Nile makes as it comes toward the sea. Yes, the townsmen said, a great army had passed in the early hours of the morning on the opposite bank. Two ferrymen had been detained by them, their little boat on the other side of the river. The commander had wanted to send scouts across, but the boat was not big enough for horses.

I shook my head, not even dismounting. That was what I would do—put a few scouts across on horseback to ride ahead and see what we had at Camel's Fort. "I thank the Lady of the Nile that your boat was too small," I said.

The ferryman's eyes widened, and he said something to his fellow in rapid Egyptian that I did not catch. But I could guess what it was.

"I honor Her too," I said. "Aset, Isis the Lady of Egypt. Now we must ride."

With the thunder of six hundred and fifty horses we swept out of Sile, on the road south.

AFTERNOON BROUGHT US to Daphnae, which stood on the eastern bank. I called a halt and shouted out to a man fishing in a little reed boat hardly big enough for one. He turned fearfully and paddled in the opposite direction, looking over his shoulder nervously.

"They've already been," Glaukos said. "Look there. Those fields near the river."

On the other shore were empty fields, the last of the harvest long since cleaned up, waiting for the Inundation. Just below Daphnae they were littered with dead fires of dung, the smooth fields dug and hummocked where an army had been. This was their camp. They had rested here a few hours, since they had marched all night. We were less than six hours behind them.

"Ride!" I said.

Ⲛow the road curved away from the river, bending westward to Tanis and then south to Bubastis. There was a track along the river of course, but it was muddy and rutted, with tall palms shading it and crowding toward the water. We could not go at a trot, but had to walk in single file.

My horse stepped in a hole and came up lame, so I had to trade with a trooper who would lead her behind.

I chafed at the delay.

Still, before sunset we came up with them and from across the broad water I could see them at last. This was what we had looked like when we marched into India. This was what we had been. The dying sun glinted off the tips of each long sarissa, the infantry phalanxes marching in perfect order. The elephants swayed along, ten between each phalanx, caparisoned with crimson and gold, drivers on their necks watchful. The Persian infantry marched in good order, spears at the ready. Before them came the horse archers, wearing silk and leather, their bows slung at their backs, their beautiful horses dancing. And in front, away from the elephants, Companion Cavalry, the exact match of us. There was Polemon and Attalos, there Seleucus and Appolion.

And they saw us, of course. I knew Polemon was saying, "There is Lydias and Glaukos too."

I wished there might be peace between us. But peace is harder to make than war.

They could see we were not the main body, just a little more than six hundred men. They did not stop or break ranks, shout or jeer. They kept to their business. And so did we.

"Do we camp tonight?" Glaukos asked, shouldering forward in the line on his big horse.

"No," I said. "As soon as we get out of sight of them we'll stop for three hours and rest the horses and eat. Then we'll ride through the night. That should put us there in the early morning and then the horses can rest all they like inside the fort."

Another night, another night ride. This time it was not the bare red walls of the wadis that looked down upon us, the dark of the Red Land. We rode through the Delta at night, a full moon rising golden above us, large as an apple, looking near enough to touch. Palm trees blew in the wind, their leaves making a soft sound. We rode through little villages, dogs and sleepy children starting up as we came, their parents pulling them back inside as we passed through like spirits. Beside us, the river ran northward, hungry for the sea and Pelousion, the last few miles of a journey that had spanned who knew how far, from distant jungles no man had mapped. Above us, the moon rose high at last, cool and clear at its zenith.

Gods rode with us, not almost made flesh and shadow as they had been in that last mad ride with the hearse, but as a presence scarcely felt, a wind at my back, a whisper behind me.

*Are you afraid, Lydias?* the lioness whispered. *Do not be.*

"I am not afraid, Lady," I said. "Perdiccas has brought a Persian army onto Egyptian soil. It is your cause as well as our own we serve."

*Son of Egypt, you are home,* She whispered, and I knew it was true. I had dreamed this place, yearned for it though I never knew its name. Avaris and Tanis, Bubastis and Sais, Heliopolis and Memphis, I could call the Delta home. Alexandria.

As the eastern sky flushed with dawn Orion the Hunter slipped over the horizon, but the Dogs were not quite clear. Sothis stayed just out of sight.

*It is not quite time,* She whispered. *Nine days. You must give us nine days.* And for a moment, dozing on my horse, I saw the world from above, the sharp line of the Nile cutting like a rich green serpent through the Red Land, leaping down from the cataracts, twining back on itself as it twisted through the deserts of Nubia far to the south. I saw it as though I stood aloft on the wind, higher than hawk ever flew. Green lands, emerald beneath a hot sun, waterfalls plunging down in cascades of spume. Clouds gathering above the green lands, the first plump drops of rain falling, shivering on long green leaves. *Nine days,* She whispered, *nine days for the river to rise.*

"Nine days."

*You must give us nine days, my son,* She whispered. *And you will have your miracle.*

The sun rose golden in the east, the indigo sky rolling back before its mighty passage. And we rode.

WE CLATTERED INTO Camel's Fort in the first hour of the day.

"Walk your horses, damn it!" Glaukos was yelling as we dismounted. "Don't you turn them at those troughs yet! They'll be sick, every fucking one! Walk them, you witless wonders!"

I smiled and left him at it, going to find Artashir.

Who was as tremendously pleased to find that Perdiccas' entire army was coming down upon him as one might expect.

Artashir came up with some Persian curses that were completely new to me. "And Ptolemy's on the road?"

"He's on the road with the infantry," I confirmed. "He started just behind me, but there's no way he can be here until day after tomorrow."

"And you think we'll have Perdiccas tomorrow."

I nodded. "They were at Daphnae yesterday. I think they'll be here late tomorrow."

Artashir steepled his hands, resting his fingers on his short, trimmed beard. "If they keep a good pace," he said. "I don't think Perdiccas will send his men into an attack straight off a full day's march, do you?"

"I doubt it," I said. "I wouldn't. I especially wouldn't once I saw how lousy the fortifications were here."

"I know they are," Artashir snapped. "But what do you think I can do about it? Build a stone curtain wall in a week? I've repaired the palisades and put up cavalry traps around the sides, and laid in food for five thousand for a month."

"Or ten thousand for half a month," I said.

"How big do you think this place is?" Artashir demanded. "Look around you, Lydias. It's a squeeze to get ten thousand in here, and we're going to have a serious sanitation problem if we're all in here even half so long. This is not Pelousion!"

I put my hand to my brow. "Forgive me, Artashir," I said. "I did not mean to belittle your work. I have been riding all night and am not at my best. You have done all that can be done in a short time, and I thank you for it."

"We can't hold Perdiccas here," Artashir said. "It's not built for it. We might withstand one good attack. We can make him bleed some. But we can't win it here."

"I see that," I said.

"When Ptolemy gets here, you and I need to get out," Artashir said. "Horse archers are no use in a siege, and neither is cavalry. We need to leave the infantry and Egyptian archers in the fort and get out on the east bank, where we can harry Perdiccas' army."

"The problem with that is that he's got more horse archers and cavalry than we have," I said.

"Yes, well." Artashir grinned. "Who wants to live forever?"

"We only need to delay them nine days," I said, and Her words sounded like a bell in my mind.

"What happens in nine days?" Artashir looked perplexed.

I shook my head. "Nothing in particular. But I think your plan sounds good. As soon as Ptolemy gets here we'll lay it out."

"Agreed," Artashir said.


Ptolemy arrived at the same time as Perdiccas, having force-marched his infantry through two nights with only four-hour halts each night. The last ten hours they had seen Perdiccas' army on the other side of the river, and both armies had marched in sight of the other.

Ptolemy looked exhausted, but he sat down with me, Artashir, and the infantry commanders while his men found quarters in the fort and turned in. On the other side of the river Perdiccas' men were making camp.

"The race wore them out too," Ptolemy said, a ghost of his old grin on his face. "We kept the pressure on. We're too tired to go at it tonight, but so are they."

"And you have rested men here and he doesn't," Artashir said, gesturing to the boy who brought around watered wine that had been chilling in the lowest and coolest storeroom. The scent of roasting duck wafted up from the ovens. We sat around a table in the Persian style, but the olives and goat cheese brought around with fresh bread was pure Greek.

"Many thanks for that," Ptolemy said, as the infantry commanders dug right in. "No good food for a few days makes you appreciate it."

I looked at Artashir and him at me. It was his idea, but I might be closer to Ptolemy. Go on, I tried to signal him, you should have the credit.

"There is little use for horse archers or cavalry in a fortress," Artashir said. "I have been wondering if it would not be better for Lydias and myself to quit the fort and cross the river so that we can harass Perdiccas' army while it sits encamped."

Ptolemy nodded thoughtfully, chewing on a piece of bread. "And how would you get across, with Perdiccas now encamped on the opposite side?"

"We would have to leave under cover of night," I said. "If we continue upriver to just short of where the Bubasite branch of the Nile splits, we could get across there and come back on the eastern side. It's not a proper ford, but it's shallow except for the main channel and we could swim the horses there."

"That takes you nearly to Bubastis." Ptolemy frowned. "That's a long way out of the way. And how do you know whether it's shallow or not?"

"I remember that when we brought the hearse this way on a barge from Pelousion that the bargemen said that in the dry season it was shallow enough to cross except for the main channel, and that boats must take care not to run aground. How should I not remember where it was?"

Ptolemy looked amused. "I must remember that you have enough Egyptian to chat with the bargemen! That's useful."

"It won't take us more than a full night to get up there," Artashir said. "We can be back and working on them by midafternoon."

"On tired horses when they outnumber you with fresh cavalry?"

I spread my hands. "We wait. We rest. We fall on them the next night. And while he'll send some cavalry after us, Perdiccas won't dare chase us in force, lest we be a diversion for you making a sortie from the fort. If you and your men rest tonight, we can be gone tonight and troubling them tomorrow night."

"And if Perdiccas attacks tomorrow, you're my late afternoon relief," Ptolemy said, reaching for another piece of bread. "He won't know what you are or that you're not the advance guard of another force, so he'll break off if he's engaged so as not to face two fronts." He took a bite. "I like it."

That would buy us two days, I thought. Today and tomorrow, the first two of the nine days' run. I said nothing about that, but I believed it. How could I not believe it in my bones?

A T DAWN WE halted just outside Bubastis and rested horses and men. Another dawn, another morning when I had not seen a bed.

The sun rose livid out of the Nile. A white ibis started up from the reeds beside the road, spreading his pale wings. The smoke from the cooking fires of Bubastis stained the sky, rising from temple and town. We rested for two hours and then crossed the river.

The current was very slow, and for most of the way across the water came only to my horse's shoulder. Midstream there was a channel that was a little deeper, and we had to swim the horses for perhaps five or six lengths before their feet found purchase again.

"Look out for that," Glaukos said, as along the opposite bank several medium-sized crocodiles lowered themselves into the water.

"I can take care of that," Artashir said, taking the bow from his back and drawing it with a single smooth motion. An arrow flashed, hitting one of the crocodiles that had just splashed into the shallows. Blood blossomed in the water, the wounded crocodile thrashing madly, the arrow standing out from the top of its head.

"Nice shot," I said.

Artashir bowed from the saddle. "My pleasure."

The other crocodiles turned about, drawn by the blood in the water, attacking their wounded fellow.

"Get everybody ashore as fast as you can," I said. I leaned back, looking over my shoulder. "Come on! Get on with it!"

Several more crocodiles splashed in, but Artashir's horse archers fired to good effect, and we all reached the shore entirely without casualties, though my horse was sweating and jumping.

Later, I rode beside Artashir near the front of the column. The sun was hot, and my chiton dried to my skin beneath my breastplate, which seemed hot enough to cook on. I envied Artashir his light silks and leathers. The Persian horse archers did not wear steel.

"A long way from Babylon," he said, shading his eyes with one hand and looking ahead to where Perdiccas' men must now besiege our fort.

"A long way," I said.

Artashir looked up at a movement, but it was only a hawk turning slowly on the wing over the lands of the Delta. "I swore my oaths to Alexander at Ecbatana," he said softly. "Before that, I was just one of the men, following my kinsman, Oxathres, as was my duty." Artashir looked at me sideways. "We expected to die. We were the conquered, and we expected that Alexander would behave as a conqueror does. That he embraced Oxathres as a brother, that he ruled as Great King for the good of Persia as well, was something entirely unexpected. It cost him, of course. How could it not?"

"Not more than he was willing to pay," I said.

Artashir nodded. "No, not more. And that is the thing I still do not understand. When so many of his own men hated that he treated us as civilized people, not barbarians, when they hated and resented our officers taking their place among them, he still persisted."

"Perhaps it was only common sense," I said. "After all, the Persian Empire is vast. If Oxathres and others had not made peace we should still be at war, trying to put down one rebellion after another. Alexander wanted to be Great King. Once he was and was recognized as such, why then should he make war on his own subjects or take what was theirs? Is it not better to be given allegiance freely, and have a proud people as allies rather than enemies?"

"You may think so," Artashir said, "but very few of your countrymen agree. They saw Persia as a source of rich spoils, and still do. They were incensed when Alexander took Princess Stateira as his wife, that he should mingle his blood with that of the Achaemenids."

"They are not my countrymen," I said. "Remember, I am no part of Macedon, Artashir. I am Carian, and perhaps Greek if you stretch a point of blood. But I am no more Macedonian than you."

"Ptolemy is," Artashir said.

"And so was Alexander," I replied. "So it is not about Macedon. It is about two different kinds of men, and I think those are found in any land."

Artashir sighed. "Yes, there are certainly those in Persia who hate that which is not of us. And I see that they have had the governing of Egypt recently and have made our names a curse throughout the Black Land. But it was not always thus, you know. Darius the Great ruled Egypt fairly and well, and his wife Artystone was the daughter of an Egyptian princess from Sais. It was only his descendants who became so hated, in lesser days when weaker men ruled. And they ruled Persia as poorly as Egypt."

My eyebrows rose. I had never heard Artashir criticize the Great Kings, even obliquely.

"Even though we are taught to reject the Lie, and to worship the

Truth as Auramazda created it, there are always men who do not. Evil exists, my friend, whether we like it or not. And more often than not it is petty evil, the selfishness of men for more than that which they deserve, but it is the Lie all the same." Artashir shrugged, his hands on his reins. "When I saw Alexander, and knew how he was, that he had spared the family of Darius and that he opposed Bessos the usurper who had killed Darius by treachery, I said, there is one who serves the Truth. And whatever his country, I am on his side for I am choosing the side of Truth. In Ecbatana I made my own oaths."

I swallowed. "Before or after Hephaistion died?"

Artashir looked at me sideways. "Before, of course," he said. "There was no after."

"Do you think it was poison?" I asked.

Artashir was silent a moment, swaying slightly with the movement of his walking horse. "No. Yes. Who knows? He had enemies enough, but a poison that takes so long to kill and is so much like illnesses many others have had? It does not matter why he died, only that he did."

"If Hephaistion had not died, perhaps the empire would not have crumbled."

"And perhaps Roxane would have killed him with Queen Stateira," Artashir said grimly. "Or Perdiccas, wanting the Regency."

"I think he was harder to kill than that," I said. It made my chest ache still. We had been at the games. The boys' footrace had ended, and a messenger came for the King, saying that he must come at once. I sat in my seat, watching Alexander hurry after the squire, feeling the sudden sense of foreboding that comes when something turns, something goes terribly wrong.

"We painted the roofs black," Artashir said, still in his own memory. "All those pitched roofs, each one painted another brilliant color, golds and reds and purples and greens, the great summer palace of Darius the Great. We painted all the roofs black in mourning. The King said to, that we should do it in memory of Hephaistion."

"I remember," I said. "It was a beautiful palace before then."

"It still is," Artashir said. "It should have stayed a place of joy."

"Yes," I said, and for a moment I could imagine it as it should be decked for a wedding, with Damascene roses in bloom in the courtyards and the meadows of the mountains above green with summer, the temple of their goddess Anahita alight with lamps.

Artashir looked at me sideways. "When did you take your Companion's oaths?" he asked.

"Well, I joined the Companions after Gaugamela," I said.

"That's not what I mean."

"I know," I said. I stretched my cramped left hand against my leg, the reins in my right. "Not long before the end. In Babylon."

THE AIR OF Babylon was moist and humid, at least in the gardens. An ancient king had built them about the palaces and temples, and they were accounted a great wonder, holding plants from all the known world. At least all the world that king had known. There were no Indian peach trees until we brought them, and none of the wild berries the Macedonians said they missed. Our world was larger than his had been.

It was an honor to guard the King, even in the middle of the night, even when there was nothing going on. Since an assassination attempt years ago there had always been one Companion on duty besides the regular guards, and rotating as the duty did. It was a rare and occasional honor that tonight was mine.

I stood outside the bathhouse, looking out over the gardens. Below, on the walk that curved around ornamental plants of this paradise, I saw the regular guards on watch waiting. I stood by the fretted door, unobtrusive and quiet. We had all heard the King was ill. The water eased him, and so he was spending the night in the bathhouse, with only an attendant or two. He would be well soon, surely. Many men had the summer flux in the heat of Babylon, or had brought malaria back from the marshes. The King would be well soon.

It was long past midnight. Above, the stars were wheeling on toward dawn. I heard a movement behind me and turned, thinking perhaps it was one of the attendants, slipping out to get something.

It was the King. His blond hair was damp, as though he had come from the bathing pool, and he wore a plain white chiton that anyone might have worn.

"My Lord," I said.

He looked at me and half smiled. "Lydias of Miletus, is it? How do you fare?" Of course he knew the names of every man. He had put his arm around me himself, when Sati and Sikander lay on the pyre.

"Well enough, my Lord," I said, as what else can one say?

Alexander shrugged, and stretched his hands out to lean on the carved railing that separated the bathhouse door from the garden below. "They are all asleep, in there. I do not like to wake Bagoas. He has not slept much since I was ill."

"I hope you are better now," I said, though he did not look it. I did not like the flush to his face.

He leaned on the rail, looking out, and in the light of the cresset along the wall his profile looked like a cameo, cut against the darkness beyond. "When I came out just now you looked sad."

"I suppose I do, my Lord," I said. How else should I look, when there had been nothing but grief in my heart these many months?

He nodded but did not look at me. "You mourned the Chiliarch Hephaistion. I saw you at the funeral."

I took a breath. The night made me bold and sorrow made me reckless. "Yes, my Lord. Had he never known you, Hephaistion should have been a great man."

Alexander smiled. "You saw that too, did you? I think you see too many things sometimes, Lydias of Miletus, a gift and a curse both. And a wise man does not ask for oracles when he does not wish to know."

His mouth twisted in an expression that could have been rueful, or could have been the answer to some pain. "The choice of Achilles is easy. It's living and ruling that's hard." He looked at me and his eyes were fever-bright. "Shall I tell you a story?"

"If you like, my Lord," I said. I thought that he really should not be out of bed in the night air, and wondered how I could call Bagoas the eunuch unobtrusively.

His voice was quiet, like a dreaming child. "There was once a Titan named Prometheus who loved men more than he should, and thought that they could be more than insensible animals, always at the mercy of their fears and hungers. He watched them for a long time. And that fascination turned to love, the thing that undoes all men. At last the thought came to him that he might give them forbidden knowledge that would set them free. And so he stole fire from heaven and gave it to men. For that he was condemned to spend eternity in torment, sacrificed again and again, reborn to begin it over. Do you know that story, Lydias?"

"Yes," I said, and a chill ran down my back, as though someone had put a cold hand on me. "And yet was it not worth it, if all the hearths in the world are kindled from that stolen fire?"

Alexander nodded slowly, his eyes on mine, gray and rimmed with black, eyes to see eternity with. "It was indeed worth it."

I laid my heart on the earth, like a libation, though it thundered in my breast. "My Lord, will you accept my oath?"

"Yes," he said gravely as I knelt.

The crushed stone of the path was rough beneath my knees and above the careless stars turned on in their wheeling dance. "I, Lydias of Miletus, do give my word to you, Alexander, to be your true man waking and sleeping, in all things great and small, to obey you and die at your command, for all time."

"All time is too long," he said. "Say rather while life and breath lasts, as otherwise there may come a time when you regret these words."

"Then I will regret," I said, and raised my eyes to his.

Alexander searched my face, and I did not know what he sought and found there. "Rise, Lydias, true Companion, and know that I understand the full worth of your gift." His hand when he touched me burned with fever.

"You should go and lie down, my Lord," I said. "Or perhaps return to the pool if it eases you."

"I will," he said, turning, then stopped with one hand on the bath-house door, his eyes bright. "I will see you again, Lydias," he said.

"Of course, my Lord," I said. Of course he would see me often, in the natural order of things.

Instead, he died four days later.

# THE BATTLE OF CAMEL'S FORT

We heard the battle before we saw it. There is no sound like it—the rumble of so many hooves and feet, the shouts of thousands of men, the crash and scream of arms. It was midafternoon, and the sun had slipped westward from its zenith.

Awkwardly, I wrapped the reins around my left hand, passing them between thumb and fingers, and drew sword with my right. "Forward!"

I held my horse to a walk as the two Iles formed up, the first with Glaukos on the point, myself in the rear between the Companion Cavalry and the fifty horse archers. I would follow the charge, not lead it. I swept the sword point forward, my voice carrying over the din. "Ptolemy and Egypt!"

And let it go.

We came in like a loosed arrow, straight into their flank.

On the other side of the ford, our fort still held, but that was about all one could say for it. The wooden palisades Artashir had repaired were torn and gaping, huge gaps between trampled sections. Perdiccas had let the elephants at them, and the results were unmistakable.

Half of his men were across the river, scaling ladders raised to the walls, a full phalanx of infantry about the base of the ladders, shields raised above their heads to ward off the Egyptian archers on the wall above. The other half of his men were either midstream or still on our bank, horse archers held in reserve and some others. Twenty men or so were struggling with a massive elephant, its eyes streaming blood and gore. Our defenders on the wall had blinded the lead elephant, and in its pain it rampaged through their lines while its handlers tried to calm it. Another elephant stood some distance away on the opposite shore, its flanks heaving. The platform on its back was smashed to splinters and its driver dangled head down, dead, from its neck, still held on by the straps of his harness.

As the first Ile of our cavalry plunged like a knife into the flank of the men on our side of the river, I saw something I could not have seen had I been in the front of the charge. To our right Perdiccas' camp lay open.

Artashir and the horse archers were still behind me. They were not meant for the shock of a charge against heavy infantry.

"Artashir!" I shouted. "The camp!"

He could see where I pointed — the elaborate tents with their gilded posts that must surely belong to Perdiccas. To Perdiccas, or to the boy king and his mother.

Artashir met my eyes, and there was no need for further words. "I'll get the child," he said, and with a shout his men formed up around him, riding hard for the camp and Alexander's son.

I followed the charge instead. We were pressing deep into the side of Perdiccas' reserve phalanx, and had come down on them so fast that they hadn't had time to change facing. A sarissa is twice a man's height in length, and as the phalanx advances the ranks are staggered, so that each sarissa goes between the men of the rank ahead of it. In order to turn the entire formation, each man must be able to lift his sarissa free and rotate ninety degrees, maintaining proper distance and dress between ranks, and then lower his sarissa again between the men now before him. This is a maneuver practiced over and over on the drill field, because it is difficult to do without someone fouling up and blocking others. It is doubly difficult to do on the battlefield, especially with cavalry crowding into the front ranks, swords in hand.

They had not managed to do it, and as always happens in these situations, some men had dropped their sarissas and drawn sword as our horsemen got in too close. Which meant those sarissas now fouled other men, lying across theirs at wrong angles and preventing them from turning to the new facing, or just released without being put properly down. This was the right chaos. This was good chaos. And it benefited us.

I raised my sword again. "Ptolemy and Egypt! Press it home!" We were giving a lot better than we were taking, but a seasoned phalanx wouldn't break easily.

My horse screamed and shied, and I fought to stay with her, the reins still wound around my left hand. I hadn't the strength in the hand. I couldn't hold her as she fought. Their horse archers had engaged, and an arrow had burned along her side, lodging nearly spent in the fleshy part of her rump. It was far from a mortal wound, but she struggled and panicked.

I got the rein loose and slid down her off side, trying to get clear of her before she threw me entirely, my feet skidding in the dust. I made a better target for their horse archers than our men, who were now hopelessly tangled up with their phalanx.

I saw his shadow move along the ground rather than saw him, and without even thinking turned, my sword in guard. The infantryman who had come at me was one of the Silver Shields, his beard threaded with gray. I saw his eyes flicker to my left hand as our blades connected. He saw I had a bad hand. Would that translate to a bad side?

He feinted to my left, testing me, but I had seen his eyes and blocked to the right instead, catching the return strongly. And then it was cut and thrust, guard and block, the deadly dance. I was younger than he, but I had been up all night. Thrust and block, neither with the advantage, sweat running down my brow.

I do not know how it would have ended if not for the horns and shouting. Perdiccas was ordering the recall. Still horsed and able to see somewhat above the fray, he must have seen Artashir sprinting for the camp. Now he shouted the recall, that all the infantry on this side of the river must rally immediately to prevent losing the prize.

My opponent hesitated for half a second, then turned and charged off toward the camp. I did not pursue. My chest heaved with my breath. Too many months on leave, I thought, if one combat should wear me out!

I looked about for my horse, but she was nowhere to be seen. "Fuck," I said under my breath. Dismounted I couldn't tell what was going on, nor could I give orders. One of my troopers was some little distance away, but I could not make him hear me in the din. I had always thought that squires and bodyservants were an affectation in battle, but now I could see the use of them. A general who can't see what's going on is useless.

There was a thunder of hooves, and a dozen horse archers thundered down on me. It took a moment to distinguish that these were ours, not theirs, since all were clad alike.

"I need a horse!" I shouted in Persian, and one of them pulled up and extended a hand to me.

I came up behind him. "Many thanks!" I shouted in his ear. "Where is Artashir?"

"Right behind," he yelled back. "We did not get through to the tent because the heavy infantry got back before we were done with the guards. Artashir said to disengage."

I looked about, but in the dust and chaos I could see nothing, certainly not Artashir.

"Make for the river," I shouted. "We need to get back across to the fort." If we got stuck on the wrong side of the river with their superior numbers of both cavalry and horse archers, we'd get crushed.

By now, the flow of troops was in reverse, Perdiccas' men breaking off the attack and returning to their camp, and our men going the other way. Fortunately, at this point the ford was quite shallow, hardly up to the horses' bellies. We floundered across at the southernmost end.

By the time we were on the opposite shore a few of my own men had joined us, and I traded for the horse of a trooper who had been wounded. He was a youngish stallion and he had been spooked quite a bit, so it took my good hand to hold him in and get him to bear a new rider. Really, I thought, as I walked him in a circle where we were forming up, he was too green for this, but we had run through the remounts quickly. We were going to need more horses, good Nisean blooded horses that had the size for a man in steel. The little horses the archers used were not large enough. I doubted there was a Nisean broodmare in all Egypt. Another problem for another day.

"Form up!" I yelled. Our men were still crossing over, and even though ours and theirs were passing in midstream everyone looked too exhausted to trade blows.

They formed up in a ragged line halfway up the bank, three ranks of them, some of them nursing wounds but still horsed. Six of Artashir's men. Seventy-seven of my own.

Not good at all, I thought grimly, scanning the battlefield. Not good at all.

The sun was behind the fort, and I heard at last the gate opening when none of Perdiccas' men remained on this side of the river.

"Wounded to the rear!" I ordered. "Everyone else, stay mounted and guard the ford." The last thing we needed was a late sortie when we had the gates open. We paced down the bank a little way, until the first rank stood with their ankles in the water, a barrier across the ford.

Behind us were the terrible sounds of the wounded. The cries for help were not so bad. Men who have both wits and strength to cry for help may live to see another day. It was the groans and the rasping breaths, the choking cries like children that were dreadful. I did not have to look. I stood with my men, our backs to them, guarding the ford while our servants and doctors came down.

A few more of our men straggled across in ones and twos, all cavalry and horse archers, though some were now dismounted. A big Nisean stallion, ten years old or more from the look of him, came trotting up with no rider, his saddle blanket drenched with blood though he looked fresh as rain. He came to me and I caught his bridle in my bad hand

and he came and stood beside me without pulling or fussing. I thought that he looked relieved to be doing something that made sense, standing around with a bunch of other horses. If it hadn't been for the blood I would have changed horses then and there.

Fourteen horse archers. A hundred and forty-five of my men. The stragglers were coming in. That meant we were missing thirty-six archers and five hundred and five cavalrymen, the bulk of our force.

Surely we hadn't lost so many? I wouldn't have thought so. Sixty, seventy, even a hundred I would accept, but we could not have lost so many. What had happened when I could not see?

At last, when full night fell, I gave the order to dismount and walk the horses back to the fort.

Ptolemy was waiting for me in the courtyard, talking with one of the infantry officers, while the servants were laying out the wounded in the courtyard, the lightly wounded to the right, the dying to the left. The men in the middle were taken straight into the shed they were using for a surgery.

Ptolemy's breastplate was streaked with gore, and blood had dried stiff in his hair where he had run his hands through it with his reddened hands. "What have you got?"

"Fourteen archers and a hundred and forty-five cavalry," I said wearily. "And I've lost Artashir and Glaukos. You?"

Ptolemy looked grave. "Not as bad as that. Eighty-one killed or wounded on the parapets. I'd guess four or five times that number for them. But we were about to get overwhelmed by the elephants when you showed up. That was a good plan. We needed them to break off exactly then."

"I don't know how we lost so many," I said, and I could hear my voice choking. "Ptolemy, I don't. I don't know what happened. I was unhorsed and I couldn't see, but I don't think it should be that bad." To have lost almost my entire command...

He put his hand on my shoulder, dark circles of dried blood under his nails. "It's probably not. From the walls of the fort I could see the gambit going for the tent, and when they had to break off from that because Perdiccas turned, a bunch of men were on the wrong side. They couldn't get back to the river because Perdiccas' horse archers were between them. I saw a bunch reel away into the trees to the east, those palm groves along the canal over there. Some of them were in breastplates, so it wasn't all Artashir's men."

I took a breath. I must think. I must not despair. "If there weren't enough to break through, they did the right thing," I said. "And there may have been some others who disengaged at the end but couldn't get back across the ford."

"We've more tomorrow," Ptolemy said grimly. He squeezed my shoulder. "You tell your men to stand down and get something to eat. I know they've not slept last night, so they're excused from the watch tonight. And you get some rest too. The infantry is in better shape, and we'll shore up the defenses."

"Don't you need me awake?" I said. "I can—"

"Go to bed," Ptolemy said. "I'll need you more tomorrow, and you've already been up a full night. I'll see you in the morning."


I LAY DOWN on a rough straw-filled mattress in one of the upper rooms of the fortress, certain that I would not sleep while the bustle of the work and the moans of the wounded below continued. Of course I did. I was asleep almost before I stretched out, and did not open my eyes until one of the squires shook me.

"Sir? General Ptolemy sent me to get you. They're gone again."

I hurried up to the walls, once again to be met with the sight of a deserted camp.

Ptolemy looked bemused. "We had the same master, Perdiccas and I. He knows better than to waste his men trying to take Camel's Fort when the real prize is Memphis. All he needs is a place to cross the river. It doesn't need to be this place."

I blew out a breath. "Head for Bubastis?"

Ptolemy shook his head. "No. We can keep doing this, pushing back at every river ford, but that's not going to win anything. We've tested each other now. We know where he's going. And Memphis has the strongest fortifications in the Delta. Let's do this on our terms, not just react to Perdiccas."

I nodded slowly. The walls of Memphis were as impenetrable as any I had ever seen, except perhaps Babylon. It would take Perdiccas five or six days at least to get there, maybe more. And we had seven days to run of the nine the goddess had promised. I looked at him sideways. I had not dared to mention it before, but now there was so little time left. "Sir? I was wondering…when we were lost in the desert when Cleomenes tried to kill you…"

Ptolemy bowed his head, still looking out over the walls. "If you're asking if you dreamed it, no. No, Lydias, you didn't."

I didn't think I had, as Thais had told me that Ptolemy remembered it too, but I didn't say that. "What are you going to do?"

Ptolemy turned about, leaning back against the parapet. "What would you do, if you were me?"

"I would take the gods' bargain," I said quietly. "But then you already know that."

"And what about that child there?" He gestured with his chin toward the way Perdiccas had gone.

"Make him your heir," I said. "He is too young to rule now, and you have no legitimate son that you would name. You've already made it clear that you can't name Lagos or Leontiscus. So name Alexander the son of Alexander your heir. Or rule in his name as satrap as long as you can. But this land needs a pharaoh, and the King needs release. Take what is offered to you and make your nephew your heir."

Ptolemy looked at me sharply.

"I have seen Chloe," I said. "Do you think I can't add it up?"

He let out a sigh. "You and plenty of other men." He paced a few steps along the wall. "I do not want my children to grow up the way I did, knowing that every gift, every bite of food might conceal a deadly purpose. Olympias could have had me killed if she had ever deemed me a threat. Sometimes I thought she did, and the only thing I could do was to be less and less interesting to her. Fortunately, when Phillip remarried it gave her other heirs to think about, legitimate sons of Phillip's new queen, rather than the colorless young man who was nothing but the son of Arsinoe, a girl Phillip had loved when they were boy and girl together. I do not want my children to grow up fearing their family." He turned at the end of the walk and came back. "And Chloe is too easy to proclaim Alexander's daughter, too easy for some unscrupulous man to use."

"That is a problem for another day," I said. "She was a brave child, and she will be a capable woman, as her mother is."

Ptolemy smiled, as men do when their daughter is praised. "You like her, then?"

"I do," I said. "I saw her when I visited Thais last. She said you must win for her, and I promised her that we should."

"Well, if you have promised Chloe, we must be about it," Ptolemy said, but he did not laugh. "Get your men ready to march this afternoon. We are going down the western bank to Memphis."

"Yes, sir," I said and turned to go.

Ptolemy stopped me. "And promote an aide. You need one now."

And a remount, I thought. I had not recognized the big black horse as belonging to one of my men, so I presumed he must belong to some member of Perdiccas' Companion Cavalry. In which case he was mine. My horse hadn't turned up, but I thought he might be better, actually. I had not been very fond of that remount, as she was inclined to be nervous. I called him Perseus, and he did not seem to object.

We marched four hours in the afternoon, leading the column and scouting both before and behind, providing a screen for the infantry. At the first stop my scouts to the rear came up. "Sir? We are being shadowed by a group of horsemen. We saw them behind us a little while ago."

"Form up!" I ordered, getting the scant hundred and forty-five into line across the road, while the infantry phalanx that was last in column went into square in preparation.

We waited. A fly settled on Perseus' ear, and he twitched.

Around the curve of the river behind us came a company of men, some three hundred, all mounted. They checked when they saw us. I raised my hand and shaded my eyes. Heavy cavalry, I thought. Here and there a flash of bright silk. And then I recognized them as the pair in front came forward at a walk, a big man in steel, his head bare in the sun, and a light bearded man with a bow slung at his back.

"Artashir! Glaukos!"

They came up to us, and there was much shouting and pounding each other on the back—most of the shouting from me, and most of the pounding from Glaukos.

Ptolemy came back while we were standing about and embraced them both like brothers. "What happened to you?"

"We couldn't get through," Artashir said, drawing himself up. "When we had to break off the attack on the camp, we had the main body of Perdiccas' infantry between us and you. So I pulled us out to the east, and we lurked in the woods. Just before dawn Glaukos came along."

Glaukos nodded. "We got stuck too. I saw you give the order, Lydias, but we couldn't disengage and get over there. So I picked what looked like the clearest route out, and we went south. Around midnight we heard them breaking camp and coming our way, so we swung east to stay clear of them. I'm not about to take on fifteen hundred cavalry or so with two hundred and fifty. We waited for their vanguard to go by, and then slipped around the east side through the farms. And ran into Artashir. We got some rest and then midmorning went to see what had happened at the fort. They told us you were on the road south, so we left our wounded there with the others and followed."

"That was well done," Ptolemy said. "Very well done, both of you. How many sound men do you have?"

"Twenty-four horse archers," Artashir said. "And two hundred and sixty-one cavalry."

I let out a breath I hadn't been aware I was holding. That meant I had a little over four hundred men left out of six hundred and fifty.

Which was not terrible after two battles. Many of our casualties were wounded and would eventually return, and still more were probably sound themselves but dismounted due to injury to the horses. Once again we did not have enough remounts.

"Tell them to come join their fellows," Ptolemy said. "And you two come have a drink. You deserve it."

"What's next?" Artashir asked.

"Memphis," I said. "We ride to Memphis."

# THE DESCENT
## OF KINGS

We came to Memphis in evening on the fourth day, having crossed the Saite branch of the Nile at Abusir and then marched down the good road on the western side. Perdiccas was now behind us. He could not get across the Nile yet, as he had no way across the Bubasite branch of the river, and the terrain was much more rugged on the eastern side and the roads less certain. We thought that he would not come up to the eastern side opposite Memphis until afternoon the next day at least, and would not attack so late in the day.

It was with considerable relief that I saw the walls of Memphis. The greatest city of Egypt, she takes her name from them, and is known in the Egyptian tongue as "The Lady of White Walls." They were sixty feet high and thirty feet thick, with enormous flanking towers about each gate. The walls loomed over the river and the docks that lay in their shadow. In the dry season when the water was low there were shallow sandy beaches along that side.

Perdiccas would have to be mad to try to cross directly to them, however. There was not so much as a fingernail's width of beach and docks that was not covered by the towers and walls. Every step that a man could take would be under devastating fire from above.

Fortunately or unfortunately depending on one's point of view, cavalry has little to do in the siege of a walled city, so once my men had their horses stabled I had no further duties for the evening, and might go and get some dinner while Ptolemy and the infantry officers consulted with the city guard far into the night.

I went to find Bagoas.

His room was a haven of light and peace, and his smile when he saw me warmed me to the bone. He did not ply me with a million questions, only said, "Come and rest." And so I did.

I woke beside him in the early hours of morning from dreams I could not quite remember. There had been a lady with a veil of silver over her long black hair, and I would have thought her Egyptian or Indian except that her eyes were as blue as the heavens. She stood before closed doors marked with ancient words I could not read, and no matter how I tried to go around her and through them she blocked my way, a sad little smile on her face, and shook her head as my mother had when I was a child.

I woke, and lay on my back staring up at the ceiling above. The first rays of the sun came slanting through the window. It was after dawn.

I woke Bagoas gently. "Come on, my dear. It's late. We must see what Ptolemy has for us to do." Ten hours off duty was all I could expect.

Ptolemy was breakfasting with Artashir in one of the small gardens. He looked groggy still, as though he had not been to bed until well after midnight. The infantry officers were nowhere in sight. I imagined they had already received their orders, and so had no need to turn out so early after a long march.

To my surprise, Manetho was also there, as well as another priest I did not know and a plump young woman who wore a green gown in the Egyptian style, its broad straps barely concealing her breasts. I was more than a little taken aback to see a woman sitting in council with men and wondered who she might be.

Artashir stood up as we came in. "That's it, then," he said. "I'll be about it right away."

The young woman nodded. "I will have my servants send the sarcophagus to you. It is the one that was intended for Nectanebo, but he died far away in Upper Egypt and never used it."

Bagoas stiffened. "What are you doing with my Lord?"

Ptolemy looked up. "Come in, Bagoas. We are moving him from the temple that is near the river to the tombs of the Sacred Bulls in the hills at Saqqara. It is too dangerous in the city, and he will lie in the company of Serapis."

I had never seen Bagoas challenge anybody about anything, but this was the thing he would do it for. "Surely you do not expect to lose Memphis, that you need to do such a thing and take him from the hearse that was prepared for him and lay him in the coffin of another man?"

"No," Ptolemy said, "I do not expect to lose Memphis." He and Manetho exchanged a look.

"I'll be going, then," Artashir said, and fled.

I hesitated, torn between a decision I should have no part in and Bagoas. I stayed.

Ptolemy took a breath, his eyes flicking once to me, and then back to Bagoas. "It's more than that. Much more. I am not sure how to begin to explain."

It all added up to me suddenly, Manetho and the other priest, and the woman I didn't know who must also be one of the Egyptian clergy, and the need for Alexander's body. "You are accepting the gods' bargain," I said.

Bagoas turned and looked at me.

"Yes," Ptolemy said. "You already know Manetho. This is the Hierophant of Osiris from Abydos and the Adoratrice of Bastet from Bubastis. They are here to assist with what needs to be done."

"What has this to do with my Lord's body," Bagoas demanded, "that you should take him out of his coffin and carry him around?"

Ptolemy looked at me, one eyebrow quirked.

"It is partly for the King that this must be done," I said. "Bagoas, he was crowned in Memphis by the old rites, the ones designed to call the godhead of Horus down upon the Pharaoh and commingle their spirits. When Pharaoh dies, there is supposed to be a rite to transfer Horus into the new king. Until this is done, the old pharaoh is not released from the body he has inhabited."

His eyes searched my face. This was not at all what Persians are taught about life and death. "You believe this?"

"I do," I said, "and I believe it must be done, both for the King and for Egypt."

"To release his spirit."

"And to give Ptolemy the power to defeat Perdiccas and rule Egypt."

"We intend your king no disrespect," the Adoratrice said in halting Greek. "He was our pharaoh too. He gave us our freedom. I bring the coffin that was for our last pharaoh, who died in exile. It is no shame but our greatest gift to offer it to Alexander."

"And that he lie for a while among the gods, among the sacred avatars of Osiris," Manetho said. "Until Ptolemy has built his tomb, as is proper."

Bagoas nodded then, dropping his eyes.

"We must do it tonight," Ptolemy said. "We have no more time."

"It shall be tonight," Manetho said. "We have prepared already, and as you say you do not want the rite of coronation…"

"No." Ptolemy shook his head. "I will stand as proxy for Alexander's son. No more than that."

"I understand," Manetho said. "You shall be the sem-priest, but we will not call Horus to dwell within you. That shall be as you say. Is there any other you would like to walk with you as your companion? It is traditional that there be two such to walk through the Gates of Amenti with you and to come forth by day."

"I would have Lydias," Ptolemy said.

I gulped. I had never imagined such. "Surely that is the office of a kinsman," I sputtered.

"I have no kinsmen here," Ptolemy said. "And besides, did you not stand with me once before, when we came to Memphis?"

"Yes," I said. We had stood together in that strange place both of Egypt and not, in the desert when Cleomenes tried to kill him.

"Will you stand with me now?" Ptolemy asked, extending his hand.

I took it wrist to wrist, and his flesh was warm in my hand. "I will, and I am honored."

Manetho nodded. "That is well done. Artashir has been sent to get the coffin that the Adoratrice brought. When evening comes we will go out to Saqqara as funeral processions do, just a few of us so as not to attract attention, looking like a family of mourners and a priest, carrying the body with us on a funeral wagon. That is what people do when they go to the tombs and it will not signal to Perdiccas that there is anything unusual going on."

"You are not taking my Lord anywhere without me," Bagoas said.

"Bagoas," I began.

Bagoas looked straight at Manetho. "Am I not a funerary priest of Alexander? Is that not what you have named me these many months? Then how should I be barred from his funeral, and from the office you have already acknowledged?"

"He is Persian," the Adoratrice said. "His presence would be offensive to the Sacred Bulls."

"Bagoas was not yet born when Artaxerxes killed the Apis bull," Ptolemy snapped. "We all need to be a little bit flexible here."

Manetho shifted from one foot to another, clearly disliking it but not wanting to naysay Ptolemy, who would be his king. "Then you would allow this?"

Ptolemy nodded, his eyes on Bagoas not Manetho. "Alexander should have someone by his bier besides me who loved him."

Bagoas' breath caught, though he made no sound.

Ptolemy stretched out his other hand to Bagoas. "We are a strange company, and I do not say this is not ill considered. But will you walk with me into the darkness for Alexander's sake?"

"I will," Bagoas said, grave as a bridegroom.

"Then we will try the Gates of Amenti, the three of us," Ptolemy said. "And we will free the King, and hopefully Egypt besides."

We left the city as the sun sank westward toward the hills above Saqqara. Three priests and Manetho walked in front, while a pair of oxen led a funeral cart draped in white. A pall lay over the mummy case on it, which was well as it seemed to be covered in gold leaf. Ptolemy walked behind it, and Bagoas and I behind him, followed by the Adoratrice, another woman I did not know, and three young priests.

Dressed in Egyptian clothes, I supposed that from a distance we looked like a family going out to the tombs, a common enough occurrence. It looked like the funeral of an ordinary man.

Hephaistion had been given a funeral fit for a god.

Alexander had built in Babylon the greatest funeral pyre the world had ever seen. Four months were spent building it, while preserved by the embalmer's art Hephaistion lay in state. It was as large as a temple, seven stories from base to top, each more splendid than the last. There were entire trunks of palm trees supporting it, the prows of ships made of fragrant cedar wood with gilded archers on their decks, banners of crimson felt, eagles and serpents, lions and bulls all carved in wood with the most exquisite lifelike detail. There were Macedonian and Persian arms, and four great statues of sirens cunningly made so that they could seem to sing a lament for the dead, their voices those of four eunuchs known for their beautiful voices who would stand concealed within them for the first part of the funeral, before the pyre was lit. At last, at the top on a bier draped with Tyrian purple bordered in gold, lay Hephaistion.

His chiton was purple as though he were a king, and his breastplate was worked with precious gems, his sword by his hand. I know, as I saw him there. We paid our respects before the pyre was kindled, and I too had my part to play. I saw him there, gold coins with Alexander's likeness on his eyes, his long red hair combed on his shoulders. I saw him there, and I did not have to pretend to sadness. I looked upon his face and thought that he would smile.

"Hephaistion," I whispered. "Sir. If you are there with them, watch over Sati and Sikander for me. Please, sir." I was blind with tears and could speak no more. If he could, he would. He would do so much for me.

The man beside me had to nudge me to do my part.

The sacrifices were being brought to the pyre to pour out their blood, sacrifices for a king. A black bull, his horns gilded. A ram.

Walking with proud gait, steady as ever on parade, his saddle blanket of purple wool, was Ghost Dancer. I went to him and stood at his head, and he looked me in the eye.

"There, my darling," I said. "I knew you were the finest. You were the finest ever. Go now with your master and serve him forever. Here in the world above you will live on in your fleet-footed foals."

He bent his head to me, and I could swear I saw understanding in his dark eyes. When the priest came with the knife he did not struggle, only stood with his head high, baring his throat. His blood splashed over me and he died in my arms.

I died that day too, while the flames enveloped them. I was dead already when Alexander died.

AND YET I walked under the sun. I followed the funeral cart up the hill to Saqqara, where ancient pyramids of stone were etched against the western sky, along the main processional way. We did not go toward the pyramids, but turned off to the right, going around the lake with its lotus flowers and lilies, toward the Serapeum and the tombs of the Sacred Bulls.

We did not speak, Ptolemy and Bagoas and I. I wondered what my life would have been if Alexander had never come to Miletus, or if I had not gone with him. No, I thought, I did not regret it, even with all the sorrow that came after. I have seen the peaks of the Hindu Kush mountains in bright morning, and the distant sea at the end of the Indus, where there is no farther shore. I have talked with sages and priests in a dozen lands, and have walked the plains of Scythia toward the rising sun. I have ridden on elephants and sailed on great galleys. I have loved and I have lost and I have come to Egypt with stolen fire in a gilded coffin, walking with gods.

I looked up, and the hillside loomed over the door to the Serapeum, a black hole into the earth. Not for anything, I thought, would I want to pass that door forever. There is still too much to see. I have not been up the Nile beyond Thebes, nor been to Greece, nor seen my daughter wed in a saffron veil or watched my grandchildren grow. I could not read the Egyptian language, and I did not know where the sun sets beyond the Gates of Hercules.

*I know*, Isis whispered. *You want to live.*

At that a tear broke loose and ran down my cheek.

I want to live, Lady of Egypt, I thought. I cannot help it, but I want to live. I took a breath, and it seemed something loosened in my chest.

Before me, Ptolemy walked gravely, his head down. Beside me, Bagoas lifted his face to the first stars appearing in the sky, his green eyes glittering with tears. I mourned a king who had changed my life. He mourned the one he had loved. I understood that now. Loyalty and pride would have caused him to speak no ill of the King, but this grief came from love.

And how not, I thought. Was it such a strange thing that any who served him, even come into his service as a spoil of war, should not in the end love him? Whoever had scarred Bagoas had not been Alexander. This grief was real.

I felt no jealousy, for how should I? It was I who had come after, with my own memories and my own scars. Above the dry cliffs the sky still flared in the west with the fading colors of the sun's passage.

We came to the doors of the Serapeum, and Manetho stepped forward to face us. The funeral cart passed him and went within, disappearing into the darkness. We watched it go. We would see it again, later in the rite.

"This is the place of the Sacred Bulls," Manetho said. "For more than a thousand years, the Apis bulls have been laid in this place when it was their time to go down into the West, to the Halls of Amenti. Will you pass the doors of Amenti, Ptolemy of Egypt?"

"I will pass," Ptolemy said. "I am seeking Alexander the son of Phillip."

I saw Bagoas' eyebrow quirk, that even now and here Ptolemy named him in the Macedonian style.

Manetho looked at me and Bagoas. "And will you accompany him?"

"I will," we said together. I hoped there were not many more lines that could not be easily guessed, as I had not ever seen such a rite before, nor had anyone prepare me as Manetho had Ptolemy.

Manetho turned and led us in, under the massive lintel carved in the very stone of the hills. This was no entirely manmade place, but a cave wrought by the gods, old as time. We passed into its shadow.

We went down a long sloping passageway that went straight back into the hill, vaulted and wide enough for four men to walk abreast. It was not entirely dark. At intervals along the passage oil lamps had been set on stands so that they threw their light up onto the walls. I wondered for a moment why they had put them so far apart if they were going to the trouble of bringing in lamps, but then realized that it was so parts of the passage would remain in shadow.

We had gone only a short distance when a young woman stepped out carrying a golden scale in her hands and exchanged words with Ptolemy. "I am Justice," she said in Greek, a conciliation to Ptolemy not speaking Egyptian. "Any who seek to rule the Black Land must pledge to uphold Justice for all who dwell within her borders. Will you so swear?"

"I will," Ptolemy said, and she stepped back against the wall.

As we passed, he let me catch up and said to me, "Don't worry so, Lydias. It's not so very different from the Eleusinian Mysteries, is it?"

"I wouldn't know," I said. "Nor did I know you were an initiate."

Ptolemy dropped his voice. "I became one long ago, when I was a young man in Athens with Alexander. Thais had already become an initiate, and she sponsored me."

"Oh," I said. Truly, there was a great deal I did not know of Ptolemy. But I had never been to Eleusis, or anywhere else in Greece. Nor could I imagine what a mystery should look like that was open to women as well as men.

Now two people dressed as peasants stepped forward, asking for Ptolemy's promise to watch over the poor of Egypt, those who labored in the fields with little reward. Once again he gave his word, and once again we went on.

We came to a broad cross corridor where there was yet another tableau, then turned left down it. The flickering lamps, the jumping shadows did make it feel rather strange. The hairs stood up on the back of my neck. We came to another, still broader junction, and there was another priestess, this time asking Ptolemy to affirm his dedication to the gods of Egypt. I thought this priestess was the Adoratrice I had seen earlier, though now she wore a heavy wig with many plaits, each braided with gold beads. She caught my eye and gave me a little smile, almost flirtatious, like a girl at a festival. I felt myself blushing.

On either side of this corridor were great arches sealed with blocks of stone, elaborate carvings on them saying something I could not understand.

"We have come to the Passage of the Bulls," Manetho said, standing with his staff in the left-hand side. "Here lie the Sacred Bulls in their tombs." He touched the archway to his left. "Here lies Apis, who died in the twenty-third year of Ahmose Khnemibre, who you call Amasis. There beside him lies Apis, who died in the sixteenth year of Nekau. That way," he gestured with his chin, "lies Apis who died in the fifth year of Alexander the Son of Amon, who you call the son of Phillip. They go into Amenti, as all men do." He raised his arms, and the lamps threw his shadow tall on the wall behind. "Hear, oh gods! Hear us knock, for we come on behalf of Alexander, the son of Amon!"

At this a young priest with a shaven head came forward with a basin and held it so Ptolemy could wash his hands and dry them on a piece of linen, then stepped behind him and did the same for me and Bagoas.

"Come into the presence of Pharaoh that was," Manetho said.

We walked a short distance down the corridor. One arch was unblocked, and within on the lid of a sarcophagus of green granite lay the golden coffin. The lid was off, and I heard Bagoas make a sound.

Alexander lay as if sleeping, his hands crossed on his breast just as I had seen him when I looked in the coffin after I had taken the hearse. His hands looked perfectly lifelike, if a little waxy, and in the glow of the lamps it seemed that he had the glow of health. He looked as though in a moment he would wake.

Bagoas should not have come, I thought. Surely he has already had enough of this. But he did not move, only stood silent and reverent.

"Frankincense and myrrh we offer, gifts for a king," Manetho said. Another young priest came in with a censer and passed it slowly around the room, the smoke curling in living tendrils around Alexander's body.

"Gold we offer, gift for a king," Manetho said. He brought forth a diadem, and I drew a sharp breath. The kings of Macedon wear diadems, not the heavy double crowns of Egypt. Alexander, when he was here, wore the double crown only once. For other occasions he had a diadem made, a simple circlet of gold such as Macedonians wear, only with the rearing cobra's head, the uraeus, in the front. It was this that Manetho brought forth and carefully arranged on Alexander's head.

Bagoas closed his eyes.

"Oil we bring you, scent of life." Manetho lifted a small glass vessel and unstopped it, the heady scent of roses filling the room like a breeze of summer. He put a single drop on the King's forehead.

"Bread and beer and the flesh of birds we bring you," Manetho said as again the young priest stepped forward carrying dishes for a feast, roasted duck and other good things, and laid them on the sarcophagus at Alexander's feet.

"Breath of life we bring you," Manetho said, and the censer swung his smoke again. "We bring all we have to you, to our king and god." He brought his hands together in front of his chest.

He took a step back, and then spoke to Ptolemy. "These things we do in any funeral, to greater or lesser degree, so that all who pass the Gates of Amenti shall be remembered and shall be blessed with all good things. From this point, however, we depart from what is done for any man besides Pharaoh. We shall do the Opening of the Mouth as is common, but then we must call forth Horus who is still indwelling in the body of Alexander the King, that his ka and that of the Pharaoh That Was may become separate. First, Ptah must give him breath."

An older priest stepped forward, and Manetho gave way gracefully. From a box presented by an assistant he took forth a stone chisel, and then began a long recitation that was not translated into Greek. I understood parts of it, I thought. "Awake! May you be as a living man once more! May you be rested every day, healthy and whole…" When he finished he barely touched the tip of the chisel to Alexander's lips.

"And then Sokar must give him sight," Manetho said.

The young priest stepped forward, taking from the box a stone of clear quartz and one of black obsidian. He began a long prayer in Egyptian as well. The smoke from the incense was thick in the confined space, and it made my head spin. "…may the gods protect you. May they weave protection about you every day. May you open your eyes to the blessings of Ra." Carefully, he touched each still eyelid with the black stone, then with the white.

I blinked. It should be warm in here with all of us pressed into the small room. And yet I felt a chill down my back, as though someone stood just behind me. I could almost see how Alexander would be, bemused and a little pleased, I thought. I could almost see how he would be.

"Now it is for you," Manetho said. "This is for the sem-priest to do. Take up the knife."

The last item in the box was a small flat dagger, its blade dark and vaguely mottled, as though it had a light sheen of oil on it. Ptolemy lifted it gently. "What is it?" he asked.

"Forged of meteoric iron," Manetho said. "When I say, touch it to his lips." He cleared his throat and began in Greek, his words slightly accented. "Come forth, Alexander son of Phillip! Come forth, Horus of Egypt! Come to those who call you, to the sem-priest who is your son, to those who wait for you. Come and speak. Let your mouth be loosened. Come forth, Alexander and Horus!"

Meteoric iron, I thought. Fire stolen from the gods, as Prometheus had done. There was a layer that Manetho did not know, more than one layer. And he did not know that Ptolemy was blood kin, brother in fact to Alexander. And he did not know…something. I had no time to even formulate what I would say before Ptolemy bent and gently touched the tip of the iron blade to Alexander's lips.

Stolen fire.

My head reeled, the room reeled around me. The lamps flickered, their shadows moving across the King's face.

He was there. He was standing behind me and a little to the side, just behind Bagoas. There was nothing I could see. There was no flesh I could touch, but the sense of him, the pure, vital thing that had animated him, that was nothing to do with the mummified body in the coffin, was there.

Alexander stood beside me, and I knew what he asked. There could be no doubt of my assent. I was a Companion, my oaths binding beyond death.

I felt my mouth open, heard my voice issue forth changed in timbre and tone. "You have called me. Why?"

# THE ⊙PENING ⊙F THE MOUTH

Bagoas spun around, his brows knitting together as though he wondered if this were some part of the rite that I had been rehearsed in, some ritual repetition of lines. Ptolemy, who doubtless thought that unlikely, looked at me as though he could not credit what he had heard. It was Manetho, who knew this was no part of the preparations, who openly gaped.

"If you call me, why are you surprised when I answer?" I said. Or he said. Perhaps we said was the most accurate. It was a very strange sensation, as though Alexander were both by my side and within me. I could hear him, though it was more than that. It was as though I shared his thoughts as if he'd said them, and yet remained entirely separate. I was myself and he was himself, though he used my voice.

*Though you allow me use your voice*, he thought in my head. *I cannot make you do or say anything. And I am grateful that you allow it.* For a moment Alexander sounded amused. *This is more usually the job of oracles than cavalry!*

*My Lord*, I thought, *you have no idea how many strange things have happened since I stood beside your bier. I do not know what I am anymore.*

It was Manetho who recovered his presence of mind first, and he bowed from the waist. "All hail Alexander, Lord of the Two Lands,

Beloved of Amon, Chosen of Ra. All hail Alexander, Pharaoh of Egypt."

Bagoas stared at me in absolute disbelief.

Ptolemy frowned. "What is going on here?"

"You called me," we said. "Did you not have a reason for it, Ptolemy? You seem to have gone to a good deal of trouble to do it." We looked around the tomb chamber, the priests crowding in with their implements, Manetho with his cheetah skin draped across his chest. And of course the body lying in the coffin. We did not quite like to look at that.

Bagoas' voice was flat. "This is cruel and has no point."

The part of me that was me recoiled at the anger and hurt in his eyes, thinking that I played with him thus. It did not bode well for Lydias.

*It's like that, is it?* Alexander sounded almost wistful.

*My Lord, you have been dead three years,* I replied a bit defensively.

*I know,* he said. *And I do not wish him unhappiness. He never gave less than the best of himself to me.*

"Lydias, what are you doing?" Ptolemy demanded. "Manetho, is this part of the rite? Is he acting? Did you rehearse him?"

Manetho spread his hands, his customary confidence deserting him. "No, Gracious Lord. Not in the least. He is a soldier, and I have never heard of such a thing happening when there was not a trained priest or priestess involved. Indeed we have priests here! I cannot imagine why Pharaoh would choose a soldier instead."

"Possibly because your priests do not speak Greek," we said. "Besides, I prefer to rely upon my own men." We tilted my head just a bit, the way Alexander always did when he spoke to someone taller than he. "Ptolemy, what leads you and Bagoas to this? And what is going on?"

Ptolemy's mouth opened and closed.

"Gracious Lord, you should address him just as you would have," Manetho said. "We invited him to speak, and while it is unusual that the dead would want to converse with the living, such things do happen. Though usually through a proper oracle."

"Talk to him as though he were Alexander?"

"I don't believe this," Bagoas said flatly.

"Is it so strange that I might speak to you?" we asked. "Are there not rites and prayers to me? Are there not men who call upon my name as a god?"

"Pharaoh is a god," Manetho said, recovering somewhat. "Horus indwelling. And when he dies he becomes Osiris and passes into the Uttermost West. I have never spoken with a dead pharaoh before, though I have seen accounts of such. Seti is particularly voluble, I understand."

"There are men who invoke you as a god, yes," Ptolemy said. "Does that matter?"

"It should," Manetho said. "That is why we pray before statues—to call the god's attention to where we are, to bring their wandering consciousness to bear on us. The god Alexander is as real as any other." He looked at us and shrugged. "And he is still trapped by it, not free to pass from here into Amenti should he so choose."

Our head lifted again, keenly, like a hunting dog on a scent. "Should I so choose? What are my choices then, priest?"

Manetho took a breath, his eyes on ours. "These are deep waters, my Pharaoh. But once you are released, I believe you have a choice. To remain here, an invoked being, exactly as you are now, feeding upon the energy of offerings and belief."

"An immortal hero?" we asked.

"Rather a daimon," Manetho said. "If I have your word correctly. A spirit disincarnate, unchanging and unaging, a benefactor of mortals."

We nodded slowly. "Or?"

"You may pass into the Halls of Amenti," Manetho said. "Where you will stand before Isis and Osiris, and Ma'at will weigh your heart."

*Or before Death and his Queen, and return to the wheel once more,* I thought to him. *To return to this life in all its pains and sorrows, like Prometheus chained to the peak devoured again each day.*

I felt him smile within me. *The world is not all sorrow, Lydias. Surely you cannot say so when Bagoas is your friend?*

"But that is a question Isis should put to you," Manetho said. "Not I."

"Then what question is it that you called me for?" we asked.

Ptolemy looked us in the eye. Ever practical, he would play this the way it came. "To ask you to give up the governing of the Black Land and the control of its creatures so that it may be taken up by another."

"By whom?"

"By your son, Alexander son of Alexander. I stand as proxy until such time as he can rule," he said evenly.

*If he rules*, I thought. I tried to keep it to myself, but that was impossible.

Alexander was not surprised, though I felt the thread of regret run through him. *You have said nothing I did not know*, he thought. *Bagoas has told me much, in his empty hours.*

I thought with an ache of Bagoas sitting beside the golden coffin, telling stories and news and court gossip to ears that could not hear.

We spoke, and our voice was firm and unexpectedly gentle. "You cannot be a little bit of a king, my brother."

Bagoas' head shot up and we heard Manetho take a swift breath.

"You must be king, or not be king," we said.

To my astonishment Ptolemy's eyes were filled with tears. "I promised you when you were six years old that I should never take anything that was yours, that I should never betray you or plot against you. I promised you that you were my little brother, and that you would never have reason to mistrust me. I swore, Alexander!"

"You are taking nothing from me," we said. "Nothing." I heard my voice choke, and swallowed hard. "My son does not have Egypt, and he never will. Persia may be his, and Macedon if Roxane is strong enough. You didn't see why I wanted to marry her, said that she was unsuitable. You did not say, she is just like your mother, Alexander, though you thought it. Do you think I didn't know that? Do you think I thought that any one less strong and ruthless would be able to keep our children alive? I did not want to see my children murdered any more than you do."

Bagoas drew a breath that was almost a sob.

"Roxane has her fight, and you have yours. Egypt is a small enough gift out of all the vast empire." Our eyes met Ptolemy's, and a rueful smile touched our lips. "You had no patrimony from our father. I had it all. Always, I had it all, his care, his effort, even his name. Most men would hate a younger brother who had everything while they had nothing. And yet you were true, the truest brother who ever lived. Take this then from me, a patrimony long delayed."

We raised our voice, addressing Manetho and all who stood there. "I relinquish the kingdom of Egypt into the care of my beloved brother Ptolemy, so that he may reign and wield the power of Pharaoh, he and his descendants who come after him. Does that do it?"

Manetho bent his head. "I think so, Gracious King."

"And may you know what a good bargain you have got in Ptolemy," we said, smiling.

"We know that, Gracious King," Manetho said.

"Bagoas."

He lifted his eyes to ours, and I saw that he at last believed. "I know," he said.

"You do."

"Good night, my sweet Lord," he whispered.

"Sleep sound, beautiful one," we said, and I watched his eyes overflow at last. Bagoas closed his eyes and lifted his chin, the light playing across his face, and I was not sure whether it was Lydias or Alexander who ached.

We turned to Manetho. "What do we do to let go?"

"I call Horus from you," he said, "and when the sem-priest touches your lips with the knife, Horus will come out from you and rest in him."

"Do it then," we said. "And Ptolemy?"

"Yes?"

"Remember me to Thais."

Ptolemy shook his head, looking for once entirely like an exasperated big brother. "I will, Alexander."

We took a step back and Manetho spread his arms, beginning to speak aloud in the Egyptian tongue. It was very odd, as we understood some parts of it and didn't understand at the same time.

*I have learned some here in Egypt*, I said.

*I never had the chance*, he replied as Manetho went on and on.

*Perhaps next time*, I thought.

I felt a broad grin cross his face. *You do not think I will choose to be a daimon?*

If I could have blushed I would have, but I answered straight. *My Lord, did not the oracle at Siwah reply when you sent to them asking if Hephaistion would be a god that he was not? That he was a hero, but he was not a god? I do not think you would choose to go where he cannot follow. You are a wind through this world, and I do not think you are done with it.*

Manetho's voice grew louder, ringing in our ears.

*I will see you again, Lydias of Miletus*, he said.

*I do not see how you can help it*, I replied.

"Now," Manetho said.

Ptolemy lifted the blade of meteoric iron, and as it touched my lips the room twisted and at last went dark.

I woke to darkness and the stars reeling overhead. For a long moment I had no idea where I was, or what might be happening. There were just the moving stars. Then I was aware of the sound of hooves, the quiet clopping of a horse on a sandswept road, and it came to me. I lay in the cart on which we had brought Alexander's body to Saqqara. We must now be on the way back to the walls of Memphis.

Someone bent over me and I saw that it was Manetho. "What?" I asked.

He looked relieved. "Ah. You're awake. Do you know who you are?"

"The Hipparch Lydias," I said, trying to push myself up on my elbows. "Where is Ptolemy?"

"He has gone ahead to the city," Manetho said. "A messenger came a few minutes ago and said that Perdiccas' men had been sighted."

"He's gone to the walls then." I sat up, though the world tilted around me. "What's wrong with me?"

"To hold a daimon within you requires a great deal of energy," Manetho said. "For an unprepared man with no training at all to do so is frankly unusual. Generally oracles and the like are trained from childhood, in Egypt anyway. I've never seen it happen in a grown man and a soldier. You are exhausted. But it is nothing that normal rest will not mend. You should eat a meal including meat, and you should go to bed."

"I need to go to the walls," I said, still clutching the boards of the wagon. I felt as though I had lost blood, though there was no wound on me.

"You will not," Bagoas said, appearing on the other side of the wagon. "Ptolemy said you were to rest and not to try to report to him until tomorrow, that you had done enough in his service for one night."

"Bagoas." I did not know what to say to him. Certainly I had never intended to cause him pain.

"Sit still and don't fall over," he said. "We will get you a meal and a good night's sleep, and tomorrow you can see Ptolemy."

His tone of voice left me nothing to say that would not start a very personal scene in front of Manetho and all the junior priests, so I subsided. Wordlessly I rode in the cart as we approached the walls of Memphis, shining whitely in the light of the waning moon. How many days had it been? Eight? Morning would bring the ninth day. And then what?

The movement of the cart was soothing, and I nearly went to sleep before we got to Bagoas' rooms. He asked one of the priests to fetch some food, and helped me in and settled me on the couch as though I were an invalid.

I looked at him, ready to say I knew not what, but the priest came back with two bowls of hearty fish stew, goat cheese, bread, and beer.

The smell of the food was almost overwhelming. I could have come off a two-day march from the way I tucked into it. The fish stew was thick and rich, redolent of dill and other herbs. I thought I had never had something so good. The bread was the perfect texture, and the beer was cool and good even to the dregs in the bottom. Food is life, I thought. And I am hungry.

At last I put the bowl down. "Bagoas," I began. "I had no idea that would happen. Please believe that."

He looked at me clear-eyed, an earring dangling in one ear despite the white Egyptian shenti he had worn for the rite. It looked well on him, showing off the fine muscles of his arms and chest. Persians were more modest. I had never seen him out and around without a shirt before. "It wasn't your fault, Lydias."

"He wanted to speak," I said. "And I would not refuse him. How could I?"

"Of course you should not have refused him," Bagoas said.

"I would not have hurt you for all the world," I said.

Bagoas shook his head. "Lydias, I already know he's dead. He's been dead three years. Believe me, I already know that." He stood up, pacing over to the door and back. "He is gone, and I must find something else to do with the rest of my life, or else die. And I have little taste for death. I do not want it, not now."

"Bagoas," I said, and did not know how to continue.

"There was a time I wished to die," he said, his back still to me. "When I was young and thought that death was my only release. I was not born a slave, you see, nor gelded as a child too young to remember. I knew, and I mourned the life I should have had, the man I should have been, even more than I detested my lot. But time passed, and if I did not die then I must live. And living I must find some pride and some hope." His shoulders moved in what might have been a shrug. "All that was long ago, before I came to Alexander with the rest of Darius' trappings. Like you, I invented myself, created someone entirely different from the man I was born to be, the man my father would have called his son, a man more like Artashir." Bagoas raised his head, and there were no tears in his eyes. "I am not a man, and I am not that man. I am Bagoas who was Alexander's. But now I must be something else again, something more besides, and I do not know how to go on."

"Let me speak to Ptolemy about coming to Alexandria. He needs a chamberlain, a master of the palace. Come to Alexandria, Bagoas." I had not thought that he might consider death. But that arrow had passed before I even knew it was there. "You are needed. And it is not your beauty or your grace that are needed, but your wits and your diplomacy. Ptolemy needs such as you, the one you are now, not some dream of who you might have been, or who you were to Alexander."

He hesitated, and I thought I knew why. "I am not doing favors for you, Bagoas. You are truly needed."

I saw him weighing it. He nodded slowly, his eyes never leaving my face. "I will come to Alexandria if…" He held up a hand. "If you win and there is still Ptolemy to serve. If you win, I will come if Ptolemy wants me. But he must ask me, not you, Lydias. I do not want that between us, that I owe you my livelihood."

"If we lose we'll probably all be dead," I said.

"Well, yes." Perdiccas would not be happy with him either, since Bagoas had betrayed the hearse into Ptolemy's hands. He came and brought a blanket, which he tucked around me. "Then you will have to win."


In the morning we faced Perdiccas.

At Memphis the Nile is a formidable river, even shrunken in the dry season as it was. Even now, just before the Inundation, the river remained perfectly navigable to all except the largest and heaviest of craft. We had borne Alexander's hearse to Memphis during the flood because the barge was exceptionally big and unwieldy, but normal river traffic did not cease in the dry season. Directly opposite the walls the river was still wider than the best archer might shoot, and the water was easily over a man's head.

However, just upriver of Memphis there was an island anchored by palm trees that cut the Nile in half. The westward side was shallower, and in the dry season boats stayed to the eastward side where even then the water came to a man's neck. Also, the westward bank was broad and flat, divided into rich fields that surrounded the city. In a few months those fields would be green with grain, but now they lay fallow waiting for the flood.

When I came onto the walls the next morning, it was already clear what Perdiccas was doing. Sheltered from our side of the river by the island, he was trying to cross his troops over to the island. Twenty or thirty cavalry had already crossed over by swimming the horses, and now several officers were dismounted, examining the banks of the island on either side and poking at the river with the poles of a couple of sarissas.

Ptolemy was on the walls with Artashir, who was shaking his head.

"We would have to be in the water to hit them," Artashir said. "There are too many trees on the island. If we go out on the western bank we still won't be able to hit them crossing over to the island from the eastern side."

"On the other hand," Ptolemy said, "that means they can't hit us. Would you agree?"

Artashir lifted his hand to his eyes to shade them from the rising sun and looked east again. "No, they can't hit us from the island either. If they massed on this side they might get a few arrows in the bank, but it's extreme range. They wouldn't hit anyone. This isn't an archery duel, sir. Our best bet would be to stay on the western bank and cover the water between the island and us. We could hit targets in the water easily."

"When they try to cross from the island to our side of the river," Ptolemy said, nodding.

"Good morning," I said.

Ptolemy looked around. "Good morning, Lydias. Feeling better?"

"Entirely myself, sir," I said.

Ptolemy laughed. "That's almost a pity. We could have used you the other way!"

Artashir looked from one of us to the other.

"I'm afraid that's not an experiment to be repeated," I said. "Even for the tactical advantage. All you have is me."

"Then you'll have to do," Ptolemy said.

I thought that he looked rested and confident, more so than I had seen the last few weeks. If the ritual had done nothing else, it seemed to have put Ptolemy on his best form.

"Artashir was just saying that he doesn't think he can hit them from the shore while they're crossing over to the island," he said.

I nodded. "I see that. So what's the plan then?"

"They're looking for a place to cross and they'll probably find one. That's the shallower side and the river is all the way down."

I looked across again. The river was all the way down, low and relatively slow between its banks. Now was the time. The river was supposed to be rising. But there was no sign of anything happening. It looked just as it had every other day, and not even my most fervent hopes could imagine that the waterline was higher on the opposite shore. I did not see a miracle.

Ptolemy put his hands on the parapet. "We're going to have to resist him on the riverbank. It gives us enough of an advantage. They'll be wading out of the Nile and won't be able to keep in formation. And they'll have to go straight into massed infantry. That's a tough fight."

"And we can hit them with arrows as soon as they get in the water," Artashir said. "I can bring some of the Egyptian archers down off the walls and put them behind our infantry."

"That's a tough crossing for them," I agreed. "But they've still got most of their elephants."

"That's a job for you and Artashir, isn't it?" Ptolemy said.

I winced. "I was afraid you'd say that." Cavalry on elephants was the worst imaginable scenario from my point of view, but heavy cavalry was about the only thing that could deal with elephants. Elephants would tear through a packed phalanx doing an incredible amount of damage.

Artashir nodded grimly. "If we shoot for the handlers and the elephants' eyes, we can do it. But I've only got about thirty horse archers left."

"I'll hold you in reserve, then," Ptolemy said. "And send you after the elephants when they come ashore. Lydias, you do the same. I need you both on the elephants. Artashir hasn't enough men."

I nodded. "We're ready."

Of course there would be enemy cavalry too, but if they had to wade out of the river through a formed-up phalanx that was less pressing. If we had cavalry already through the phalanx then we had worse problems than elephants.

"We need to make it hurt," Ptolemy said. "We can retire on Memphis if we need to, but we can't afford to do that unless we've hurt him too badly for him to make a serious assault on the city."

"And he doesn't have anywhere to go," I said. "While we have supplies and walls at our back."

Artashir nodded. "We can do this."

"Then let's go. Make sure everyone gets a good meal now. Perdiccas won't be over on the island until noon, and I don't want everyone standing around for seven or eight hours without having eaten. We've got time. Let's take it."

As I went down the stairs from the wall to brief Glaukos and the troop leaders about the plan, I reflected that this was just like Ptolemy. Younger, less experienced commanders would rush everyone onto the field in harness to stand in the sun from dawn until afternoon growing restive, tired, and hungry. Ptolemy would mosey onto the field at the point where it was necessary, as though he were in no hurry at all.

By midmorning Perdiccas had moved all of his men except the rearguard onto the island. We saw when the elephants crossed. Though the water was high enough that horses needed to swim, the backs of the elephants stayed dry. From the walls I saw one with its platform decked with scarlet curtains. I had seen that before, in India.

"Ptolemy," I said, and pointed.

He nodded. He had seen them too, steeds for great princes or more often queens.

I thought I saw the curtains move, as though a curious child tried to look out. He is there, I thought. Alexander's son. Perdiccas does not dare leave him behind.

"To arms," Ptolemy said in a conversational tone. "It's time."

İ HAD MY new horse, Perseus, and together we stood behind the cavalry formation on a little hillock, where a few almond trees marked the edge of the farmer's field. The sun beat down in the hottest part of the year. The Black Land baked under the sun.

Glaukos sat beside me on his horse. When the time came he would take his place at the front. To my right were Artashir and his horse archers, and to my left the Egyptian archers in their linen stood impassive behind our massed infantry.

Ptolemy came along the front of the lines at a walk, his horse perfectly in hand, his helmet off and his forehead reddening with sun.

"Time for the speech," Glaukos said wearily.

"He'll be short and sweet," I said.

"Men of Egypt! Companions all! We stand together before Memphis, before Alexander who lies in state. But we stand before more than that. We stand before Alexandria, and our homes, our families."

Our lines were silent. No one shouted. In that moment I realized the genius of him. Alexander had promised glory. He had promised an adventure the like of which the world had never known. But in the end we were all tired. In the end, the ends of the earth were too far for our mortal feet. Ptolemy did not promise us glory. He promised home at the end of the road. In giving land in Alexandria he had taken the temper of his men exactly. They could see themselves citizens of a proud new city, fathers and men of substance, not forever questing after some far horizon. He gave them a future to fight for.

"We stand before our own. Together." Ptolemy's voice carried, not beautiful but serviceable, like the rest of him. "Let's do this. And then go home."

The roar began at the back of the infantry, but it swelled, rising into a loud cheer, the banging of sarissa butts on shields in counterpoint.

Ptolemy rode down the line and passed through, and we cheered him as never before, as though he were Alexander.

As though he were Pharaoh.

Blessed Lady of Egypt, I prayed, keep him safe. Let us win.

Ptolemy came back to where we were, his face flushed.

"That went well," I said.

He looked surprised and pleased. "Thank you."

"Ah-ha!" said Artashir, looking out over the river. "They've found something."

"A shallow place, I think," I said, raising my hand to my eyes.

They were sending a line of elephants into the water a little way upstream of us, each right behind the other, seven of them, while downstream from the elephants a troop leader waded out. The water was only waist deep.

"They've found a sandbar," Ptolemy said. "And put the elephants upstream to break the current. I wonder if—" He broke off. "Yes, there."

Downstream of the place where the troop leader stood, ten or twelve horsemen waded out into the water. To catch anyone swept away, I thought, as they must cross in full armor with sarissas leveled. I did think the river was running faster, the current stronger.

On the opposite bank the first phalanx formed up and began to wade into the water.

"Artashir," Ptolemy said.

Artashir nodded to his men and began directing them around, getting into position to cover where they would come.

Knee-deep in the water as they waded out, the first of Perdiccas' phalanxes raised their shields above their heads.

"Ready," Artashir said.

As one every bow was drawn.

"Fire." Black arrows swooped across the sky and the battle was joined.

# RIVER GODS

The first volleys were not effective. With their shields over their heads the arrows that dropped down upon them largely clanged off the steel. Here and there one slipped through gaps between shields, but did little damage. Still, there was the effect of being under fire, which was not something to underestimate.

Artashir called hold after the third volley. They were coming close to the shore, and the first lines of our infantry stepped forward to meet them, sarissas leveled. Like two enormous crashing behemoths, our infantry and theirs locked together. The noise was tremendous, the clash of steel and the shouts of men, the grunts and groans as they strained with main force to push the other back, sometimes literally shoving shield to shield.

We had the advantage. Our men stood on solid ground, while the back of their phalanx was knee-deep in water with a sandy bottom. Slowly, a handspan at a time, we began to push them back. Our first ranks splashed into the river.

A second phalanx was crossing, trying to swing into position upstream to the right of the first, and Ptolemy shifted the line to meet it.

They locked shield to shield, struggling at the very edge of the Nile. And our men began to push.

I gentled my restive horse. He smelled blood. "Not our turn yet, boy," I said. I waited, cool and collected as Ptolemy, watching the battle.

Above, people had gathered on the walls of Memphis. I wondered if Bagoas were there. I thought he probably was. He would want to see, would not be able to bear sitting quietly somewhere while everything unfolded.

Step by step, our men were forcing them back, pushing them slowly into the river. Muscles strained, and from where I sat I could hear the groans of men and metal as our men shoved with all their strength. The first two ranks were in the water now, the river running around their ankles, carrying their blood away. The fallen lay trapped by the feet of their comrades. The current could not seize them yet.

"Form up," I said to Glaukos.

He looked at me questioningly.

"He's got to break through, man," I said. "That means either cavalry or elephants. And either one is our job."

Perdiccas chose cavalry. Almost before Glaukos got to the front of the formation, his horsemen were in the water, wading through the river that came up to the horses' chests.

"Stand to receive!" Glaukos shouted, glancing back over his shoulder at me.

What? I thought. Wait for them to come out of the water and form up before we hit them?

I had my reins in my right hand, and raised my left, catching Glaukos' eye. "Form to the right!" I ordered. "Get around the right end of our infantry!" I pointed to the troop leader of the farthest left file. "Go down to the other end. Get on the far right." There was no point in having men who were behind our own phalanx. "Get round the flank."

I trotted along the back of the line behind them. Out in the water, the men of Perdiccas' cavalry were halfway across. We wanted to hit them just when they started to form up. And from what I could see of the speed of the shallow water, they wouldn't get into anything approaching formation until they got almost ashore.

"Form up!" I shouted, and the Ile responded. The horses were restive, ready to go.

Glaukos looked relieved.

I raised my empty left hand again. He kept his eyes on it.

Almost to shore. Almost. The first ones of them were knee deep in the water, the rest of the cavalry strung out across the river on the sandbar. Almost.

"Forward!" I shouted. "Ptolemy and Egypt!"

With a spring, all Ptolemy's Ile leapt forward.

Perseus took off too, and I lurched at the unexpected charge. "Oh shit," I said, fumbling with my left hand trying to get my sword out and hauling on Perseus' head at the same time. He was a trained warhorse, and he'd been in charges before. He knew his place was in the middle of the fray and he wasn't going to hang back.

I pulled him up, swearing, just short of the river, right behind the last of my men. It took all my strength to hold him in, turning his head sharply so that he wasn't facing the same direction as the other horses. Which left me broadside to the battle.

"You stupid ass," I said, as he sidled around to the right, trying to get back into it. "Cut it out."

Too close. I was in too close, and my men had opened gaps in their ranks as they engaged in groups. I barely got my sword in hand and the reins transferred to my bad hand before the first of the enemy was upon me.

He came in against my right side, any momentum he might have had blunted by the water. His horse couldn't charge, and coming at me at a walk didn't give him much. I met the first blow, then disengaged below his guard. My thrust hit him in the fleshy part of the shoulder just below the harness, digging into the muscle as he tried to turn his horse away.

And then he was past me and I was facing the next one, guard and thrust, guard and thrust, the rhythm of steel on steel. I finally got in, hitting the back of his hand hard enough to break fingers and knock his sword from him.

Perseus lurched, and I barely held on with my left hand. In the process I lost the opportunity. My opponent got clear.

I pulled Perseus around, facing the river once again. "You idiot. I'm beginning to change my mind about you," I said to him. Perhaps he was too much horse for a man with a bad hand. I should have to have some gentle beast suitable for an invalid.

The thought made me snarl. I put my heels to his side and urged him straight into the fray.

Guard and cut and slash, the familiar dance, with Perseus beneath me and the world narrowing to the length of my sword, death blossoming where I was. For a few moments there was nothing else.

And then I was clear, standing with the water about Perseus' knees. I could not do this, I thought. I needed to see better, to be more than a soldier. I could not simply surrender to battle madness and forget all else. I was responsible.

I backed Perseus a few paces and looked about.

To my left, their infantry was locked with ours in the water just short of the riverbank, our front lines completely entangled. We were pushing them back slowly and surely, the water almost to the waists of the men in our front rank. They struggled in the water, chest to chest, shield to shield.

Before me, our cavalry had engaged theirs in the water upstream of the rest. The bottom was farther here and the water more swift-flowing. As I looked I saw a soldier, one of ours or theirs I could not tell, fall from his horse. I did not think his wound was mortal, but the water drew him under and away, the current running strong and hard.

For a moment I stared, and then I realized what was happening. So many men and animals on the sandbar were destroying it. Horses and elephants were stirring up the bottom, and once disturbed the sand was carrying away in the swift current. The Nile could not be trifled with, and She fought for Egypt.

At that moment Perdiccas ordered the elephants forward.

Elephants do not mind deep water. Indeed, in India where they live one may see whole herds of elephants bathing and playing like children in water that a man would be foolish to dare. Perdiccas' elephants plunged into the water, twenty of them, bearing straight down upon our infantry lines. His own men were entangled with ours and doubt-less could not get free, but that didn't matter to Perdiccas. He had never shown much concern for lives when victory hung in the balance.

To my left, behind the infantry lines, I heard Ptolemy shouting, but could not understand his words.

"Lydias' Ile," I yelled, "form up!" We must disengage as best we could. Elephants are almost impossible to fight from the ground, and our men would be up to their necks in water that would not bother the elephants at all.

"Form up!" I heard Glaukos' voice echoing mine.

All our men would not be able to disengage, but those who could needed to now.

There was a buzzing overhead, and the first flight of Artashir's arrows passed over us. His thirty horse archers were drawn up in a tight formation on the riverbank, targeting the drivers of the first elephants. Their horses stood as though they had been carved from stone, trained for years thus so that they will not twitch and spoil their riders' shots. But there were so few. There were only thirty of them left.

There were ten of my men about me now, forming up as though I were the troop leader. And the first elephant was almost upon us, plow-ing through the water, great plumes of spume flying from his feet.

"All right, men," I said. "You've done this before and you know the drill. Get the drivers. Or go for the eyes. And keep loose. We have to confuse them and stay out of their way."

"Easier on dry land, sir," one wit said.

"So's fucking," I said, "but you take the opportunity when it arises."

They laughed, as I meant them to. It takes nerve to stand when ele-phants charge down upon you.

And then they were upon us, the lead animal plowing through the river, his long tusks held high.

I dodged to the right with the wit, Perseus plunging through the water. Most horses will not abide elephants, though our more experi-enced warhorses had seen them before. I was glad to know that at least he wasn't going to pitch me off and run away.

As I passed the elephant's side, I slashed at it, but my sword did no damage to its thick hide. Which was, of course, the trouble with elephants.

We had opened, as we should, letting them pass between us and taking what blows we could land. Now we closed behind them, trying to get around them and get at the drivers.

I nearly fell as the elephant swung about, his tusks passing just over my head as Perseus plunged beneath his nose. The elephant trumpeted in anger.

Well enough, I thought. While he is playing lion baiting with me, he is doing nothing else. I had the reins in my good hand, and did not try to strike, just ride like a spirit about and beneath him, bedeviling the animal.

The elephant wheeled about, more angered by our attacks than hurt. He turned, lowering his head like a bull.

Not too far away, Artashir sat on his horse like a statue, only his arm moving as he drew and released, drew and released.

The elephant came down upon him.

He held the arrow at the notch, and even his horse did not flinch, her ears forward and pointed at the elephant.

I shouted. I kicked Perseus hard and we took after the elephant, driving hard through the sheets of water the mighty beast threw up.

He was waiting too long. He was waiting too late, waiting for the perfect shot.

And then Artashir released. The arrow flew straight and true, catching the handler in the throat. Blood fountained from severed arteries, and he pitched backward.

At last Artashir moved as the vast unguided beast bore down upon him, his little horse struggling in the mud of the riverbank. She slipped, scrambling, and stumbled to her knees.

"Faster, boy," I said, digging my heels into Perseus so that we were right beside the elephant, and I struck with all my strength at him.

Time elongated. It seemed forever, the lift of my arm, the brave movement of Perseus' legs. Ears, Sati had said. Something about ears.

She had said it long ago, but I heard her again, as though she said it now, just behind me, a smile in her voice. *Their drivers strike them on the ears to direct them.*

I hit the elephant's left ear as hard as I could with the flat of my sword.

Raising his long trunk, he veered off to the right, plunging past Artashir and his horse where they floundered in the water.

I pulled Perseus up just short of Artashir. He was out of the saddle, trying to coax his mare to rise. From the way she moved, favoring her right foreleg, I thought she had definitely sprained something.

"Thanks."

"Anytime," I said. "That was quite a shot. Once in a lifetime."

"Let's hope," Artashir said.

I turned Perseus about, looking out over the river. Several other elephants were engaged by my men, weaving and splashing in a wild melee in the river. Off to my left, our infantry was still fully engaged, though on the far end an elephant had broken through and was creating havoc in our lines. Ptolemy was down there. I saw the red crest of his helmet.

The sandbar must have been nearly gone. Men struggled in water chest deep. Bodies swirled on the current or, dragged down by armor, bumped along the bottom, pulled toward Memphis and the distant sea beyond. As I looked, I saw a man suddenly scream and disappear under the water.

I blinked. No arrow had hit him. No soldier of ours had been near him.

The water roiled. Beneath its surface churned a long, reptilian shape, gray-green and three times the length of a man.

"Oh Lady of Egypt," I whispered, looking frantically toward the walls of Memphis.

The grate was up. They had released the sacred crocodiles. And the water was full of blood.

"Everybody get back! Everybody back!" I shouted. "Men of Ptolemy's Ile! Get out of the water! Everybody back on the bank!" I rode through the water toward my men, shouting at the top of my voice. "Form up on shore! Everybody back!"

We had a riverbank to retire to. Perdiccas' men had only the island, and the way there was deeper now, and much more deadly.

Down the line I could hear Ptolemy's voice raised as well. "Out of the water! Get back!"

Another man screamed as he was pulled under by an unseen shape, the water boiling with blood and bits of his flesh.

"Everybody back!"

Perseus splashed toward the shore. Now the water was up to his shoulders, now only to his knees.

I stopped. "Everybody back! Form up!"

"Form up on shore, you sons of bitches," Glaukos was shouting. I couldn't see him, but I heard him clearly above the din.

Perdiccas' men were in a panic. Some were throwing arms and harness away, swimming madly for the island. Some of them even made it.

Others plunged forward into us, dropping swords and sarissas, begging for quarter. They should rather a hundred times surrender to our men than face the monsters in the water.

Soaked to the skin, I stood on Perseus and felt it flow through me like lightning, like rain in distant lands, the ancient power of Egypt. Sobek, the defender, embodied in all his children, fought for Memphis.

*Egypt has Horus again*, the lioness whispered beside me. *The powers obey Pharaoh, Our son, Our hands on earth.*

About Perseus' knees I felt the river rise.

The current had been swifter, but now came the water, the Nile rising fingerwidth by fingerwidth, swollen with rain fallen nine days ago a thousand miles away.

The river rose.

"Get out of the water!" Ptolemy's horse was ankle-deep, cantering through the very edge of the flood, as he swept down the lines. "Everybody out! Grant quarter if they drop their weapons! Everybody out of the water. You there, surrender and you will be spared!"

The sun did not make a halo about him, and no god touched him with fire, but I felt the power crackle around Ptolemy, felt it bending to his will. Pharaoh commanded, and Egypt herself answered.

"Out of the water! Drop your sword, man. Quarter is given."

They were surrendering to him in tens and twenties now, casting away sarissas and flinging themselves face down on dry land, when two or three of them could easily have dragged him from his horse and killed him. He was one man among many of them, but none raised a hand to him. Instead they threw down their arms and begged for quarter.

"Quarter is given," Ptolemy shouted. "Throw down your weapons and get out of the water!"

The river was running swift and dangerous now. Crocodiles roiled the depths, as in darkness at the dawn of the world. Men swept away did not surface again.

I shouldered my way to Ptolemy. "All right?"

"Not a scratch," Ptolemy said. He looked me up and down. "You need a better horse. I saw you spinning around out there."

I felt the blood rising in my face. "I apologize, sir," I said stiffly.

He leaned forward and clapped me on the shoulder. "No need for that. You did well. Get that end of the line formed up. Let's see what we've got and where we are. And get Glaukos over here to take charge of prisoners. We're going to have plenty."

"Quarter to all who ask it?" I said. That wasn't usual, and I wanted to make sure.

Ptolemy nodded. "Quarter to all. Let's get these men rounded up."

I went back down to the right. Past the end of our lines, four elephants were standing exhausted in the date grove on the edge of a farmer's field, their drivers dead and their tack smashed to splinters, though none of them seemed gravely injured. I thought I would just let them alone for the time being.

Glaukos and five or six others were still mounted, trying to get the last of our men out of the water, mostly infantrymen who were bogged down by their heavy breastplates.

A little farther along a group of my men had formed up on the shore. The troop leader called to me, "Orders, Hipparch?"

"Get the wounded back into the walls of Memphis. Give quarter to all who ask. And keep out of the water," I said.

"Don't have to say that twice," he said, grinning with the strange euphoria that comes over men when they expected to die and instead have lived.

On the island, Perdiccas' rearguard still waited. Some of the men who had tried to cross had struggled back to the island, but now there was nowhere to go. On both sides the river ran fast and strong, patrolled by the sacred crocodiles of Sobek. They would have a long, cold, wet night of it, I thought. And no way off without boats. Perdiccas was more than welcome to it.

I counted men, took tallies of prisoners and wounded, and went to report to Ptolemy.

"I've four hundred and two men fit to fight, sir," I said. "Another eighty-eight wounded and seventy-six dismounted. Artashir is dismounted, but he's not hurt. I don't think his men were too cut up. I've thirty dead confirmed, though there are men missing."

Ptolemy nodded. "The river," he said.

"Yes," I said. "We can look for bodies downstream. What are we doing tonight?"

Ptolemy glanced across the water. "We wait," he said finally. "They can't leave. Let's give Perdiccas a while to think about the predicament he's in. Get our wounded in to the surgeons and get everybody a square meal and a rest. In the morning we'll be good, and Perdiccas won't be."

"There's something else," I said. "We've also got between Glaukos and me over eight hundred prisoners."

Ptolemy blinked. "Eight hundred?"

"Yes," I said. "Mostly Silver Shields infantry. They were in the vanguard, so most of them were on our side of the river when they got cut off. We've basically got the whole phalanx except for their dead."

Ptolemy whistled. The Silver Shields had been Alexander's crack infantry, veterans of all his campaigns back to Chaeronea. Some had served since Alexander's father's time. "That's what? Half or a little more of the total?"

I nodded. "I'd say five hundred. The other three hundred are from assorted units. Some of this, some of that. I've given quarter as you said, and ordered that their wounded should be treated."

"Good. Because they're on our side now."

I raised an eyebrow. "Are they?"

"They will be when I'm done talking to them." Ptolemy clasped my wrist, and went past me to where the prisoners sat at the edge of the field, their hands folded before them, looking out across the river in flood toward Perdiccas' banners on the island.

The setting sun cast shadows across us as it westered behind Saqqara. Above, a desert falcon turned on the air.

"Horus of Egypt," I said.

I lifted my head and felt the wind of victory.

# THE BARGAIN OF THE PTOLEMIES

I dreamed, and in my dream I fought again. I fought not beside the Nile in flood, but in the streets of Alexandria. Warships crowded the harbor, men landing sword in hand, while above all our half-completed buildings burned, streamers of flame shooting up to the sky. Showers of sparks fell around me as I struggled hand to hand in our streets. The curve of the harbor was engulfed.

I was looking for someone, but I didn't know who. About me our city burned.

Smoke billowed, acrid and thick. My head spun, my chest heaved.

She stepped from the flames, a woman wreathed in red sparks with the head of a lioness. "Ptolemy grasped the fire," She said. "And a new world dies aborning."

"No!" I ran toward her, shaking my watering eyes. "No! I tell you this will not be!"

Her golden eyes were sad. "So passes another Great King. So passes another might have been."

"This will not be, I tell you!" I shouted. "This must not be!"

"That is not yours to decide, Lydias of Miletus," She said. "That rests with Ptolemy. It is up to him whether or not this comes to pass."

"We didn't lose," I said. "We won."

"The danger lies not in losing, but in winning," She said.

I stood beside her in the burning street, but the blowing cinders did not injure me. "Why do I dream this?"

"It is one of the paths of the future," She said. "Something that might be."

I lifted my head, and it seemed I had known forever how it might work. "But not necessarily be," I said. "Visions of the future don't work that way. The gods do not see the future."

I thought that the lioness smiled at me, Her great teeth gleaming. "Only mortals see the future. And you, oracle, know that what you see are paths only, things that may be changed by the will of men."

"Then this may be changed," I said.

"If Ptolemy takes what is offered, this will be," She said. "If he seizes that fatal fire. It is up to him."

"I do not know what choice you mean, Lady," I said.

"You will," She said, and for a moment as the dream faded I thought the clouds of smoke gave way, clearing as if in a strong wind.

Instead of burning, a white city circled a cerulean harbor, green parks glittering like gems, while on the island off the coast a bright beacon gleamed clad in marble, light flashing from its pinnacle.

Lydias? Lydias?" Bagoas was shaking me. "It's a dream. Wake up."

I opened my eyes. It was still dark, and I lay in Bagoas' room in Memphis. He sat beside me, one hand on my shoulder, frowning with worry.

"It's a dream, Lydias. Wake up now."

I blinked. The burning city had seemed so real. It had seemed so tangible. My heart pounded still. "War," I said. "War that goes on and on and on. And in the end we will lose. In the end Alexandria will burn."

Bagoas looked nonplussed. "It's a dream, Lydias. When a man has been in battle, often he goes on fighting in his sleep long after the battle is ended."

"I do not know how to avoid it," I said. "I do not know what choice."

Bagoas put his hand to my shoulder, gentling me as though I were a nervous horse. "Calmly, dear. You dreamed, still fighting though the battle is over. It's over. You won."

"Winning is more dangerous than losing," I said. I swung my legs over the edge of the bed. "I need to go find Ptolemy."

"If it will make you feel better," Bagoas said. "Though Ptolemy may be asleep too. It's an hour or more until dawn."

"He won't be," I said. I dressed and, putting on harness and sword, went to the walls of Memphis.

Across and upriver on the island I could see the faint glow of a few campfires. There would not have been much to burn on the island. At my feet, the city of Memphis slept, houses and temples and markets and all, silent in the night. Only a few lights burned here and there fitfully, at the temples and about the courtyard of the House of Life where the wounded lay.

I do not know how long I stood upon the walls, half waiting and half dreaming. It cannot have been long before Ptolemy came.

"Anything going on over there?" he asked, and my eyes popped open. No doubt he thought I was only tired.

"Not that I can see," I said. "Their fires are dying down."

"There was some fuss and commotion a few hours ago," Ptolemy said. "The watch said something was happening, but who can tell what from this distance?"

"Maybe some crocodiles came ashore on the island," I guessed. "That ought to cause some trouble."

"Could be." Ptolemy shrugged. "We'll find out in a few hours. After sunrise we're going over in boats under a truce and see what Perdiccas is willing to give up to get out of the trap he's put himself in."

"Do you think he'll treat with you?" I asked. Perdiccas was known as a stubborn man, and a ruthless one.

Ptolemy nodded. "I think he'll treat. Or he can keep sitting on the island. Or he can try to wade to shore. Those are pretty much his choices right now. At least until the flood goes down. How long does that usually take, Lydias? Do you know for certain?"

"Two to three weeks after the flood peaks before the water starts going down," I said. "That's a long time for him to sit on the island. And it's hard to tell in the dark, but I'm pretty sure the river is still rising."

"He's not going to be able to sit there for more than a few days," Ptolemy said. "No food to speak of. So let's see if he's ready to make a deal. Tell Artashir I want him to come too. My Persian's not good, and somebody needs to be able to talk to the Persian officers."

"I'll let him know, sir," I said. "And it doesn't hurt to have that someone be of the house of Darius the Great. They can't say he's a nobody who's on the lookout for the main chance, not when he's got a distant claim on the throne himself."

"I know," Ptolemy said. "And a blood feud with Roxane. We'll just see how this all shakes out."

Two hours after the sun rose we set forth on an Egyptian ship, one of the lateen-sailed rivercraft that they have made from time immemorial, with a good, experienced captain from Memphis. Artashir and ten of his men came with us, as well as ten of our infantrymen, steady men who knew their business and would not start a fight.

The river was running fast and deep. It took thirty oarsmen to beat dead upstream, as there was no wind to carry us. The water flowed swift and true. I did not see any crocodiles beneath its smooth surface, but I supposed they were still there.

As soon as we got within bowshot we hailed them. "We come under truce! Ptolemy, Satrap of Egypt, would like to speak with the Regent!"

There was a movement among the people on the bank, and I recognized Polemon, who had chased after me so well when I had stolen the hearse. Beside him was an older, slighter man, a Companion I recognized as Seleucus, one of the infantry officers. He had been one of the most Persian of the Macedonian officers, marrying a lady of the Persian nobility by whom he now had a number of children. From the things our prisoners had said, it seemed he was now Perdiccas' second in command.

Now he leaned out from the crowd and called across the water to us. "If Ptolemy would like to speak, he is welcome to come ashore and speak with me. I will grant him safe passage and truce."

Ptolemy mounted the bow himself as we came closer. "Ho, Seleucus! My men are coming ashore too."

Seleucus shook his head. "No."

"Twenty men among your five thousand?" Ptolemy called back. "Don't be ridiculous. The risk is mine, not yours."

Polemon bent his head and said something to Seleucus, who straightened. "All right, Ptolemy. Agreed. Your men can come ashore."

Artashir and I exchanged a look. We would be entirely surrounded and outnumbered. Then again, they couldn't get off the island without us, and taking us hostage was not much of a plan. Memphis would hardly throw its gates open in exchange for Ptolemy.

Ptolemy turned, dropping his voice. He didn't sound worried at all. "Artashir, I want you to talk to the Persians. Anybody who might defect to us will be treated as honorable gentlemen, and serve with us under the same terms as my other men. I'll rely on you to say the right things."

Artashir nodded.

"Lydias, keep your eyes open. If you get a chance, talk to the drivers of the other elephants. You used to speak some of the Indian languages, yes?"

"I did," I said. That had been five years ago, and I had not been entirely fluent. But I imagined it was more than most men knew.

"Talk the drivers around. The elephants won't serve just any man. If we get the drivers, we get them. Promise them good pay and land in Alexandria. We need some elephants of our own. Let's see if we can hire some."

"I will," I said.

The boat came to shore slowly, the oarsmen careful. The river had risen a great deal, and the roots of the largest trees were now underwater. I didn't suppose it would hurt them. This must happen every year, and some of those trees were decades old. However, it would certainly damage the bottom of the boat to run into them, so the captain was very careful in bringing us close. Even so, we could not step directly ashore, but must step out in shallow water not quite to our knees.

I flinched at its cold touch, though I knew full well that all the blood and bodies had by now been carried downstream. I was not stepping through our dead.

The men on the shore looked battered, as though they had passed a mostly sleepless night. They were all in full harness and armed, and the camp had a makeshift look about it, as though it had been squeezed together by the rising river, and the smell of death hung about it. They had had no place to take their wounded.

Artashir and I flanked Ptolemy, one on the left, the other on the right. "I'd like to speak with the Regent," Ptolemy said to Seleucus pleasantly.

Seleucus' chin rose. "Perdiccas is dead," he said shortly, jerking his head toward the camp. "His body's in the tent over there. You talk to us."

"Did he die of his wounds?" Ptolemy asked.

"You could say that," Seleucus replied dryly. "He took quite a few before we were done."

Ptolemy nodded. "I see," he said evenly. "That does change a few things."

"Perdiccas was a fool," Seleucus said. "We're ready to come to terms."

"What are you offering?" Ptolemy asked.

There was a stir at the back of the crowd, and soldiers pushed them through, a young woman beautiful still, her long hair falling from its combs, her elaborate Persian dress muddy about the hem. Shoved, she stumbled to her knees but did not drop the child. A little boy about three years old looked up at Ptolemy.

"Them," Seleucus said. "Roxane and her son. We give them to you to do what you like with in return for our pardon, our arms, and our freedom. We will acclaim you as Regent."

Roxane watched him, her eyes smoldering. On her shoulder, the boy seemed more curious than frightened.

Artashir took a breath.

It seemed for a moment that time stopped. Here all the strands of what had been and what might be met, and turning from this place departed never to converge again. The burning city, the white city by the sea, both were real in this moment, both equally likely. The gods themselves were listening.

Seleucus spoke again. "We'll acclaim you as Regent, or if you want to get rid of them right away, we'll proclaim you Great King. With our backing too, you can have it all, the Persian Empire, Macedon, everything that was Alexander's. Antipatros is an old man. He can't stand against us all."

"It's mine anyway," Ptolemy said quietly, though his voice carried far enough. "They're mine, whether you give them to me or not. You're all trapped on this island until my men let you go. If I want the Regency, I can have it. If I want to be Great King, I can have it with you or without you."

And he could, I thought. I could see him enthroned, the mitre on his head. I could see him thus, crowned in Babylon. That fire was within his grasp. That path was clear before him.

Seleucus spread his hands. "Easier to have it with us, don't you think? My wife is Artashir's cousin," he said, with a nod to Artashir. "You'd rather have the Persian nobility back you. It would cost you far less. If we acclaim you Regent, you'll have it without a fight. Or kill the boy and be Great King tomorrow."

I saw Roxane's eyes go from Seleucus to Ptolemy. She was more angry than anything else, not cowed in the least. Alexander had married courage.

"But you can't be Regent without the boy," Ptolemy said. "Without him you have war with Antipatros and with Roxane's kin in Bactria as well. Not to mention that you'll have Olympias as your enemy. There's only one thing she wants, and that's her grandson on the throne of Macedon. And you'll never be sure of me. Your best chance is to come to terms with the Lady Roxane." His tone was still light and pleasant, as though he were discussing some ordinary piece of business, not the fate of kingdoms. Not a bit of tension showed in his face.

"True enough," Seleucus said. "But if we swear ourselves to you, you have it all. It's all yours, Ptolemy."

Ptolemy bent his head, and there was a small, rueful smile on his face.

The very wind in the trees died. Far overhead, the desert falcon twisted in the air, gyring and diving.

I saw its shadow cross his face, and then he looked up. His plain brown eyes were very bright. The world moved again.

"Hail Alexander, son of Alexander, Great King of Persia." He reached for Roxane and took her hand, drawing her to her feet. "Lady, you are free to go, you and your son, and such men and servants as wish to accompany you. I have no wish to be Regent, or Great King either. Your son is Great King, as was his father before him, and worthier men than I shall serve as Regent and guard his minority. Though I am sure none shall guard him so well as you do yourself."

Roxane stared at him, her dirty hand in his. "What?"

"You may leave, Lady," Ptolemy said. "My men will escort you and your son to the shore, with whatever soldiers and servants pledge themselves to you. You are free to return to Persia or wherever else you desire."

Seleucus gaped. "You are giving up Persia?"

Ptolemy shrugged with a look around, a look that seemed to encompass draggled date trees and swollen river and sky, and perhaps our white city by the sea as well. "I don't need Persia," he said. "Egypt is plenty for me."

He knelt down before the child, who stood beside his mother's skirts. Three years old, I thought, born just after I left Babylon. He had his mother's dark eyes and hair, but in the shape of his face there was Alexander. I knew the look. I had seen it in Chloe and her little brothers.

"And you, Alexander," Ptolemy said, his eyes searching the boy's face. "I hope that we will meet again, as man to man. I know your father would be very proud of you."

Seleucus shook his head. "You are giving up the Regency?"

"I am," Ptolemy said. "I'm sure you and Antipatros and the others will come to some terms. That is, if you're there to do so." Ptolemy grinned. "If you'd like a way off the island, I suggest you start making deals with the Lady Roxane. I've offered her free passage, not you. And she's probably more amenable to deals than the crocodiles are."

Roxane's eyes did not leave him. "Why?"

For a moment I thought he would give an easy answer, but he did not. "Because we must be better than our worst selves."

She shook her head. "I don't understand."

Gently, he placed her hand at her side and let go. "Because it's what Alexander would have done."

# SOTHIS RISING

Of course it was not so simple. There were wounded to be tended and the dead to be burned. I led a party downriver the next day, looking for bodies carried up on shore by the flood, asking farmers along the river if they had found any cast up in their fields. We found them nearly as far as Bubastis, and there were many we did not find, whether eaten by crocodiles or carried out to sea, or lost somewhere in the quagmires of the Delta to rot. Some we found whole, and some not. The crocodiles of Sobek had eaten their fill.

More than two thousand of Perdiccas' men were dead. We had lost less than four hundred.

We burned them on pyres before Memphis, and the black smoke went up to the sky. The Egyptians thought it horrible of course, for there is no greater blasphemy to them than to destroy the bodies of the dead, but they knew it was our way. I think they thought Ptolemy very rough indeed, like one old pharaoh on the walls of their temples who had counted his victory in the cut-off foreskins of his enemies.

The Greeks and Persians did not find it so at all. Ptolemy had each man's ashes put in an urn with his name on it to be brought to his family and friends in Persia. Those who we could not name, or those bodies that were incomplete, we burned together and buried at Saqqara with a stone above them that said they had been soldiers of Alexander. I did not think he would mind sharing his resting place with them, or that they could seek greater than to lie with him.

While we would not permit the living to enter the city, we had food brought out to the fields across the river and fodder for their animals. We feasted them as though this were the meeting of dear kinsmen. They ate and drank with gusto, as provisions had been scarce for them. And while they did our men went among them, talking in their own languages and praising the benefits of serving Ptolemy. Yes, soldiering is an uncertain life, but how much less so under such a general? How much less so, when there is ample pay and ample food, friendly territory beneath one's feet, and no long marches to the ends of the earth? How much better, when the pay is good and regular, and there are house lots to be had for free in Alexandria, where one can be a citizen and own something real?

I was proud that in the end all of the Indians stayed. There were twenty-eight elephants surviving, and four more with no drivers. All twenty-eight crews consulted together and decided to stay as a single unit. Home was a thousand miles away, over deserts and mountains, through the heart of an empire at war. Better to stay, they said, and risk their chances here. And so was born Ptolemy's elephant corps.

Nearly six hundred of the horse archers stayed as well. "Do you think," Artashir asked them, "that the empire will not dissolve into civil war? That we will not see kin pitted against kin?" He stood before them, handsome and well turned out in his archer's silks, and he spoke to them of honor. "I am of the house of Darius the Great. You know that Cyrus found us tribesmen, no more than rude men who warred with one another over every little piece of land. He made us into a great empire, and Darius made us the greatest in the world. What will happen when once again we break along tribal lines? Will you kill your mother's kin, or your father's? Will you go to war against your wives' brothers, or against your sisters' husbands? That is the question that awaits us in Persia, for make no mistake the empire is crumbling. You know as I do that to slay your kin is not only dishonorable, but is also a violation of the Truth. What can an honorable man do in these times except step away from it, and in doing so serve the Light?"

I had not quite seen it that way before, but now I saw it was so. Artashir and Amina, his first wife, were of different houses, and their son of both. Who could he serve without wrongdoing besides Ptolemy of Egypt?

Many of them seemed to agree, for almost half of them signed with Ptolemy, to serve beneath Artashir, a nobleman of their own people.

The infantry were a tougher case. Many of them had been long years under their officers and had families in Babylon. Most of them chose to go.

All in all, it was nine days before they marched northward up the eastern bank of the Nile. Artashir and an escort rode with them, ushering them to the ancient boundaries of Egypt.

Seleucus, Polemon, and a Companion named Peithon had sworn their service to Roxane, to support the claims of Alexander son of Alexander above all else. Seleucus and Peithon shared the Regency, until such time as all the other players could meet together and elect a new Regent, as they had the first days in Babylon.

I did not go, as I had far too much to do in Memphis. I found some old abandoned barracks buildings along the river outside the city walls to the south and set about buying the site for the crown. It would be a good place to keep the elephants, though the buildings would need a lot of repair.

From the walls Glaukos and I watched them go, a long column snaking its way northward beside the swollen river.

Glaukos leaned over and put his elbows on the wall. "How long do you suppose the boy will last?"

"I don't know," I said, looking where the banners at the center of the column marked Roxane and her son. "But longer than he would have a few days ago. Ptolemy's given him a chance. And I wouldn't underestimate his mother."

Glaukos spat over the walls, then looked down to make sure it hadn't hit anyone below. "The one he ought not underestimate is Seleucus. He shouldn't have let that snake go. Mark my words, there will be trouble from that."

"Maybe so," I said. I looked out over the valley of the Nile from the walls of Memphis on a beautiful day in the summer, and it was hard to think of anything terrible. "But we can't foresee all ends, Glaukos."

Glaukos looked at me sideways, a rather keen expression on his bearded face. "And what do you see?"

I flinched. "See?" I asked.

Glaukos grinned. "Do you think I don't know you're god-touched? Serving under you as long as I have? Do you think I didn't notice? Especially when you did things like tell us to stand to receive before the enemy was in sight?"

I opened my mouth and then shut it again.

Glaukos shrugged. "My old auntie back in Macedon had a bit of it. Could tell you what the weather would be, and whether a babe was boy or girl. It's not so strange as that. So what do you see, Lydias? Come on, man. It's for a friend."

"It is at that," I said, and leaned beside him on the wall. I should know better, I thought, than to hold back from old friends. I had done that too much, these past years. I looked out over the river, the sun catching fire like sparks from the surface of the water. The sparkles danced, the memory of fire. I had not tried to do this before, but it was easy. It was simply knowing.

"It's not over," I said quietly. "We'll fight and fight again. But Alexandria won't burn and Ptolemy won't be Great King. If he had taken the throne he couldn't have held it, and in reaching for more would have lost all we had."

Glaukos sighed. "Pity. He'd have been a damn fine Great King."

"Yes," I said. "But it's like a dice game, Glaukos. There's a time to walk away from the table with your winnings."

He nodded. "And if you stay too long, you'll be worse off than you started. Myself, I'd rather keep my winnings than gamble on a better pot."

"Ptolemy too," I said. "Men will ruin themselves grasping for Alexander's empire. Best not to crave that."

"And what's to happen to us?"

"I don't know," I began, but I could see Glaukos then, silver threads in his beard, rushing ashore in a beleaguered town, his men fighting their way through to mine to relieve the siege. I saw the sea before me, white mountains capped with snow, green rolling plains under a golden sunrise, caves beneath the earth in far-off lands. And I knew in that moment that our stories were not over. We stood at the beginning of the rest, not at the end of Alexander's world, but in the beginning of a new world.

"We go home to Alexandria," I said, and clapped him on the shoulder. "We go home, Glaukos."

WE DID NOT go just yet. There was one more thing to do.

At Saqqara a special temple was erected just beside the tombs of the Sacred Bulls. It would hold Alexander's body for now, until the sea defenses at Alexandria made it safe to bring him there. The gilded hearse was dragged there one last time, and then its wheels removed so that it could remain as the innermost shrine. About the outside plinths were to be erected so that a full circle of the greatest men of any age, Greek, Persian, and Egyptian sages alike, would surround the King.

The statues were not done yet when I walked that circle with Bagoas. Inside, in his golden coffin, Alexander rested, the uraeus still upon his brow. I did not need to open the sarcophagus to see him. He was not there any longer. Wherever he was, in Amenti or the lands beneath the earth, or walking once more behind the eyes of an innocent child, Alexander was not here. No daimon answered any call.

Bagoas seemed tranquil, though there was a hint of sadness in his eyes that he did not speak of. I flexed my hand and rubbed it where it ached.

"How is your hand?" Bagoas asked, a frown between his brows.

I stretched my fingers, still knobbed and bent. "Better," I said. "But I do not think it will ever be completely whole."

He put his hand on my shoulder. "I am sorry," he said. "But it is not as though Ptolemy is going to turn you off. Not with the things you have done. You are not a horseboy anymore, who is worth no more than the work of two good hands."

I nodded. "I know." I raised my hand, trying to close it. It did not, quite. "And if this is the price for it, then I am content. Not many men can say that they have stolen a god."

I heard a step behind me and turned.

It was Ptolemy who stood in the entrance of the tomb. "Oh, Lydias. I didn't expect you here. I was looking for Bagoas."

"I am here," Bagoas said, stepping forward. "Do you wish to visit with the King?"

"No, I wanted to talk to you," Ptolemy said. He hesitated. "I know that I promised you that you could serve the King forever, and that I would never part you from him or from his service. So I am reluctant to ask something as a favor of you, and I will completely understand if you refuse me."

Bagoas' face was bland. "What does my Pharaoh desire?"

"Would you be willing to come to Alexandria for a while? I am in dire need of a chamberlain who understands how palaces are run and who can make things work. I would be happy to give you the title of Master of the Palace or any other you prefer, and to pay you well for it. You made Alexander's court run more smoothly. Since I seem to have a court now, I would like you to do the same for mine."

Bagoas said nothing, apparently struck dumb.

Ptolemy looked almost sheepish. "Of course if you'd rather not, if you'd rather stay here in Memphis with the King, I understand that. I just thought that I would ask."

Bagoas found his voice. "I will come," he said. "It will be an honor to serve you." He glanced at me, then back at Ptolemy. "I can serve my Lord best by making sure he is well remembered, and that those futures he desired do not die with him."

"Alexander will lie in Alexandria, the city of his founding, when his great tomb is ready," Ptolemy said. "You only go ahead of him to prepare his place for him, as you did so often in life."

"And to serve his brother and his nephews who will come after," Bagoas said. "I will come to Alexandria, Ptolemy of Egypt."

So it was that we sailed down the Nile in the end of the Inundation, bound for Alexandria. Beside us on both sides of the river the water was receding, leaving a layer of rich brown silt. In the upper fields farthest from the river farmers were planting grain and other things. They stopped and waved as we passed in a great ship painted gold and red, like that of the pharaohs of old. Egypt had a Pharaoh again, this quiet man of forty-four, born in the mountains of Macedon. A strange fate, but it seemed to be working so far.

A new beginning, I thought, watching the first seedlings quicken in the fields. Ptolemy has changed, and so will Egypt. Alexandria will change her forever, Black Land, Red Land, and the City. A thousand strands of the future stretched before us on this morning, a thousand dizzying possibilities of all that could be.

I lifted my head and felt the sun on my face. Egypt had kept her promise to me. When I had crossed her borders she had promised that I too would be changed. I had not feared it, having nothing to lose, but now standing beside Bagoas on the ship I found myself wondering about the future for the first time in years.

"What are you thinking?" Bagoas asked, looking out over the greening land. The wind of our passage teased at his hair, a few strands blowing about his face, beautiful still for all that he was twenty-eight years old.

"That I should find out what number they have put on my lot in the city," I said. "And find out where it is. I suppose I will need a house."

Building anything would take time. We came back to an Alexandria full of scaffolding, buildings half raised, the foundations of a few temples laid and the work on the great public markets begun.

The squat, stoalike building that had been serving for the palace was being expanded. Two stories with a colonnade faced the sea over a long terrace covered in sandstone pavers. It looked stark, but more elegant than previously. I thought that maybe some plants would help. And the view of harbor and sea was amazing.

Out on the breakwater a wooden watchtower had been built with a beacon to warn ships that they were coming into shallow water. I thought that was a good idea, though it was very vulnerable in wood alone. If it could be fortified and armed it would be a good way to put any unwelcome ship entering the harbor into a crossfire.

One more project, I thought. It would take a lifetime to get to them all. More than a lifetime.

I HAD ONLY been back a few days, staying in the palace for want of anywhere else to stay yet, when I came down to breakfast in the morning to meet Artashir on the stairs.

"Artashir! When did you get back? I thought you had escorted Roxane to Pelousion?" I asked.

"I did," he said. "But she's away, so I came back to Alexandria as quickly as I could. I got in yesterday. And I was looking for you, actually."

"You've found me," I said.

"I've got something I want to show you. Are you busy, or can you come outside for a minute?"

"No, I'm not busy," I said. I followed him downstairs. "What is it?"

He turned at the bottom under the colonnade at the terrace. "This," Artashir said cheerfully.

A beautiful chestnut mare stood by one of the columns, her scarlet leather reins looped around it. She was small-boned and high-crested, so dark she was almost black, with a white star on her forehead. Her ears pricked forward and she looked at me with her intelligent dark eyes, lifting her head curiously.

I laughed. "Oh, she's a beauty!" I came out and walked around her to have a look at her, stopping in front of her. She snuffled at the front of my chiton hopefully, one delicate leg forward. Her coat shone with glossy health, and her mane was braided into tiny plaits, each decorated with red ribbon. She was built for speed.

"Her name is Desert Wind," Artashir said, lounging back against the column with a grin on his face.

"She's gorgeous," I said, letting her mouth at my palm and then raising my hand to her warm neck. Her coat was like silk. "Your new horse, Artashir?"

Artashir shook his head. "No, she belongs to the widow of one of my men who was killed at Memphis. I said I'd help her look for a buyer who would give her a fair price."

"You ought not have trouble getting that," I said, walking around her and admiring her again. "By all the gods, she's built to run! And young enough from the look of her to have several foals ahead of her, if a man wanted to breed her."

Artashir nodded. "She's eight years old, an archer's horse, not one of those big stubborn stallions you cavalry ride. She's completely trained to knee commands. You don't have to touch her reins in battle."

I looked up at him sharply. "What?"

"I said, she's completely trained to knee commands." Artashir looked pleased with himself. "How do you think we do it, firing a bow from the saddle? They have to be trained not to need the reins. You can loop them over your arm, or lay them across her back. Makes no difference to her. She'll answer to your knees like an absolute professional. I put her through her paces this morning, and there's nothing I'd ask for except maybe a little more power in the jump."

"Artashir," I began, and was embarrassed that I was blinking back tears. I stood beside her, swallowing.

Desert Wind looked round at me, her beautiful ears pricked forward.

"Think she'll do for you, Lydias?" Artashir asked.

"I think she's wonderful," I said.

---

I woke in the hour before dawn and knew I could rest no more. I left Bagoas sleeping, curled like a cat in his warm bed, while I stood and dressed.

No spirits, no nightmares moved, no creatures out of the Red Land troubled our dreams. Egypt had a Pharaoh, and the last hour of the night held no terror. I went down and walked out onto the terrace.

Before me the sea piled against the breakwater, sighing softly against the rocks we had placed there, dark and restless under the moonless sky. The harbor was a curve of white sand. Only a few lights showed here and there in the city, where some tradesman rose before dawn to begin his work, and along the harbor where three fishing boats were setting sail so that they would be well out to sea before the sun rose. On the island the beacon shone faintly, warning them away from the shallow water.

Above, the sky stretched clear and cloudless, more stars than there are numbers glittering in sooty darkness. On the eastern horizon Sothis rose pale and bright, following in the Hunter's track, heralding the dawn.

I took a long breath and let it out, pierced to the core.

I did not have a libation, and the words were hard to find. "Lady of Egypt, Gracious Ones. I am not a priest nor a healer nor a magician. But what I have, I place in Your hands. Help me to live, and living be Your instrument."

I closed my eyes and heard Her voice, as though She stood behind me with Her hand on my back, as though it were my mother's voice, filled with pride and love. *My dear boy, you always have been.*

I felt peace steal over me, not victory, not respite, but the bone-deep peace of the Black Land, still and sure as the bones of the earth. It filled me, and I rested upon it like a child at his mother's breast. Peace is not without, but within.

I do not know how long I had stood there when I heard footsteps on the terrace behind me and turned. Ptolemy came and stood beside me, his dark-colored chiton blending into the shadows. For a long time he said nothing, just stood beside me looking out at the waves. In the east there was the faintest flush of pink, the stars paling. The fishing boats were rounding the island, their sails glimmering against the dark water.

At last he spoke. "Lydias, have you thought about getting married?"

"Not really," I said. "Bagoas thinks I should. But I haven't considered it much."

"I'd like you to marry Chloe."

I turned and looked at him. "What?"

"Marry Chloe," he said. "You're an honorable man and a kind one. And you're strong enough to protect her. You know what kind of prize she would be for an ambitious man. He could marry Chloe, proclaim her Alexander's daughter, and go after a throne."

"She's not Alexander's daughter," I said. "That's ridiculous."

Ptolemy sighed. "But we were all friendly in Persepolis. Yes, Thais sat on my couch and Bagoas on his. But Thais is a hetaira, and if Alexander had asked for her she would have gone. It didn't happen, but as Aristotle taught us, you can't prove a negative. I know Chloe is my daughter, and I know why she looks like Alexander, but a man with Chloe in his power, the father of her children, could make whatever claims he liked and there would be plenty who would believe him. Nor can I give her to some green boy her own age with powerful kin of his own who might do the same."

"I have no kin," I said slowly. "And I am the last man who would seek your throne, Ptolemy, much less Alexander's."

"And I want her to be happy," he said, his eyes straying again to the beacon, which winked out, the light extinguished as the dawn light grew. "I want her to marry someone who will cherish her, and who will love her children and treat her with respect and friendship. Of course she's still too young, and I wouldn't want you to bed her right away, but I trust that you will wait until the proper time."

I blinked. "You would trust me with this? You would trust me with Chloe?"

Ptolemy shrugged, but there was something deeper in his eyes. "I trusted you with her before, didn't I?"

I closed my eyes. I remembered a wild flight from Babylon under Ishtar's moon, that fearless child held before me on my horse as we fled from death and chaos into the unknown, from Alexander's bier to a fortress that might be held by friend or foe. She was that child no longer, of course, but a girl on the edge of womanhood, with her father's quick wits and her mother's courage. A dynastic prize for a noble companion. A child of the baggage train. A hetaira's daughter now a princess of Egypt. She was herself, a story that was only begun.

Ptolemy put his hand on my arm. "Lydias," he said, "this is as close as you will come to stealing fire."

We had all sought it through these years, some remnant of the divine spark, some touch of grace, some breath of destiny from beyond the world, sought it like a man seeks a dream after he has awakened. We were building it here, in walls of stone, a city where none had been before, Ptolemy and I, and Thais too with her bower of transplanted roses. Fire had touched, like a purifying bolt from heaven, searing everything in its path. And in its wake, the flowers bloomed.

"Yes," I said, and opened my eyes. "I will marry Chloe."

*I*T ENDS AS *all the stories end.*

*Once there was a slave boy who became a soldier. He served an immortal hero and then a worthy king. He fought in epic battles from one end of the world to the other, through terror and pain and strife, through frozen mountains and haunted deserts. He became a general and he married a princess, twice royal. And in due course of time she bore him two sons and three daughters and they lived together in a white city by the sea.*

*All the stories end so.*

# PEOPLE, PLACES,
# AND THINGS

**Abydos**—a city in Egypt between Memphis and Thebes, site of many temples including the Osirion.

**Adoratrice of Bastet**—the senior priestess of Bastet in Bubastis.

**Alexander III of Macedon (the Great)**—born in 356 BCE, and rising to the throne of Macedon at the age of twenty upon the assassination of his father, Phillip II. The son of Phillip's queen, Olympias, he embarked on the expedition against the Persian Empire that Phillip had planned. In 334 he fought a major battle at the Granicus River, which gave him control of most of present-day Turkey, and a year later defeated Darius III, Great King of Persia, at the Battle of Issos. Tyre fell before him by siege, and he entered Egypt as a liberator. In 331 he once again defeated Darius decisively at the Battle of Gaugamela, which essentially gave him the entire Persian Empire. Later campaigns included expeditions in Bactria and Sogdiana, present-day Uzbekistan and Tajikistan, and into the Indian states now in Pakistan and Kashmir. He died in 323 BCE, just short of his thirty-third birthday, leaving an empire thrown into chaos by his passing.

**Alexander IV**—son of Alexander the Great and Roxane. He was born in the fall of 323 BCE, a few months after his father's death. He reigned as Great King in name only.

**Alexandria (in Egypt)**—the most successful of the many cities that Alexander founded in his name. It became one of the great metropolises of the ancient world and has continued to the present day as an important city on the Mediterranean. It was founded in 334 BCE, though most of the actual construction took place a decade later, under Ptolemy I Soter.

**Ambhi, Raja** — known in Greek as King Omphis, ruler of an Indian kingdom in the northern part of the Pakistani Punjab and the enemy of Raja Puru. He became an ally of Alexander the Great, and was still active as a player in the political scene several years after Alexander's death, though his ultimate fate is unknown.

**Amenti** — the Egyptian Land of the Dead, ruled by Osiris and Isis.

**Amina** — a Persian noblewoman who is the first wife of Artashir.

**Antipatros** — a Macedonian noble and contemporary of Phillip II. He was one of Phillip's most trusted supporters. When Alexander left Macedon, he left Antipatros as Regent despite the constant friction between Antipatros and Alexander's mother, Olympias. He is the father of Cassander, one of the Companions, and Eurydice.

**Artashir** — a Persian nobleman and Companion, commander of the troop of horse archers that are loyal to Ptolemy. He is the grandson of Artontes, the son of General Mardunaya and his wife Artazostre, the daughter of Darius the Great, and hence a royal kinsman. His wives are Amina and Rania.

**Ashkelon** — a city under Persian rule in Alexander's time, now Migdol Ashquelon in Israel.

**Babylon** — a city just south of present-day Baghdad, one of the great cities of the ancient world. Formerly the capital of the Neo-Babylonian Empire, in the fourth century BCE it was a seat of the Persian Empire, and home to perhaps as many as half a million people.

**Bagoas** — a eunuch courtier of Alexander the Great. He appears to have been a royal favorite of Alexander's as he reputedly had been of Darius'.

**Bastet** — an Egyptian goddess who often took the form of a cat, goddess of hearth, home, and childbirth.

**Berenice** — Eurydice's maternal aunt who accompanied her to Alexandria to marry Ptolemy.

**Black Land** — the part of Egypt touched by the Nile floods or by irrigation, the part that has rich soil deposits from the river and is fertile, also more generally Egypt as a whole.

**Bubastis** — a medium-size city in the eastern Nile Delta.

**Camel's Fort** — a small fort on the Bubasite branch of the Nile at a fordable river crossing.

**Cassander** — one of Alexander's Companions, son of the Regent in Macedon, Antipatros, and brother of Eurydice.

**Chiliarch** — the Grand Vizier of Alexander's empire, held in his lifetime by Hephaistion and then Perdiccas.

**chiton** — a basic article of clothing worn by both men and women, like a tunic. Young men usually wore a short chiton, which came to mid-thigh and might be ornamented with embroidery or colored borders. Women and older men might wear a full-length chiton. For women this was usually gathered at the waist and bloused out over a belt. Chitons could be anything from a shift of coarse linen or wool to elaborately decorated silks, depending on the status of the wearer. Even with a short chiton, men did not wear trousers under it, as trousers were seen as effeminate and foreign.

**Chloe** — Ptolemy and Thais' oldest daughter, born in late 331 BCE.

**Cleomenes** — Alexander's governor in Memphis, a friend of Perdiccas.

**Companion** — one of Alexander's personal friends who have binding oaths to him.

**Companion Cavalry** — Alexander's elite cavalry units, originally made up entirely of Macedonians who had served with him there, but later including replacements from across the empire. The Companions did not use shields, but fought with spear and sword. Their armor consisted of a breastplate and helmet, and sometimes greaves for the lower legs. They did not use either saddles or stirrups, as neither had been invented yet.

**Cyaxara** — the daughter of Artashir and Amina, born around 325 BCE.

**daimons** — spirits between gods and humans, such as minor deities or heroes who are worthy of worship, or guardian spirits of particular places.

**Darius III (Great King of Persia)** — born circa 380 BCE to a cadet line of the Achaemenid royal house, and rising to the throne in 336 in a period of crisis, after several heirs had been killed successively. After being defeated by Alexander twice, he was deposed by a group of his own nobles led by Bessos, Satrap of Bactria, and killed in 330.

**Dead City** — the mound known today as Amarna, the city of Akhetaten built by the heretic pharaoh Akhenaten in the fourteenth century BCE. After Akhenaten's death the city was abandoned within a few years.

**Drypetis** — the younger daughter of Darius III, married to Hephaistion.

**Ecbatana** — a mountain city in what is now northern Iraq, site of the summer palace of the Persian kings.

**eunuch** — a castrated man, particularly one castrated before puberty. Eunuchs served as courtiers, servants, priests, and prostitutes in much of the ancient world, in some places constituting a third gender distinct from both men and women.

**Eurydice** — the daughter of Antipatros, sister of Cassander, later married to Ptolemy.

**facing** — the direction that an infantry unit is pointing their sarissas. Because the sarissas are very long and heavy, it is a complicated series of drill maneuvers to change a phalanx's facing, i.e., which way they're going.

**flying wedge** — a cavalry formation created by Phillip II of Macedon and used extensively by Alexander the Great in which cavalry charges in a formation like an arrowhead in order to break through lines of defenders. This classic tactic is still used today with tanks.

**Gaugamela** — a site near Mosul in modern Iraq where Alexander defeated Darius III for the second and decisive time in 331 BCE.

**Gedrosia** — a desert in the Persian Empire, in what is now southern Iran.

**Ghost Dancer** — the horse that Lydias raised, bought from Tehwaz by Hephaistion.

**Glaukos** — an officer of Hephaistion's Ile in the Companion Cavalry.

**Hephaistion (son of Amyntor)**—born around 356 BCE and schooled with Alexander, and Alexander's closest friend and probable lover from an early date. A leader among the Companions who supported the pro-assimilation policies, he was also a gifted military commander and eventual Chiliarch, or Grand Vizier, of the empire. Married to Drypetis, the younger daughter of Darius III, he died at an early age in Ecbatana in 324. The cause of his death is unknown, and speculation ranges from poison to the more prosaic explanation of typhus.

**hetaira**—a courtesan, literally "a companion."

**hetairos**—a Companion.

**Hipparch**—the officer in command of an Ile, also later the title of a cavalry general.

**Horus**—an Egyptian god often portrayed as a falcon or desert hawk, or as a man with a hawk's head. Horus is the son of Isis and Osiris, the prince who redeems Egypt from his uncle's evil rule and restores peace and justice. Pharaoh was often seen as Horus incarnate.

**Ile**—a cavalry unit consisting of roughly 600–800 men, depending on unit strength.

**Inundation**—the annual flooding of the Nile that fertilized Egypt and began the growing season.

**Isis**—an Egyptian goddess, wife of Osiris and mother of Horus, queen of the heavens. Isis was one of the principal gods of the Egyptian pantheon, and in the Hellenistic period became a universal goddess.

**Issos**—the site of Alexander's first major defeat of Darius III, in 333 BCE, in present-day Turkey.

**Jio**—Lydias of Miletus' original boyhood name.

**Kalanos**—an Indian sage who met Alexander in India and decided to return to Persia with him so that they could continue their conversations. He was advanced in years and died shortly after his arrival.

**Khemet**—the realm of Egypt.

**Krateros**—one of Alexander's Companions from schooldays, and a trusted soldier. It is speculated that Alexander intended to leave the Regency to him upon his death, but Krateros was instead ousted by Perdiccas. He died in battle in 321 BCE.

**Lagos (1)** — a Macedonian noble and adherent of Phillip II who married Arsinoe and was the purported father of Ptolemy.

**Lagos (2)** — Ptolemy and Thais' oldest son, born in early 325 BCE and named for Ptolemy's father. Called Bunny by his older sister, he lived to adulthood and won a chariot race in the Arcadian festival in 307, a visit to Greece that coincides with Ptolemy's. It is likely his father came to see him race.

**Lake Mareotis** — a brackish lake behind the city of Alexandria. Its position relative to Alexandria is very similar to that of Lake Ponchartrain to New Orleans.

**Leontiscus** — Ptolemy and Thais' younger son, born in 322 BCE. In 306 he was taken as a prisoner of war during a naval engagement and ransomed by his father for a huge sum.

**Lochias Peninsula** — a peninsula on the eastern side of the harbor of Alexandria that jutted far out into the sea. Its remains today are known as Silsileh.

**Lydias of Miletus** — an officer of Hephaistion's Ile in the Companion Cavalry. Unlike many of the men he serves with, Lydias is not Macedonian but Carian.

**Magi** — the Zoroastrian priests, augers, and astrologers of Persia.

**Manetho** — an Egyptian priest of Thoth and supporter of Ptolemy. He is best known for his later history of Egypt, in which he provided an overview of three thousand years of history. Modern archaeologists are amazed at the accuracy of his dating, and it is likely that he had access to an unbroken line of documents.

**Mardonias (Mardunaya)** — the son of Artashir and Amina, born around 330 BCE and named for his great-great-grandfather, who was a general of Xerxes.

**Memphis** — an Egyptian city at the base of the Nile Delta, near modern-day Cairo.

**Miletus** — a city on the Aegean coast of Asia Minor, in Hittite times called Millawanda of the mighty walls, more recently under Persian rule.

**Nectanebo II** — the last Pharaoh of Egypt before the second Persian occupation, reigning 360–343 BCE.

Nisean—an ancient breed of horses from Persia, renowned for their strength and fearlessness. Larger than most contemporary breeds, they were tall and strong enough to fight with a rider in armor. Known for their smooth gait and high-crested neck like a modern Arabian, they came in colors including black, bay, "red," chestnut, a light palomino color, and white. Their closest modern equivalents may be the Andalusians and Lusitanians.

Nysa—a town in the Punjab where Lydias was stationed during Alexander's Indian campaign.

Olympias—Queen of Macedon and Alexander's mother. She was often at odds with her husband, Phillip II, and with the Regent in Macedon, Antipatros.

Osiris—Egyptian god of the dead, husband of Isis and father of Horus. He is the ruler of Amenti, the Uttermost West where the dead dwell.

Oxathres—younger half brother of Darius III, a Persian noble who became one of Alexander's Companions.

Pelousion—an ancient Egyptian port and fortress near modern-day Port Said, at the easternmost edge of the Nile Delta.

Perdiccas—one of the Companions. He was a close friend of Alexander and a supporter of his later policies of assimilation with conquered peoples. After Hephaistion's death, Perdiccas was named Chiliarch, or Grand Vizier, in his place, though not given Hephaistion's full army commands, which were split between him and Krateros. Upon Alexander's death he emerged as the Regent, and the closest ally of Alexander's wife Roxane.

Persepolis—the Persian capital city, the palace of which was partially burned by Alexander at the urging of Thais the Athenian.

Perseus—Lydias' horse.

phalanx—an infantry formation consisting of men marching and drilling in close order, in the Hellenistic period usually using sarissas as their primary weapon.

Phillip II of Macedon—born in 382 BCE, and one of the most successful kings of Macedon. During his twenty-three-year reign expanded the kingdom through a series of military campaigns, including the defeat of Athens and Thebes at the Battle of Chaeronea in 338. He had several wives, including Olympias, the Epirote princess who was the mother of his heir, Alexander the Great. He was assassinated shortly before his planned campaign against the Persian Empire was to begin, in 336.

**Polemon** — a Companion and cavalry veteran loyal to Perdiccas.

**Ptolemy (Ptolemy I Soter)** — a general and Companion of Alexander the Great, later Satrap of Egypt and then the first Pharaoh of the Ptolemaic dynasty. He may or may not have been the illegitimate son of Phillip II of Macedon, and hence Alexander's half brother. He lived into his eighties, and founded the most stable and lasting of the Successor states. He was also known in ancient times for his memoirs, which were one of the primary sources concerning the campaigns of Alexander.

**Puru, Raja** — known in Greek as King Porus, king of an Indian state in the Punjab, with his capital near present-day Lahore. He fought against Alexander the Great and Raja Ambhi at the Battle of the Hydaspes River (Jhelum River) and was defeated, but was pardoned by Alexander and became an ally. He was killed in 317 BCE defending Chandragupta Maurya during an assassination attempt.

**Rania** — an Indian woman who is the second wife of Artashir.

**Red Land** — the part of Egypt not touched by the yearly Inundation or by irrigation; the desert.

**Roxane** — the daughter of a Sogdian chieftain in what is now Uzebeki-stan. She became Alexander the Great's first wife and the mother of his heir, Alexander IV.

**Royal Road** — one of the highways across the Persian Empire main-tained by the Great King for the use of his armies and commerce.

**Saqqara** — a hillside district west of Memphis, site of several Old King-dom pyramids as well as an extensive temple and tomb complex, including the tombs of the Apis bulls.

**sarissa** — the pike used by hoplite infantry in phalanx, roughly thir-teen feet long in Alexander's day, and topped with a sharp spear point. A phalanx armed with sarissas was considered unstoppable; however, drill was vitally important for maneuver and combat.

Sati — Lydias' wife, who was killed in Gedrosia with their son Sikander.

satrap — the Persian title for the governor of a province, adopted by Alexander the Great for his regional governors.

Seleucus — a Companion who supported Perdiccas after Alexander's death.

Sikander — Lydias' son, killed in Gedrosia at the age of ten months.

Silver Shields — a crack infantry phalanx of Alexander's, made up of veterans.

Sisygambis — the queen mother of Persia, mother of Darius III.

Siwah — an oasis in the Egyptian Western Desert where the Oracle of Amon dwells. It was consulted by Alexander the Great when he was in Egypt and held in high esteem by the King.

Sobek — Egyptian crocodile god, ruling over, among other things, justice on earth.

Sothis — Sirius, the dog star. Its heliacal rising marked the beginning of the Inundation in Egypt.

Stateira — the elder daughter of Darius III, wife and queen of Alexander the Great. She was murdered following her husband's death.

Tehwaz — a merchant and horse trader of Miletus who was Jio's master.

Thais the Athenian — a hetaira of renowned beauty. She was Ptolemy's companion for many years, traveling with him on Alexander's campaigns. She is best known for inciting Alexander to burn the palace at Persepolis during a banquet there in revenge for the Persian burning of the acropolis at Athens in the previous century. Thais and Ptolemy had at least three children who grew to adulthood.

Thebes — a former capital of Egypt, in Upper Egypt south of Memphis.

Thoth — the Egyptian god of knowledge and lore.

uraeus — the Egyptian symbol of kingship, a rearing cobra head, usually worn on the front of a headdress or crown.

Zephyr — Hephaistion's warhorse.

# FOR FURTHER READING

Many excellent books have been written about Alexander the Great and his times. He has been the subject of exhaustive study from his own lifetime until the present day, a subject of intense fascination to ancient and modern writers alike. Unfortunately, not one single contemporary source survives out of all the old soldiers who wrote memoirs, detractors who wrote polemics, and historians who attempted to record events they were part of.

Of the ancient sources written after Alexander's lifetime, I have leaned most heavily on Arrian's *Campaigns of Alexander*. Though Arrian was a Roman writing several centuries after Alexander's death, he used the memoirs of Ptolemy as his primary source, who is of course one of my main characters and whose attitudes about Alexander and his Companions would be closest to those of Lydias. I have also leaned on the ancient biographies of Alexander supplied by Plutarch, Diodorus, and Quintus Curtius Rufus. They, like Arrian, are available in several excellent modern translations.

The modern biographies of Alexander are myriad. Unfortunately, most of them end with Alexander's death and do little to illuminate the period immediately after, which is the subject of *Stealing Fire*. Therefore I found the following books most useful.

*Ptolemy of Egypt* by Walter Ellis (London; Routledge, 1994) is the only English-language biography of Ptolemy, and as such was invaluable. *The Successors of Alexander the Great: Ptolemy I, Pyrrhus of Epirus, Hiero of*

*Syracuse and Antiochus* by C. A. Kincaid (Chicago: Ares Publishers, 1985) was also extremely helpful. For the tale of the theft of Alexander's body and its subsequent adventures, I am indebted to Nicholas J. Saunders' *Alexander's Tomb* (New York: Basic Books, 2006).

Egypt as Ptolemy found it is a fascinating subject, and again there are many excellent resources. I would especially point out Karol Mysliwiec's *The Twilight of Ancient Egypt* (Ithaca, NY: Cornell University Press, 2000). For the tombs of the Apis bulls, including an excellent map of the catacombs, I recommend *Divine Creatures: Animal Mummies in Ancient Egypt*, edited by Salima Ikram (Cairo: American University in Cairo Press, 2005).

I am also indebted to the inspiration of some online resources, most notably "Hephaistion Philalexandros," which can be found at http://myweb.unomaha.edu/~mreames/Hephaistion/hephaistion.html, and www.neosalexandria.org.

# ACKNOWLEDGMENTS

There are a number of people without whom this book would not have been written. Foremost on that list must be Anne-Elisabeth Moutet, who decided it had to be a book when I wrote my first short story with Lydias, and who has unfailingly encouraged me at every step of the way. She is very much the godmother of this book!

I am also deeply appreciative to Suzanne Griswold, who helped me with Lydias' horsemanship. All errors, of course, are mine.

There are many others whose help I am deeply grateful for in the writing of *Stealing Fire*: Lesley Arnold, Gretchen Brinkerhoff, Katy Catlin, Mary Day, Danielle D'Onofrio, Phoebe Duncan, Lynn Foster, Imogen Hardy, Nathan Jensen, Tanja Kinkel, Anna Kiwiel, Wanda Lybarger, Kathryn McCulley, Anjali Salvador, Melissa Scott, Erin Simonich, Lena Strid, Jeff Tan, Casimira Walker-Smith, and Robert Waters.

I am also grateful to my editor, Devi Pillai, who once again decided to take a chance on a strange journey with me, and my agent, Robin Rue.

Most of all, I must thank my wonderful partner, Amy, who has spent a great deal of time with Lydias recently!

# extras

orbit

# meet the author

Robert Waters

Jo Graham lives in North Carolina with her family and worked in politics for many years. To learn more about the author, visit her website at http://jo-graham.livejournal.com/.

# interview

***Why did you decide to write a book about the death of Alexander the Great and its aftermath?***

I've been interested in the story of Alexander for a long time, at least since I read Mary Renault's *Fire from Heaven* when I was in high school. But the story of Alexander has been done and done, and it's been tackled by some of my favorite authors both living and dead, so I hesitated to cover the same ground. It's a fabulous subject, and of course the recent Oliver Stone movie sparked a lot of interest from people who had never been familiar with Alexander before.

I thought it would be interesting to do something different — instead of talking about Alexander and speculating on his character and feelings, to talk instead about the world he created. In many ways, our modern world is the product of his life, of the ideas and the cross-cultural pollination that began with Alexander and his Successors. I wanted to write about the beginnings of that world, of our world.

***Your two previous books have women narrators. What was different about writing with a man as the narrator?***

The biggest thing is that there could be a lot more action! I've had a challenge in the last two books writing around the battle scenes for the most part, because there was no good reason for Gull or Charmian to be in the thick of the action. Lydias not only could be, but could lead it. He's a warrior.

Also this time there are no childbirth scenes! Lydias can see more of one side of life, and less of another, because he has no good

313

reason to be part of that aspect of things. If I had chosen Thais as the narrator it would have been very different.

**You've said that you greatly admire the work of Mary Renault. How did you feel about writing some of her most iconic historical characters, Alexander, Hephaistion, and Bagoas?**

That was my biggest hesitation in starting *Stealing Fire*, but fortunately I had my partner, Amy, and my friends Anne-Elisabeth and Tanja to urge me forward. To write the same historical figures that Mary Renault did is a huge challenge. I had to try very hard to find my own vision of them, to find a different interpretation of some things. For example, what is Bagoas like after Alexander's death? What is he going to do with the rest of his life? He's not but about twenty-five at the time. And so the story of Bagoas searching for a way to reinvent himself outside of being Alexander's favorite became an important part of the story.

**What other authors who have written Alexander do you admire?**

Many authors have done a wonderful job with Alexander, but there are a few that really stand out to me besides Mary Renault. I am a huge fan of Judith Tarr, and her *Lord of the Two Lands* is one of my very favorite Alexanders. I also love Melissa Scott's Alexander in *A Choice of Destinies*. I'm also very fond of the not-quite-Alexander, Demetrios Asterius, in Jacqueline Carey's *Kushiel's Chosen*.

**You've talked before about being inspired by various songs, that you have a "playlist" that goes with each of your books. What's your Lydias playlist?**

I have quite a few songs on my Lydias playlist! Elton John's "The One" is the first, because it so sums up Lydias at the end of the book, but his "Original Sin" is pretty much the ultimate Lydias song, though I think you'd have to twist it around to Hephaistion's point of view! Other things on the list include the Rolling Stones'

"Continental Drift," Grateful Dead's "Touch of Grey," and Sting's "A Thousand Years." The last one may be the most important, as I think it encapsulates Lydias perfectly!

*Lydias has several important relationships in his life—with Sati, Hephaistion, and now Bagoas. Do you see any conflicts in his having relationships with both men and women?*

Not a bit! We tend to see sexual orientation as an on/off switch—you're straight or you're gay. But these are new concepts and a way of looking at things that are by no means universal. This idea is peculiar to our culture and would have been utterly meaningless to Lydias, as it would be to most people in the history of the world! In Lydias' culture, male bisexuality is the norm. Men are supposed to like sex, and the gender of the partner is really beside the point. The point is the social role that one is playing.

*In* Stealing Fire *there's a lot of horsemanship, training, and cavalry tactics. Did you make that up? Where did it come from?*

Fortunately, we have a manual of horsemanship, which, while not quite contemporary with Lydias, is in the same culture and within the same time frame! Xenophon, an Athenian soldier and general, wrote a fascinating book called *On Horsemanship* about a hundred years earlier, when the warhorse was just becoming an important part of Greek culture. He talks about buying and training a horse, about the maneuvers, about tack and conformation—everything Lydias would need to know! It's a wonderful resource.

Also, I was fortunate to have Suzanne Griswold, a professional equestrian, look over the book for me and correct various bits of horsemanship. All the errors, of course, are mine.

*How long did it take you to write* Stealing Fire? *What are some of your writing habits?*

Six months, from July 2008 to December 2008, but I had done much of the research beforehand, while I was working on *Hand of Isis* and before. I work every day, though how much I get done varies. When I'm really rolling I can do five-thousand words a day. I've done twenty-five thousand words a week at my best, when I know what the story is and I'm almost possessed by it. But then I don't really eat or sleep or do anything else! I have to be patient, though, because for every week like that there are three when I stumble through a couple of thousand words and just can't seem to catch the flow of it. When that happens I have to try to chill out and realize that it will break loose again when I'm ready.

**In your last book,** Hand of Isis, *Charmian remembers her past life as Lydias. Did you plan this book before you wrote* Hand of Isis? *How did all that work?*

Yes, to a certain extent. I already knew who Lydias was and what the bones of his adventures were before I started *Hand of Isis*. I already knew before I started *Black Ships*, for that matter. I have twenty or more stories in my head, all the places this soul has been and all the things Lydias/Charmian/Gull has done, and I've only begun to explore them. There are a couple of additional books written that have not been bought yet, and more where I've played with it and done some scenes and short stories. I hope I have the opportunity to do them all!

It's really necessary for internal consistency that I know all the stories. The things that happen to these people in each life have lasting impact on everything down the line, so I have to know what already happened even if the reader doesn't yet. For example, in *Hand of Isis* the relationship between Charmian and Agrippa is seriously influenced by what passed between Lydias and Hephaistion, even if neither Charmian nor Agrippa is really aware of it. There's a scene in that book, a dream sequence with Charmian and Agrippa in dream Ecbatana where she says, "I was nothing but a pretty face to you," and he says, "Never only that." Yes, they're talking about what happened in Egypt between

Charmian and Agrippa, but also what happened between Lydias and Hephaistion.

And of course when Charmian calls Caesar "by his bones in Alexandria" this is lent power because Lydias stole those bones, stole Alexander's body, and is partially responsible for the fact that Alexander lies in Alexandria!

So I have to know how all the pieces fit. I think it's safe to say that there are a lot of "dangling strings" right now that attach to things! I hope you'll come along with me in the rest of my travels through the Numinous World.

# reading group guide

1. What is your first impression of Lydias and how does that change or not change in the course of the book?
2. Fatherhood is very important to several of the characters in the book. How do Ptolemy, Artashir, and Lydias exemplify fatherhood? What are the characteristics of good fathers, and how are they the same or different from one another?
3. In Persia, Bagoas is considered to be a third gender, neither male nor female. In Egypt, there is no third gender. How does Bagoas cope with this change? How do we look at gender today? Is our view simpler or more complicated than Lydias' world?
4. If Ptolemy and Alexander knew for years that they were really half brothers, how did this affect their relationship? Who else do you think knew, besides their parents? How do you think growing up in Alexander's shadow affected Ptolemy?
5. Lydias in *Stealing Fire* was Gull in *Black Ships* in a previous life, and will be Charmian in *Hand of Isis*. How do you think the different incarnations are similar? How are they different?
6. At the beginning of *Stealing Fire*, Lydias is grieving the death of his wife and son, and also the death of Hephaistion and his beloved horse. Over the course of the book, he comes to terms with his losses. Why do you think he decides to build a new life? What are the decisive moments in coming to terms with his grief?
7. In *Stealing Fire* we see several different models of marriage—Lydias' marriage to Sati, Ptolemy's arranged marriage to Eurydice, Artashir's polygamous marriage with Amina and Rania, and Alexander's

marriage to Roxane, as well as a number of other commitments, including Alexander and Hephaistion, Ptolemy and Thais, and Lydias and Bagoas. Which relationships do you think work the best? Which ones were you most surprised by? Which ones do you think are the happiest and why?

8. One of Lydias' greatest strengths is his cultural flexibility, his ability to understand and work with people from different backgrounds. Do you think his own background, as the child of two cultures, Greek and Carian, is the cause of this? What insights do his experiences give him?

9. In *Hand of Isis* we see the mature city of Alexandria, which is only just beginning in *Stealing Fire*. How does or does not that city live up to what its founders intended? How does it go beyond what its founders intended?

10. Do you think Lydias' decision to marry Chloe at the end of the book at Ptolemy's request is a good decision or a bad one? What do you think will happen?

# introducing

**If you enjoyed
STEALING FIRE,
look out for**

## BLACK SHIPS

*by Jo Graham*

"Are you afraid of the dark?" she asked.

"No," I said.

"Good," she said, and smothered the fire with ashes until only a few coals glowed. It was very dark within the cave. I had never been somewhere there was not even starlight. I heard her moving in the dark, the rustling of cloth.

"Sit here," she said, and I felt her putting a cushion at my back. I sat up upon it. It raised me so that I sat, my legs crossed, leaning almost over the brazier. She put another cushion behind me so that I might lean back against the wall.

There was more rustling, and I smelled the acrid scent of herbs crumbled over the coals. Rosemary. Laurel. And something richer, like resin, like pine carpets beneath my feet. Something heady, like smoke.

"There," Pythia said. "Look into the fire and tell me what you see."

My eyes itched. It was hard to keep them open. They watered. The smoke wavered. The tiny glowing lines of coals blurred. I didn't know what to say.

She was still talking, but I wasn't really hearing her. I was looking at the darkness between the glowing lines. At the blackness in the heart of the fire.

"Black ships," I said, and I hardly knew my own voice.

"Where?" Pythia said.

"Black ships," I said. I could see them in the darkness of the coals. "Black ships and a burning city. A great city on a headland. Some of the ships are small, not much more than one sail or a few rowers. But some of them are big. Painted black. They're coming out from land, from the burning city. But there are other ships in the way, between the black ships and the sea."

My voice caught with the emotion of what I saw. "There are so few of them! I can see them coming, rowing hard. The one in front has seven stars on her prow, *Seven Sisters*, like the constellation. That's her name. The soldiers on the other ships have archers. They're shooting at them."

One of the sailors was struck in the eye by an arrow. He screamed and plunged into the sea. One of the ships' boys was hit in the leg and went down with a high, keening sound, his blood spurting across the deck.

One of the small boats was rammed and capsized.

"There are people in the water. They're not sailors, not on the little boats. Children. Women." I could see them struggling. The archers were shooting them in the water.

"One of the big ships is turning back. She's turning around." I could see the dolphin on her prow, white and red on black.

There was a girl in the water, her slim, naked body cutting through the waves like a dolphin herself. She was almost to the big ship. Now she was there. One of the rowers shipped his oar as she reached for it, stretching her arms up the shaft. She got one foot on the top of the paddle, pulled herself half out of the water. Hands reached down to haul her aboard.

"*Seven Sisters* has come about," I said. "She's bearing down on one of the ships of archers, and they're hauling at the oars to get out of the way."

*Seven Sisters* swung past, close enough that I could see the young man at her tiller, his sandy hair pulled back from his face with a leather thong, lips set in concentration, the wind kissing him.

"They have fire arrows," I gasped. "The blockaders. They're lighting them."

One fell hissing into the sea. Another dropped on the foredeck of *Dolphin* and was quickly extinguished with a bucket of water. A young man with long black hair was hauling one of the children from the fishing boat aboard.

The rest of the fishing boats were either sunk or out to sea, sails spread to catch the land breeze carrying them away.

I heard shouted words, saw the captain of *Seven Sisters* waving.

A fire arrow struck the captain of *Dolphin* full in the chest, his beard igniting. He fell away from the tiller, his face on fire and his chest exploding. The young man with black hair swung the child into the shelter of the rowers' rail and leapt for the tiller. *Seven Sisters* swung away, her course between *Dolphin* and the nearest blockader.

*Dolphin's* sail unfurled, red dolphin painted on white. It filled with the land breeze. A moment later *Seven Sisters'* spread, black stars against white. Behind them the city burned. Ahead was only open sea.